Just Once

in a

Verra

Blue Moon

A Highland Gardens Novel
Book 2

Dawn Marie Hamilton

ISBN: 978-0-9899642-4-1

This novel is dedicated to
the cousins.

Sarah, Ian, Kimberly, Scott, Krystle, and my godson, Tyler.

ACKNOWLEDGMENTS

So many individuals helped bring this book to fruition, and I thank you.

Thank you to Cindy Davis for editorial guidance. To the Celtic Critters, past and present, for critiques and vital encouragement. A special thank you to Derek Dodson, Cathy Macrae, and Cate Parke. Words cannot convey how important you are to me.

Thank you to the members of Celtic Hearts Romance Writers and From the Heart Romance Writers for keeping me sane. To all the judges who've judged the manuscript for *Just Once in a Verra Blue Moon* in RWA® chapter contests and provided constructive feedback. Priceless.

With all my heart, I thank Frank, my husband, best friend, and personal hero.

PROLOGUE

Castle Lachlan, Strathlachlan, Scottish Highlands, 1490

Fae? Mairi stilled, senses alert. Along with stifling afternoon heat, a curious fragrance pervaded the airless bedchamber, making her nose twitch. What interest had the *Sithichean* here? Her faerie protector, Caitrina, traveled far from Castle Lachlan on a private errand. There was nae reason for fae interference.

Mairi MacLachlan shifted the *bairn* nursing at her breast to the crook of her arm and fidgeted with the sleepy babe's wrappings. Angst swelled in her chest. *Could they be after the babe?*

The old folk whispered tales of malicious faeries stealing infants and replacing them with *changelings*—sadly misshapen souls. Mairi scanned the room in panic. She and the *bairn* must escape.

While Mairi struggled to untangle herself from the bedding, a white-haired woman appeared afore her, an elder, a reader of destiny. Mairi held the child close and swallowed uneasily. The *bairn* let out a disgruntled yelp, and she eased her hold.

"M'lady." The fae woman's voice garnered attention.

"You honor us with your presence." Mairi inclined her head briefly in deference to the faerie's status, though apprehension shivered over her skin. She searched the woman's features, hoping to ascertain the intent of the unexpected visit.

A sweet smile curved the faerie's lips and the edges of her ageless, green eyes crinkled.

Mairi relaxed against the pillows. The woman didn't bring warnings of ill fortune. The faerie's gray silk gown reminded Mairi of the ever-present Highland mists—a thought that made her frown.

"Why so sad, mistress? You have a bonnie wee one in your arms." The faerie glided to the side of the bed and peered at the bundle Mairi cradled.

Why, indeed? The answer troubled Mairi more than the woman's sudden appearance. Less than a sennight had passed since their child's birth, yet her husband left this morn in anger. She hadn't meant to quarrel with him, but he had set his course.

"My stubborn man is off to meet with the Campbell to secure a contract for the babe to wed one of his grandsons."

She didn't want such an arrangement for her *bairn*. She begged Iain that when the time came for the child to wed, he allow the lass to choose a husband of her own. Mairi wanted wee Elspeth to find love in the marriage bed, as she herself had.

"Be at peace." The old woman reached down to move the swaddling away from the babe's face, distracting Mairi from her glum thoughts. The faerie ran a finger along the *bairn's* tender cheek. A pleasant smile transformed her as she gazed upon the perfect features of the precious lass. She glanced at Mairi and in a raspy voice said, "Just once in a verra blue moon love will…" The faerie's brow puckered. "Oh, dear." She tapped a finger against her wrinkled chin. "I simply cannot remember what I am to say."

"Ah, yes." Her face beamed. "When three, seven-year cycles of the moon wane…" The wise one placed her hand on the wee babe's forehead and gazed into the infant's eyes. "A strange warrior from an unknown far-off place will come wielding the mighty lost sword of the fae to save you from despair, dear one. *Just once in a verra blue moon love will triumph.*"

As silently and swiftly as she arrived, the faerie woman disappeared. The only evidence remaining from her visit was the sweet, otherworldly fragrance clinging to the air.

Mairi caressed her daughter's smooth cheek, and the child cooed. "Well, my wee Elspeth, your da will not be pleased to learn the fae guide your future."

CHAPTER ONE

Present Day, Manhattan

*H*umid July air slammed into Finn as he rushed from the steel and glass high-rise of his family's prestigious business consulting firm. The fine linen shirt he wore instantly stuck to his chest. He tugged at the fabric and surveyed the heavy afternoon traffic. The shrill horn from a passing vehicle blared, starting a frenzy of honking.

Finn released a heavy sigh and loosened his silk tie. If he didn't find a cab right away, he'd be late for his flight.

He flicked his gaze at the empty curbside stand then hurried along Madison Avenue in search of a taxi. Sudden tingling on the back of his neck alerted him someone followed. A glance over his shoulder confirmed his suspicion.

Damn. To be stalked by beautiful women would be most men's fantasy dream, but it was his worst nightmare and all too real. The debutante following him was only the most recent in a barrage of overzealous females set on making his life hell.

He clutched his shoulder bag filled with his reenactment gear and quickened his pace. He didn't have the time or the inclination to deal with the woman's intrigues.

Finn had a games to attend. Damn good thing he'd sent his claymore on ahead.

In an effort to lose her, he sprinted for several blocks, weaving in and out of hordes of pedestrians, and ducked into a side street. He jumped into the first cab he came across. "LaGuardia, and make it quick."

When he looked back, a second cabby pulled in behind them, the darned woman was the passenger. His gut burned with dread. He told her he wouldn't marry her. Why did she persist in pursuing him?

"You've earned an extra hundred if you lose the yellow following us."

The driver accelerated into the flow of vehicles. The taxi careened through midtown traffic, running red lights and barely missing bystanders. Finn darted glances behind him. The other cab tailed them as if attached to their bumper.

Finn jerked forward. "What the—"

The other taxi had rammed them. Then it rammed them again, several times. His driver yelled a rapid-fire succession of what he assumed obscenities in a foreign language and maneuvered around several cars to get out of reach.

At the Queensboro Bridge, traffic slowed to a crawl. Finn tapped his fingers on the armrest. Antsy, he twisted to see out the rear window. The other vehicle was two cars behind.

Once on the boulevard, things opened up. He checked his watch. "Hurry, dammit."

On the expressway, they raced along straight-aways, darted between cars, skidded around curves. Tires squealed. Horns blared. An abrupt twist of the steering wheel hurled Finn across the black vinyl. He used his arms and legs to brace himself, determined to keep his seat.

When he entered the airport terminal, the woman wasn't far behind. Zigzagging through the crowd, he lost her at security.

Finn boarded his flight, slumped into his first-class seat, and ordered a whisky. While the crew prepared for takeoff, he spied the woman watching through the large plate-glass window of the waiting area. She must have used her security credentials to get through the checkpoint. Her audacity made him shudder.

The 737 taxied, took off, gained altitude. He stared out the small window at the wispy clouds. He could imagine the look of defeat in her dark eyes when the aircraft pulled back from the jetway to speed him off to North Carolina and the Highland games at Grandfather Mountain.

Blue Ridge Mountains, near the Village of Anderson Creek

Finn inhaled deeply. His lungs filled with fresh mountain air. For the first time in months, he was free of fawning women. Free of the awkward position they put him in.

Patrick's sword sliced past his face, drawing him from his thoughts. Rain streamed over his bare chest, mixing with sweat. He needed to pay attention. If he weren't more careful, he'd do a face-plant in the mud.

"You fight like a lass, MacIntyre," Patrick taunted.

"Hilt is slippery." Finn cursed under his breath and sought a better grip.

"You must learn to fight under every circumstance. That includes rain. Could save your miserable life someday."

Grunting, Finn barely ducked the next assault.

Patrick pulled back. "Enough!" He dropped the point of his claymore to the ground and scowled. "'Tis obvious you are not paying attention."

Trying to catch his breath, Finn gulped air. He glared at his cousin-in-law. "This is supposed to be just for fun."

"Ach, then. You must try harder to have fun, lad." Humor lit Patrick's blue eyes, and he unloosed the leather strip holding back his long chestnut hair. Patrick MacLachlan was a primitive man; to him a workout with the large two-handed sword was child's play. "At times I forget we live in a modern world."

Finn shook his head. *"You are my fiercest opponent."*

Patrick laughed and placed a hand on Finn's wet shoulder. "Come. The *bairns* are at the inn for Rory's Thursday morning story time. Let us go and warm ourselves by the fire and listen to the old Highlander tell his tales."

Finn yanked on a soaked t-shirt and followed Patrick across the wet lawn.

About twenty-five eagerly waiting children sat on the plush carpet in the parlor of the *Whispering Pines Inn* while gossiping moms relaxed on overstuffed floral sofas. A few dads stood nearby, appearing disinterested. Finn knew better. Everyone loved hearing Rory's stories.

The crackling fire brought much-needed warmth to the dreary mountain morning. Finn joined Patrick at the hearth, hoping his clothes would dry.

Conversation ended when Rory MacNaughton entered from the rear door, his carved walking stick at his side. The elderly gentleman wore dress slacks, a brown tweed jacket with leather patches at the elbows, and a tam covering his white hair. He greeted individuals as he crossed the room and eased onto the tall stool at the center of the parlor. With an age-spotted hand, he motioned for his audience to move closer.

Alert eyes sparkling, Rory glanced at Finn and grinned. One of the men standing nearby snickered. Finn groaned, sure he knew the yarn the storyteller would regale them with.

Taking a deep breath, Rory began…

"The *Sithichean*, the faeries of the ancient Highlands, had a special affinity for moonstones. Enamored by the pale, lustrous, blue color resembling that of moonlight, they found the best of these unique stones on the shores of their sensuous faerie paradise *Tir-nan-Óg*—land o' heart's desire—having washed ashore on the tides when the sun god and moon maiden were in a particular heavenly harmony."

Rory leaned forward. "Ye ken this miraculous occurrence happens only once in three, seven-year cycles of the moon…"

He held up an index finger. "Just once in a verra blue moon," he whispered.

A hush fell across the parlor.

"Handfuls of these precious stones belonged to a beautiful flame-haired faerie with eyes the color and brightness of the most costly emeralds."

"Caitrina?" a precocious little girl, with red curls and freckles sprinkled across her nose, whispered. Her blond-haired friend giggled, and Rory smiled at the pair.

"She bestowed upon the moonstones magical powers, gifting them to deserving mortals. Some of these charmed stones had the ability to reunite lost lovers. Others gave the bearer the gift of second sight. One especially large gemstone she forged into the hilt of a magnificent Highland claymore, and with a kiss enchanted it with extraordinary power."

His eyes wide, a boy in front pointed at Finn.

Finn glanced down. He must be a sight, his soaked shirt clinging to his chest and his wet kilt slung low on his hips. He'd grown his hair long and now the knotty, wet strands hung around his shoulders in disarray. Beside him, his sheathed sword leaned against the stone of the fireplace, the large moonstone in its cross-section plain to see.

Rory chuckled, locking gazes with him. With tight lips, Finn shook his head *no*. He didn't want the kids to think his sword was the one of which Rory spoke.

"Over the ages, the sword brought many a worthy warrior fame and fortune. That was until the day an evil, dark power used it." Rory's voice rose and his pace quickened. "This could not be borne. With green eyes shooting flames of fire, the one who fashioned the splendid weapon cast it far away to vanish in the *Sands of Time*."

The storyteller lowered his voice an octave and slowed his speech. "There are those who believe the lost sword of the fae has been found."

Finn refused to listen to more of the man's fantasy. He signaled to Patrick he was leaving.

Patrick followed him into the foyer. "Why the rush, lad?"

"My claymore doesn't have supernatural powers. It's just an antique sword."

"Ach, well. Dinnae take offense. Rory means nae insult. He merely wishes for the *bairns* to believe in a wee bit of magic. Nae harm in that."

Finn shrugged. "Guess not."

"Will you be staying for the midday meal?" Patrick asked.

"No. I'll change out of these wet clothes then head to the mountain for a nap before the festival begins."

"I will meet you at the game field for the picnic along with Laurie and the *bairns.*"

"See you there." Finn crossed the parking lot to the truck he kept in North Carolina for when he visited.

Less than an hour later, he walked along the camping area's muddy gravel road past travel trailers, water dripping from his rain gear. Why hadn't he thought to rent an RV? He'd be about to enjoy a dry warm bed instead of a damp sleeping bag. He continued down the road, swerving to sidestep one exceptionally large puddle.

There were few people about. The afternoon rain kept most from exploring. Those who had ventured outdoors huddled beneath ugly blue tarps, sat around smoldering campfires that made him want to sneeze, or were garbed in bright-colored raingear from head to toe.

Striding down the hill past pop-up trailers, he walked into what some had named *Flag Town*. Wet banners and flags flapped in the wind, hanging mostly everywhere, from ropes strung across the road, from poles in campsites, from trees. Stars and Stripes, St. Andrew's Crosses, and Lion Rampants hung together among the multitude of Clan banners. He inhaled a deep breath of moist air. The display roused his ancestral pride.

He waved to a couple of fellow reenactors then jumped over a fast running stream that hadn't been there yesterday. The flow weaved its way across the road, along the edge, through the center of someone's campsite, to cross the road again around the bend. There the water rushed into the woods, into the faerie glen where his friends, the MacRae sisters, camped.

Farther along the road, he eyed his tent where it stood in the woods at the edge of the camping area, behind the campsite of a bunch of good ole boys, alumni of the University of Tennessee. Fortunately, he'd pitched his humble abode on the hill and dug a trench around the upward side. His efforts paid off. The water flowed around the tent instead of through it. But there was too much rain, making it impossible for anything to stay completely dry.

Finn bent to unzip the fly and entered the vestibule. Hunched over, he re-zipped the flap and took off his raingear, hanging the wet jacket and pants on the line he strung inside. After removing his muddy boots, he unzipped the tent and climbed in. His sleeping bag wasn't wet, just damp.

He didn't care. He needed sleep.

Rolling his shoulders, he tried to ease the tension in his muscles from his workout with Patrick. He reached for a ditty bag and took out an aspirin, popped the pill into his mouth, and washed it down with water from his sport bottle.

Wrapped in a fleece blanket, he lay on the sleeping bag and allowed the distant skirl of pipes lull him toward sleep. He began to snore, the sound startling him, almost fully waking him again, before he drifted into oblivion.

She called to him.

The young woman stood alone on a heather-covered hill, as if surrounded by a halo, her long strawberry blond hair aglow in the sunshine. A puff of air blew the sheer gown she wore, causing the gossamer fabric to cling to feminine curves, teasing his imagination.

He wanted to reach out, touch her cheek, kiss her lips, sweep his palms over her sensuous form. Desire pooled low, tightening his groin.

As he strode closer, she floated farther away.

The lilting sound of her voice came to him on the breeze, soft and alluring.

At first, he couldn't make out her words. She spoke a language he didn't understand yet sounded familiar. And then…

"Come to me, my warrior…save me…come to me."

CHAPTER TWO

*T*he *pop* of a firecracker jolted Finn awake. Disoriented, he blinked several times before remembering he lay in his tent at Grandfather Mountain. With a hard-on, no less. *Shit.* He'd better get a move on if he planned to meet his cousin Laurie's family for the picnic and opening ceremonies of the Highland Games and Gathering of the Scottish Clans.

Dressed and ready, he poked his head out of the tent. The rain had stopped and late afternoon sunshine blessed the North Carolina Mountains.

Finn sauntered up the road, taking on the persona of the reenactment costume he wore. Impersonating a sixteenth century Highland warrior provided the opportunity to be someone else for a while. Forget the demands of his business. With the added bonus of venting pent-up energy in mock sword fights.

When hailed, he stopped at the campsite of four women from South Carolina, exchanged pleasantries and quickly continued on his way.

It wasn't that he didn't like women. He did. But ever since a trendy New York City gossip rag named him the *Best Catch of the Year*, women relentlessly pursued him, trying to lure him into a loveless marriage. If that wasn't bad enough, the paper renewed the insult by adding his name to their *Top Ten Eligible Bachelors in Manhattan List* every year.

Thank God, only a few people at this year's Scottish gathering were aware of his status and wealth. Others knew him merely as a member of the MacIntyre clan. And dammit. That was the way he wanted it.

Amy Ferguson stepped from her tent. Dressed in belly-baring jeans, her tight strappy t-shirt sported a Celtic logo with the words: *Celtic Woman—Goddess With An Attitude.*

"Finn, you look fetching this evening." Amy moistened her lips and smiled.

He inwardly cringed. He'd hoped to avoid her.

"Really, you look great…so authentic."

He glanced down at his saffron-colored knee length *leine* and the MacIntyre hunting plaid of green and blue he'd draped over the linen. He shifted the heavy weight of the claymore hung across his back and murmured, "Thanks."

The costume he wore wasn't what interested the brazen brunette. She always came on to him despite his overt attempts to discourage her.

"Let me see your claymore."

He didn't want to oblige, but to be polite he reached over his shoulder, pulled his sword free of its sheath and held it forward, balancing the weight across his palms.

She gasped and her brown eyes bugged as she took in the size of the moonstone imbedded in the cross-section of the sword. "My God! Is that real?"

"Nah. An imitation." The lie tasted bad, but the calculating glint in her eyes gave him no alternative. He returned the sword to the leather sheath strapped to his back. She'd not even noticed the beautiful Celtic symbols etched into the blade.

"Hey, Finn." Krystle, a fellow reenactor's college-aged daughter, emerged from a pop-up trailer across the way and ran over to join them. "Wow. You look way cool."

"Ach, you're a comely wench." He smiled, glad for the interruption.

Dipping into a quick curtsy, Krystle giggled, obviously enjoying their role-playing. She spun in a circle. "Do you think Jamesie will notice me?"

Even though it wasn't what she asked of him, Finn inspected her costume for historical accuracy. Dressed in the ancient way, a white linen *leine* graced her ankles with a belted *arisaid* overtop, fastened at her breast with a Celtic brooch. Her eating knife, secured in a decorative leather sheath, hung from the belt at her waist. When he raised his gaze, her blond French braid pulled his attention to her expressive crystalline eyes, and he remembered what she asked.

No way would Jamesie, the popular drummer from a Scottish tribal band, fail to take notice.

"Aye, lass, I'm sure he'll be enthralled."

She blushed sweetly.

Finn gave her a formal bow as her brother Tyler approached the group. Tyler was also dressed in costume, wearing a baggy white tunic under a great kilt of red, white, and blue Hamilton plaid. He wore a dirk in a leather sheath at his waist and carried a studded leather *targe*.

"Don't encourage her," he said. "She's already full of herself."

Krystle punched her brother in the arm and they all shared a good-natured laugh.

"I must be off. I'm meeting my cousin's family at the field for the picnic." Finn turned and strode several steps.

"I'd love to get under his kilt." Amy's words set his teeth on edge.

He stopped and twisted around. Tyler and Krystle rolled their eyes and walked away, leaving Amy standing in the road, staring at him, sporting a speculative expression.

Finn refrained from rolling his eyes also and waved farewell, pretending he hadn't heard. However, as he headed on up the road toward the festival grounds, he distinctly felt the heat of Amy's gaze on his back. With that, an uncomfortable chill reached down deep into the very marrow of his bones.

He shook off the cold feeling. He was lucky she didn't know he was the CEO and President of *MacIntyre Consulting*, the number-two privately held business-consulting firm in the United States. She'd made it perfectly clear on the one date they had last summer she planned to marry for money.

Recently the demands of his career had become overwhelming. He now understood why his father had years earlier dumped the responsibility of running the family firm on his shoulders and disappeared for months at a time to dig ancient artifacts in some godforsaken desert in Africa. Lately, Finn found himself, more often than not, escaping the city whenever possible and leaving the running of the firm to his two new partners.

They were more than willing to have him out of their way, encouraging him to take a less hands-on role in the business.

Maybe—probably—he should take a serious look at his life and make some major changes.

Laurie often teased him about flaunting his wealth. He learned his lesson when that stupid magazine did the first article on him. So whenever he visited North Carolina, he kept a low profile. He dressed down, drove an old-beater pickup truck, and slept in a tent while attending the games.

He sighed. One of these days, he'd find balance in his life.

Entering the meadow from the wooded camping area, Finn stopped for a moment to take in the view. The spectacle of colorful clan tents impressed, but the sight of Grandfather's summit as a backdrop to the festival grounds was humbling indeed. The bronze light of the setting sun played across the old man's features. Nature at her awe-inspiring best.

Finn crossed the running track and found Laurie and Patrick, their baby daughter, and their two, wild toddlers. The twins, Scott and Young Iain, ran around the picnic blanket, playing warrior with wooden swords. They were cute boys, and Finn enjoyed hanging with them. Someday he hoped to have a couple kids of his own.

Geez. He needed to forget his problems and find out what

had Laurie so tense when she picked him up at the airport. He feared bad memories had surfaced, and she had Post Traumatic Stress Disorder. Now wasn't the right time to ask questions though. Tomorrow he'd sit her down and find out what was going on in her head.

He saw red every time he thought of what was done to her. He unclenched his fists and inhaled a deep, calming breath.

By the time he ate and settled on the blanket, it was almost dark. The torchlight ceremony would soon begin. When Laurie managed to get the boys quieted down, Scott came over and climbed onto Finn's lap.

"Having fun?"

"Em hmm." The boy leaned back, and his small body relaxed.

Finn tousled the imp's blond curls, inhaling the lad's rough and tumble little-boy scent. Stubby fingers gripped his shirt, and his heart squeezed. He glanced at Laurie holding her daughter, leaning against Patrick, Young Iain curled on his father's lap. This was what Finn craved, a harmonious family life—here in these mountains.

If only the woman from my dreams was real. He sighed heavily and pushed that impossible wish out of his mind.

Darkness fell and the ceremony began. A deep voice came across the loud speaker, explaining the historic significance of the torch ceremony.

"The saltire cross of Saint Andrew is recognized as Scotland's ancient symbol. Tonight, we call the clans to rendezvous as our ancestors were once summoned to battle."

The speaker fell silent…

His voice thundered. *"Raise the Clans."*

Chills played along Finn's spine, as one by one, the resonant voice called the names. "Anderson… Armstrong… Baird… Barcley… Bell… Bruce…" As he called each clan's name, a representing member crossed the field, carrying a lit torch to add to the fiery cross of flames in the center of the field.

"MacIntyre."

Finn leapt to his feet, hugging the excited Scott to his chest. Laurie and Patrick joined them along with Young Iain. They all screamed as loud as they could, jumping up and down. They did the same again, a few minutes later, when the call was for Clan MacLachlan.

"Life or Death!" Patrick yelled the MacLachlan battle cry, his fist extended in the air.

After they sat, Scott climbed off Finn's lap to go to his mother. Finn distinctly felt the loss, a barren place in the center of his chest. He rubbed his palm over the spot. He'd better get himself in-gear and find a woman who could love him. Undoubtedly, the task would be difficult.

The curse he choked on came from deep within the aching void near his heart. He wanted to have children and be young enough to enjoy rough housing with his boys. At thirty-six, he was past the age when he should have started a family, and he wasn't getting any younger.

He swallowed, targeting his attention on the clan emissaries walking across the field and the rich baritone coming from the loudspeakers.

"Stewart... Sutherland... Turnbull... Wallace... Young."

"The clans have come once again to celebrate who they are," the speaker called out when the last torch was set.

The torches burned brightly. The haunting sounds of pipes filled the air.

Finn experienced a sense of belonging he never imagined. A feeling of rightness.

The abundance of twinkling stars overhead added to the magic.

Patrick broke the spell when he nudged Finn while attempting to gather up the twins and their belongings.

"I'll help you carry this stuff to your car." Finn bent and picked up the picnic basket.

As they walked along the path toward the parking lot, Laurie grabbed his arm. The beam from his flashlight bobbed crazily across the ground. "I hope you didn't forget my garden party is tonight at eleven," she said.

He nodded with a grunt.

"I expect you to be there on time and to still be in costume. And for heaven sakes, please be nice to Jillian."

Finn groaned, and Patrick snorted.

Lively fiddle tunes greeted Finn as he parked his truck in the gravel lot near Laurie's home and garden center. A portion of her garden and the crowd were visible through the iron gate. He was tempted to leave. He didn't feel like making nice-nice with her business associates, but she'd never forgive him if he didn't make an appearance.

The anniversary of opening her garden center meant a lot to her. He couldn't hurt her feelings. And she just didn't seem herself lately.

They had a falling-out several years ago when she handed him her resignation and moved to Anderson Creek. At the time, the thought of her in the country seemed ludicrous. But since she survived her adventure—at least physically—and married Patrick, damn if she hadn't proved him wrong. Her garden center and gift shop, *Foxgloves*, had grown into a successful local enterprise.

He'd been a real jerk back then. So, yeah, he'd stay tonight. Laurie needed to know she could depend on him.

Finn got out of the pickup and entered the garden through the front gate. *Geez.* He hoped he could dodge Laurie's two business partners, Jillian and Caitrina, for the rest of the evening.

His luck, Jillian was the first guest he saw. She leaned against the side of the tool shed, watching the musicians. Whenever they were thrown together, she tripped over herself to get his attention. Although it would make his cousin happy, he'd no desire to pursue a relationship with the mousy woman.

She had a kind heart and nice eyes yet the chemistry wasn't there. No way could he picture her as the mother of his sons.

"Finn." She waved her arms and lunged forward, knocking over a planted urn. The ceramic pot shattered on the stone patio, scattering shards and soil. She stared at him then bent to clean up the mess.

Shit, he should offer assistance. He struggled with his conscience. Good manners won, but before he moved, a couple of other guests jumped to her aid. Finn grasped the opportunity and strolled in the opposite direction.

He stumbled upon Caitrina almost hidden within the lush foliage near the rear gate. Their gazes met. An impish smile played on her lips.

The fine hairs on the back of his neck stood on end. He wasn't sure what it was about her. Beautiful, tall and willowy, she had intense green eyes. Her long auburn hair would set any man's heart racing. In fact, his buddy Douglas was in love with her. Nevertheless, there was something unusual about her. Something out of the ordinary he couldn't quite identify, which made him damn uncomfortable.

Caitrina always watched him, staring with her piercing emerald eyes, as if she knew something he didn't.

She probably did. But still—

Annoyed he allowed her to unnerve him he tore his gaze away.

Before long, Jillian bore down on him.

He sidestepped a server with a tray of champagne flutes and strode to the sanctuary of the house, to the refrigerator for a cold beer, hoping she wouldn't follow.

Caitrina stood amongst the rose-colored foxgloves, alone in the shadows near the garden's rear gate. She smiled when Finn evaded Jillian's clumsy attempt to attract his attention. As he disappeared into the house, Caitrina turned away to gaze at the silvery haze surrounding the full moon. The time neared, and she'd work to do.

She would set the match into action before the High

Queen of the Fae learned the game had begun. Caitrina could almost taste victory. This round and one more—she'd earn her freedom and be returned to the royal realm.

She inhaled a deep breath and uncurled her fists.

From her peripheral vision, she glimpsed Douglas MacKinnon watching her. Didn't he understand he no longer aroused her curiosity?

She pressed her palm against her chest. She must have ingested a stimulant with an unusual property capable of causing a faerie heart to beat too fast.

Douglas raised a dark eyebrow in question.

What a meddlesome man. Caitrina glanced heavenward, wishing he'd go away.

When she looked in his direction again, he gave her one of his devastating smiles, saluted, and walked off.

Oh, how she wanted to turn him into a horny toad. But she couldn't waste time thinking about the beguiling man. She'd a challenge to win.

Taking note of the other guests, she made sure no one noticed as she shimmered, faded, dissolved into a fragrant fae mist.

A large hand clamped on Finn's shoulder as he reached into the fridge.

He tensed then relaxed, realizing who joined him. He'd practiced swordplay with Douglas long enough to know the man's distinctive scent.

"Grab one for me." Douglas squeezed his shoulder before releasing him and stepping away.

Finn removed two bottles of beer from the refrigerator and faced his best buddy.

Douglas scraped his palm across the late night shadow of whiskers on his jaw that gave him a hard look. Five inches taller than Finn at six foot seven, he did his heritage proud. He wore a reenactment costume similar to Finn's, a gilt unicorn holding his predominantly red and green plaid in place. He wore his long black hair pulled back in a ponytail and a cynical smile curled his lips. When he stared through his tiger-like eyes, you knew he meant business. His one weakness seemed to be Caitrina.

Finn was glad to call the man friend. "Hey. How's things?"

"Great." Douglas grabbed the offered beer and pried off the cap. "This is my busiest week. Sales at my shop are solid."

No surprise. Douglas owned the *Celtic Image* shop in the village of Anderson Creek where he stocked antique and new merchandise from Scotland, Ireland, and Wales. When Finn bought his claymore in the store the first time he visited the area, he and Douglas became quick friends.

"I bet. Everyone who attends the games visits your shop." After prying off the cap from his beer, Finn raised the bottle. "*Slàinte mhór!*"

"Good health!" Douglas returned.

The bottles clinked.

"I need to tell you something," Douglas said, his tone serious.

Unease tightened Finn's gut. He gave his buddy his full attention. "What gives?"

"You know I don't usually get involved in other people's business. But…"

"Spill it."

"Patrick told me Laurie's been anxious lately. She's having nightmares about the time she was abducted. He's worried."

"She seemed nervous the other day when she picked me up at the airport in Asheville. I sensed something was wrong, but wasn't sure what." Finn fiddled with the label on his beer bottle. "Thanks for mentioning it."

"Sure."

"I plan to talk to her again tomorrow and see if there's any way I can help. I've been trying to convince her to see a professional, but she doesn't want to talk to a stranger about her experience. She's afraid she'd slip, say something about her time-traveling adventure and they'd think she's a lunatic.

Who would believe she was tortured by a sixteenth century warrior and nearly beaten to death?"

Sometimes it still amazed him that Laurie had simply walked through her garden gate and traveled back in time to sixteenth century Scotland.

He winced when he thought of the thin scars crisscrossing her back. She'd met Patrick in the past, and his enemy, a man by the name of Malcolm Maclay, kidnapped and tortured her. Fortunately, she was rescued and wed Patrick before they traveled forward in time to present day North Carolina. What a surprise they had. His parents already lived there, running a B&B. The old adage held. Truth really was stranger than fiction.

"Can't blame her for her fear." A furrow marred Douglas's forehead. "She's right. We need to be the ones to provide help."

"Yeah. I agree." Finn's chest tightened. "There are times I wish I could travel back in time and do away with her tormentor."

Douglas glanced toward the screen door then grasped hold of his upper arm and squeezed. "Guard that thought."

Finn nodded, aware he'd received a veiled warning. Douglas released him and stepped back, his expression inscrutable.

"Damn that bastard Maclay!" Finn took a deep swig from his bottle, allowing the hearty dark brew to wash away his anger.

"Forget it." Douglas set his bottle on the counter. "Come on. Let's join the rest of the party in the garden. I'll help you keep Jillian at bay." He flicked him a conspiratorial wink.

Finn adjusted the sword on his back as he and Douglas joined Patrick's parents, Mairi and Iain, and the guests standing around their host.

"Quiet. Please." Patrick smiled at the crowd and held up his glass. "A toast to my sweet wife—"

He stared at Laurie. She gaped toward the back of the garden, to the gate and beyond, her face turned ashen.

A stranger stood on the knoll beyond the gate, brandishing a claymore in the air. After a few seconds, the man's watery image faded, vanishing into swirling mist.

"Maclay!" Patrick darted toward the gate.

Before he ran through, his father grabbed his arm, holding him back with a don't-even-think-it grip. "You cannot go. You have *bairns* and a wife now. We dinnae ken whether you could ever return here."

Finn's temper flared. He slipped past Patrick and bolted for the gate.

"No, Finn. You mustn't," Laurie cried.

The entreaty came too late. He sprinted through the gate and into a dense fog.

"*He will not be alone.*" As if from a great distance, he heard Patrick's words.

Then the world spun, or so it seemed. The pressure was unbearable and the pain almost more than he could endure. He pressed his hands against the sides of his head, afraid his brain would explode.

A bright light burst behind his eyelids.

He fell. The sensation of weightlessness overcame him. Changing colors swirled around in slow motion, flashing and dulling erratically. His mind separated from his physical body. He watched, as if from another realm.

Falling downward, down…down…down, into a black expanse of nothingness. All color faded from existence. His mind merged with the dark. Blackness surrounded him, enveloping him, frightening him. He thought to scream, but the sound choked on the lump in his throat.

The speed of his descent increased.

Colors erupted. Lights flashed.

"What the—"

He sped toward a narrow opening, and once there was sucked through into a dull gray sky. Still, he fell.

Water flowed below him—a rushing river.

His body took on weight, becoming heavier as he dropped. He slammed hard against the water and plunged into the cold, murky depths.

CHAPTER THREE

Fir-wood, Strathlachlan, 1511

*H*e dare not assault me." Elspeth MacLachlan leaned forward in her saddle and eyed the trail. She didn't want to end the search for the precious herbs she sought.

"Lass, this place is not safe." The redheaded Jamie MacEwen wasn't of the same mind.

He should be accustomed to her strange ways by now, having been her guard for many years. She often came to this magical place, to Fir-wood, to the knoll near the deserted hut. The old folk warned that faeries inhabited the spot, and she had reason to believe the tales to be true. Her parents vanished there years before.

Elspeth held the impossible dream close to her heart of them one day reappearing.

Jamie scratched the back of his neck while he glanced around. "I never should have ridden out alone with you. Maclay was seen here not but a sennight ago. And you ken how dangerous he is. He nearly raped and killed your brother's lady-wife. You saw the Lady Laurie yourself after Archie rescued her from Maclay's lair."

Elspeth cringed at the reminder. She'd terrible memories

of that day. Of her brother Archibald carrying Laurie's bruised and bloodied body into the hall, and the pained bellow of her other brother Patrick when he saw his ladylove. Even so, the memory wouldn't deter her. She needed to find the medicinal herbs for Aine, who unselfishly looked after the comfort of those living in the castle. Elspeth promised. Besides, Laurie's abduction happened more than a year ago. Patrick and Laurie had since wed and moved...*somewhere.*

Jamie scowled. "I should have at least brought Duncan along to watch our backs."

"Please, a moment longer. There is a spot along the burn where I always find the plants I need."

She walked her chestnut palfrey to the edge of the stream and dismounted. As she knelt to look for herbs, she reached in front of her and pushed aside some brush.

Peering around a bush, she screamed.

In a flash, Jamie stood beside her with his sword drawn.

She gaped at the man lying there, facedown, the lower half of his body submerged in water. Sunlight glinted off the large milky gem imbedded in the hilt of the sword lying next to the man.

Elspeth gasped, her chest tightening. She leaned closer. "Who is he?"

Jamie hunkered down next to the warrior and examined the soaking wet man. He rolled him over. "I have never seen him afore."

At the sight of the man's face, her heart fluttered. She reached her hand down and gently caressed his cheek. A tingling sensation raced through her, and she quickly pulled her fingers away, clutching them over her heart.

Afraid Jamie might notice her agitation, she stood. "We must take him to the castle to tend him properly." Unable to stop herself, she bent again to examine the stranger. "He does not appear to be wounded. How do you think he came to be here?"

Jamie rubbed his jaw and glanced toward the burn. "He appears to have been in the water for some time. Mayhap he was injured and floated down stream."

At the sound of an approaching rider, Jamie dragged Elspeth away to hide in the trees.

She peeked around the trunk of a large fir as Duncan cautiously rode his horse close to the injured man lying on the ground while searching the wood with keen eyes.

"I ken you are there, Jamie. Come out of hiding."

Her escort gave a hearty sigh of relief. He grasped her by the elbow, and they left the protection of the trees to stand at Duncan's side.

"Ach. What did you find, brother?" Duncan asked.

"A stranger. Elspeth wishes to take him to the castle."

"Aye, sure. Help me get him onto my mount. We can throw him into the pit until we learn who he is."

Elspeth fisted hands on hips and did her best to glare at the brothers. "Nae, you must not do such a thing. The poor man is injured and needs tending."

After dismounting, Duncan examined the man, nudging him several times. "Where do you think he came from?"

"Could not say." Jamie shrugged. "Though he must be of good birth by the look of his sword."

"Could be stolen. Think you, mayhap, he be one of Maclay's men?"

"Nae. His garments are too fine," Jamie said.

"Would you two stop? He needs help." They'd be there forever if the twins continued their conjecture.

Duncan and Jamie exchanged glances. Jamie raised his eyes heavenward and acted put upon. Even so, he helped his brother toss the sodden stranger across the horse with Duncan swinging up behind.

"Jamie, you should not have ridden out with Elspeth alone. We have had more dire warnings of Maclay."

"What hear you?" Jamie picked up the man's sword and hooked it with his own on the flank of his stallion. Then he gave her a leg up before mounting his steed.

Duncan reined his horse 'round and started to ride. "Alexander Campbell and his men rode in with tales of finding Maclay's camp and chasing the cur, but the mongrel eluded capture again," he said, once Jamie and Elspeth were abreast.

Clearing his throat, he peered at her. "Your betrothed is distraught you were not at the castle to greet him. Your brother sent me to fetch you."

She frowned. "Alexander is at the castle?"

"Aye, that he is. He was not happy to find you gone. He is bellowing like an injured mountain cat, threatening to take a whip to your backside." Duncan winked at Jamie.

"I am not afraid of him." She rode with proud posture, but unease settled in her belly.

This didn't bode well. Alexander could be prickly at the best of times. She'd have to think of something to soothe his misplaced anger.

Her mouth tasted sour all of a sudden.

When she'd been younger, and he traveled for the king, she'd believed herself in love with Alexander. Since they spent more time together, she learned to rather dislike her betrothed.

She tightened her grip on the reins and braced for the feared confrontation.

It wasn't long before her thoughts and gaze wandered to the man hanging across Duncan's saddle. Why did the sight of him make her feel…things a betrothed woman shouldn't feel?

Caitrina shimmered onto the center of the *Sithichean Sluaigh*, conjuring a heavy mist to maintain her glamour of invisibility. She sensed the presence of the *brunaidh* in a coppice of trees near the edge of the Fir-wood and the faerie knoll. Foolish wee man, as if he could remain hidden from a fae.

Munn, the MacLachlan clan brownie, barely stood three feet tall and, dressed as he was in baggy brown leather *trews*, a knee length *leine* and a forest green *brat*, almost blended into the foliage. His unusual blue-green eyes searched the area before he stepped onto the grassy knoll. He certainly didn't see her, but when he sniffed the air, his ancient, whiskery, brown face scrunched even more than usual into a nasty grimace.

"I hate that exotic fragrance, the scents of peony and freesia and sandalwood." He sneezed and wiped his big nose with the back of a brown hand. "She has returned. It must be she. That irritating *sithiche* is back."

Even though he mumbled, Caitrina heard his rant.

He knelt and studied the tracks still fresh in the rich grass. He scanned the area before rising and following the imprints to the edge of the stream.

"What mischief have you conjured, princess?" His face reddened and he clenched his fists. "Ach, I must warn the chief before something terrible happens."

He spun in a circle and disappeared into the haze.

This time, Caitrina would ensure the wee man not interfere with her tasks. She would mate the MacIntyre lad with the MacLachlan lass and win the queen's challenge.

Caitrina smiled, but as she dissolved into the mist, her skin prickled in warning.

Hours after returning home, Elspeth sat in the guest chamber waiting for the stranger to wake. She shifted her weight in the chair. Her ears still flamed from the scolding she received earlier from her betrothed. He acted as if they'd already wed.

Alexander's temper had exploded, but the reprimand could have been worse. In the course of what she'd expected to be a lengthy tirade, his face paled as if he'd seen a *banshee*. Then a smile brightened his face, the kind that broadened his lips when he got what he wanted. He and his men rode out shortly thereafter, leaving the castle in unprecedented haste.

How had she once believed herself in love with the man?

She tapped her fingernails on the wooden bed frame.

Oh, bother. With the excitement of finding the stranger, she forgot the herbs she intended to collect. Well, they'd have to make do with what had been dried and put into storage. Her brother wouldn't allow her to ride out again. Not with Maclay in the area.

Besides, she wasn't inclined to expose herself to more danger.

She stared at the stranger who lay motionless on the mattress and studied the contours of his face. Handsome with a firm, square jaw. The tips of her breasts tingled from the naughty images prancing through her mind while she gazed upon his lush lips.

Moistening hers, she could hardly wait for his eyes to open so she'd discover their color. She reached her hand out and touched his hair. Now dry, the soft strands slipped through her fingers. The warm honey color contrasted nicely with his sun-bronzed skin.

She liked the look of him.

There were other things she liked about him as well. Things she'd seen earlier while examining him for injuries. He had a hard, muscular body. That a man who appeared to possess so much strength could be free of scars amazed her. *For shame.* Admiring his body surely was wrong. She was to wed Alexander.

An uneasy chill swept down her spine, and she shivered.

But she couldn't stop her wayward gaze from straying to the stranger's hands. Strong hands. She released a small cry when one of those hands wrapped tightly around her wrist.

She jerked her gaze to the man's face.

The stranger quickly released her. "Where am I?" he demanded.

Unable to catch her breath, she raised a hand to her chest to calm her racing heart. His eyes were a lovely shade of hazel.

Disturbed to realize he glared at her, she knit her brow.

"You are a guest at Castle Lachlan," Aine MacTamhais said as she entered the chamber.

The stranger's tense muscles relaxed upon hearing that wee bit of news.

"Did you bring broth?" Elspeth jumped to her feet. She hoped the older woman didn't notice the flush guilt brought to her cheeks.

"Aye. You ken I did." Aine stared at her oddly.

Elspeth bit her bottom lip and stepped away from the bed. "Then I will take my leave." She hurried to the door, but before she fled the bedchamber, she stole one more look at the handsome warrior.

The bold man winked at her.

Finn caught the scowl of the plump older woman.

Disappointment surged through him and he frowned. He hadn't meant to chase the girl away. It was just that…this was all a bit unnerving. He'd been more than surprised when he woke to see her there, staring at him as if she wanted to…*taste him*.

Now that was an intriguing thought. One he'd certainly enjoy experiencing.

She was the petite woman from his dreams. Of that, he was certain. She looked younger, but possessed the same desirable curves. Her strawberry-blond hair, pulled back in a long braid, was the same lustrous silk he remembered from his dreams. And her eyes, those mesmerizing silver eyes, definitely belonged to the angel of his memories.

The thrill he'd felt when he touched her still coursed through him, a tremor sizzling along his spine. He tugged at the fabric of his kilt to hide his erection.

The older woman, whom the girl called Aine, slammed the tray down on the chest next to the bed. She gave him a disapproving look. "What did you do to frighten the lass so?"

She could glower at him all she wanted. He felt damn lucky to be there. He'd ended up exactly where he wanted to be. Castle Lachlan was the hereditary home of the MacLachlans, which meant these people were members of Patrick's clan.

Finn sat up straight, giving the woman what he hoped was his most winning smile. "I didn't mean to frighten the...*lass*. I'm Finn MacIntyre. Is this the home of Archibald MacLachlan?"

Aine's eyes narrowed. "Aye, that it be."

"I must speak with him immediately."

"Demanding, you are." She gave a nearly indiscernible nod to the ginger-haired warrior who Finn now noticed stood in the doorway. The enigmatic hulk of a man stared at Finn for a moment before departing.

"The chief is busy with more important matters than strange warriors. He will see you when he is ready. Aye. In good time. Now you will drink this broth I brought you." She held the cup out to him.

A persistent knocking at the door interrupted Archibald MacLachlan from his bleak thoughts. Immersed in the complicated tangle of his problems, he imagined the pounding had been going on for some time.

He'd become chief of the clan when his twin brother Patrick gave up the position to leave Scotland with his outlander wife. In all that time, Archibald still hadn't convinced Iain Lamont, the chief of his feuding neighbors, to allow him to wed his daughter Isobell.

Archibald rubbed the stiffness from his neck. "Enter."

He recognized the heavy footfalls. Duncan entered his study, his private chamber. The place where the successive chiefs of Clan MacLachlan found solace, or not, depending on the individual challenges they faced.

Today, Archibald came here to brood.

Disappointed by the disturbance, he turned away from the window, where he'd been looking toward his beloved Scottish hills without truly seeing them. "What has happened to Elspeth? I am sure you have an interesting tale to tell."

"I found *Herself* and Jamie in Fir-wood near the old deserted hut." Duncan shuffled his feet.

"At the *Sithichean Sluaigh*, that cursed faerie knoll?" Archibald grimaced.

"Aye." Duncan awkwardly cleared his throat "They searched for herbs, but they found something more disturbing."

Unease slithered along Archibald's spine. "And what would that be?"

"A man who claims to be Finn MacIntyre."

"Lady Laurie's cousin? Are you sure?" Archibald reached for a chair to sit. Could the day spawn any more unexpected events?

"I heard him say so myself."

"Bring him to me."

Finn smiled at Aine, believing he found an ally. Over the past half-hour, he gleaned quite a bit from her about the household. Most importantly, he discovered the woman who tended him was Elspeth, the chief's younger sister.

And the sister of Finn's cousin-in-law, Patrick MacLachlan.

Damned complication.

At the sound of approaching footsteps, he raised his gaze. The warrior Aine had earlier named Duncan reappeared. She said he was a strong man, but one with a gentle heart.

Her face flushed when she noticed the glaring man hovering in the doorway.

Finn studied Duncan and grinned. The red-haired warrior was probably six foot four and solid like a linebacker. *This is the guy Laurie thought of as a teddy bear?*

Hardly. Finn shook his head.

"Our chief is ready to see you. Are you feeling well enough to go below stairs?"

"The dizziness has passed." Finn stood on rubbery legs, his sense of balance off. He struggled to hide his weakness from Duncan. Finn didn't want the man to think him incapable. After a few moments, his equilibrium returned, and he followed the warrior from the chamber, down the narrow circular stairs, to the level below.

He ran a hand along the cold gray stone wall of the passageway. From the smooth stone, to the torches burning in metal stands, to the sturdy-looking wood furniture, to the colorful tapestries gracing the walls, all roused his insatiable curiosity. He visited castles before—dank and musty places—but never one like this. Here everything appeared new, or at least newer than the dusty relics found in museums. This was an opportunity to see how castles actually functioned in their own time period.

He chuckled to himself. He'd become obsessed with history. *I guess I've more in common with my father than I thought.*

David MacIntyre's African digs were famous in archeology circles and over the years spurred resentment from Finn. Maybe he shouldn't have been so hard on his father. He'd have to reconcile with the old man when he returned to the future.

*If...*he could return to the future. He brushed away the unwanted thought before it weakened his determination. Instead, he focused on the broad back of the man he followed.

When they entered one of the dim passageways, Elspeth approached. As she brushed by, a shy smile brightened her heart-shaped face. Her heat penetrated his clothing to touch his very soul, branding him. He shot a glance over his shoulder to watch as, with a swish of her hips, she moved on along the passageway, her backside swaying provocatively, her long gown clinging to generous curves.

Inhaling sharply, he averted his eyes. He didn't dare allow the lust he felt for such a young woman, for his cousin-in-law's sister, no less.

Duncan's lips thinned. "Lad, you had best forget her. She is betrothed to Alexander Campbell. You will not want to make an enemy of him. If you have an argument with one Campbell, you have an argument with the whole clan. That is the way of it."

"Understood." He would put her out of his mind and concentrate on revenge.

Keeping pace with Duncan as they moved along the passageway, Finn anticipated the meeting. He would be the last person the MacLachlan expected to see today.

Finn wasn't sure why he found the situation amusing. He should be frightened, or at least concerned, but he wasn't. Something happened to him while traveling through time. Something lightened his heart. Even his step seemed springier.

He'd fallen into an unexpected adventure and he planned to enjoy every minute of his time in the past. Then he would take his vengeance and return to the future.

When Duncan banged on the heavy oak door in front of them, a deep voice called from within, bidding them enter.

At the window stood Archibald MacLachlan, staring outward toward the reflected glow of the waning moon on the glass-like surface of the bay, his broad shoulders rigid and unyielding. When the man turned around, Finn found it hard to refrain from smiling. It was as if he looked at his cousin-in-law. The man who stood before him was Patrick's identical twin.

Standing tall, his long chestnut hair pulled back in a ponytail, his features void of emotion, Archibald was the picture of a powerful Highland chief. The only noticeable difference was Archibald appeared more severe than Patrick. Finn doubted this man ever smiled. And there was one other difference. This man's eyes were icy silver-blue, whereas Patrick's were a startling sapphire.

Archibald motioned with his arm to one of the two chairs before the hearth. Finn casually sat. His host stiffly took the other seat, his back ramrod straight.

Duncan backed out of the door, closing it behind him; the soft thud sounded overly loud in the quiet room.

"My man kens his duty. He will wait outside the door, ready if I am in need of him." Archibald's forehead furrowed as if he remembered something and he lunged to his feet. A couple of steps took him to a nearby table where he filled two cups with a ruby-red liquid. Returning, he handed one to Finn.

Finn accepted the wine with a nod, and Archibald returned to his chair. "You are Finn MacIntyre, cousin to the Lady Laurie MacLachlan?"

"Aye."

Archibald pointed to the cup in Finn's hand. "Try the wine. Tis a fine claret I acquired in France."

Both men drank.

Feeling the chill of the other's gaze, Finn sensed Archibald observing him.

The man put his cup down. "Why are you here?"

Also setting aside his wine, Finn looked directly into Archibald's eyes. "Patrick sent me after Maclay." He inwardly winced. He hated to lie, but he needed this man to believe he had Patrick's approval.

Archibald's eyes narrowed. "Where is my twin?"

"France."

"Ah, they did go to the Continent. I told Elspeth as much."

"Good." Finn shifted his weight in his chair.

Archibald seemed to relax then raised a brow. "You say Patrick sent you. Why now? I have not heard from my brother for more than a year. How did he ken we have not yet captured Maclay?"

"Patrick has had word."

His host's glower was a blatant attempt to intimidate. Finn didn't flinch under the intense scrutiny. He'd faced worse across many a boardroom table.

"I see." Archibald's voice rose and his glance measured Finn. "He sent you to achieve something none of our lads have. You dinnae look like much of a warrior."

A tingling of unease crept along Finn's spine. Maybe pretending to be a sixteenth-century warrior wouldn't be as painless as he hoped. He hadn't thought his actions through. He'd been impulsive to run through the time gate. But the fear etched in Laurie's face enraged him, causing him to act blindly.

The need for retribution burned hot in his blood.

"How did you come to be here on MacLachlan lands and out of your head?" Archibald continued the interrogation before Finn could respond to his previous comment.

"I was attacked."

"You have nae injuries. How do you explain that? And you still have your sword. I hear tell it is a fine piece of weaponry with a large moonstone in its hilt. Your claymore would be a grand prize for a thief."

"I escaped. However, I was weak from the struggle and fell into the water. The next thing I remember is your beautiful sister standing over me."

"Interesting tale." Archibald stroked his chin and rose from his seat. "We shall see. The night is growing late, and we should be for bed-going. On the morrow, you can prove your vigor with a trial on the practice field."

Finn also stood.

"Sleep well." The other man gave him a crooked half-grin. "You are going to need your rest."

Finn inclined his head and walked to the door.

"'Twould be best to stay away from my sister," Archibald added as Finn's hand hovered over the door latch.

When Elspeth returned to the bedchamber, she found Aine examining the stranger's claymore, rubbing callused fingers reverently over the large moonstone in the sword's cross-section. Elspeth touched her mother's silver brooch pinned at her breast. The brooch contained the same lustrous, pale blue stones.

Her father gave the token of his love to her mother when they'd wed. The brooch was a beautiful piece of craftsmanship, adorned with six small moonstones entwined with animals and spiral filigrees. Each gemstone represented one of the children Mairi MacLachlan had come to mother, three from her husband's first marriage and three from their union.

Elspeth's mother had been wearing the brooch when she disappeared along with Elspeth's father, never to be heard from again.

That happened nearly five years ago. Elspeth sighed. She missed them so. Her heart still ached, her sorrow held deep within.

Then Lady Laurie arrived with the brooch pinned to her *plaide*, claiming to be from the future. Having grown up with tales of faeries and brownies, Elspeth believed her friend, happy to have her mother's brooch returned. The one she now wore instead of her own.

Aine laid the sword on the chest and raised her eyes to Elspeth. "I served your mother when you were born. I hid in the shadows when the faerie appeared to her and gave the prophecy." Aine moved closer, leaning into Elspeth to whisper. "The elder said a stranger bearing the faerie-kissed sword would come for you from a far-off distant place." Aine straightened to stare at Elspeth with age-worn eyes.

"That is naught but a *bairn's* tale. I dinnae believe it true. I am to wed Alexander come the harvest, as my father wished."

Aine made a tsking sound. "The man you brought home from the wood is not of these hills and glens. He carries a claymore with a moonstone in the hilt. He claims to be a MacIntyre. Cousin to the Lady Laurie. Do you not think that odd, lass?"

"If this man is of the prophecy, I would have foreseen his coming. I did not. We must not speak of this again."

"'Tis likely you refuse to see."

Elspeth dropped into one of the chairs before the hearth. Could it be possible? Could he be the one? Did she dare hope?

Maybe it was time she embrace her gift.

CHAPTER FOUR

Time draws near.

Elspeth jolted awake, sat up, and jerked her eyes open. "Who?"

Dim light peeked through slits in closed shutters. In the gloom, she identified familiar furniture shapes. Bed frame, chairs, chests.

Just a dream, or had it been...a *vision?*

She shivered and rubbed the gooseflesh prickling her arms. The room had grown chill during the night. Swinging her legs over the edge of the bed, she reached for the flint and lit a candle. She padded across the cold floor and tossed kindling on the embers. When the twigs lit, she added a couple pieces of firewood.

Was a vision trying to break through her blocks?

She glared at the ornate chest at the end of the bed. Should she embrace her gift? Last night she'd thought so. This morning...

Lifting the lid, she rifled through the contents and pulled out a small intricately carved wooden box. She clutched her prized possession to her bosom and sat. For a brief moment, she savored the meager warmth from the fire burning in the hearth.

Elspeth opened the box and removed a tiny parcel. Setting the box aside, she laid the leather-wrapped package on her lap and undid the knot securing it. A silver brooch fell into the crease of her skirt. Picking up the delicate piece, she held it tenderly in her hand.

A tear escaped her eye and ran along her cheek. She wiped at the moisture with the palm of her free hand as she remembered.

Cold wind blew across Loch Fyne the day her womanly flux began. Her mother surprised her with a present to celebrate her becoming a woman. The beautiful silver brooch was embellished with a single moonstone in the center surrounded by silver flowers and interwoven spirals. Her mother told her the faerie-blessed stone would help clarify the meaning of the visions that would come to her as her womanhood blossomed.

Her mother had been right. As with the other females of her line, the visions came and she learned to ken their meaning. A burden at times, the aftermath of her gift often painful.

The other tale her ma told her that day was of the prophecy given at Elspeth's birth. According to her mother, the moonstone in the brooch represented the man who would come to love Elspeth.

She knew the story well. Her mother's eyes had clouded as she relived that time of birthing and in a whispered voice told the tale.

When three, seven-year cycles of the moon wane, a strange warrior from an unknown far-off place will come wielding the mighty, lost sword of the fae to save you from despair. Just once in a verra blue moon love will triumph.

Elspeth wanted to believe the tale of nonsense, but she was nearly a score and one summers. Many believed her too old to be desirable to wed. Yet she was to marry Alexander Campbell on the eve of her next birth celebration.

Her father refused to heed the faerie magic at the time of her birth. He wanted her wed to the son of an influential

Highland chief. Thus, he secured a marriage contract with the Campbell, the great Chief of Clan Diarmaid, second Earl of Argyll, binding her to his grandson, Alexander.

As decreed by her father, she would wed the wretch at the end of summer when he received the grant of keepership for Skipness Castle.

Elspeth grasped the brooch until the pressure of the metal against her tender palm caused pain. *Come autumn, will I truly be chained to the pompous bore?*

Caitrina laughed, amusement bubbling up her throat. Foolish human. She'd drawn the arrogant man away from Castle Lachlan and led him on a merry chase through the night. She wouldn't allow him to threaten her plans any more than she'd allow the damn brownie to get in her way.

With Alexander Campbell busy, pursuing an illusion, she concentrated on her task.

Filtered morning light fell on the path. She stepped lightly, leaving not a footprint. The forest animals' silence meant she was close. After several more minutes, the rancid smell of damp wood smoke made her nose itch. She stifled a sneeze.

Donning the glamour of invisibility with a thought, she shimmered to the edge of the clearing and peered into the camp.

"Wake up, you miserable dogs." Malcolm Maclay kicked one of his sleeping men.

The others scrambled to rise, avoiding similar abuse.

"You idiots, I should kill the lot of you." Maclay's white knuckled fingers tightened on the pole he held. His face mottled to a deep shade of purple, the horrendous scars a light pink in contrast. "I send you to perform a simple task. To bring me one man and one sword. You cannot even manage that."

Four of his men shuffled their feet and stared at the ground. The one who stood nearest dared look Maclay in the eye. "But the man's claymore, 'tis magic. The sword glows with an unholy light and when we touched it, the cursed thing burned us." He held out his hands and showed the black on the tips of singed fingers.

A smile tugged at Caitrina's lips, but she forced aside the merriment. It had been the work of a moment to push the soaking wet Finn back into the rushing water, away from his attackers.

"I will not abide fools!"

With a swift motion, the blunt end of Maclay's pole slammed into the man's chest. The man crumpled to the ground, gasping for breath. Maclay kicked him hard in the ribs and walked away.

Caitrina giggled, sending a musical note on the breeze.

Goosebumps bubbled on Maclay's forearms. His wide-eyed gaze darted around the clearing. Then he narrowed his eyes, shook his head and continued into the wood away from his men. "Magic? Paah," he muttered. "Capture the man. Control the sword."

Alarm tightened Caitrina's chest, and she sobered. How had the bastard learned about the enchanted blade? No matter. She'd continue to use him. Though caution would be prudent. Previously, Maclay proved difficult to manipulate.

She pursed her lips. She could handle him. Unless—

Had the queen interfered? Already?

Trepidation-laced excitement vibrated through Caitrina. Unable to remain still, she paced. Once Oonagh learned the game had begun, Caitrina would need to orchestrate carefully calculated moves to remain in play. She refused to lose everything to the queen's whims.

Caitrina would see Finn and Elspeth matched.

Someone played drums on his skull. Finn groaned and pulled the pillow over his head. The down did little to silence the thump.

"Gah!" His head ached and nausea threatened. Finn tossed the pillow aside. Laurie never mentioned a post time-travel hangover when she described her fall into the past. When he managed to pry his eyes open and shake some of the fuzz from his mind, he discovered the annoying sound came from a heavy hand banging on the bedchamber door. He glanced through the unshuttered window at the gray sky. The sun hadn't yet cleared the horizon. Who would wake him at such a ghastly hour?

Two hearty warriors burst into the chamber, two identical, heavily muscled men dressed in battle gear. Great. This would be fun.

Doubtful.

Was the conceiving of twins an epidemic in the Highlands?

One of the ginger-haired men stepped forward. Finn eyed him suspiciously, suspecting he was Duncan. Was surprising they waited as long as they had before barging in.

"Time to break your fast." The man laughed.

He moved to the chest where Finn's clothes lay and handed them over. The twin picked up Finn's sheathed sword and strode to the door.

"Hey, what goes on here?" Finn demanded.

"My brother Jamie and I are to take you to the hall to break your fast. Then to the practice field," Duncan gave his brother an exaggerated wink, "to watch Archie put you on your arse."

"Archie? Archibald?"

"Aye, our Elspeth's pet name for her brother," Jamie answered.

Finn fought the smile threatening to curl his lips at the thought of his angel. He dressed in a rush. Before Jamie strode away with his sword, Finn grabbed the leather-encased claymore and strapped it to his back.

They made their way from the eastern wing to the western and descended the circular stairs. Even with the early hour, the hall bustled with activity. The great hall ran the entire length of the castle's first floor and was half as wide. On one side, several heavy wooden chairs with elaborate velvet cushions fronted an immense fireplace, eight feet tall and about twelve feet wide. Across the room, a long table with thirteen chairs on the far side sat atop a dais from where the diners could view the rest of the hall.

Finn ignored the curious eyes observing him.

On the wall behind the head table hung several brightly colored tapestries depicting mythical scenes with dragons. The shimmering blue scales of one of the beasts held his attention until Duncan nudged him forward.

While crossing the stone floor, they passed a number of multi-branched wrought iron stands supporting drippy candles, which cast a sickly yellow light and putrefied the air.

Finn scrunched his nose, trying not to sneeze.

The men escorted him to a table below the dais where they sat on a rough-hewn bench. A young serving girl brushed her breasts across his upper arm while placing a trencher heaped with food on the table in front of him. Before strutting away, she flicked her dark lashes suggestively.

A grunt of disgust slipped from his throat when his body reacted. He refused to look at the twins. He didn't want to see their smirks.

Finn's stomach growled, and he dug into the food, though went light on the ale. He never drank in the morning and suspected the twins attempted to get him drunk before the festivities.

Since *he* was the entertainment, he wasn't about to accommodate.

Sensing someone watching, he glanced at the table on the dais. Silver eyes stared at him. A spark of indefinable emotion flickered, and a rosy blush flushed Elspeth's cheeks. He inclined his head, and she averted her gaze.

What was his angel thinking? His? What was he thinking?

He didn't have much of a chance to contemplate the intricacies of his and Elspeth's thoughts. Duncan pulled him from his seat, and they strode off for the trial of vigor.

The sun rose on the horizon. Archibald studied the view as streaks of crimson merged with the blue of the sky. He needed to collect his weapons and head to the field to grind that arrogant MacIntyre into the ground.

He hunched his shoulders, bone weary.

He'd come to his private chamber earlier than usual on this morn, wanting to reassure himself all was as it should be. With Maclay thieving cattle, he'd reason for concern. His seneschal had only recently locked away the ledgers and left the chamber.

Flexing the muscles in his back, Archibald attempted to relieve the stiffness from sitting so long. He still wasn't used to the long hours required to deal with clan business. He was more accustomed to being out-of-doors, practicing warrior skills, and traveling for the king.

Lucky for him, his father, and then his brother Patrick had left clan matters in good order. Archibald had little to distress him in the managing of the clan lands and castles. However, there'd be problems come winter if they didn't capture Maclay and end the thieving.

Archibald heaved a frustrated sigh and ran fingers through his thick hair. What truly vexed him remained the problem dearest to his heart. His efforts to convince Iain Lamont to contract a marriage agreement with him for Lady Isobell's hand had been futile. He missed her and was certain she must be bereft without him. No matter how determined, he hadn't yet thought of a way to resolve the matter to his satisfaction. The longer the negotiations dragged on, the angrier he became.

A crash from behind him disturbed his troubled thoughts. When he twisted around, he saw a small table overturned, and Munn, the clan brownie, emerging into solid form. The little man spun in frenzied circles until finally stopping to fall into a sit upon the floor.

"What are you about, wee man?" Archibald hid his smile behind a hand.

Munn stood and brushed the dust from his arse. "That

meddling *sithiche* Caitrina has returned to plague us."

Boldly smiling, Archibald remembered with pleasure his one encounter with the fae Caitrina. Her beauty had so captivated him, convincing him to follow her. Thank Saint Columba he had, for he saved Lady Laurie from Maclay's clutches that day.

"And what would she want with us? The Lady Laurie is on the Continent with my brother Patrick. Her faerie-protector should be there with them." He squeezed his jaw and stroked. "Unless... Might she have come with MacIntyre?"

Munn leapt onto a chair and leaned forward, his gnarled face mere inches from that of Archibald. "Ach, chief. Have you forgotten my warnings he would come? He will take our Elspeth away. He will."

"Never mind you that." Archibald stepped back. "MacIntyre claims Patrick sent him to rid us of that bastard Maclay. Do you ken if he speaks the truth?"

"You must break the marriage contract with the Campbell. Lady Elspeth must not wed Alexander. She must not wed a Campbell. 'Twill bring ruin to the clan." Munn shook his head, ignoring the question about MacIntyre.

"Dire warnings, indeed. Breaking marriage contracts is not for me. Entering one with Lamont is what I have planned."

"More. Keep our lady from the MacIntyre warrior. He plans to steal her away."

"Ach, Munn." Archibald frowned. The brownie drove him mad with his inability to focus on one subject.

"Do you not hear the warning on the wind? Ach! You must listen. Lady Elspeth must not wed a Campbell."

Then again, maybe the little man was obsessed with one thing.

"Nonsense." Archibald reached for his claymore and strapped the leather sheath to his back. He'd heard enough of Munn's annoying counsel. Archibald was determined to see his sister wed to Alexander Campbell as their father's contract dictated. No one, especially a bothersome brownie, would change his mind on the matter.

"Be gone, wee man. I am to the field to grind that arrogant MacIntyre warrior into the mud." He strode from the chamber, leaving the loyal yet annoying Munn behind to rant about the Campbells and all things dire.

Finn rubbed his sweaty palms on his plaid, swearing under his breath. If he couldn't keep his hands dry, he'd have difficulty maintaining his grip on the hilt of his sword.

Watching the men practicing on the field, he swallowed. Strong and well trained, these men were seasoned warriors. Unlike himself—a weekend warrior, fighting mock battles, pretending to be something he wasn't.

Bluffing came easy to him in the business world. Would he be able to deceive these men? He shifted from one foot to the other. Waiting frazzled his nerves. Where was MacLachlan?

From the corner of his eye, Finn caught the grim countenances of his two watchdogs. The twins were large brawny men, as were most of the men on the field. Following their gazes to the two men now battling with claymores cheered on by an enthusiastic crowd, Finn became fixated too. The fighters appeared well matched, slicked with sweat, their massive chests heaving with exertion.

The men circled each other until one stepped forward aggressively, swinging his sword in a horizontal arc. The second warrior defensively blocked the cut aimed at his torso. The high-pitched clank of metal buzzed in Finn's ears. His eyes blurred. The dance of the warriors played before him in painfully slow motion, blades striking and cutting and chopping, blinding sunlight glaring off polished metal. Finally, to his relief, the battle ended. The large two-handed swords stilled point-down in the dirt. Warriors exclaimed victory and conceded defeat.

Finn wiped his hands down the length of his *leine*, declaring himself the biggest fool. Just because he trained with Patrick and Iain MacLachlan in the twenty-first century didn't mean he could best either man or anyone else for that matter. Especially when it would really count, when his skill, or lack of, would be a matter of life or death, his or his opponent's.

His escape from the thieves who attacked him at the stream after his trip through the time gate had been a matter of luck. Four thugs threatened him, but the men had been clumsy, and only one carried a sword. One man almost wrestled the claymore away from Finn, instead to pull back in unexplained pain, causing Finn to lose his balance. Stumbling, he'd fallen into the rapids and been whisked downstream away from his assailants before they inflicted more harm.

He glanced at the huddle of warriors again. In an attempt to ease his anxiety, he used the deep-breathing exercises taught to him by his good friend, Douglas.

Calming some, he walked away from the enthusiastic congratulations and primitive backslapping. Finding a secluded space away from the others, he began the martial arts exercises meant to prepare his body for battle. The ones he practiced every day, for years, ever since his discharge from the Marines. The fluid movements soothed his fears.

He'd be ready when Archibald arrived.

Jaw clenched, Elspeth had watched the newcomer leave the hall. Now, she searched the room for her least favorite serving woman. The buxom wench giggled with a warrior in the corner.

Good. The woman's interest in the newcomer was fleeting.

Hoping no one noticed her departure, Elspeth hurried from the great hall. She ran up the stairs as fast as her skirts allowed. Sometimes she wished she could wear *trews* like a man.

She rushed into her solar and flew to the window. The practice field below hummed with activity. The idle chatter in the hall this morn had been rife with what would take place there. Her brother intended to test the newcomer.

Wondering why she cared, she moved closer to the opening. He meant nothing to her. She'd barely met the man. Refused to consider she might be attracted to him. Nor would she believe he'd anything to do with the prophecy given at her birth. *Impossible.*

Convinced her only interest in the man's fate was due to his relationship to Lady Laurie—not for any other reason— Elspeth leaned over the sill to get a better view.

She couldn't find Finn among the warriors, but the men she did see were in different degrees of undress, fighting with an array of sharp, pointy weapons. There were also several young lads on the field at singlestick practice, striking hard ash sticks against straw men.

Patrick once explained the importance of the constant practice. He believed the continuous training helped the men develop such a high level of proficiency with each weapon they became skilled enough to avoid bloodshed.

Her brothers abhorred killing, except when absolutely necessary.

Elspeth leaned even farther over the sill, her toes rising off the floor. She dangled precariously out the window trying to locate Finn in the crowd. A large warrior moved to the side. *There he is!* Finn faced Archibald, his sword raised to strike.

"What are you doing there, lass?" came a panicked voice from behind Elspeth.

CHAPTER FIVE

*M*uscles straining, Finn raised his sword, the tip pointed toward Archibald's eyes. An odd tingling sensation raced along his outstretched arms, coalescing around his heart. *Nerves.* A bad time for a panic attack.

Swallowing hard, he held his stance.

Archibald attacked.

Finn warded off the first cut with the flat of his blade. Counterattacking, his feet firmly planted, he used his hips to bring power to his blow. The large two-handed sword was heavy. He heard Iain's instructions in his head. *"Bring the fight to an end swiftly, lad, before you become overly fatigued and are injured, or accidentally wound your opponent."*

Archibald grunted. The clang of steel rang in Finn's ears. Sun reflecting off polished metal nearly blinded him. Ignoring the distraction, he reached within to pull forth his inner-warrior.

Lightning flashed. Rolling thunder reverberated in his ears.

Each clash of his sword sent vibrations shooting up his arms, thrumming inside his chest, racing down his spine, spreading through his nervous system. Instead of weakening him, the pulsating energy made him more powerful.

With every stroke, he wielded his sword with renewed

strength, his senses enhanced. He moved from one blow to the next, his blade in constant motion.

A blur of silver fabric startled him, but he deflected the next strike with finesse.

Elspeth ran to the edge of the grassy field still embarrassed from the teasing she received from Aine who'd caught her hanging out her bedchamber window in a most unladylike fashion. She smoothed the front of her wrinkled silver gown and tried to see through the growing crowd.

"Devil of a fighter for a MacIntyre."

"Aye, the man can warm my bed on an eve."

Did the guardsmen and servants discuss her stranger? Hers?

She mustn't think of him as belonging to her. Need she remind herself she would soon wed? She should return to the castle.

"Bold attack. Near felled the chief."

She rose onto the balls of her feet, trying to see, but a broad warrior blocked her view of the action. Each time he moved, flinging his arms with excitement, he forced her to weave in the opposite direction.

"Lady Elspeth. Here." A young maid tugged her forward to the front of the ogling crowd.

Elspeth wasn't prepared for the scene unfolding, or for the unexpected emotions raging through her. She stared, mesmerized, white knuckles pressed against her mouth, the ring of steel against steel grating along her spine. Fear leapt into her throat. With every move the men made she tasted her fright.

She prayed for Finn. Guilt brought heat to her cheeks. She never supported her brothers' opponents.

Why now? Why this man?

Finn breathed deeply, dragging air into his lungs. Oxygen

pumped through his veins.

He warded another blow, pushing forward as he did. Archibald stumbled, his chest heaving from the effort.

Taking advantage, Finn released his left hand from the hilt of his sword and struck his opponent in the throat. Staggering backward, Archibald fell to one knee.

The crowd roared. Shock registered in the man's eyes.

Finn dropped his sword and bent over, panting. Holy shit. He'd bested Archibald.

The other warriors pressed forward. Someone pounded Finn on the back, cheering him. His vision blurred. He thought he might lose his breakfast, pass out.

He managed to stand firm.

Through a haze, Finn watched Duncan assist Archibald to his feet. His sword held tightly in his right hand, the Chief of Clan MacLachlan moved forward.

Finn blinked to clear his vision and braced for retribution.

Archibald handed his sword to Duncan and grabbed Finn's forearm, honoring him with a warrior's embrace. Finn returned the arm grasp with a strong grip. Their gazes locked. They came to a wordless accord.

When they broke apart, a young lad handed them both mugs filled to the brim, foam sloshing over the edge. They slammed their cups together and drank deeply.

"Well done! We will talk later." Archibald turned away and graciously accepted ribbing from his men.

Wiping the froth from his mouth with the back of his forearm, Finn noticed Elspeth standing beside her brother. He caught her gaze and smiled. She blushed and looked away.

Was for the best. He didn't dare mark time with her.

Within the mass of warriors, Finn received slaps on the back, the MacLachlan men showing their approval. Some maybe more grudgingly than others, but still, he'd never expected to be accepted, at least not so soon.

He scanned the crowd. What the heck? A medieval-dressed Caitrina stood off to the side, a smug smile set on her lips.

How the hell—

He must be seeing things. Finn rubbed his eyes with sweat-drenched fingers. When he looked again, she was gone, as if she dissolved into fine particles to scatter with the pollen on the breeze.

Duncan called to him, and Finn jerked his gaze away from the vacant spot. His stomach heaved. He twisted toward the grinning MacLachlan warrior and swallowed sour bile. What was wrong with him? He'd never before imagined such a strange thing after a fight.

Had Caitrina followed him through the gate? He hoped not.

At the evening meal in the great hall, Finn found himself seated at the head table with the family and their inner circle of retainers. Elspeth sat to the left of her brother and Finn to Archibald's right as an honored guest. Duncan sprawled on a chair to Finn's other side.

"You fought well. Moved faster than lightning. And when…" Duncan shook his head.

Finn grunted.

"When you grabbed for Archie—"

Finn glanced away from the man, unable to resist gazing at Elspeth. She was resplendent, dressed in a silver-blue gown matching the color of her bright eyes. Pink flushed her cheeks as she merrily conversed with Jamie, using delicate, long fingers to illustrate a point here and there.

Duncan's voice droned on. Finn lost the gist of the man's words until Duncan punched his arm. "I told you. You best not think of the lass. She is promised to another."

"Who is this Alexander fellow she is to marry?"

Duncan glanced around them. Only a serving lad stood nearby, so he leaned closer to whisper, "You best stay out of the man's way. His father is the Campbell and has the ear of King Jamie. The marriage is a political arrangement. 'Twill bring Archie closer to the crown."

Finn frowned and continued to watch Elspeth. Could she possibly be happy with such a match?

The thunk of the heavy oak door slamming against the wall of the great hall brought Finn's attention to the entrance where several armed men forcibly barged in, shoving MacLachlan men out of the way as they passed. Behind them strode an older man who bore a strong resemblance to Archibald and Patrick.

Voices rose in anger. Men seated at tables around the room jumped to their feet to stare at the fracas.

The older man marched to the dais and grinned.

"Silence!" Archibald stood.

Leaning forward, he pressed his hands flat on the table with such force his knuckles turned white. His twisted glare made Finn shudder.

"How dare you enter my hall?" A dark flush crept up Archibald's neck and reddened his face. "I should slay you for your treachery."

"Is that any way to greet your long absent uncle?"

"Aye 'tis, when a man's uncle is a traitor."

Patrick's uncle, Donald. Every muscle in Finn's body clenched. He gripped the edge of the table. He had to keep a tight rein on his anger or he'd jump across the board and strangle the man for what he'd done to Laurie.

Donald feigned hurt. "The king has given his pardon." He tossed a rolled document on the table. "Note the royal seal."

The hall remained silent as if those in attendance held their collective breath.

Archibald's jaw tightened and he continued to glare at his uncle. "Duncan, escort my uncle to my private chamber. I will join him momentarily."

Duncan shoved away from the table and rounded the dais.

"Nae need. I ken the way." Donald dismissed him with a jerk of his hand.

"Aye, and I will just see that you have not forgotten." Duncan moved in tight.

When they were gone, Archibald addressed Jamie with a

clipped tone, "See to my uncle's companions. Ensure they stay out of trouble."

Jamie eyed the men with distaste. "Aye. I will see they cause nae mischief." He stood and ushered the warriors to a lower table, the one furthest from the dais.

"Beth, please entertain our guest." He twisted and faced Finn. "If you will excuse me? I must see to this matter." He grabbed the document from the table and strode from the hall.

Finn let out a deep breath and took the opportunity to move over into Jamie's seat next to Elspeth. He made every effort to remain levelheaded. The situation required he be careful and take his cues from the MacLachlans. Although he wanted to understand what was going on, he didn't want to garner unwanted attention from the men who had accompanied Patrick's uncle. Finn hoped Elspeth would explain.

She didn't disappoint.

"You must think these events quite peculiar." Elspeth looked down at her folded hands.

"That was your Uncle Donald, correct?" Finn's jaw felt so taut he thought it might snap.

"Aye. Do you ken him?"

Finn released another heavy breath. "I know he was suspected of having my cousin Laurie kidnapped before she fell into the hands of that madman Malcolm Maclay."

"Aye, that he was, although 'twas never proved. Still, my brothers believe it so. My uncle has been known in the past to be...shall I say, untrustworthy. We have not seen him since Patrick and Lady Laurie went away." Elspeth raised her gaze to Finn. Her silver eyes were that of an angel. "Are they well?"

"They're quite happy in France with their three children." He cleared his throat uncomfortably. More lies.

"*Bairns?*"

Elspeth's face glowed when she grinned. Finn thought his heart would melt. How could he mislead the young woman?

He was certainly a lowlife. But he doubted she was aware Patrick and Laurie had traveled forward in time. How could he explain such to her without risking his cover? He couldn't. Besides, how could she possibly believe the story?

The last thing he wanted was someone thinking he was a sorcerer and having him condemned to death by fire.

Finn forced a smile and reached over and squeezed Elspeth's fingers. "Aye. Rambunctious twin boys and a sweet baby girl."

Caught in the magic of her gaze, he held onto her hand longer than appropriate. When he released her fingers, Elspeth's blush turned scarlet.

Feeling awkward himself, he moved to shove his hands into his pockets, but his kilt didn't have any. "Listen, it's getting late…" He hesitated, unsure of how to politely excuse himself.

"Aye, you best retire," Elspeth said. "Duncan is signaling you from the other side of the hall."

When he reached Duncan, the man gripped his upper arm. "Heed my warning, lad."

Finn nodded and continued to the stairs. As he made his way to his assigned bedchamber, he brushed past a small man with beady eyes. The brief contact made his skin crawl. He wondered if Archibald was aware unsavory characters stalked his halls.

Elspeth's gaze tracked Finn's progress across the hall. She wondered at Duncan's aggression. When Finn brushed past him and headed for the stairs, she stood to follow, but hesitated. She brought her fingers to her nose and inhaled the lingering, masculine scent, hardly believing she'd allowed a near stranger hold her hand. Her betrothed would surely be furious if he knew another man dared touch her.

Finn had a way about him that put her at ease, made her feel…safe.

Voices around her escalated—the clan consumed with the

intent of her uncle's visit. Elspeth hated to believe her relative had been as cruel as the rumors accused. Had he been involved with Laurie's abduction…he had nerve to return to Castle Lachlan.

Several of her brother's men fingered their swords while glaring at her uncle's men.

Her uncle was lucky Archibald had traveled for the king and learned to control his anger over the years. Had he not, a fight to the death could have erupted in the middle of the great hall.

Might have turned into a melee.

Men could be foolish at times. Tempers lost. Mistakes made.

Of course, none of the men would care to hear her opinion. Elspeth made her way to the stairs and through the passageways, stopping outside Finn's chamber. With a glance in both directions, she ascertained no one lurked nearby. She doubted anyone paid any heed to her whereabouts. The castle folk were too busy speculating about her uncle's sudden appearance to bother with the activities of a mere woman.

In front of the rough oak door, she bit her lower lip. She shouldn't be here. Alexander surely would be angry, as would Archie. But she was a Highlander bred to hospitality. As a good hostess she should ensure her guest's comfort.

Shouldn't she?

She hesitated only for a moment more before tapping softly on the door.

Finn leaned against the windowsill, enjoying the view of twilight over the sea loch. He found the way the rising moon glistened on the calm water a spectacular sight.

A knock intruded on his thoughts. Wasn't Duncan getting tired of lecturing him?

"Enter."

His breath hissed through his teeth when he spun to find Elspeth stepping across the threshold. "Lass, why are you here? If your brother learns you visited my room…my bedchamber, he'll be angry."

Elspeth's mouth curved into a tentative smile. "I came to see that you have all you require."

Well, wasn't that a loaded statement?

He stared at her kissable lips. Everything he required, huh. How about his need to smother her mouth with possessive kisses? He swallowed hard and looked away from her delectable smile.

"Lass, I thank you for your concern. I'm well. But I think you should leave before we come to regret this evening."

She tensed and her eyes widened.

Shucks. He hadn't meant to insult her. He stepped forward, his arm outstretched. "I'm sorry. I mean…"

"I am sorry. I should not have intruded on your privacy."

"You didn't. It's just… I understand you're betrothed," he blurted.

Elspeth hesitated. Opened her mouth and shut it.

Finn took another step toward her.

"Have a good eve." She spun on her heel and stepped through the doorway.

"Wait." He strode toward her.

Elspeth looked over her shoulder. There gazes met and locked.

"I'm glad you stopped by to check on me," he said.

She smiled and closed the oak panel.

Shit. Why hadn't he left it alone? Sometimes he was such a jerk. Finn leaned his forehead against the inside of the door. *A narrow escape.* He'd almost blown it and invited her to stay. He rubbed his groin thankful he wore a *leine* instead of tight jeans. It wouldn't do to make time with Elspeth. He'd never forgive himself if he betrayed Patrick's friendship for nothing more than a tumble in the sheets with his affianced sister. Never mind the fact Finn liked and respected Elspeth and didn't want to cause her trouble.

He hoped when next Alexander Campbell visited the gossips wouldn't be too harsh.

Finn determined to keep his distance from Elspeth.

After watching Elspeth enter Finn's chamber, Caitrina smiled. They were making this match much easier than Laurie and Patrick made theirs.

Perhaps Elspeth and Finn would consummate their union this very evening, then Caitrina could return to the twenty-first century and plot the last of the queen's challenges. The thought tempted her to cloak herself and enter the chamber to move things along, but she refrained...just barely.

The door flew open way too soon; she jumped into the shadows.

After the panel shut again, Elspeth leaned back against the solid wood, oblivious to the faerie's presence. A soft sigh escaped the young woman's lips and her eyes misted. She stood there for several minutes, smiling, and then slowly walked away along the passage.

Caitrina caught the scent of the couple's arousal. Maybe their union wouldn't happen tonight, but soon. Well-pleased, she grinned, until she felt a drain on her powers. Her instincts demanded she fight the unearthly pull, but she refused to allow the queen to learn just how powerful she'd become. Instead, she willed herself calm as the unnatural energy pulled her through time and space.

CHAPTER SIX

*N*ot a patient man, Alexander Campbell paced the confines of the small clearing within a grove of trees at the edge of the Fir-wood. He couldn't wait for these loathsome dealings to be at an end. He clenched and unclenched his fists, vexed a night and day had been wasted chasing a fae woman who remained illusive, vexed Elspeth had more backbone than he wanted in a wife, vexed the swine he was to meet made him wait. Rain soaked through his *plaide*, chilling his skin. Could the night be any fouler?

Malcolm Maclay sidled up next to him. Startled, Alexander strangled a gasp in his throat before it reached his lips. He found the silent way Maclay moved unnerving.

Alexander jerked his gaze away from the repulsive sight of the man's numerous scars, many the handiwork of Patrick MacLachlan's sword. One of the advantages Alexander counted on was Maclay's hatred for the MacLachlans. Alexander masked his expression before looking back at Maclay. "Did you come alone? I cannot afford to be seen meeting with the likes of you."

A little weasel-like man with beady eyes stepped out from behind a tree.

"I told you to come alone!" Alexander scowled at Maclay,

annoyed his orders hadn't been followed.

"You will be wanting to hear what my man has to say."

Alexander shot a glare at the distasteful stranger. "What have you to tell me?"

The man stepped close, his beady eyes darting from side to side. "I learned of things that will displease m'lord."

"Then speak."

"Aye. I heard plenty of tales this night."

The reek of the loathsome stranger's breath sickened Alexander. He leaned away. "Get on with it, man."

"I 'ave needs."

Alexander glowered before reaching under the drape of his *plaide* to his belt and pulled out a small pouch. From the leather bag, he withdrew a coin and held it forward.

Faster than his eyes could follow, the man snatched the coin and hid it somewhere within his filthy garments. "Aye, I saw many happenings mayhap ye would want to ken."

The insolence. Alexander clamped down on his annoyance. He wanted information. He ground his teeth. "Tell me. If I think your information of worth, I will give you another coin.

"There was much talk o' the stranger's claymore. The warriors believe the embedded moonstone is magic. They be saying the sword o' the fae has been found," the fool said, spit flying as he spoke.

Wiping spittle from his cheek, Alexander stepped back. So the stories were true. He couldn't wait to get his hands on the sword. "What else?"

"Yer lass." The weasel looked behind him as if he feared someone had followed him.

Alexander stiffened. "What do you ken of my betrothed?"

"She was at the high table, cozying up to the stranger. They clasped hands." The fool smirked. "Later I saw her outside his chamber, just before she entered. I did not see her come out."

Alexander backhanded the man. "You will not repeat this tale or I will see you hanging gutless from nearby tree."

How dare the bitch sneak around behind his back? He gnashed his jaw until he thought of the pleasure he'd have in teaching Elspeth her place on his return to Castle Lachlan. Though he'd need to tread carefully around Archibald. His good friend didn't understand women were immoral by nature and required guidance from a heavy hand.

Alexander turned his glare on Maclay and shoved a finger into the man's chest. "I want that sword. I dinnae care what happens to the man beyond making him suffer. Dinnae fail me in this."

A tic throbbed over Archibald's left eye. He hesitated outside the closed door of his private chamber while he tried to rein in his tumultuous emotions. It was hard to believe his uncle was in there. Archibald had never imagined the man would have the audacity to show his face here. How was he to handle Donald, especially if the king's pardon proved authentic?

Archibald was sure his uncle had been involved in Lady Laurie's abduction and torture at the hands of Malcolm Maclay. However, they'd never been able to prove his duplicity, having found the involved serving wench dead.

Archibald slapped the king's document against his palm. At times like this, he missed his brother Patrick more than he wanted to admit. The fact his twin had never seen fit to send word of his whereabouts stung. Not a single letter from Patrick. Nary a one.

He opened the door to find Donald propped before a roaring fire, enjoying a cup of Castle Lachlan's best claret. Taking a deep breath, Archibald joined his uncle, tossing the document he carried onto the worktable before pouring himself a cup of his finest. "So why are you here?"

Donald sipped from his cup then placed it on the mantel and faced him. "Can a man nae wish to see his kin?"

"You must surely ken you are not welcome here after the offences you committed against my brother and his lady-wife."

"You make too much of my involvement. 'Tis why the king pardoned me. He nae believes the charges you brought against me."

Archibald picked up the document and stared at the royal seal. "What did you promise King Jamie to gain his support?"

"Lad, why do you always think poorly of me? There was little need to sway the king's thinking. James recognized I had naught to do with the outlander's abduction. 'Twas all the doing of Maclay. 'Tis not my fault your brother Patrick made a bitter enemy of the cur."

Archibald eyed his uncle with disdain. He could never tell when the man spoke the truth. They were both well aware of the policies of their king. James the IV attempted to do in the Highlands what had been so effective with his lowland lairds. Pit one clan against the other, perpetuate ancient feuds, create new bitterness, and thus ensure control over his Highland chiefs.

King Jamie would be more than happy for strife to continue within the MacLachlan clan and for the feud to carry on between the MacLachlans and the Lamonts.

Archibald sat heavily onto one of the chairs in front of the hearth. "What do you want?"

"I have come to offer my assistance." Donald reached for his mug from the mantle and took a swig.

Archibald rubbed the back of his neck. The nerve of the man. To stand before him after what he'd done. "Just what kind of assistance do you think to offer?"

"I understand you wish to wed the Lamont wench. Iain Lamont was in Edinburgh with me two fortnights ago. I believe, if certain requirements are met, he will end the feuding and agree to your marriage." Donald drank more of his wine, and then stared at Archibald. "Lad, I offer my help to negotiate the terms of your betrothal to Lamont's daughter."

Archibald stiffened. His hands clenched the arms of his chair. He stood, glared at his uncle, and paced away. Was it possible Donald held sway with Lamont?

"Archie, I can give you what you want." Donald's voice taunted.

His back rigid, his hands in tight fists, Archibald turned to face his uncle. "What do you require from me in return?"

Donald smiled. "Naught, lad. My only wish is to see you happy."

Archibald feared he'd come to regret this decision. But if his uncle could give him what he wanted…if his uncle could gain him a betrothal contract with Lamont, he'd give Donald almost anything.

What if the man lied? What if his offer was some kind of trick?

Stroking his chin, Archibald resumed pacing. At one time, Donald had been all for Patrick wedding Isobell. Had actually tried to force Patrick's hand. Would Donald benefit in some way from a match between the two clans? Something other than a truce in the feud?

Archibald contemplated the questions swirling in his mind. Did he really care if his uncle benefited from his union with Isobell? Did it matter, as long as he got what he wanted?

Isobell as his wife.

He spun to face his uncle, pinning him with a fierce stare. "Then let the negotiations begin."

Caitrina fought the urge to curl her lip in distaste as she glanced around the queen's brightly lit antechamber. Plush pillows of the deepest blue velvet provided visual contrast to the chamber's stark whiteness. Her gaze drifted from the pillows to the open wall draped by lucent curtains. Farther to the veranda with its tranquil azure pool, the water a mirror image of the perfect sky above. The beauty of the surroundings did little more than annoy her. She'd prefer to be anywhere other than here.

She leaned against a crystal pillar and crossed her arms, forcing a bored expression to her features.

"My Princess, so good of you to attend me," purred Oonagh from her perch on the edge of her favorite white brocade chaise.

Sunlight glinted off cut glass bowls filled with exquisite sapphires of the purest blue. Everything in the room contrived to enhance the queen's silvery splendor.

Oonagh rose, tall and lissome. When the high queen of the fae moved, her liquid silver gown cut low to her navel draped open to expose the rosy nipples of her rounded breasts. She reached up to release the silver brooch at one shoulder and her gown pooled at her feet. Her glorious white-gold hair fell in glimmering curls to her ankles, providing a teasing peek at her sumptuous form.

Caitrina looked away from Oonagh's flawless white skin with its dusting of silver powder, her heart racing, her human-half appalled by the queen's display. Her fae-half intrigued. Her gut tightened. With what? Certainly not desire.

Damn the queen for her allure.

Oonagh's seductive fragrance teased Caitrina's senses, and she felt her sex clench. She ground her teeth, annoyed the queen tested her sexuality.

All Caitrina needed do was recall the pain of her banishment and her unwanted desire quelled. She sighed with relief as her muscles relaxed. "Why have you summoned me?"

With a smug smile on her luscious red lips, Oonagh shrugged and with a mere thought garbed herself in a fresh gown of argent oriental silk. "I gave you a challenge. Will you concede defeat and serve me as the bargain demands?" The queen's eyes sparkled, a dazzling blue.

"I haven't failed yet. The contract gives me until the blue moon to succeed. And I will."

"That remains to be seen."

"Finn MacIntyre will wed Elspeth MacLachlan and she shall conceive a child." Caitrina curled her hands into tight fists.

Oonagh pointed a slender finger. "Remember, the mortals

are merely pawns in our game. I don't want any of our toys permanently damaged. I wasn't pleased when I was required to journey to the earth realm during our last skirmish to bring Patrick MacLachlan back from the edge of death."

"This is but a game to you?"

"Aye. With your fate the prize."

"It wasn't my fault you threw that foolish brownie in my way when I matched Laurie with Patrick." Caitrina couldn't help but remind the queen of the bargain Oonagh had previously made with Munn, the MacLachlan clan brownie.

"The wee man was entertaining, but worthless for my needs. I'd not anticipated the MacLachlan chief would interfere with the brownie's punishment and transfer the slow death spell to himself. I'll not make the same mistake again." The queen smiled with what Caitrina could only imagine was ill intent. "Shall we play?"

Oonagh glided across the room, stopping beside a silver table, which displayed a crystal and sapphire chess set. Set upon the game board, checked in ivory and ebony squares, the crystal queen with her knights and pawns stood ready to battle her opposing sapphire queen's men.

The fae queen waved her arm. The gemstone chess pieces fell away. The game board vibrated, levitating above its stand to spin in the air. Tilting to one side, the panel became translucent before it spun on its axis like a gyroscope.

Caitrina wanted to ask what this thing was she observed, but she didn't wish to please the queen with her curiosity. When the board stopped spinning and again lay flat, it took on the appearance of polished steel. On its surface, colors swirled to coalesce into images, and images into scenes of battle.

Unease swept through Caitrina when she realized what she viewed. The chessboard had become a scrying mirror displaying potential futures. As she stared, Finn's image appeared. Then the surface of the board changed in front of her eyes to a vivid red. Color dripped from the edges like blood before the entire panel shattered into millions of tiny pieces, which turned to rusty dust and blew away on the breeze.

Caitrina glanced away, swallowing her displeasure. When she turned back, the gemstone chess set sat in its original position on the molded silver stand, the crystal queen once again poised to do battle with the sapphire queen.

And Oonagh lounged upon her chaise like a contented feline.

CHAPTER SEVEN

*F*inn entered the armory, pleased to find the large room empty of men. Most of the MacLachlan warriors gathered in the hall eating breakfast. Earlier, Finn had grabbed a couple of apples on his way outside to workout. Though ravenous since arriving in the sixteenth-century, he preferred to eat light in the morning.

Rising in the early chill gave him quiet time to work through his martial arts exercises and enjoy a solitary run. To return home in one piece once his adventure played out required he stayed fit and healthy.

He rolled his neck. The exercise helped. He felt much better.

Last night when Donald MacLachlan approached the dais, Finn almost lost control and lunged across the table for the man. This morning he learned the Scottish king had indeed pardoned Donald. Had Finn tried to kill the man he would've found himself in the MacLachlan pit—a prisoner.

God, he was lucky.

Finn stepped over to the rough-hewn table dominating the center of the room and laid his sword on top of the work surface. From a nearby rack, he withdrew the sharpening stones and strop he intended to use to remove the nicks his sword received during yesterday's practice.

He plopped onto a bench, intent on his task.

Early morning sun from the high window reflected off the polished surface of his claymore to shine on the far wall of the armory. He stared at the spot, and his mind wandered to Elspeth. He didn't want to go there. With a shake of the head, he jerked his gaze back to his task and pulled the sharpening stone along the edge of the blade.

Better to think about his reason for being in the past.

Winning the competition against Archibald still amazed him. When the mock battle began, he thought he'd pass out from the panic attack strangling his breath. Intense pain in his chest almost forced him to his knees. The unexpected energy surge that shot through him was something he never experienced before.

Finn made another pass along the steel with the fine-gritted stone.

The strange thing was he never fought so well before. Never had he felt so powerful or so in-sync with his claymore. The sword had become an extension of himself.

He glanced up from his task as Duncan joined him. "You put on quite a show on the practice field yesterday. You are sure to have many challengers from here on."

Finn groaned. He hadn't intended for that consequence. His only thought had been to impress Archibald so the man would invite him into his inner circle. Well, at least he achieved his goal. This morning Archibald offered him a position within his *Lèine-chneas*—Archibald's elite bodyguard. Finn would be one of the men who made up Archibald's tail. Finn understood the honor bestowed on him and knew he'd be in good company.

Jamie and Duncan belonged to the handpicked group of men. When the warriors went after Maclay, Finn would be with them. Everything seemed to be fitting into place.

Duncan sat across the room, working to sharpen his sword.

"What happened to Stephen MacEwen?" Finn asked, the

question popping into his head from who knew where. Laurie often mentioned the man who'd been Patrick's personal bodyguard yet Duncan performed the service for Archibald.

"You ken him?"

"No. Though my cousin spoke fondly of him."

"After Patrick left, there was nae reason for Stephen to stay on at Castle Lachlan. I think it troubled him when Patrick did not request he join him on the Continent. Stephen traveled for a time, finding himself after a time settled with our cousin Allaine in Glasrie near the old fort at Dunadd."

Finn laid aside the stone and started with the leather strop, working to put a razor sharp edge on the blade. When he finished, he ran his finger along the edge and drew blood.

He was probably in over his head. Time would certainly tell.

A scraping noise sent a chill down his spine, and he twisted toward the sound. "Did you hear that?"

Duncan set aside his sword and strode to the rack of weapons. After searching about, he looked at Finn over his shoulder. "Probably a rat. I will tell Archie's man to see traps are set."

Munn left the armory in a huff, determined to find Caitrina. Believing the *Sithichean Sluaigh*, the faerie knoll near the Fir-wood, the best place to find the she-devil, he traveled through space and materialized on a tree limb above the grassy hill.

Caitrina appeared to sleep on the bright green turf, her head pillowed on an enormous toadstool. Munn jumped down from his branch. As he approached, she opened one eye. "What do you want?"

He glared at her. "How did the MacIntyre warrior get your claymore?"

Caitrina sat up and stretched, but didn't respond to his

question.

He clenched his fists at his sides. "The enchanted sword has been hidden for centuries. If the weapon falls into the wrong hands like it did once before…" Munn shuddered. "Ach, I nae want to think of what could happen."

"Nae concern of yours. I choose to whom I gift the stone's powers."

Caitrina rose to her feet and smiled beguilingly.

Damn her!

"But to give the sword to another mortal. What if he is unworthy?"

"I chose well."

"How can you ken that?"

"Finn MacIntyre and his son will fulfill the ancient prophecies."

Munn's jaw fell open. Caitrina placed a finger beneath his chin and closed his mouth.

"Ach, then, you will be needing my assistance." He rocked back and forth on the balls of his feet, near to bursting with excitement.

"What help would you be? You bungle everything you do."

Munn wrinkled his nose. The spiteful faerie was unjust. There were many things he could do, and had. "Then I won't tell you who stalks the man and his weapon." She'd need to find the traitor on her own. In a fit of anger, Munn spun and flashed away.

Elspeth slid her legs over the edge of the mattress and brushed stray hair from her face. She noted the height of the sun and realized she'd slept later than usual, having tossed restlessly during the night. She shouldn't think about Finn so much. Her musings were highly improper.

With a heavy sigh, she padded across the floor. From the ewer, she poured water into the basin to wash the sleep from her eyes. After completing her ablutions, she dressed in a plain gray linen gown and with a yawn made her way to the kitchen, where one of the maids helped her don an apron. The heavy garment protected her gown from dirt or a wayward thorn while she worked in the garden.

As she passed the cook's worktable, she snatched a piece of cheese and a small hunk of bread. She dropped them into one of the voluminous pockets of her apron, planning to break her fast in the garden.

Before leaving, she grabbed her gloves from a door side table and stuffed those into another pocket.

Jamie fell in behind as she crossed the courtyard. "Good morn to you, lass."

"And to you, Jamie MacEwen."

Through the castle gate and into the sunshine, Elspeth skipped along the path to the castle garden with Jamie at her back. As always, he remained outside the arched entrance to stand guard while she worked within.

The herbs' heady scents tickled her nose. She smiled and glanced at the bright blue sky. 'Twas a fair day. Although she'd felt the breeze on her cheeks when she made her way along the path, all was calm and peaceful within the high stone walls of the garden.

She sighed happily.

Laid out in a geometric design, wooden planks held back the soil in the beds, most of which were filled with medicinal herbs and vegetables bordered by white and lavender violets. A large strawberry bed took up one end and a rose garden sat off to the other side, the pink and white blooms displayed against shiny green foliage.

Elspeth brushed her fingers along the edge of a planting of lemon balm, releasing the pungent scent as she made her way to the rose bed with its flowering turf bench of chamomile. Her favorite place for a picnic.

She sat and munched the cheese and bread, wishing she'd thought to bring a skin of cider along. *Oh, bother.* She'd quench her thirst with water from the well at the center of the garden.

Elspeth gazed over the beds with a sense of accomplishment. She tended this space—mostly alone—ever since her mother and father had disappeared. Then Laurie had arrived and helped a bit.

On occasion, Aine joined Elspeth in her tasks. For the most part, though, she worked the garden alone—in memory of her mother. Who would tend the garden after she married?

Brushing the unwanted thought away, she giggled when a wren scampered across the ground in search of crumbs. The crunch of gravel startled her, and she shot her gaze to the path.

Finn approached and stopped a few feet short of where she sat. A small smile curved his mouth. Her chest tightened. Such an odd feeling. Frightening and exciting at the same time.

She shouldn't be staring at his lips. She raised her gaze to his hazel eyes and sighed.

His stare flared, and he stepped forward, stopping close enough she could touch him. She tightened her grasp on the hunk of bread, refusing to give in to temptation.

"Lady Elspeth." Finn bowed.

Her entire body tingled from his nearness. "Good morn' to you, sir."

"Please, call me Finn." He glanced around. "I was exploring and stumbled upon your garden. Laurie told me how beautiful it was. She was right. This is a peaceful place."

"Aye, 'tis." She tilted her head to one side.

Finn cleared his throat. "I hope you don't mind I've intruded on your privacy."

"We shouldn't be alone."

Shrugging, Finn pointed toward the archway. "We're not completely alone. Jamie stands guard outside the wall."

Elspeth smiled, and Finn smiled back. An awkward silence hung between them. She chewed her bottom lip. "If you wish, I could show you the castle grounds."

"I would like that."

"Where shall we begin?" She started to rise. Finn reached

for her hand and helped her to her feet. Her skin tingled where he touched. A sense of loss followed when he released her.

"How about the beach?" he said.

"I am sure you have seen for yourself Castle Lachlan sits upon a small islet a short distance from the mainland. There is beach all around us."

Finn's eyes twinkled. "Then it's a good place to start a tour. Don't you think?"

Elspeth giggled. "Aye, sure. We will start on the northwest side then. Come."

They passed Jamie on their way to the sea loch path. To Elspeth's surprise, he didn't follow. Finn took her arm and helped her around a group of smooth boulders. "Duncan tells me you're betrothed."

"Aye, since my birth. I am to wed Alexander Campbell at the end of the summer. But I should not speak with thee of such."

"Why not?"

"It…'tis just not done," Elspeth stammered.

Finn grinned, deciding he liked the pink blush on Elspeth's cheeks. "What's not done?" he teased.

Elspeth's face went a brighter shade of red. "Speak to strange men of such. 'Tis not proper."

"Do you have women friends to speak with?"

"Aye. Jonet Stewart is my good friend. Though she travels much these past years and I have not seen her for a verra long time." Elspeth wrinkled her nose. "Nae. I have nae women to gossip with. Nae matter, Castle Lachlan keeps me verra busy."

"When you wed will you not move away?"

"Aye, sure. Alexander will receive keepership of Skipness Castle on Kintyre Penninsula when we wed. We will reside there in the new towerhouse."

"Will you miss your family?"

"Aye, my brothers. But other than Archie, they seldom

visit Castle Lachlan these days. Suibne resides in Glasgow at University and Iain the Younger fosters with the Campbells of Glen Orchy." She lifted the hem of her skirt to step over a large root jutting into the path. "Archie will marry soon, so there will be little need for me to remain here."

Heat flared with the flash of ankle and calf. Finn swallowed uneasily, shocked the simple exposure of skin turned him on. His mind easily filled in what the rest of Elspeth would look like naked and lounging on his bed. An instantaneous hard-on forced him to stifle a groan.

This wouldn't do. He wracked his brain for something boring to think about. Playing cricket, a slow moving sport. Very tedious.

They reached the edge of the beach, and he assisted Elspeth to sit upon a large boulder. Then he leaned against a nearby broken tree trunk, feeling more in control. "See, it wasn't difficult to talk to me."

Elspeth lowered her gaze before looking away toward the water's edge, where gentle waves lapped the pebbly beach.

"Lady Elspeth, I'd like to be your friend."

She raised her gaze to his, and he watched several emotions flick across the soft silver of her eyes. He got lost in the depths.

The harsh sound of a masculine throat clearing broke the spell. Finn jerked his gaze to an angry Archibald.

"Beth, Aine is fretting for your help. Be off with you."

Elspeth jumped up, curtsied, and hurried along the trail toward the castle.

"Stay away from my sister. I will not warn you again."

Finn hadn't meant to seek her out. He'd stumbled upon the garden and the sight of Elspeth, so beautiful amidst the flowers, stole his resolve to stay away. Now that he knew a mere glimpse of skin brought him to the edge, he'd need to triple his resolve to keep her at a distance.

He straightened from the tree trunk and opened his mouth to retort, but Archibald stopped him with a raised hand. "Her betrothed arrives on the morrow. I dinnae want him after your blood. Are we understood?"

Finn nodded once.

"Good. Now, will you oblige me with a wee bit of sport on the practice field?"

CHAPTER EIGHT

You must not get up. You are still too ill." Elspeth *attempted to push him back against the down pillows. Finn wouldn't listen. He kept staring at her with hungry hazel eyes. She sensed he might leap from the bed and devour her, like a wild mountain cat.*

A part of her wished he would.

Her skin burned where he held her wrist. She thought to pull away, yet wanted him to touch more of her.

Touch her everywhere.

He reached for her braid and tugged her head closer. Their lips a breath apart. He was going to kiss her. Her heart pounded so loud she thought he'd hear.

She closed her eyes.

His mouth softly grazed hers. Her insides went soft.

His tongue moved over her lips, gently, yet the velvety touch demanded entrance. She popped her eyes open and gasped. His tongue swept across her teeth, and then their tongues danced. The grip on her arm tightened and he pulled her down on top of him.

She squeezed her eyes shut.

Finn's hands roamed everywhere. Stroking. Exploring. Scorching her skin through the cloth of her gown. He reached inside the bodice and found her breasts. A rough, calloused finger rubbed across a nipple. Then his lips replaced his finger and something clenched inside of her as he took possession of her soul.

Outside, lightning flashed across a stormy sky. Thunder rumbled, ricocheting through the hills.

Elspeth jolted straight up in bed. Her heart raced the way it did after a long run. Silvery moonlight spilled through the unshuttered window and across the coverlet. She shivered as the cool breeze kissed her overheated, moist skin.

Odd. An unfamiliar fragrance scented the room.

She lay back on the mattress and pulled the linen sheet up around her neck with a trembling hand.

Vision?

A dream. Naught but a dream. A wonderfully marvelous dream of which she should be ashamed. Aching with shameful cravings, she punched the pillow, unable to fall back to sleep.

The remainder of the night she spent praying to God for forgiveness. Several hours later, she joined Aine in the solar.

Elspeth's stomach ached the moment she looked out the window and spotted the large cloud of dust rising from the long line of riders galloping across the moor. The Campbell banner flapped in the wind as the procession made its way to the stables. Soon the men would row across the bay to the castle. The thought of dealing with Alexander this day made her queasy. She twisted away from the window and clutched her belly.

No wonder dark clouds plundered the sky.

"Lass, what is the matter?" Aine jumped up from where she sat and quickly crossed the solar to stand at Elspeth's side.

Elspeth leaned against the back of a chair and inhaled a deep breath, trying to calm her racing heart and ease the turmoil churning in her stomach. What had come over her? Alexander was the man she was to wed. Why did she fear seeing him?

In her heart, she knew the answer. She'd sinned. During the night, she dreamt of another man. Her wayward thoughts would be her ruin if she weren't careful. Finn was not the man for her. Whether he carried the fae sword, or nae, mattered not. As her father decreed at her birth, she'd wed Alexander at the end of the summer. Move to the new towerhouse at Skipness Castle and give Alexander an heir. What more could she possibly want? She was the luckiest lass in all the Highlands. Everyone thought so. Why then did she feel so miserable?

She straightened. "I am fine."

Aine looked out the window and then back at Elspeth. "You are as pale as fresh fallen snow, lass. Just like after one of your visions. I will go to the kitchen and make you some of my special willow bark tea. A few swigs will put the blush back into your cheeks." Aine walked away muttering, "And give you some fortification to deal with your boorish betrothed."

A knock sounded as Finn strapped his claymore to his back. He opened the door to find Aine standing in the threshold, her arms filled with sheets for the bed. He reached forward.

"Here. Let me help you with those." Taking the bundle from her, he placed it on the carved wooden chest at the foot of the bed.

"Thank you." Aine followed him into the room, shutting the door behind her.

"You're wel—" The word died on his tongue when he turned around and found her standing in front of him, arms crossed over chest as she tapped her foot in rapid rhythm on the stone floor. A speculative gleam burned in her eyes while she raked him from head to toe.

He inwardly cringed, familiar with the look. What could the old lady want?

Finn reached down to put his hands in his pockets, but *leines* don't have pockets. He fought the urge to cross his arms and left them hanging at his sides instead.

Aine moved around Finn, continuing to size him up.

Just when he thought he'd have to break the awkward silence, Aine said, "Aye. You will do nicely."

"Excuse me?"

Aine fixed him with an intent stare. "Do you ken why you are here?"

Finn hesitated. He couldn't very well tell her he planned to kill a man. Even in this time, they'd laws against such acts.

Hoping to hedge, he opened his mouth—

"Nae? Hush and listen to what I have to say."

Crossing his arms, he leaned against one of the bedposts.

"Our Elspeth was born on a hot summer evening. Nearly a score and one summers ago. A sennight later, our chief, Iain, Elspeth's father, made an agreement with the second Earl of Argyll for our wee lass to wed with his grandson, Alexander. While Iain was away from Castle Lachlan making his foolish contract with the Campbell, a learned woman of the fae appeared to Mairi, Elspeth's mother, and prophesized your coming."

Finn swallowed hard. None of this could be true. Aine wasn't aware he knew Mairi and Iain MacLachlan, and they'd never once mentioned any such gibberish. Rory MacNaughton, on the other hand, may have told a yarn or two of such. But never Iain or Mairi. And Rory's stories were make-believe tales of myth meant to entertain.

"When three, seven-year cycles of the moon wane, a strange warrior from an unknown far-off place will come, wielding the mighty lost sword of the fae, to save our Elspeth from despair. Just once in a verra blue moon love will triumph," she continued.

Finn didn't know how to respond to the woman's foolishness.

"Lad, dinnae you ken? You are the warrior foretold in the prophecy."

"I'm afraid you have the wrong guy." He had the maddening desire to squirm beneath the woman's penetrating regard.

"You can deny it all you want now. But you will be called

to fulfill your destiny."

"Faeries? Prophecies? I don't believe in all that mumbo-jumbo magic stuff."

"Then how is it possible you are here?"

All he could do was gape at the older woman as she opened the door.

"Tsk, tsk. You are a thick one," Aine muttered as she walked out of the chamber.

Due to the arrival of the large Campbell entourage, Finn found himself relegated to one of the tables below the dais, where he sat with several heavily imbibing warriors. Didn't matter. From this vantage point, he could see the entire head table, especially Elspeth who sat between her brother and her fiancé.

Finn took a bite of the salmon in cream sauce and savored the flavors on his tongue.

Although he couldn't hear what they said, he could see Archibald and Alexander were in a heated conversation with good ole Uncle Donald. The three men completely ignored Elspeth, who smiled serenely at others in the hall.

It shouldn't bother him, but he noticed she seemed to avoid glancing in his direction, though he made several attempts to catch her eye.

Grudgingly, he had to admit, Elspeth's fiancé was an attractive man. An inch or two shorter than Finn, he kept a neat appearance. Alexander's clothes were of good quality. He was clean-shaven and wore his reddish-brown hair pulled back in a ponytail as most of the men did. However, there was something disturbing about his eyes.

Finn had the distinct feeling Alexander hid many unsavory secrets.

A disturbance to his left had Finn moving his chair away from his closest dining companion, who enthusiastically waved his arms as he told a story. The warrior spoke in the Gaelic tongue, and although Finn had spent some time attempting to learn the language from Patrick, this man's words came too quickly for Finn to understand. He could pick out only a few terms.

By the time the *ghillies* served the venison course, he was bored and his mind wandered.

Over the past couple of years, he'd read extensively about Scottish history. He knew in two years' time Scotland's current sense of peace and prosperity would end. The redheaded king, King James IV of Scotland, would die in battle against the English at Flodden Field, taking with him over ten thousand of the bravest and best of Scotland's young men. Finn worried the MacLachlan warriors might be caught in the chaos. Would Duncan, Jamie or Archibald lose their lives?

Finn couldn't tell them what he knew. He couldn't warn them. The laws of the universe forbade him from messing with history.

But if that were true, what was he doing here?

He glanced at Elspeth. He'd dreamt of her on more than one occasion. Was she his destiny?

Aine insisted he was here to fulfill a prophecy given at Elspeth's birth. That wasn't why he'd run through the time-gate. His only reason for traveling to the past was to kill Malcolm Maclay and avenge Laurie.

If he succeeded, would he change history? He didn't want to think so. Yet wasn't it true, just the fact Laurie had been here, and now he was, had changed history? Or was their coming to sixteenth century Scotland predestined, part of what was supposed to happen?

What a riddle this time traveling created.

A ghillie removed the trenchers from the table, and Finn noticed people began to leave the hall. A hand clamped down hard on his shoulder. "You have been invited to join the family at the hearth for the entertainment," Duncan said.

He followed Duncan across the hall as servants removed tables and constructed privacy screens. They joined a small group near the fire where Elspeth sat holding a lute.

Alexander stood behind her, his hands possessively placed on her shoulders.

Archibald clapped his hands and the group quieted. "Beth, please begin."

She took a deep breath and sang, accompanying herself on the lute. Her voice was that of an angel. Finn found himself caught in the web she wove with her words, her song a soulful love ballad. Unable to shift his gaze from her, he more than likely smiled like an idiot.

When she finished several enchanting songs, she attempted to coax Archibald to sing along with her. He refused, but Jamie volunteered and together they sang a merrier ditty about four drunken warriors and one sassy wench.

Shortly thereafter, Elspeth curtsied to her audience. "I will leave you men to your claret." She stood.

Finn had the desire to follow her, but Alexander grasped her hand and walked her to the circular stair where he pressed a kiss upon her palm.

Finn tensed. Something about Alexander struck him wrong. For one thing, Finn didn't like the man touching Elspeth, which was foolish since he himself had no claim on her.

Alexander returned to the group of men, and Archibald slapped him on the back. "'Tis great to see you again, friend. Though I wish you'd brought different tidings. My Uncle Donald has left for Toward Keep to meet with Lamont to negotiate the terms of my betrothal to Isobell. I had it in my mind to go with him, but Maclay is on my northern border, and I must go after him instead."

"If only I could join you to eradicate the cur. However, I must race off at sunrise to deliver the king's missives to my father," Alexander said.

"Certainly, I understand the importance of your mission." Archibald reached for one of many goblets of wine that sat atop a side table along with several full flagons. "Please, join us in a drink."

Alexander poured wine into a goblet, holding it for several moments before handing it to Finn. "I understand you are the cousin of our Lady Laurie."

Finn accepted the offered drink. "Aye. Finn MacIntyre. A pleasure to meet you, m'lord." The hairs on the back of his neck tingled, and he fought to keep a calm expression on his face. He hated playing nice with the guy.

Alexander reached for another goblet and poured for himself. "The pleasure is mine. Archie has bragged of your skill with the claymore. On my return, perhaps, you would give me a demonstration by meeting me on the practice field."

"As you wish." Finn inclined his head politely and sipped the wine, surprised to find the claret had a bitter aftertaste. He was tempted to cast it aside, but Alexander made several toasts to which he felt obliged to drink.

By the time his cup was empty, his tongue felt thick and he was unsteady on his feet. How strange the wine had such a weird effect on him. He attempted to sit, but Alexander took his arm. "I think our friend here is in his cups."

Finn stumbled and almost fell.

"Connor," Alexander called to his henchman.

"Aye, Lord Alexander."

"Help Duncan put this fool to bed."

Duncan put a beefy arm around Finn to steady him. The other fellow supported his other side. Even with their help, Finn tripped up the steps.

Duncan leaned in close to his ear. "What is wrong with you?"

"The lad is drunk," Connor snapped.

"I wonder," Duncan murmured.

Returning from the garderobe, Elspeth found her bedchamber door ajar. She didn't remember having left it open. Perhaps Aine had returned for some reason while Elspeth was gone. She eased the heavy wooden door the remainder of the way open and gasped, her right hand rising to her chest when she saw the man standing afore the hearth.

Alexander slowly turned and held the goblet in his hand out to her. "Good eve'n, m'lady."

Elspeth curtsied, pulling the wool *plaide* she'd draped about her shoulders tighter to cover her breasts, which were visible through her sheer bed gown. "And to you, m'lord." She glanced behind her and then back to Alexander. "You shouldn't be here in my bedchamber."

Alexander stepped around her and shut the door. "Did you nae foresee my coming?"

Elspeth hesitated, disturbed by his mocking tone. "Nae. I dinnae understand."

"There is nae need." Alexander walked back to the hearth and sat in one of the two chairs. "Come. Sit with me."

Elspeth tried to swallow, but her mouth had gone dry. She couldn't move, unable to decide what she should do.

"Come, now. We are to wed soon. You are not afraid of your future husband, are you?"

She jerked her gaze to his. "Nae."

"Ach, then. Come sit with me by the fire and we shall share some private conversation. Like husband and wife." He patted the seat next to him.

Elspeth's heart quickened its beat. His smile didn't quite reach his eyes. Something ugly lurked in those dark orbs. The last thing she wanted to do this night was to join him. "I dinnae think Archie would approve."

"Soon it will not matter what he thinks. I will be your lord and master."

Elspeth made a move for the door, but before she reached it, Alexander stood beside her, gripping her wrist in a vise-like hold. "Nae, you will sit and tell me what you ken about the stranger and his sword."

Alexander pulled her toward one of the chairs and pushed her down into it, then released his grip on her. Rubbing her sore wrist, she leaned back against the velvet cushion, and glared at him.

"I ken you have spent time alone with him. Are you still pure?"

She gasped and swept a hand to her throat.

"No matter. I will wed you anyway. But never doubt, I will have him flogged if he touches you again."

Elspeth swallowed impulsively, fear a living thing in her belly. She'd need to convince Alexander naught wayward transpired between her and Finn. She couldn't allow Finn to suffer for her impure thoughts.

Alexander grinned as he sat next to her and crossed his leg over his knee. "Now, lass. Tell me what you ken of MacIntyre."

She fought back revulsion, placed her hand on his arm, and rubbed in a circular motion. Alexander raised his brows and she could tell he liked the attention. She continued to stroke his arm, moving to the muscle in his shoulder when she felt him relax. "You ken you are the only man for me."

CHAPTER NINE

*F*inn woke to a pounding in his head. *Damn. What the hell is the matter with me?* He couldn't remember ever feeling this shitty. Not even after he drank that bottle of tequila the night of his discharge from the Marines had he felt this awful.

When he finally managed to pry his crusty eyes open, he heaved up onto his elbows and groaned. Duncan and Jamie stood over him, grinning.

"What?" Finn demanded.

"We are going after Maclay," Jamie said.

"Archie is waiting for you." Duncan pulled the blanket off Finn and from the bed.

Finn leapt up and reached for his *leine*, his headache all but forgotten. He'd finally have the opportunity to avenge Laurie.

"I brought these for you. We might be in the saddle for several days." Duncan held out a pair of brown leather *trews*.

Finn eyed Duncan. There was no way he'd fit into the big man's pants.

"I found them in a chest Patrick left behind."

Finn grabbed the pants and stepped into them. The deerskin fit snug, but the supple fabric stretched when he flexed his muscles. The leather would be comfortable in the saddle. He strapped a wide belt around his waist, and sat on the bed to put on his rough hide boots in which he tucked his knife. When he finished dressing, he tossed his plaid over his shoulder and went to the chest at the end of the bed to retrieve his claymore.

He opened the lid and reached in.

His heart slammed against his ribs, his headache returning full force. "Damn!" His sword wasn't there. He was sure it had been on top of a pile of clothes, lying catty-cornered within the wide chest.

He rushed around the room, looking into all the nooks and crannies, lifting things and searching under them, trying to figure out what he'd done with his weapon. Although he was certain he put it in the chest after his workout yesterday.

Jamie grabbed his arm. "What are you doing? We dinnae have time to waste. Get your claymore and let us be on our way."

"It's gone!"

"What?"

Finn stormed to the foot of the bed and pointed. "You heard me. I put my claymore in this chest after practice yesterday. And it's not there now."

Jamie and Duncan both looked into the wooden chest and then at each other.

"How'd I get to bed last night?" Finn scowled at the twins.

Duncan shrugged. "You were in your cups, so Connor Campbell helped me drag your sorry arse up here."

"And they lovingly tucked you into bed," Jamie said, sarcastically.

"Well, someone stole my sword. Do you think it might have been Connor?"

"I did not leave him here alone." Duncan scratched the side of his head. "'Tis possible though. He could have come back after I left. I really dinnae ken."

"Now what do I do?" Finn's chest clenched as anger merged with panic.

Alexander rode his gray stallion at the front of the line of Campbell warriors as they crossed Glen Sluain. His gaze continually scanned the terrain to their right for a lone rider. The glaring high noon sun caused him to squint as he searched the ridge. His patience worn thin he stood in his stirrups to gain a better view.

He caught the glint of sun on metal. A few moments later, his henchman maneuvered his horse across a nearby hill and rode toward them. Easing back onto the saddle again, Alexander halted and waved the others on, wanting to converse privately with Connor.

"Did you run into any trouble?" Alexander asked when his man reined in next to him.

"Nae. The MacIntyre warrior passed out cold. Once Duncan retired 'twas easy to sneak back to the chamber and search for the sword. "'Twas in a chest with nae lock." Connor handed the long, leather-wrapped parcel into Alexander's trembling hands.

Finally, it's mine.

Alexander laid the package across his thighs. He waited a moment to compose himself. With steadier hands, he unwrapped the covering, careful not to touch the claymore within. Until he understood better the secret of the sword's power, he wasn't about to risk his skin. Rumors claimed by merely touching the blade one could suffer burns that never healed.

The milky blue stone in the claymore's cross-section glowed when the sun's rays hit the gem. Fearful he'd invoke the sword's magic, Alexander quickly rewrapped the weapon of the fae in the protective leather covering.

"Did you discover what you needed?" Connor asked.

"I learned little of value from my wench." She'd surprised him with a back rub and he'd put off grilling her, never expecting to fall asleep. When he woke, the wench had gone and he couldn't locate her. He'd not let her make a fool of him again. A good beating would put her in her place. "'Tis of nae consequence, *we* possess the claymore. You will take the sword to Seumas at Carrick Castle. He will ken what to do."

Anticipation slid along Alexander's spine. He would be a power to contend with once the old wizard uncovered the sword's secrets.

Finn shifted his weight on the uncomfortable saddle. Muscles he never realized he had ached. He'd be sore for days after this excursion. Thank God, his father insisted he and Laurie learned to ride. He dug his knees in and galloped after Jamie across the heather covered moor.

The MacLachlan warriors rode until dusk. They found a small clearing deep within an evergreen forest. A bubbling brook ran nearby. While some of the men set camp for the night and built a fire, others set off to catch fish for dinner. Finn helped Jamie tether the horses near a grassy hill.

"I thought you were Elspeth's personal guard. I'm surprised you rode out with us to hunt Maclay." Finn held the reins of one of the stallions while Jamie worked with the rope.

"Aye, well. That was true. However, since the lass will wed soon, Alexander has convinced Archie that one of the Campbell men should guard Elspeth, a lad by the name of Hector. My services for such are nae longer required. My duty now lies with my chief and my brother." Jamie wrapped the end of the tether line around a tree trunk, securing it with a tight knot.

Something about Alexander Campbell didn't sit well with Finn. He suspected, as he believed Duncan did, that Campbell's henchman stole his claymore. Archibald ardently disagreed, blaming Finn's drunken clumsiness for the loss of his sword. But he hadn't been drunk at dinner. At least not until after he drank the one goblet of wine Alexander gave him.

Suspicious. Very suspicious.

If the MacLachlans hadn't chosen this morning to go after Maclay, Finn would have tracked down Connor Campbell. One of Archibald's men who guarded the castle gate confirmed Connor had ridden out in the middle of the night, claiming to be on a mission for Alexander. Thus for the king.

And reportedly, Alexander and the rest of the Campbell men departed at first light with the same excuse.

When Finn continued to assert that Connor had likely stolen the sword, Archibald grudgingly agreed to send out a couple of lads to trail the man and see what they could learn. Then he ordered Finn to join him in the hunt. Since finding Maclay was Finn's purpose for being in sixteenth century Scotland in the first place, he hadn't argued.

Finn and Jamie joined the warriors at the fire, where they shared a skin of wine. Wine tasting remarkably less bitter than what he drank the night before.

Soon the others returned with their catch, and the men set to cooking the trout on a spit over the flames. When the meal ended, Finn walked away from the others and followed a path through the woods to the brook. Several semi-submerged boulders jutted out into the water from the edge. He carefully stepped from one to the other until he was about a quarter of the way out into the flow. He squatted, cupped his hands and filled them. Splashing the cold water on his face refreshed him.

The sound of a twig snapping set him on alert. He slowly pulled his knife from his boot and twisted toward shore, relieved to find Jamie standing there. Behind Jamie, Archibald leaned against a tree trunk, his arms crossed over his chest.

Finn hopped across the stones back to shore to join them.

"I ken you're upset about your claymore," Archibald said. "But I believe we will learn the sword was not stolen, merely misplaced. 'Tis bound to show up somewhere in the castle."

Finn didn't believe that for a minute, but he gave Archibald a half-smile anyway. "I hope you're right."

"I am convinced I am. Alexander is above reproach. After all, I have traveled with him extensively for the king. I am certain his man is trustworthy too." Archibald moved away from the tree toward Finn. "Are you comfortable with the sword from the armory?"

"I'll make the best of it."

"Good."

Rustling leaves attracted the men's attention. A gnome-like creature appeared, spinning in frenzied circles before stopping to become a solid, breathing man. A small man, at that.

Jamie chuckled. "Welcome, Munn."

Finn had thought Laurie teased him when she described Munn. But here he was, for real. The strange little man jumped up and down. "I ken. I ken where Maclay camps."

Archibald stepped forward. "Where?"

"In the greenwood below the waterfalls in Glen Sluain."

They broke camp and rode out immediately, hoping to take advantage of the cover of darkness. The plan was to spread out through the wood, encircle Maclay's camp, and on Archibald's signal, attack. Before the MacLachlan warriors were in place, men dropped from the trees to surround them. Had they been expected? Had someone told Maclay they were coming? Had Munn betrayed them?

The MacLachlan men were outnumbered two to one.

Three warriors circled Archibald. Finn didn't have time to think before a man attacked him. His stomach lurched. The borrowed claymore felt clumsy in his hands, the weapon lacking the same balance as his own. He wielded the sword as he'd been taught, but the skill he'd built faith in over the last few years failed him. He floundered under the assault.

His attacker's sword slashed his left thigh, the blade slicing deep through the leather *trews* he wore, leaving a burning gash. Finn continued to fight, moving as best he could with his injury.

He blocked another cut. His arms ached. The pain in his leg throbbed. Blood oozed from the wound. His muscles were on fire. He weakened. He backed away. Maclay's man pursued. The force of the next blow shot through Finn like a speeding freight train, shocking every nerve in his body. He stumbled and fell.

Would he die here today?

Thank God Jamie stepped in, raising his sword. With one stroke, Maclay's man lay dead. His severed head rested next to his still twitching body.

Jamie pivoted to battle another warrior. Using his arms and his one good leg, Finn grabbed handfuls of turf and rock, pulling and pushing himself across the field, away from the gruesome sight of death and the dreadful sounds of battle. In the bushes, he lost the contents of his stomach before he collapsed.

He lay there alone, his cheek pressed against cool grass, cursing himself the biggest fool.

In the middle of the night, an urgent need to use the garderobe woke Elspeth. She used the moonlight entering the chamber through the unshuttered window to find a *plaide*, wrapped the length of wool around her shoulders for warmth, and lit the lantern sitting on a table at the side of the bed. Stepping from the woven rush mat onto the cold stone floor, she shivered and searched for her shoes. Then put them on one by one.

She hurried along the passageway to the garderobe. The cold had her making haste. Feeling much relieved when she finished, she made her way along the corridor, tripping when a sharp pain sliced through her stomach. She fell onto her hands and knees, panting as visions seized her. Scenes of bloody battle played before her mind's eye.

Through a murky fog, images formed, dissolved and reappeared. Warriors with hidden faces swung claymores and axes. They cut and chopped, steel clanging against steel.

Screams hurt her ears.

Blood ran. Men fell.

One face came clearly—Finn.

Elspeth curled into a ball, clutching her belly and moaning.

Aine found her thus. On creaking joints, the older woman eased down beside her. "Lass, are you sick?"

"Oh, Aine. I ken he is not the man I will wed, but he is a good man. He cannot be dead." Elspeth threw her arms around the older woman's waist.

"Of what do you speak, child?"

"A bloody battle. I saw Finn lying on the grass." A strangled sob ripped from Elspeth's throat. "Dead."

Aine rubbed her back. "Mayhap he is merely injured."

"My visions are never wrong."

Two days after the battle, in the early hours of dawn, the MacLachlan warriors brought Finn back to the castle. With Aine's help, Elspeth tended him. Her vision had been wrong so far. She prayed it remained that way.

Fear for Finn clawed at her heart.

Even after they cleaned and wrapped his wound, Elspeth remained at his side. She didn't care what others thought. As soon as Finn was well—she needed to believe it would be so—she would go to Archie and demand her betrothal to Alexander be broken. She refused to wed the brute.

At midday, Jamie quietly entered the chamber, his brow creased with concern. "How is the lad?"

Finn lay within the curtained bed, his complexion pale in contrast to the dark furs covering him. They had done everything they could. Yet still, he lay unmoving, burning with fever.

Elspeth wet his heated brow with a cool, damp cloth. "He is dying." She choked on a sob.

Munn hovered in the shadows of the chamber, wringing his hands.

Jamie turned to the wee man. "Is there naught you can do?"

The wee man shook his head before spinning in a circle and disappearing.

Tears sprang to Elspeth's eyes. She didn't care if Jamie saw them. Her heart was breaking.

Caitrina traveled through the wood in silence. Leaves on the limbs quivered and danced in the wind. She paused, opening her senses.

She felt a tremor of unease. A slight change to the balance of the universe, the weight tipping toward the dark. Something had gone terribly awry.

A current of air carried a message from Munn.

She made haste, traveling through time and space to Castle Lachlan. She found Elspeth asleep, holding Finn's limp hand, the young woman's head resting atop his sunken chest.

Elspeth's eyes slowly opened. "Is he gone? Have you come to take him?"

"Nae, I am nae *banshee* to harbinger death."

"Then who are you?"

"A healer. I've come to care for the lad." Caitrina moved forward.

Elspeth appeared skeptical, blocking her from reaching for Finn. "Who sent you?"

There wasn't time for this. Caitrina edged closer to the bed. "Your wee man."

The young woman hesitated for another moment. Knowledge dawned in the depth of her silver eyes and she stepped away to allow Caitrina access to the wounded man.

She leaned down and blew her fae breath into Finn's mouth. His chest rose and then flattened. She did the same again. His lungs puffed full of air and then released. Finally, his chest rose on its own, his breathing easier.

Munn spun into the chamber, banging against the chair in the corner where Jamie napped. Jamie's eyes widened at the sight of Caitrina.

She turned her attention to Munn. "I'll need a snippet of *gymnoderma lineare.*"

The brownie frowned. "Ach, 'tis dangerous for you to return to the future before your task is complete here in the past. 'Twill be easy to forget your quest."

"I'll not be distracted."

"What is it you need?" Elspeth asked.

"A wee lichen."

Jamie stood. "Lichen, you say? I will climb the crags and return with a bundle."

"Nae. I require special lichen, which grows in a far off place only I can go." Caitrina wiped her hand along Finn's cheek, deepening his slumber. She smiled at Elspeth. "Nae fear. I'll return with a potion for your braw man."

Elspeth tucked the covers around Finn's fevered body. "Then I entrust his life to you."

Caitrina dissolved into mist.

CHAPTER TEN

Present Day, Grandfather Mountain, North Carolina

Planning to go to the field to see the hunky contestants toss the caber, Caitrina slid off the huge rock on which she'd been sitting. At the edge of her vision, Douglas MacKinnon walked through the Celtic Grove where her favorite band just finished performing.

She stopped and stood motionless.

At six foot seven, the man was hard to miss. What was he up to? Why wasn't he at his store where he belonged, doing whatever work human shopkeepers were supposed to do?

Caitrina cloaked herself with the glamour of invisibility.

Such an annoyance. She'd only meant to come forward in time for a moment. Get what she needed and return to the past and Castle Lachlan. But the tribal beats of the entertainers' drums lured her to the grove and kept her longer in the twenty-first century than she'd intended.

Douglas was another distraction she could ill afford.

At the band's sales tent, he picked up a box filled with CD's. The afternoon sunlight glistened on the crystal cases. Maybe he planned to sell them in his store.

He spoke to the band's lead vocalist. Despite her keen

hearing, Caitrina couldn't make out the words. The buxom redhead with the sweet lilting voice laughed at whatever he said. If nothing else, Douglas was consistent. Caitrina touched her auburn locks and snarled.

The smile on the annoying man's face looked almost like a smirk.

Did he wink in her direction?

She narrowed her eyes. 'Twas impossible. He couldn't see her. Her power wasn't weakening but getting stronger. He couldn't know she watched.

Continuing with the flirting, Douglas placed the box on the table and leaned in close to the singer. He gently touched the young woman's arm and whispered into her ear. Caitrina stared through a green haze while heat sizzled up her spine. How dare he? She twirled around and headed away from the stage and sales tent. Once she strode deep in the dense woods, she stopped and closed her eyes. Sparks flew in every direction as she tried to take control over her anger.

"I should turn him into a leathery lizard."

"You love me too dearly, my lass." The sound of Douglas's deep voice snapped her eyes open. He stood in front of her, bare-chested, wearing a red and green kilt and hide boots, a boar's head fur sporran strung around his waist. Hands fisted on hips, he roared with laughter. Long ebony hair fell loose onto a bronzed chest. The sight of his well-defined six-pack had her licking her lips.

His sensual growl vibrated through her.

She resisted the impulse to seek shelter in his warmth. "How did you find me?"

"You left a trail of embers any man could follow. Someone needed to make sure you didn't start a forest fire with that fae temper of yours."

"Damn you, Douglas." Wait. There was no way he knew what she was. "Fae? What are you talking about?"

"No one else smells as beautiful as you. The tantalizing fragrance of peony, freesia, and sandalwood sets my loins aflame."

"Stop with the flowery words. What do you want?"

"You know we're meant to be together." His tawny gaze seared her flesh.

"No we aren't." Caitrina stepped back, wanting to put distance between them. "Really, why are you here?"

"I want to know what you did with Finn. I can't find him anywhere. Lass, don't deny you had a hand in the events at Laurie's party."

"Finn's gone on a journey and so must I." Caitrina raced behind a grove of fir and disappeared before her desire for the devilish man got in the way of the tasks she must perform.

The rare rock gnome lichen grew in only one place to her knowledge: high on the rocky summit of Grandfather Mountain. Scattered amidst the cliffs, small colonies of the reindeer moss she sought clung to vertical rock faces, where water seeped through crevices and frequent fogs nourished the blue-gray foliage.

Caitrina inhaled the fresh mountain air, allowing it to cleanse her lungs. Feeling exhilarated, she made her way through a cool, moist spruce and fir forest, past gnarled thickets of pink-blossomed rhododendron, along an ancient path used by Cherokee Indians in the past, but known by few in the present. Skirting gray-green boulders and yellow birch, the rambling trail climbed higher. Breaking out onto a wind swept ridge, she glanced up at the racing clouds crossing the powder blue sky.

She marched across the ridge, her hair blowing in the wind. A loud, rapid kek kek kek kek kek sounded before the whish of wings and the large bird landed on her outstretched arm.

"Trystan, you've returned to our mountain. I'm glad to see you, my friend."

The peregrine falcon murmured close to Caitrina's ear.

"Ah, you want to feel the sun on your face again. Aye, I imagine the northern tundra was verra cold."

Trystan raised one clawed foot, stepped back, then raised

the other, replacing it on Caitrina's sleeve. He nuzzled her neck before she lifted her arm to release him to the air. She watched the bird of prey surf air currents as clouds swept up the ridge and over Grandfather's rocky spire.

Time was running out. She needed to hurry.

Unexpected pain shot through her chest.

She closed her eyes, falling to her knees. Her temples throbbed. She could barely think. Could hardly see the land before her or the rocky black cliffs where she would find her prize.

"So easily distracted, Princess." Oonagh's piercing laugh shot down Caitrina's spine. "If Finn MacIntyre dies, you'll lose the challenge and feel my wrath."

The fae queen's voice penetrated her mind. Her eardrums felt like they would burst.

"Stop!" Caitrina covered her ears with her hands, attempting to block the horrific sound.

Munn had been right. Returning to the future was perilous. Especially since the queen wanted her to fail.

Suddenly Caitrina's pain ceased. When she opened her eyes, Douglas stood over her, a concerned expression on his handsome face.

"Are you hurt?" He reached out to assist her to her feet.

How had he found her again? She refused him and stood without aid. "You followed me. Why?"

"Dammit, lass. What are you doing up here alone?"

"None of your concern. Go back down the mountain where you belong and flirt some more with your singer." Caitrina turned and strode away.

Douglas grabbed her arm, swinging her around to face him. His eyes flamed golden. "Do not turn your back on me."

She tried to pull away, but the queen's attack must have weakened her, for she couldn't get away from his tight grip. He grasped her other arm and shook. "Tell me why you're here or so help me, I'll throw you over my shoulder and carry you down this mountain."

Caitrina ground her teeth. The infuriating man had no rights where she was concerned. But time was running out. "I need to collect an herb for a project I'm working on."

"I'll go with you."

"I don't need your help." She clenched her fists in an attempt to control her temper.

"That may be true, but I will join you anyway. You should not be on this mountain alone."

She attempted to pull out of his grip with no success. Giving in to him went against everything within her. But what choice did she have? In her weakened state, he overpowered her.

"All right. Come on."

Douglas released her arm, and Caitrina led the way across the exposed ridge, her hair blowing into her eyes as she walked. She ignored him and concentrated on what she needed to do.

She would take but a snippet of the rare plant, use her power to rejuvenate its growth, return to the past, and prepare the powerful potion required to save Finn's life.

When they reached an odd shaped outcrop of rock, Caitrina knelt, pulled clippers from her pocket, and reached for the foliage.

"Lass, what do you think you're doing? That's rock gnome lichen. It's rare and needs to be protected."

"I ken it. I'll only take a little."

"You're not allowed to take any."

Caitrina risked all, allowing Douglas to see her use her power. She counted on the fact that he was in love with her, hoping his feelings for her were strong enough to keep him from spreading the tale. She'd deal with the consequences after she saved Finn.

She snipped a tiny piece of the lichen and in her heart heard the plant cry out in pain.

"I beseech the great Goddess Dana, mother of this earth, to lend your power to mine," she implored. "Stimulate this lean soil and renew verdant growth. This I beg of thee as your conduit."

Caitrina raised her arms and used the power flowing through her to take the hurt away and begin the regeneration.

Like a plant in a time-lapse film, the diminutive lichen grew fresh, healthy tissue replacing the small piece she'd removed. Within moments, the reindeer moss sang.

When Caitrina ventured a look at Douglas, he stood with his arms crossed over his chest, a wide smile on his very kissable lips. "What?" She shook her head unable to believe her vision.

"We make progress, I think." He reached out his hand. "Come. It will be dark soon."

"I'm sorry," she said and vanished.

CHAPTER ELEVEN

Castle Lachlan 1511

A moan escaped Finn's lips.

Two angels floated over him, coming close, and then slipping away. One with hair like fire hovered to his right, just out of reach. The other—

My God. There was something about her that made him want to touch her.

Blond hair. Silver eyes.

He tried with all his might to move his hand. Nothing. He couldn't even will his fingers to twitch. Speech eluded him as well. He knew what he wanted to say, yet his parched lips couldn't form the words.

A glass of water. What he wouldn't do for a glass of cool, sweet water. If only he could tell them what he wanted.

Never mind. He could watch them and listen to them forever.

The angels spoke to each other with voices so enchanting they touched his soul. He could almost comprehend what they said, but not quite. The words wavered at the edge of his mind then flitted away without his understanding.

Heaven wasn't what he expected.

He made another effort to reach out. Only to find, once again, he was caught in a web of silky mist.

"His fever has lessened some." Elspeth removed the damp cloth from Finn's forehead.

"Aye. The potion removed the poisons from his body, yet he needs time to recover fully. He'll rest now." Caitrina moved away from the curtained bed. "Try to get some broth into him."

Before Elspeth could ask any questions, Caitrina disappeared. It then occurred to Elspeth the fragrance lingering in the chamber seemed familiar. She'd smelled that fragrance—

A groan from Finn distracted her from her remembering.

"Please send for Aine," Elspeth called to Hector, who stood guard outside the door.

The watchdog Elspeth's betrothed had set upon her stared down his nose in distaste. "Lord Alexander will be angry when he learns you spend so much time with this," he waved his hand toward the large bed where Finn lay fitfully sleeping, "lad."

Sighing, Elspeth tried to maintain her patience. "Please, Sir Hector. Call for Aine."

For once, the man did as she asked.

Moments later, Aine bustled into the room carrying a bowl of broth. "How is the lad?"

The stern-faced Hector peered into the chamber, glared at Elspeth, and then shut the door. She guessed he remained in the passage to stand guard. As if she needed a protector in her brother's home.

"The fever is still with him."

"He is sure to waken soon and fulfill the prophecy." Aine squeezed Elspeth's hand.

Elspeth glanced heavenward, shaking her head, refusing to encourage the old woman's imaginings.

Finn woke, yet he remained in a state of confusion. Aine tried to get him to drink some of the broth and he complained he wanted the other angel to feed him.

When Elspeth attempted to give the warm liquid to him, he refused to open his mouth. Instead, he stared at her with a big grin on his flushed face, like a village idiot. The deed took much effort, but the two women finally coaxed Finn into swallowing every drop of the broth. After which, he fell into a deep slumber.

Elspeth pulled the covers over him. "I pray his fever continues to lessen."

Aine patted her arm. "He will be himself again soon."

With a bob of her head, the woman left the chamber.

Alone with Finn, Elspeth succumbed to uncontrollable emotions—thankful he remained alive yet fearful he might die. This man had come to mean so much to her. Hector was right, Alexander would be furious when he learned of it.

She couldn't help herself. She needed to be near Finn. She wanted to touch him. Hold him close and make sure no one ever hurt him again.

Elspeth worried her bottom lip, wondering when Alexander would return from his trip to meet with his father at Inveraray Castle. He'd not said when he planned to return to Castle Lachlan. She dreaded the day he did. Alexander would expect her to leave Finn's care to someone else. Something she didn't want to do.

Days passed. The routine remained the same. Finn woke and shouted out things that made no sense. He ranted about mergers and acquisitions. Elspeth had no knowledge of the words he spoke and feared for others to hear his ranting.

She attempted to make him eat. Afterward, he fell back to sleep, only to repeat the cycle the next time he awakened.

Hector continually chastised her, saying her actions were unbecoming of the future bride of a Campbell lord. Finn's care should be left to servants, he reminded her on more than one occasion. Rather than argue, she chose to ignore the man and do what she wanted anyway. As much as Hector's warnings of Alexander's wrath concerned her, she wasn't about to give up her time with Finn. Especially not before he became well.

Her confused thoughts made her head ache. She'd always believed she would wed Alexander. Now she yearned for something different. She wished the prophecy were true and Finn would save her from her fate. Alas, it couldn't be. Her marriage to Alexander loomed before her, an unwanted destiny.

Finally, one morning, she found Finn sitting up against the down pillows, a soft smile upon his cracked lips, his hazel eyes completely free of fever.

"Good morn to you, Lady Elspeth." Finn marveled at the beauty of the woman who stood before him. He knew she'd taken care of him while he'd been sick, yet she didn't appear fatigued, as he would have expected. Her bright silver eyes matched her gown. She wore her hair in a thick braid that hung over the front of one shoulder, falling almost down to where Finn thought her knees might be covered by the gown. The healthy glow in her cheeks reddened under his inspection.

"Good morn to you, sir."

"I hope I wasn't too much trouble." Finn pulled the sheet higher up on his chest, suddenly embarrassed to think Elspeth had seen him nude.

She glanced away and fiddled with the tray she carried, placing it on the table at the side of the large bed. Then sat in a nearby chair. "I brought broth."

"Can I have something more substantial?"

Elspeth walked to the doorway, spoke to someone then returned to her seat.

Finn cleared his throat. "I wonder if I could speak with your brother."

"Archie is not here. He has gone to Toward Castle to meet with the Lamont about his betrothal."

"Did Duncan go with him?"

"Aye."

"Jamie?" Finn asked.

"He also."

Finn didn't want to upset Elspeth, but there were things he needed to know. "What of Maclay? Was he captured or killed?"

She bit her lower lip, hesitating.

The sight of her teeth grazing her lip had Finn hardening. He adjusted himself under the covers to hide his sudden arousal.

Well, then, he inwardly smiled. He certainly was getting healthier.

"Maclay was not with the group of men who attacked you," Elspeth finally answered.

Finn frowned. What would it take to kill the man? From what he'd been told, many warriors had gone after the elusive bastard over the last two years. No one had succeeded in capturing the damned man, never mind, killing the son of a bitch.

"You look much better," Elspeth said.

Heat crept up Finn's neck and he almost squirmed. "Aye, I feel much better."

Their gazes met and held.

Surprisingly, he looked away first. "Lady Elspeth?"

"Aye."

"Would you leave so I can put my clothes on?"

"Nae. You must stay abed until you are fully well."

"If I stay in this bed any longer, I'll never get my strength back."

Elspeth gave him a perturbed look. "As you wish. But only if you will wait until I send for someone to help you."

"Agreed."

Elspeth hefted the tray and glided to the door. She glanced over her shoulder, her stare measuring. As if she'd come to some conclusion, she slipped through the doorway.

The thunk of the heavy wood panel shutting allowed Finn a moment of respite. He thought about cricket, his most despised sport. So slow. So boring. He needed to get his body back under control.

Shortly after Elspeth departed, a knock sounded on the door and a portly older man with a grizzly beard entered, carrying a tray containing real food. He gave Finn the once-over. "I be Angus MacTamhais. Aine's husband. The lass be telling me you wish to clothe yourself."

"Will you assist me?"

"Aye, sure." Angus put the tray on the bed next to Finn. "Eat these victuals, and then we will get you into your garments. Keep in mind, it will not be easy. Your leg will be paining you a wee bit, I be thinking."

Finn savored every bite of the fine stew Angus brought. "This is really good. What is it?"

"Rabbit." Angus took the empty bowl from Finn, placed it on the tray, and moved the finished meal to the side table.

"Really? I've never eaten rabbit before. It's good." Finn had heard rabbit had a gamey taste, but the stew was actually quite tasty.

Angus nodded. "Aye. Our cook prepares good victuals."

Finn pulled the *leine* Angus gave him over his head and made ready to stand.

"Here. Lean on me, lad."

Placing his hand on the older man's shoulder, Finn stepped down onto his right leg. *So far, so good.* When he stepped onto his left leg, the pain that shot through him was much greater than a wee bit. His head spun, and he quickly sat onto the bed.

"The lass be right. You are not ready to be up and about."

"I can't endure staying in bed any longer," Finn said with a growl.

Angus blinked.

Finn sighed. "If you'll put a chair by the window and help me to it, I'll be content to sit and look out at the countryside."

"Aye, lad. That makes good sense. However, you must not try to get up without help." Angus moved the chair and assisted Finn to sit in it. "I will find a sturdy limb in the wood and make a walking staff for you to use. Then you can get around a wee bit on your own."

"Thank you. I appreciate your efforts."

With a nod, the old man left him to his thoughts.

Gazing out the window, he saw across the small bay to the mainland stable, to the heather covered hill above, which edged the woods.

Finn turned away from the view. He needed to find out what happened to his claymore, get the sword back and go after Maclay. He flexed his injured leg and winced. Well, maybe he should add regaining his strength to the plan.

Several weeks into his convalescence, Finn walked along the path, using the beautifully carved rowan staff Angus had gifted him for support. The man had taken great pains with the walking stick, carving bands of intricate Celtic knots for decoration. Finn hoped to take the staff with him through the time gate when he returned home.

That is, if the gate allowed him through. Laurie had tried several times before she'd made it back home. The keys were a full moon and satisfying your destiny. His destiny in this time period would be fulfilled when Malcolm Maclay died. After the man's demise, Finn would walk through the gate on a full moon.

And poof, he'd be in Laurie's garden.

He took a clumsy step over a fallen limb, leaning heavily on the staff. Most of his strength had returned, but his injured leg remained stiff and sometimes gave out on him, ergo his need for the walking stick. It would be quite awhile before he could run again, never mind go after Maclay.

His pace slow, he peered up at the golden sun shining brightly in the pristine blue sky. The lack of planes or contrails still unnerved him on occasion. The urgency of his adventure settled heavily on his chest. Wishing to relieve the pressure, he drew in a deep breath, allowing his lungs to fill completely with fresh air before he exhaled.

Finn stifled his frustration. He was alive and being out of the castle raised his spirits.

With a shake of his head, he stepped through the arched

entrance of the garden. Elspeth worked amongst the roses, bushes covered with shiny green leaves and pink and white blooms. Unfortunately, her guard Hector leaned against a nearby wall.

Weary of the nuisance's presence, Finn maneuvered the paths, startling Elspeth when his staff scraped across the gravel not far from her. A sweet smile crossed her lips and her silver eyes brightened when she glanced up from where she knelt. Warmth invaded him with the knowledge his presence delighted her.

Now if only he could get rid of the silent Hector with the condescending mannerisms and the too-observant eyes. Alexander was sure to hear a pack of lies when he returned for a visit.

Doing his best to ignore Hector, Finn returned her smile. "Good day, Lady Elspeth."

"You make much progress." Elspeth jumped up before he could offer assistance.

"You are kind, my lady."

She seemed nervous and when she glanced at Hector, he glowered. She lowered her gaze and fiddled with her apron, wiping away nonexistent dirt.

Finn stiffened, stifling an urge to punch the man. He wasn't about to allow Elspeth's guard to ruin the fine day though. Finn attempted to put Hector out of his thoughts.

"Would it disturb you if I sit a spell and enjoy the lovely sights of the garden?"

She was the lovely sight he wished to enjoy.

Elspeth's cheeks colored a pleasant pink. "Please, take your ease." She pointed to the blooming turf bench a few feet away with its small white daisy-like flowers. Finn sat, releasing the apple-like fragrance of chamomile, which mingled with the heady scent of roses.

Not turning to glare at Hector was harder than Finn imagined. And having the man standing behind his back might even be dangerous. Who knew if Hector would think to rid the lady of a possible suitor by putting a knife in Finn's back.

Finn twisted in such a manner as to covertly observe Hector to his right while still enjoying the view of Elspeth.

She hummed softly while weeding around a thorny bush. When she knelt to reach farther into the bed, her apron fell open in back, exposing to Finn's appreciative eye a perfectly sculpted backside. He barely refrained from groaning over the luscious sight covered by nothing more than thin linen. He certainly didn't want her to know he ogled her tush.

He had to admit, if only to himself, it wasn't only her physical assets he found appealing. Being in her company comforted him.

A surprising sense of contentment wrapped around him like a tender embrace, and with shock, he realized he'd fallen in love with the girl. How inappropriate. Not only was she fifteen years his junior, she was Patrick's sister.

Totally inappropriate.

Besides, after he took care of Maclay, Finn would return to the future, to his consulting firm and his real life. His adventure would end, and he'd leave Elspeth in the past.

Loneliness crept over him.

Short of breath, he got up and excused himself, cringing at the look of disappointment that crossed Elspeth's features. With an awkward gait, he made his way back to the castle, damning the circumstances that would keep him away from the one woman whom he now realized he loved. The one woman who could make him whole.

Elspeth stared after Finn as he hobbled away. Confusion marred the pleasant afternoon. Had she said something to distress him? She glanced at Hector. He quickly removed the smirk from his face and replaced the smug smile with his usual stern countenance.

Checking the position of the sun, she recognized the hour grew late. She needed to go to her chamber and change her gown before the evening meal. She gathered her gardening tools, placed them into a leather sack, and walked to the castle. Hector followed, remaining a short distance behind. Oh, how she missed Jamie. She much preferred him as her personal guard.

As she approached the castle gate, a commotion drew her attention. She shifted her gaze to the bay, where men rowed toward the beach. Apparently, her uncle returned from Lamont country. Was her brother Archibald with him? She began to run.

CHAPTER TWELVE

*F*inn gripped the rowan staff in one hand and leaned against the castle's outer wall, trying to catch his breath. The short trip from the garden left him weak. If his stamina didn't return soon, he'd go crazy. He needed to be healthy and strong so he could go after Maclay. Then he must travel home before he did something rash concerning Elspeth.

He stopped again at the castle gate and gulped air to remain standing.

Motion on the bay caught his attention. Men rowed toward the castle in several small boats of the type made from skins and wicker, the kind Highlanders called *currachs*. When the crafts beached, he recognized Donald MacLachlan as the man jumped from one, strode across the pebbly beach and headed toward him.

Suddenly a weight slammed against Finn, knocking the hard-won air from his lungs. His walking stick flew from his hand as he fell to the ground. Pain shot from his thigh, to his groin, to his chest. Gasping for breath, he found Elspeth's soft body entangled with his.

Her lush curves wrapped around him, filling his senses with all that was missing from his dreams. The scents of sunshine and roses intoxicated him. His hard-on was instantaneous.

Shit! He attempted to detangle their limbs and set her away from his ill-timed erection, but her body melded with his. She felt so right in his arms. He was tempted to hold onto her and never let her go.

Elspeth caught her breath. Everywhere Finn touched her as they tried to break apart, her skin tingled. When their gazes met, everything else faded away. The world reduced to only the two of them, and his mouth dipped toward hers.

His lips grazed hers and fire blazed through Elspeth to her toes, the moment lasting an eternity. Finn's tongue pushed between her lips, seeking entrance. Her mind reeled. With little thought, she wrapped her arms around his waist and twirled her tongue around his. *Passion.* Unlike the minimal pecks she'd received from Alexander, Finn's fierce kiss conquered, possessed.

She wanted more.

The sound of a throat clearing broke the spell, and Finn's sinful mouth pulled away, leaving behind a fracture in the foundation of Elspeth's expectations for the future.

How could she go on as before?

"Let me help you."

She gazed up through the haze of awakened sensation. Uncle Donald stared at her, a sly gleam in his eyes. He reached a hand down and helped her rise before assisting Finn. Unstable on his feet, Finn leaned on her while her uncle retrieved the walking stick.

She swayed—not from the burden of Finn's weight, but the desire awakened by their kiss.

Disappointment pinched when Uncle Donald handed the staff over, and Finn stepped aside. Elspeth jerked her gaze away from his comely form and gasped at the gathered crowd.

Hector stood to the side, glaring.

She was in trouble. Alexander would be beside himself when he learned of this. Shaking off the distressing thought, she risked a peek at Finn. He now leaned heavily on his staff.

"Are you all right?" he asked, as if their fall had been his fault.

"Fine. I am sorry. I must have tripped on a stone or…" She glanced at the ground, trying to figure out what caught her foot. Not seeing anything, she wrinkled her brow and continued, "or something and fell into you. 'Twas clumsy of me. Did I hurt you?"

She bit her lip.

Finn's eyes flared. "No worries. I'm unharmed."

Elspeth hesitated then reached for him.

"Beth, dinnae unman the lad. He is fine."

She yanked her arm back and flipped her gaze to her uncle.

Donald's stare measured Finn. "MacIntyre?"

Finn's features were inscrutable, but Elspeth noticed he held himself stiffly. "Aye."

"I am Donald MacLachlan, I have not had the pleasure to meet you, though I have heard tales of your skill on the practice field." He looked Finn up and down. "Does not seem to have done you much good on the battlefield."

Finn held his head high. "When I'm well again, I hope to give a better showing."

Donald slapped Finn's back, causing Finn to wobble. "I am sure you will." He leaned in closer and whispered, "If that Campbell lad over there does not take you down first." He tilted his head in the direction of the grim-faced Hector.

Elspeth glanced at her guard and her stomach dropped.

In his anxious state, Munn couldn't conjure an invisibility glamour. He used the speed spell instead and darted faster than a human eye could see, tripped Elspeth in passing then dashed through the castle gate before Donald reached the couple. He giggled with glee. There was more than one way to bring Elspeth and Finn together. If he must keep tripping one or the other to force them into each other's arms, so be it. He peeked around the edge of the wall.

They kissed. He howled in delight.

Caitrina would be surprised when he informed her of his success. He puffed out his chest. He couldn't wait to tell the annoying faerie. She thought he couldn't help.

She was wrong. And he proved it. Munn spun in a circle and traveled with the wind in search of the fae princess.

The memory of their kiss played havoc with his body and mind. The smell and taste of Elspeth lingered with Finn, teasing his senses. Much better than the most expensive perfume or the finest wine.

He limped along the dim corridor, leaning heavily on the walking stick. He hated to admit it, but the events of the day left him tired and in need of a rest before dinner.

He increased his pace as best he could, looking forward to reaching his bedchamber and taking the weight off his bum leg. When he hobbled around the final corner before reaching his room, Hector blocked the way.

"Excuse me," Finn said.

"You will stay away from Lady Elspeth." Hector grinned, showing rotten teeth.

"I don't take orders from you."

"I will teach you differently." Hector stepped forward.

Finn's adrenaline kicked up a notch and his muscles coiled. As much as he wanted to avoid a scuffle, he refused to allow Alexander's man to continue harassing Elspeth. Finn wouldn't tolerate Hector any longer. He widened his stance, balancing on the balls of his feet, his grip tight on his staff.

The foolish man lunged.

Finn swayed to the side and, pivoting behind Hector, slammed his staff against the back of the big man's legs. Hector fell to his knees, his hands flat to the floor in front of him. Positioning the tip of the staff on the back of one of Hector's hands, Finn pressed his weight against it.

Hector's face reddened. "Stop!"

Finn pulled the staff away and Hector sat with his butt on the stone floor, rubbing his hand, glaring at Finn.

"Here's how we're going to play this. You will continue to guard Elspeth, but you won't speak to her unless she speaks to you first. Are we understood?"

Hector nodded.

"Good."

Finn walked the short distance to his bedchamber, swinging the staff, overcompensating so as not to limp and appear weak. Once safely inside, he leaned against the closed door and slid to the floor as his leg gave out. Finn rubbed his sore thigh, wishing he had access to a hot tub for a good, bubbly soak.

Minutes passed before he felt confident enough to rise and hobble to the bed. He collapsed on the mattress with a heavy sigh. What were the chances Hector took the message to heart and no longer caused problems?

At mealtime, Elspeth walked into the passageway from her bedchamber and glanced both ways. No one lurked in the corridor. Where was Hector? She smiled, delighted not to find the irksome man hanging about her door. She made her way to the circular stair, careful of the hem of her skirt as she descended the steps to the great hall.

Loud conversation assaulted her ears as she entered, with the clan bustling to and fro in an attempt to find their places. Elspeth stepped onto the dais and sat to the right of her uncle. She looked up in surprise when Finn joined her, sitting to her right.

He leaned close and she caught a whiff of his scent, a combination of pine and fresh mountain air. "How did I earn the honor to be seated next to such a lovely lass?"

A thrill shot through Elspeth and her cheeks flamed, but she refused to look away from the man who held her heart. Said heart skipped a beat. She could hardly believe her own mind. She'd fallen in love with an unsuitable man, instead of

Alexander. She lowered her gaze to her lap as panic spiraled through her. What was she to do?

"Have you noticed, Beth? Hector nae longer haunts our halls."

She shot her gaze to her uncle.

"I wondered why he was not outside my chamber door, waiting to escort me. Where is he?" Elspeth searched the hall for Hector's intimidating presence.

"I sent him away," Donald said simply.

"How did you get rid of the pain in the ass?" Finn asked.

Donald chuckled. "I told him Alexander requested he attend him at Carrick Castle."

"Alexander did not go to Carrick," Elspeth said. "He went to Inveraray with missives for his father from the French king."

Her uncle smiled wickedly. "I ken. I lied."

Donald laughed. Finn and Elspeth joined him. However, an uncomfortable sensation chilled Elspeth. Sooner or later, Alexander would find out about the falsehood.

"MacIntyre, our lass here will need a guard. Are you up to the task?"

Finn nodded, his expression solemn.

After dinner, with one hand on his walking stick and the other on her elbow, he escorted Elspeth to her bedchamber. She wondered what mischief her uncle concocted. Not that she would complain. His action provided her with wanted freedom.

When they stopped outside her chamber, Finn opened the door, and handed her in. His fingers lingered on her arm. She wanted him to kiss her again. He pulled his hand back and gave her a half smile. "Good night, my lady."

She stared after Finn as he limped away. He was the most peculiar man...his speech and mannerisms so very strange. How odd for her to be in love with him.

Elspeth walked to the window and gazed out at the crescent moon, its silvery light reflecting on the smooth surface of the bay. Whirling away, she wrapped her arms around herself, spinning in a circle within the aura of her delight.

The excitement bubbling in her chest could put both her and Finn in danger.

Fear crept into her belly, burning a hole in her happiness. What would Alexander do if he learned her secret?

Alexander panted hard, his chest rising and falling with each labored breath. Jonet rode his shaft with the same competence as she rode her great black stallion—with skill.

When he arrived at Inveraray Castle several days prior, he was overjoyed to learn his father entertained King James IV, and Jonet Stewart was part of the king's entourage. He fisted the bed sheet at his sides, engrossed in something close to pain, holding back, forestalling the anticipated climax—until his control snapped. On an ecstatic shout, his seed roared up his cock and shot deep into her womb.

Jonet's scream echoed his and she slumped across his chest, breathing hard. Holding her close, he inhaled the heady scent of their coupling.

The loud knocking on the bedchamber door was an unwanted intrusion. He rolled Jonet to the side and pulled a sheet over them. "Enter," Alexander bellowed. "What ever you want, it better be dire."

Jonet giggled and dragged her nails over his chest. "You are so fierce, my love."

A young ghillie awkwardly stumbled into the chamber, his gaze locked on the floor, his cheeks bright red. "A missive arrived for the king, my lord."

"Dinnae glower at the poor lad, Alex. Come here, lad." Jonet accepted the missive from the ghillie and with a flick of her wrist broke the wax seal.

Recognizing the imprint, Alexander grabbed the parchment. He reread the message several times until the page turned red.

"What is it? What is wrong? Alex, speak to me," Jonet

implored.

"Naught to concern you." He threw his legs over the side of the mattress, rose and quickly dressed. He sat on the edge of the bed and pulled on his boots.

When he looked up, he noticed the ghillie remained. "If more missives arrive for the king, bring them to me."

The lad nodded and backed out of the chamber.

"Where are you going? Come to bed." Jonet ran her fingers along the back of Alexander's neck, inciting chills. Desire sliced through his anger, but he didn't have time to linger.

"I must speak with the king." Alexander gripped the missive and strode for the door.

"While with Jamie tell him you will not wed the MacLachlan wench."

He flicked his gaze over his shoulder. "Dinnae push me, lass."

"What if I am with child?"

"I will set you and your bastard up in a house and we will continue our affair."

He didn't stay for the temper tantrum. With irritated footfalls, Alexander strode through the passageways and across his father's reception hall, the heels of his boots clicking loudly on the stone floors. He dreaded relaying the information the letter contained.

He approached his king with bowed head. "I have news, sire."

King James raised his gaze from the documents he perused, his intelligent eyes curious. "What is it?"

"Donald has managed to sway Lamont to MacLachlan's cause. Archibald announces his betrothal to Isobell Lamont and requests your blessing."

The king leaned close to Alexander and spoke softly, "I thought you convinced the lass and her father against the union."

"Donald must have been more persuasive." Alexander frowned. "Your Majesty, if you would, why did you pardon

Donald?"

King James cut Alexander with a sharp look. "Do you still plan to wed the MacLachlan lass?"

"Aye." Marrying Elspeth wasn't what he wanted, but he would follow the king's mandate. However, he planned to keep Jonet Stewart as his mistress. He'd receive Elspeth's dowry and still have Jonet for his carnal pleasure.

"See that you do." With a wave of his royal arm, the king dismissed Alexander from his presence.

Resentment a bad taste in his mouth, he strode away, plotting his next move. Once he learned the secret of the fae-kissed sword, he'd never again follow anyone else's dictates. Not his overbearing father's, nor that of King Jamie. And Elspeth's gift of the sight would help him succeed.

Over the past fortnight, no mention was made of the kiss by the castle gate, but its effects hung between Elspeth and Finn. An anticipation of things that might be. If only...

Elspeth feared she'd be punished for her sin. Still, she wanted Finn to kiss her again. Desiring such was wrong. She had no choice other than to wed Alexander, but that didn't stop her from wanting more.

Finn ran along the edge of the loch from one end of the beach to the other and back again. An odd practice. The moist skin of his bronzed chest glistened in the golden afternoon light.

He healed quickly and his strength returned. The man drove himself, practicing every day with the claymore. And since Jamie and Duncan's return, they taught Finn to use his walking staff as a weapon.

Gathering the scattered victuals, Elspeth returned them to the leather satchel they used to bring the picnic goods to the beach. She smiled at Finn as he plopped onto the *plaide* next to her, sucking in her breath as his *leine* rose up on his leg, exposing the pink scar high on his thigh. She had to look away. The sight made her wish for things of which she had no right to dream. Things that could never be.

Nevertheless, her gaze wandered back to his leg. She traced his bare skin with her eyes. From above his hide boots, past his knee to his thigh, to the edge of his hiked up *leine*.

"Lass, don't look at me that way unless you want me to kiss you again."

Without much thought, she moistened her lips with the tip of her tongue.

Finn growled. Taking her by the upper arms, he pulled her closer. Their breaths mingled and his eyes seemed to search hers.

"I want to taste your sweet lips, but I won't steal the kiss. You have to let me know you want what I offer." He gently squeezed her arms, his eyes intense. "What will it be?"

She swallowed and bit her lip, never wanting anything more than for him to kiss her at this moment. Leaning forward, closer still, the warmth of his breath tickled her face. Holding his gaze, she nodded. "*Yes.*"

He pressed his mouth against hers with the lightest of touches.

When she parted her lips slightly, he sought entrance. His tongue teased, swirling around hers in a primal dance. At first, achingly slow, then faster. Her heart flew. The cadence of its beat pounded through her, throbbed in the hidden place between her thighs.

Finn fell back, pulling her down on top of him, trapping her hands between their bodies. Their lips never parted. She felt the rapid beat of his heart through the fabric of his *leine*. His heart raced in rhythm with hers.

His hands brushed over the linen covering her hips. The friction inflamed her.

Her breasts swelled, nipples hardened, chafing on the bodice of her gown, pressing against Finn's broad chest. She squirmed, wanting something she couldn't define, couldn't understand, but knew she needed.

The sound of the horn from the watchtower jarred them to their senses. They broke apart and quickly sat up, breathing heavily.

Disappointment cut through Elspeth when she recognized the Campbell device billowing from the masts of the two approaching galleys. Alexander was the last person she wanted to face. He'd know. All he'd have to do would be to look into her eyes and he'd know.

She gave another man her love.

"We must hurry to the castle," Elspeth cried.

Finn placed his hand on the nape of her neck. He looked as if he intended to kiss her again. Pressing her palm against his chest, she pushed him away.

He dropped his arms to his sides and lowered his gaze. Elspeth squeezed Finn's forearm. "Allowing you to kiss me was wrong. You must not try again." She pulled her trembling hand away and clutched the fabric over her chest. "Please understand—I must wed Alexander."

Finn inhaled sharply and stared at her for a long moment. His jaw tightened. She thought pain flickered in his eyes before he looked away, stood and wrapped his *plaide* around his muscular body. "Then we shall return to the castle unseen."

Watching the approaching galleys, she chewed on her bottom lip. On the deck of the first boat stood her greatest fear.

CHAPTER THIRTEEN

*G*olden flames greedily consumed large logs in the great hall's stone hearth. Elspeth's gaze swung from the roaring fire to Alexander as she attempted to forget Finn's passionate kiss. The beguiling man had gone to the practice field with Jamie, promising to stay away.

As to her betrothed—Alexander's uncharacteristic good mood made her wary. She no longer believed his smiles genuine. His rough handling of her on his last visit left her with a trace of fear, which rankled. She wouldn't stand for such treatment in the future. Although she hadn't as yet resolved what to do about his forceful ways.

He no longer was the man she sought to wed. Though she would do what her family expected and marry him. There must be a way to find common ground between them. If she thought hard enough, she would come up with something. She would attempt to make their union work.

At one time, he'd made her happy. However, Alexander had changed. And not for the good.

"We're on the way to Carrick Castle for the king's boar hunt," Alexander's voice interrupted Elspeth's musing. "Lady Jonet wished to visit with you before we continued the journey."

Elspeth mulled over the news and decided she would travel to Carrick with Alexander. As much as she didn't want to leave Finn, it was for the best. Putting distance between them would help keep duty to her family and clan clearly in mind. There could be no future for her and Finn. Like it or not, she had to wed Alexander.

Besides, her mother's father, Robert Campbell, was keeper of the castle at Carrick. She hadn't seen him since attending the Glasgow fair with Patrick and Lady Laurie. More than two years had passed since then. Elspeth missed her grandfather.

"Wonderful. Aine will pack my things. I can visit with my grandfather while I am there."

"I am afraid not, dearling. You will not be joining us." Alexander wore a sympathetic expression. "You have much to do here at Castle Lachlan in preparation for our nuptials. I expect all to be perfect. The celebration must be magnificent. After all, the king will arrive with my father's entourage." He patted her arm. "To have King Jamie attend our wedding is an honor not many receive."

Elspeth's contrary heart soared. Alexander wouldn't agree to take her with him. In all honesty, she didn't care about the wedding plans or the king. If she stayed at home, she could spend more time with Finn. Enjoy his company for a while longer. At least, until the wedding.

Alexander stared at her, waiting for a response.

"Aye. We are verra fortunate."

She managed to reply to him in her customary calm voice without choking on the words, but only barely. Seeming satisfied, Alexander accepted a goblet of wine from the ghillie standing by with a full tray. He scanned the hall.

"Where is my man? I am surprised not to find Hector at his post guarding my most prized possession."

Elspeth started. *What did he mean?*

Alexander raised his goblet to her. "*You, my dearling.*"

Swallowing uncomfortably, Elspeth glanced away. "My uncle said something about Hector taking a missive to

Carrick." She returned her gaze to Alexander.

"Peculiar. I gave him strict orders not to allow you out of his sight. Nae matter. He will be punished severely for his disobedience." Alexander's eyes bored into her, as if measuring her guilt.

She shivered and glanced at Jonet. The young woman wore a flattering emerald gown, which set off her pale skin, big brown eyes and red locks to their best advantage. Jonet smiled brightly, her cheeks blushing pink.

How odd. Alexander traveled with Jonet with only a young serving lass for respectability. Why? He never allowed Elspeth to travel with him, not even with an appropriate escort.

"Will you attend the hunt?" she asked Jonet.

The woman twittered, her cheeks flaming redder. Jonet's gaze flew to Alexander.

"Of course not," he said. "'Tis too dangerous. The king's boar hunt is reserved for strong warriors."

The heavy thud of boots against stone caused Elspeth to twist around toward the sound. Her brother Archibald crossed the hall to join them. He greeted his guests with a bow.

Alexander inclined his head and Jonet curtsied.

"Congratulations, Archie." Alexander clapped Archibald on the shoulder. "I was with the king when he received your missive about your betrothal. James was well pleased. When will you fetch Isobell?"

Furrows lined Archibald's forehead, and he frowned. "She has gone to Arran to visit her mother's cousin."

"If I were you, I would kidnap the lass before Lamont changes his mind." Alexander chuckled.

"How romantic that would be for Isobell. To have the love of her life whisk her away like a damsel in a ballad." Jonet sighed heavily.

Elspeth didn't think so. She didn't believe any woman would want to be stolen away from her family. "What utter nonsense."

"Always the practical one, dearling." Alexander handed her a goblet of wine. He raised his cup. "Let us drink to Archibald and Isobell. May they find the same happiness as have Elspeth and I." He raised a brow in Elspeth's direction in challenge.

She smiled, managing to refrain from comment, not wishing to encourage a quarrel.

Archibald offered a goblet to Jonet before taking one for himself. "Here. Here. I will drink to that."

They all drank, but Elspeth sensed something disturbing, something almost sinister behind Alexander's good wishes for her brother.

Late afternoon sun blazed hot over the practice field. Finn wiped his forehead to keep the sweat from dripping into his eyes. His grip tightened on the staff he held.

Damn, he made a mess of things. He never should have kissed Elspeth on the beach. He knew it was wrong. On so many levels. First, she was engaged to someone else. Even if the man was Cro-Magnon and a complete jerk, Finn's chasing after Elspeth's skirts like a randy schoolboy was wrong. Second, even if she wasn't already spoken for, she was too young for him. Third, and the worst rub of all, she was Iain's daughter. Patrick's sister. Both men Finn considered friends in the twenty-first century.

So what was he to do? The answer should be easy. Stay away from her.

Not so easy. He kicked the dirt.

She needed him.

No. Her problems with Alexander were none of his affair. He had his own problems with the man: the missing claymore. His only reason for being in sixteenth-century Scotland was to go after Maclay and make the man pay for what he did to Laurie.

Yet Finn's memory of the passionate kiss he shared with Elspeth tormented him. The longing for more teased his senses, making him ache all over. He was in love with the girl. There was absolutely nothing he could do about quelling his desire.

But that didn't mean he should act upon it.

For the moment, he had to remove her from his thoughts or Jamie would clobber him. He glanced at the other warriors standing around the practice field watching his lesson and then directed his attention to Jamie.

Finn took a deep breath.

"Are you ready? If you dinnae pay attention, I will make you eat dirt," taunted Jamie.

With a nod, Finn raised his staff. Jamie advanced, striking with his pole. Finn blocked the thrust, counterattacked, and the mock fight was on.

Elspeth bit back the resentment nearly choking her and guided Jonet to one of the guest bedchambers near her own. Ushering the other woman into the chamber, Elspeth followed and closed the door, her mind whirling. What was the matter with her? She didn't want to go to Carrick Castle.

So then why was she annoyed Jonet was going?

Elspeth didn't like the jumble of thoughts troubling her. Not in the least. She glanced at her guest.

"A lovely wee chamber with such a large bed." Jonet jounced several times on the mattress. "I am sure to be comfortable here."

"There are drying towels on the table and the ewer is filled with fresh water," Elspeth offered.

"I thank you." Jonet stroked her fingers along the furs covering the bed.

Elspeth hesitated. She didn't feel comfortable with Jonet any longer. Once, when they were young girls, they'd been the best of friends. When they visited one another's castles, they chatted and giggled into the wee hours, sharing their hopes and dreams. Now, Elspeth didn't have any idea what to say to Jonet.

Jonet hummed to herself, totally ignoring her hostess.

"Well, if there is aught else you need—"

"I am sure I have everything I desire."

"I will send Aine to help you dress for the evening meal." Elspeth opened the door to depart.

"That will not be necessary," Jonet responded in a rush.

"Then I will take my leave. Later in the hall—"

"Aye. Later. I am verra tired and wish to nap. Please, dinnae allow anyone to disturb me." Jonet turned away and fluffed one of the down pillows.

Elspeth left, closed the door and walked toward her bedchamber. Why did it seem as if Jonet had been trying to get rid of her?

Much later, when it was time for the clan to gather in the hall for the evening meal, Elspeth walked the passageway toward the wheel stair, passing Jonet's chamber. Muffled noises came from within. Elspeth stepped closer and leaned into the door to listen. There was the sound of heavy breathing, and then Jonet cried out.

Fearing the woman had taken ill, Elspeth knocked. Jonet didn't answer, so Elspeth opened the door and peered in.

She covered her mouth with her hand to muffle her gasp. She could hardly believe what the light of the flickering candles revealed. A man's bare white backside bobbed up and down as he straddled Jonet, pumping his… *thing* into her.

Her eyes wide, Jonet screamed. Alexander swung his head around and glared at Elspeth.

She backed out of the chamber, the contents of her stomach threatening to choke her. She ran along the passageway and burst into the garderobe just in time.

After retching miserably, she wiped her sweaty forehead with her sleeve. Praying no one would waylay her, she dashed from the castle.

Darting along the dimly lit garden path, she ran straight into Finn's open arms.

The unexpected impact of Elspeth's weight hurled against

his chest forced Finn back a step.

"What is it? What's happened to upset you?" Finn embraced her convulsing body, concerned by the way she shook. "Now, now. I have you. Everything will be all right." He rubbed her back in slow circles, trying to calm her so he could find out why she ran blindly along darkened paths when she should be safe within the walls of the castle.

She pulled slightly away and gazed up at him. Her eyes rimmed with red, filled with tears. "'Twill never be right. Never again."

"Tell me what happened. Maybe I can help." He brushed the loose hairs that escaped her braid from her face.

She wrapped her arms around his waist and leaned into him. He held her tight until her sobs quieted. Then he held her at arm's length.

"Now will you tell me why you're out here alone? Running as if a ghost chases you." His attempt to get a smile out of her failed miserably.

She dropped her gaze to the ground, refusing to look at him.

He wanted to shake her, but had enough sense to know it would be a mistake.

Her back stiffened and she pulled away when the crunch of heavy footsteps on the path broke the silence.

Alexander slowly walked toward them, his stare intent on Finn. "I see you have found my wayward lass."

Finn noted Alexander's disheveled appearance. The man had obviously dressed in a hurry. His long black hair was only half tied back and stray strands stuck to his sweaty face.

If Finn wasn't mistaken, Alexander sported a love bite on the side of his throat.

Elspeth's trembling increased. She appeared about to collapse.

"What have you done to her?" Finn demanded, thinking Alexander had tried to force himself on Elspeth after some innocent foreplay.

"I ken you are trying to comfort my lass, so I will not fault you for touching what is mine. I thank you for your concern, but she is my responsibility. Now come, Beth. Return to the castle, where I will explain what is expected of you."

Finn's muscles clenched. The urge to punch the man in the face erupted. He fought for control, barely stopping short of succumbing to his raging anger. He didn't want to upset Elspeth more than she already was.

At another time he would wipe that arrogant look off the man's face.

"Beth, we must discuss what you think you saw," Alexander said in a stern tone.

The plot thickens. Elspeth must have walked in on something she wasn't supposed to see.

She stepped away from Finn. With her hands on her hips, she glared at Alexander. "I ken what I saw. I never wish to see you again." Although she stood strong, her bottom lip quivered.

Alexander reached for her arm, but she darted past him and ran toward the castle.

"MacIntyre. You will never touch her again. Do you understand?"

Finn gritted his teeth.

"If you do, I will see you regret it."

Holding himself in check, Finn glared at the man.

"You have lived in France. You must understand the carnal needs of men are seldom met by delicate wives." Alexander whirled on his heel and strode back to the castle, leaving Finn where he stood.

The bastard had been with another woman. Poor Elspeth.

A seething fire raged inside Finn's belly.

Elspeth ruined a stitch. Rays of morning sunlight gleamed through the windows of the solar, highlighting the mistake. She pulled out the blue thread she used for the dragon's scales and jabbed the needle into the stretched fabric again. She glared at her needlework. The next stitch was better, but not up to her usual standard.

Well, that was to be expected. Especially since, she couldn't concentrate. She attempted to forget the horrible sight she'd seen yestereve when she walked in on Alexander and Jonet while they mated. Though Elspeth was inexperienced herself, she knew from what her mother told her, that was indeed what they'd been doing.

After Alexander retrieved her, he explained men had certain needs. Good men, like him, eased their baser needs with someone other than their wives. Wives, he said, bore heirs, and therefore should be worshipped and not required to endure the harsher side of a man's carnal lust.

Balderdash. Elspeth thought his rationalization nonsense. Before her father disappeared, he'd not taken women other than her mother.

Elspeth knew about mistresses. She wasn't naïve. Her brother Patrick had planned to take Lady Laurie as his when he faced a loveless marriage with Isobell. He hadn't loved Isobell then and Alexander didn't love Elspeth now.

How had she ever thought herself enamored of him? On occasion, when they'd spent a quiet eve before the fire, she'd enjoyed the tales he wove about his travels. However, when she really thought about those times, Archie had told the tales, not Alexander. Of course, Alexander often brought her gifts from the Continent. No, he hadn't done that either. Archie had been the one who brought her gifts of books, seeds, and plants.

So how had she allowed Alexander to charm her? Obviously, she'd been a foolish lass with silly imaginings.

As much as she tried to forget the debacle of yestereve, it proved impossible. Jonet occupied the solar with her.

Running her hand along the length of her gown, Jonet smoothed what to Elspeth's eyes were nonexistent wrinkles. Jonet moved away from her place at the window, stopping in front of Elspeth. "I dinnae wish to hurt you. You ken? But Alexander *is* the son of the Campbell." Her voice lowered to a whisper. "Even as his mistress...I will have access to the king. With my brother's excellent connections and Alexander's, we are sure to be one of the king's favored couples."

"Jonet, leave us," Alexander ordered as he entered the solar.

Jonet flinched and ran from the chamber, leaving Elspeth alone with an angry-looking Alexander. She stood ready to make her own escape, only to be grabbed by the arm and held in a tight grip until he closed the door.

When he let her go, she crossed the chamber to get as far away from him as she could. Her arm ached, but she refused to allow him to see her discomfort. "Say what you will, and then leave my sight."

"I will not allow your chill, lass. Jonet and I will leave on the tide for Carrick Castle. You will keep to our promise and prepare for our nuptials. If everything is not perfect, I will beat your arse on our wedding night until it turns blue. Then we will consummate our vows. Which, if I am angered, will not be gentle."

"I will not wed you."

"Oh, but you will." He stalked toward her.

"Nae."

"Aye. I have spoken to Archie. The contract stands. We wed on my return in a fortnight."

"But—"

"Aye. Earlier than originally planned. Until then..." With each word, his tone became more threatening. "You will stay away from Macintyre or I will see the man dead."

"Nae. I will speak to Archie. He will put an end to this farce." She brushed past Alexander on her way to the door.

He grabbed her arm and swung her around to face him. His eyes glinted with menace. "You will do as I command."

She chose to ignore the warning. "Nae."

Her head jerked back from the unexpected blow to her face, the momentum slamming her against the stone wall. Her legs gave out and she slid to the floor while rubbing the bump forming on the back of her head.

Her cheek stung where he slapped her. Stunned by the abuse, she stared at him.

"A wife should fear her husband and it is time you learned to fear me." Alexander stood over her, his jaw tight.

Fighting to hold back tears, she glared at him. "I hate you."

"I am sure you think you do at the moment. But you will see, we are well matched and together will produce a powerful heir for the Campbells. Be a good lass, Beth, and I will reward you on our wedding night."

He turned his back on her and left.

Elspeth managed to rise to her feet and as soon as his footsteps faded, she hurried in search of her brother.

"I have discussed this with Alexander," Archibald said from where he stood leaning against the hearth in his private chamber. "He kens naught of your claymore. You must search the castle again. I am quite sure your sword is somewhere within these walls."

Finn didn't trust a word of Alexander's denials. Finn's sword was gone and he believed someone stole it. He needed to find that someone and get the weapon back. Now that he'd fully recovered from his injury, it was time to go after Maclay again. "I still believe Connor Campbell took my claymore."

Archibald shook his head. "I will not allow you to chase after emissaries of the king. 'Twill only bring trouble."

A soft knock caused both men to glance toward the door.

Elspeth entered and Finn rose from his chair. Her cheek bore a large bruise and unshed tears shone in her eyes. His chest tightened.

"What happened?" He started toward her, but she held up her arms as if to ward him off.

"Please leave us. I must speak to my brother in private."

The frigid tone of her voice slid along Finn's spine, chilling him. Something was terribly wrong and he guessed it had something to do with Alexander. Finn clenched his hands into fists. Had the man struck her?

Archibald stepped away from the fireplace. "MacIntyre, our discussion is at an end. Do as my sister requests and leave us."

With a slight bow, Finn left, but anger festered.

Elspeth didn't flinch as Archibald regarded her with a stern frown. "What is it, Beth? What has happened now?"

"I nae longer wish to wed Alexander."

"You sound like Patrick when he refused to marry the one chosen for him. Why cannae you wed Alexander? He is the man father chose for you."

"He has been unfaithful. I caught him with Jonet."

"That is regrettable. But most men are unfaithful."

"Not da." Elspeth touched the sore bruise on her cheek.

Her brother's eyes flared. "Did he strike you?"

Embarrassed, Elspeth stared at the stone floor. "I tripped and fell."

"You should be more careful."

"Aye."

"Father was an exception," Archibald said. "You must wed Alexander and you ken it."

Elspeth raised her gaze. "I will not marry him. You can break the contract and pay the penalty."

"Beth, I cannae." Her brother paced away. "We need this arrangement to stay in the good graces of the king."

She had the urge to stomp her foot, but that wouldn't get her anywhere. "Archie, he struck me. You cannae mean for me to wed a wife beater."

"You said you tripped."

"I lied."

Archibald spun to face her. "You must have done something to provoke him."

"I did not."

His gaze lingered for a moment on the bruise marring her cheek. She couldn't fathom the glimpse of emotion that flashed across his features before he glanced away.

"Your betrothal stands. That is my final word. I refuse to hear more on the matter." Archibald strode to his worktable and sat. "Now, I have work to do. And you have your duty to fulfill."

CHAPTER FOURTEEN

*T*he Campbell galleys approached Carrick Castle from Loch Goil after having sailed *up the watter* from the Firth of Clyde along Loch Long. From the amount of activity about the grounds, it was evident King James and his entourage already resided at Carrick. A surprise, since they'd departed after Alexander from his father's main keep. The king's party must have made good time as they traveled across the more difficult land route from Inveraray Castle to Carrick.

Alexander clutched the gunwale, eager to set foot on land and discover what the old wizard knew of the faerie-kissed sword. He also wanted to find out why Hector had left Castle Lachlan without leaving a Campbell guard on Elspeth. If he didn't like what he learned, he'd see Hector hang.

The galley scraped the bottom and several lads jumped out to pull the boat onto the shingle. Alexander leapt over the side and set off for the castle to greet Elspeth's grandfather, Sir Robert, and to find Hector. Then he'd make his way to the caves to visit the wizard and retrieve the claymore.

Chaos reigned in the great hall. Ghillies ran hither and there. Connor approached Alexander, leaning close to his ear. "The claymore is with Seumas, but you best see the king first.

He requested you attend him as soon as you arrived."

Alexander searched the hall with his gaze. Hector sat drinking with several Campbell warriors at a table on the other side of the chamber. Before Alexander could make his way there, Sir Robert waylaid him. "The king has been eager for your arrival."

"Good eve'n to you, Sir Robert. I will go to the king forthwith."

"Nae need, lad. Your king comes to you." King James voice boomed as he and his female companion joined them.

Alexander bowed low in greeting to his monarch.

"Glad to see you have finally arrived." James gazed past Alexander as if searching for someone. Staring directly at Alexander, he raised a brow. "Where is the lovely Lady Jonet?"

Alexander stiffened. Had rumors already reached the king's ears? Maybe Jonet's contrary change of mind about joining him at Carrick had turned out for the best. James wouldn't be pleased to learn Alexander jeopardized his betrothal to Elspeth for nothing more than a tumble in the sheets with Jonet. For the king to flaunt his mistresses was one thing. For his subjects to do the same was quite another matter. Fortunately, Alexander had convinced Archibald of the many benefits the MacLachlan clan would reap from the union. The betrothal agreement would hold.

"I left Jonet at Rothesay Castle in the care of her brother. She felt squeamish about the hunt."

The king's gaze roved over the buxom form of the stunning, flame-haired woman who stood to his left. "Aye, some women are weak in that way, while others enjoy the excitement of the bloody sport."

The woman's eyes flared, proving she had a stronger will than most.

"Aye, Sire," Alexander automatically responded without much thought.

"You do still intend to wed the MacLachlan lass, aye?"

The king's words grabbed Alexander's attention. "Aye. In

a fortnight. Sooner than originally planned. Will you still attend?"

The king again looked to the lady. She gave him a sultry smile.

"I must travel north," James said. "But I think the journey can wait until after you have wed. I would see the deed done."

"Thank you, my liege." Alexander inclined his head, though he despised the need to do such.

"There is another matter on which we must speak." The king patted his mistress' hand. "Excuse us, my dear?"

His companion's chin jerked up and she tossed her mane of red hair as she whirled and strode off.

James chuckled. "Here is the earl now."

The Earl of Montrose, one of the other nobles who'd come for the hunt, joined them. The conversation took on a heated political bent. Hours passed before Alexander broke away and went in search of Hector. After speaking with his man, he found a flagon of wine to take to his chamber.

He clenched his free hand into a fist. The information he received from Hector infuriated him. Alexander should have known better than to doubt the loyalty of his man. He'd see that Donald MacLachlan and Finn MacIntyre paid for their folly. Maybe he'd also punish Elspeth for her indiscretion. No one made a fool of Alexander Campbell.

Aye, he might enjoy punishing Elspeth. His cock jerked at the thought of her tied to his bed—helpless.

Damn, he wished Jonet joined him to scratch his itch. They could have been discreet, hid their affair until after the nuptials.

Alexander climbed the stairs to his bedchamber, annoyed he'd sleep alone, annoyed he must capitulate to a monarch, annoyed the hour had grown too late for him to travel to the caves. On the morrow, he'd sneak away from the hunt.

Dawn brought clear weather. As those gathered waited for

the king to join the hunting party, Alexander's gray stallion pranced nervously, responding to the anxiety of his rider.

Seated on his white steed, King James approached with proud, straight posture. He wore his long red hair pulled back in a queue with a green velvet tie. His mistress, the infamous Flaming Janet Kennedy, sat her black mare to his left as they cantered to the group of courtiers who awaited them. Alexander smiled. Lady Janet could ride as well as any man he knew.

Along with other riders, Alexander fell in behind the king. Some of the men carried crossbows and arrows, though most held boar-spears. Alexander bore one of the cumbersome seven-foot spears in order to avoid suspicion.

The king waved enthusiastically and horns sounded.

Sir Robert joined James to his right and together they led the hunt party along a track through the forest. After several miles, the group rode into boggy terrain, past stunted trees and clumps of bushes. The hunters guided their horses with care along firm ground, avoiding deep mud mires and shallow pools.

When they spotted the first fresh sign of game, Sir Robert divided the large group into four smaller parties, providing each with a knowledgeable local ghillie as scout. As the riders rode off in different directions, Alexander slipped away. He galloped off alone. Anyone who missed him would assume he hunted with others. Hours would pass before they regrouped for the trek back to the castle. Plenty of time for what he needed to do.

Alexander made his way to a rocky outcrop, where he led his horse through a maze of large boulders. Soon, they were well hidden from anyone who might pass. He tied the reins to a branch of a tree near a large fissure in the stone and jammed the boar-spear into the ground.

After lighting the torch he found waiting for him at the mouth of the cave, he entered and made his way through a narrow tunnel and into a wide cavern. Cold burrowed into his bones. He pulled his *plaide* tight around his chest, eyeing the interior with distaste. Water dripped along the rough stone surface of the walls to fall into pools on the cave's floor, making secure footing difficult. Easing his way across the chamber, he found a thin passage and, turning sideways, edged through to another cavern.

This larger chamber was different from the first. Here the air was warmer and smelled of herbs and tonics. Crevices in the stone ceiling let in some sunlight, which glowed against pointed structures in the stone.

He placed the torch he carried into a holder on the wall and strode farther into the cavern, anticipation tightening his chest.

Seumas stood before a large rough-hewn table covered with bottles of all sorts and sizes. From a vial, the white haired man poured a thick greenish goop onto the claymore lying before him. He made inarticulate sounds and pointed a gnarled wooden wand at the sword. Smoke puffed into the air, causing the old man to sneeze three times. The sound echoed through the cavern.

The wizard glanced up at Alexander's approach. The whites of Seumas' aged eyes shone brightly from his soot covered face. He smiled, displaying perfect pearly teeth. "Ah, Alexander. You have come to fetch your claymore. Have you?"

"Aye."

"Well, you cannae take the thing. I have not yet learned the sword's secrets." Excitement shrilled the old man's voice.

Alexander slammed one fisted hand against the palm of his other. "What say you?"

Seumas took a step back. "Now dinnae be getting yourself all riled. Fae magic…" He motioned toward the sword. "Ach, well, the power contained within this claymore is greater than any I have encountered afore."

Alexander ground his back teeth.

The old man stared intently at him. "I will have more time."

"What? You cannae. I need the sword." Alexander

blustered.

"Dinnae fash yourself, lad. I just need a wee bit more time to unlock the source of the sword's power."

"How long?"

Gazing toward the ceiling, Seumas counted on his fingers. "Two moons."

Alexander paced away. He didn't want to wait to make his move, but he needed the full power of the sword to ensure success. He'd waited years for the fae sword to reappear. He could delay his plans a couple of months if it meant victory.

He spun on his heel and glared at the old man. "Nae longer."

Seumas grinned, rubbing his hands together like a *bairn* about to receive a sweet treat. He reached for a mortar and pestle. From a small container, he poured a pale yellow powder into the mortar.

The strong odor of rotten eggs reached Alexander's nostrils and he covered his nose with his arm. "When I return I expect you to have the answer," he said, his voice muffled by his sleeve.

The wiry wizard continued with his task, paying no heed.

Alexander stayed and watched for a short time, but the stench became too much to endure and he left to return to the fresh air outside the cave.

Two months and victory would be his.

The next day Alexander set out for Castle Lachlan, arriving there in three days' time. During the journey, he rethought his strategy for gaining Elspeth's cooperation. Force might not be the best approach. His famed persuasive skills, the ones that worked especially well on women, would convince Elspeth to attain and reveal the information required.

After he controlled the sword's power, he would take his revenge.

He patted the satchel he carried. Women loved receiving

expensive gifts. Although he purchased the blue, fur-lined cloak for Jonet, he'd give the mantle to Elspeth. As much as it irked him to do so, he'd consider it coin well spent for the possession of her lands, her gift of the sight, and the knowledge she'd acquire of the fae sword. Once he learned the sword's secret, he would set forth to control the MacLachlan lands along with those of the Lamonts. The Campbells would reign supreme.

He'd purchase another cloak for Jonet, one more suited to her coloring. Emerald, perhaps. She was a simple creature. Easy to love. As long as he continued to seek her bed, she'd be happy, believing their liaison brought her closer to the crown.

Alexander liked his women biddable. He'd once thought that of Elspeth. Since her association with the Lady Laurie, she'd changed. Annoyingly so. He'd bring her to heel though, once he learned what he needed to control the claymore. With the additional power of her gift, he'd be unstoppable.

"Hector." He addressed the man at his side. "Guard my lady, but keep to the shadows. Dinnae allow her to ken she is followed." *Let her have a false sense of freedom.*

"What if I catch MacIntyre sniffing at her skirts?"

"Watch, listen, report back to me." He would use a liaison to his advantage.

"As you wish, my lord."

Pleased with himself, Alexander waited for the oarsmen to beach the galley at Castle Lachlan. He looked forward to taming his woman.

CHAPTER FIFTEEN

*T*empest winds raced along Loch Fyne and slammed into the castle's walls. Lightning streaked the sky. Rolling thunder echoed through the hills. Shutters rattled and candle flames flickered.

Elspeth's thoughts were as volatile as the storm.

Torn between Finn and Alexander she didn't know how to proceed.

Aine glanced up from the sheet she mended. "What is it, lass? You are as jittery as—"

Breath ripped from her, Elspeth grabbed her stomach as an unbearable pain sliced through her belly. She slid from the chair to the floor.

Panting, she reached out for help, but a strange mist invaded the solar, wrapping around her, caressing her face, teasing her soul. As pain receded, the room spun and she whirled with it until she landed on unsteady feet.

Nausea passed quickly, but she sensed something horribly wrong.

Propelled by an unknown source, Elspeth crossed the moors, running toward she knew not what. The whinny of horses and screams of men and clank of steel striking steel grew louder with each stride. Stopping atop a ridge, she gaped at the glen below where full battle raged.

She wrapped her arms around herself, horrified by the violence. Frozen in place, she watched the scene play out in painful slow motion.

Silence signaled the end.

Elspeth walked amongst the carnage, the stench of death burrowing into her nose. Her steps sluggish, she searched, until she came to a man lying dead next to his horse. She recognized the trappings. They belonged to her brother.

"Nae!" She fell to her knees beside him and tugged at the man, praying it wasn't as she feared. The prayer went unanswered. Archibald laid before her, battered and beaten, his beloved face bloodied and bruised. His silver-blue eyes stared at her, though life had left his gaze. Then it was Duncan's face staring. Then Jamie's.

Her chest ached. Agony tore her heart.

She rose to her feet, but couldn't tear her gaze away from the mask of death.

Flesh melted away revealing bone. Beetles crawled from gaping eye sockets.

A scream of terror ripped from Elspeth's throat and she ran, blinded by the image of the grotesque sight. Stumbling, she fell forward onto the bloodstained grass and retched.

Her dearest brother and Duncan and Jamie—dead.

What had caused such tragedy?

The trill of a bird in a nearby tree seemed foreign in this meadow of death. Elspeth sat up and wiped her mouth on her sleeve. Fine loose hair teased by the breeze tickled the skin of her face.

"Come, lass, 'tis time for us to wed." Alexander sat a horse she hadn't heard approach. A large bird perched upon his shoulder, its feathers glistening in the unnatural light the same blue-black as Alexander's straight hair. Her betrothed's smile evoked pure evil.

This wasn't happening. None of this could be true. Yet the omen was clear.

She lunged to her feet, twisted away, darted across the

moor, her wild screams lost on the wind. Finn's watery image floated before her and she threw her arms out, wanting to draw him to her.

"Come to me, my warrior...save me...come to me," she cried.

When Elspeth opened her eyes, Aine knelt beside her, holding her, and rubbing her back. "Another vision?" Aine asked.

Elspeth nodded, but couldn't speak. Chills wracked her body.

"There, there, this was a bad one. 'Twill pass." Aine continued to soothe her.

With the elder woman's help, Elspeth managed to rise and slowly stumble to her bedchamber. For hours, she remained abed, eyes wide open, trembling, reliving the horrific vision.

Could Finn save them?

Until last eve, Elspeth believed she misjudged Alexander. Believed they had a chance for a happy union. He'd been so kind since his return from Carrick. Considerate. He begged for her forgiveness.

Her vision proved he couldn't be trusted.

Now to have him in her bedchamber, trying to romance her, made her ill. Elspeth pulled away from Alexander's embrace, unable to look at him.

"What is bothering you, lass?"

She moved a trembling hand to stroke the moonstone brooch pinned at her shoulder. "I had a vision this past eve. You were fighting against my brother Archie, and my clan. You wanted MacLachlan lands for your own."

Alexander stiffened. "You have acted strangely ever since you spent time with that witch your brother Patrick wed."

"Lady Laurie's not a witch. And you ken it well." Elspeth planted her fists on her hips.

"What I ken is your visions are nonsense."

"My visions are never wrong. There is always a meaning

within."

"Rubbish." Alexander stepped closer. "Hector told me you are having an affair with MacIntyre. I will not stand for such behavior."

"You are a fool to believe the liar." Elspeth held her ground, though the temptation to shrink away from his anger was strong.

"I will not tolerate your dalliance with Finn MacIntyre." Alexander jerked her into his arms.

She fought him, trying to break free. Unfortunately, he was stronger. When she looked into his eyes, fear lodged in her throat. His rage had flamed into lust. His arousal pressed against her belly.

"Stop." She struggled, pressing her hands against his chest and pushing, desperate to escape.

He cupped his hand to the back of her head and captured her mouth with his. *Wet and disgusting.* Her efforts to shove him away were futile. He forced his tongue into her mouth. *Revolting.* She could hardly breathe.

"What? You dinnae wish to kiss me like you did MacIntyre?" Moving her backwards, Alexander maneuvered her toward the bed until her thighs pressed against the frame. "I will teach you the way I like it."

Panic shot through her. Did he plan to rape her? He wouldn't dare.

Her attempts at resistance wore her down, weakening her. He seized her lips again, forcing her to accept him. With his mouth covering hers, she couldn't scream. He pressed her down onto the mattress his weight falling on top of her, holding her prisoner. While continuing his assault on her mouth, he raked her body with his hands, stopping at her breasts he squeezed her nipples painfully, causing her to buck against him.

Her resistance seemed to inflame him more. He replaced his mouth with a hand to keep her from calling out. She screamed in her mind.

Moments seemed like hours.

With his free hand, he tore at her clothing, bunching her gown around her waist. He knelt between her legs. His nails dug into the skin of her thighs as he forced them apart. She shuddered as his groping fingers crept closer to her female center.

Her efforts to escape became frantic. He released her mouth to use both hands to subdue her. She screamed with all she had in her. He slapped her hard. In shock, she quieted.

The door flew open and thunked against the wall. Archibald stood in the doorway, his sword drawn.

"What goes on here?" he bellowed.

Alexander pushed Elspeth behind him on the bed, but retained her arm in a painful grip. "Call me foul. MacIntyre dies," he whispered so only she heard.

Archibald's intense stare took in the scene. "Couldn't you wait until your wedding night? The sheets must be bloodied after the vows are said."

Alexander rolled away from Elspeth, stood and straightened his *leine*. She skittered back on the bed, pulling a cover over her torn gown.

"I beg your pardon, Archie. I am so in love with Elspeth, it was hard to wait. When she invited me to her room, I couldn't resist." He had the nerve to smile at her. "Being a virgin, she panicked and cried out. Are you better now, dearling?"

"Fine." She choked on the word. What a liar. She bit her swollen lip and glanced at her brother. She could tell by the softening of his expression that he believed the falsehood. He'd never consider she hadn't invited Alexander to her bed.

Unfortunately, Hector would corroborate the tale. Her idiot brother was blind to Alexander's shortcomings.

Frightening thoughts raced through Elspeth's mind. She needed to be careful considering Alexander's threat. She wouldn't risk Finn. She'd have to go along with the scoundrel. "I am sorry, Archie, I dinnae ken what came over me."

Archibald eyed her as if uncertain. Then a stoic expression

masked his features. "Come, Alexander. I will keep you busy until the ceremony. You have only two days to wait."

Both men left the chamber without any more notice of Elspeth. Once they were gone and the door closed, she flew off the bed. She rinsed her mouth with water from the ewer and gagged into the basin.

Her hands fisted as she paced across the chamber. There had to be a way out of this marriage. Even if she had to run away.

Dawn often shed light on things uncertain. Where could she go? How would she live? She couldn't survive on her own. Elspeth decided to try Archibald one more time. She really didn't want to run off unprotected.

She strode to his private chamber to petition him to her cause. "Archie, you cannae make me wed him."

"Beth, how many times must we go over this?"

"I had a vision. He only wants your land. He cares nothing for me or our clan."

Archibald paced to the hearth, and turned, his impassive stare boring into her. He waved his hand, swatting her words away as he would a fly. "If he wanted to harm me, he's had plenty of opportunity in the past when we traveled together for the king."

"'Twould have been too risky. Besides, you were not clan chief then. And without a marriage to me, he has nae claim to our estates. But as my husband—"

"Enough!"

"Are you not afeared for our wee brothers? What of Suibne and Iain the Younger? If an *accident* befalls you and Alexander takes claim of MacLachlan lands before you have an heir what will remain for our brothers?"

Archibald slammed his palm on the wood mantel. "I dinnae want to hear any more of these false accusations against Alexander."

"But my vision..."

"Mayhap you have lost your gift as your mother did when she wed Da."

"But, Archie—"

"Nae, lass. I have heard enough. You will wed Alexander the day after the morrow even if I must tie and gag you."

Elspeth ran for the door. Salty tears burned her eyes. Why didn't her brother understand?

"If you did not wish to wed him, why did you invite him to your bed?"

Archibald's words stopped her. She twisted around and glared at him "He was not invited." She escaped Archibald's private chamber and raced along the passageway. What was she to do? How could she stop the wedding?

The fire in the hearth sputtered and coughed. Archibald slammed his fist on the worn surface of the worktable. His day had been wretched, starting with Elspeth's visit at dawn. He didn't like the way Alexander treated her. But what was he to do about it? Men held complete control over their wives, as it should be. Alexander and Elspeth were as good as wed. The agreement that would bind them had been signed nearly a score and one summers ago. Archibald refused to go against his father's wishes and break the contract.

Alexander had been Archibald's friend for as long as he could remember. In all that time, Alexander had never shown the slightest sign of violence against women. More so, he usually persuaded them to his desires with little more than a smile and sweet words.

So what was the problem between Alexander and Elspeth? Was she so headstrong she brought out the worst in Alexander?

The man swore nothing wayward occurred between them. However, Elspeth's eyes told otherwise. She feared his friend.

With a sigh, Archibald leaned his elbows on the table and put his head in his hands, burying his fingers in his hair. He never wanted this responsibility. His father hadn't trained him to lead the clan. Donald was meant to be chief, not he. When Donald died, Patrick had easily stepped forward.

Archibald never anticipated the fate of the clan would rest on his unworthy shoulders. He'd expected to be nothing more than his brother's emissary to the king. Patrick's right hand.

Archibald raised his head to glare at the flames in the hearth. His anger with his brother was unwarranted. Yet he found it difficult to suppress his rage.

Of course, if Patrick hadn't left with Lady Laurie for the Continent, Archibald would never have been able to claim Isobell.

His lips wavered into a thin smile. Soon she would be his.

Suddenly a chill breeze blew across his skin, causing gooseflesh. Pieces of parchment slid from the table, falling in disarray on the floor. Munn spun into the chamber, landing with a thud, his arse on the stone floor.

Archibald sighed heavily. He didn't want to deal with the brownie, especially not on this eve.

"What now?" Archibald demanded.

Munn picked himself up and brushed the dust from his backside. He pointed a gnarled finger at Archibald. "Stop the wedding."

CHAPTER SIXTEEN

A chill breeze blew across Loch Fyne. The dreary morning sky matched Finn's mood. He paced a short distance away from Elspeth, his feet scraping the pebbles of the beach. The wedding was set for tomorrow night. He whirled around to face her. "Are you really going to marry the jerk?"

"Jerk?"

"Alexander."

"I must." Elspeth refused to look at Finn directly. Her hands—she tried to hide them—trembled.

"Why won't you tell me what happened last night?"

Elspeth's sad gaze flicked to him briefly before she lowered her head. "Nothing happened you need to ken."

Something unpleasant occurred to put dark shadows in her eyes. Of that, he was certain. "Why won't you talk to me?"

Elspeth twisted to the side and glanced at him from beneath her lashes. "Is that not what I have been doing?"

"No, you haven't. You've been skirting whatever upset you." Finn's hands curled into fists at his sides. Why wouldn't she confide in him?

Her marriage to Alexander. Finn didn't have the right to ask her not to go through with the wedding. He had nothing to offer as an alternative. He stalked to within a foot of her. Their gazes locked in unspoken communication. A mixture of emotions flashed between them. Mostly, *if only.*

"How can you do this thing?" he asked.

"Duty demands it."

He touched his fingers to her smooth cheek, a gentle caress. "It's wrong for you to marry a man such as him. You deserve so much more."

Elspeth backed out of reach. Her silver eyes turned molten. "Who should I wed then, Finn MacIntyre? You have not offered."

The ache in Finn's chest compounded. "I can't."

He leaned toward her, his hands hovering inches from her hips for a minute. Two. Three. Her essence lured him like a moth to the back-porch light. He grabbed her by the waist and pulled her against him, wrapping his arms around her in a needy embrace.

A gasp of surprise escaped her lips seconds before he kissed her.

He didn't hold back. His lips and tongue expressed all his frustration and longing. Need so deep, a knife-sharp pain cut through him.

The world and all its occupants faded away.

Footsteps scuffed against pebbles.

They both spun toward the sound. Archibald approached, his features twisted in an angry mask.

Elspeth stepped away. "Archie?"

Finn dropped his arms to his sides, his heart a jackhammer against the inside of his chest.

Archibald glared at them. "Beth, return to the castle." His controlled tone too menacing.

Elspeth flicked a sorrow-filled glance at Finn before she picked up the hem of her gown and dashed across the beach toward the castle.

Ready for a fight, Finn braced his legs.

"I dinnae wish to battle with you over this." Archibald's

intense silver gaze bore into Finn. "It would be best if you leave Castle Lachlan for a wee bit. Go with my uncle and his men to patrol the northern border for Maclay. Dinnae return until after Elspeth is wed."

An itch prickled across the back of Finn's neck. He shot his gaze toward the boulders bordering the beach, to the trees beyond. A shadow moved then disappeared.

Shit! Finn tensed, darting his gaze from tree to tree. Plenty of shadows and good cover.

"Are you listening to me?" Archibald's voice oozed frustration.

"I think someone spies on us. Over there, among those trees." Finn tilted his head in the direction he'd spotted movement.

Archibald cupped a hand over his eyes. "I see naught."

"Must have been mistaken." Finn didn't believe that for a minute. Someone had hidden in the trees and scurried off. Just how long they'd been there was the question. Did they spy on Elspeth, her brother or him? Or a combination of the three?

To Finn's surprise, Archibald's lips curled into a half smile and he clapped him on the back. "I believe you are a good man, Finn MacIntyre. I trust you will do the right thing and stay away until after the wedding."

Finn clamped down hard on his molars, controlling his desire to snarl at the injustice of the situation. Archibald raised a brow.

Never in his life had Finn felt this helpless, unable to change things to his advantage. He'd never before been in the midst of a losing proposition he knew he couldn't turn around to his benefit. The problem being: he was damned no matter what he did.

"I will go," he ground out.

So that would be that. Elspeth would wed Alexander, and Finn would get on with his purpose for being in the sixteenth century. He'd search for Maclay in the northern country. And when the bastard was dead, Finn would return to his own time. *Hopefully.*

Elspeth would live her life as if he'd never existed. He didn't care much for that part of the equation.

History would remain unaltered. Again, hopefully.

In frustrated silence, Finn walked with Archibald toward the castle to find Donald and his men before they left on patrol.

Unable to find Caitrina in any of the usual places, or unusual places, Munn gave up and materialized within the coppice of trees at the edge of the castle beach.

Hidden behind bushes and trees, he bounced from one foot to the other in exuberance. Like a voyeur, he watched the couple embrace and kiss. He sighed with pleasure, anticipating his meeting with Caitrina when he finally found her. She'd be impressed with his success.

Then Archibald interrupted the scene. Munn had never been so angry with his chief.

Poor Elspeth hurried off to the castle alone.

Munn warned the MacLachlan over and over again. She mustn't wed a Campbell. Ruin to the clan would be the result of such an erroneous match.

He frowned, pacing to a nearby boulder, then to a tree stump, to the boulder, and back to the stump. Again and again, to and fro, he wore a deep furrow into the earth.

With all his concentration, he sounded out an incantation to summon Caitrina.

When she didn't appear, Munn stood very still. What was he to do to stop this travesty? He couldn't allow Elspeth to wed Alexander. Just as he was about to vacate the area, he sensed he wasn't alone. Thinking Caitrina finally joined him, he spun to face her. Only it wasn't the *sithiche*. Hector slipped from behind cover and crept from shadow to shadow, following Elspeth to the castle.

What was the Campbell warrior about? Could only mean trouble for the sweet lass.

Archibald and Finn strode off unaware Hector trailed Elspeth.

Munn would take matters into his own hands. He pulled air to himself, creating a small whirlwind. Suspended within the vortex, invisible to the human eye, he traveled into the castle.

The savory aroma of roasting meats greeted Archibald upon entering the kitchen. Aine and Angus worked together, along with Cookie and her staff. The older couple inclined their heads in deference to his station and continued with their tasks.

"Good day, Chief." Cookie dipped into a curtsy with the other lasses, her girth jiggling as she rose. "All is in order for Elspeth's feast."

"Well done." He forced a smile to his lips. Elspeth usually handled such domestic matters, but she wasn't of a mind to care about a meal of which she didn't wish to partake.

Archibald came to visit the kitchen in hopes of ensuring the pre-wedding celebration set for this evening would serve to bring notoriety to the MacLachlans. Everything must be perfect for the king and his Campbell guests.

They appeared all through the day. First in small groups, and then the large entourage who traveled with the king arrived. Since the wedding would take place sooner than originally planned, there were fewer attending than invited. The important guests were above in their chambers, resting for the festivities.

Archibald nodded at his staff, pleased with the efficiency of his kitchen and those who worked within. A lad piled loaves of bread into a basket. Archibald was tempted to pilfer a loaf and enjoy a quiet repast in his private chamber, but he had much to do before this evening.

"Aine, will you see to Elspeth?" he asked. "And try to convince her to wear her wedding gown."

"Aye, sure." Aine gave him a queer look, so he felt obliged

to explain.

"Alexander requested such. He claims to have a surprise for her. Probably a piece of jewelry or some such trinket to match the gown."

Aine set off to prepare Elspeth for the pre-wedding feast.

Without anyone to turn to for support, Elspeth accepted her fate.

She'd do what duty demanded.

However, she couldn't eat a morsel of the food from the tray the serving lass was kind enough to fetch from the kitchen. Elspeth thought eating would calm the storm raging in her belly. She was wrong. Even the taste of a crumb of bread made her want to gag. How would she make it through the evening banquet?

She wandered to the window and leaned on the sill. The bay and the moors beyond glowed crimson in the early evening light. Sorrow gripped her heart. Soon this view would no longer be what she'd see when she woke.

Alexander told her that after the wedding and the bedding—the latter with a smug gleam in his eyes—they'd travel to Skipness to take up residence.

At one time, she'd been eager for such. Believed it would be an adventure. Now the thought of leaving Castle Lachlan made her want to weep. She wouldn't though. She'd deal with what was to come with her head held high, with dignity, as her mother and father would have expected.

Elspeth promised herself she wouldn't think of Finn, but she'd already broken the vow several times since he departed without saying good-bye. Watching from the window as he rode away across the moor nearly tore her heart from her chest.

"Lass, it's time to dress." Aine held out the silver wedding gown.

Wishing fate was kinder; Elspeth smoothed her hand over the precious silk fabric. The exquisite, deep blue dragon embroidery on the sleeves had lost its luster for her. She'd worked the fanciful design during the years Alexander traveled for the king. Her stitches were perfect. As she crafted the mythical creature, she'd yearned for this day to arrive. Now she wished it never came.

The guests would eat and drink, toasting the *lucky* couple, and on the morrow, she'd be forced before the priest to say vows to Alexander. She'd become the chattel of a tyrant.

Aine interrupted her thoughts, placing the gown over her head.

"Why the wedding dress?"

"His lordship requested it."

"Of course." How like Alexander, wanting to punish her the evening before the wedding took place. He'd make her wear the symbolic dress tonight and then again for the wedding.

After Elspeth donned the dress, Aine took a final stroke of a brush to her hair.

"You are beautiful, lass." A tear escaped and ran along Aine's wrinkled cheek.

Elspeth's eyes remained dry. She stiffened her back, willing herself to smile. She would do what she must. Marry Alexander. Fulfill her duty to her family and clan. No one must ever know she loved another. Or that she hated the man she wed.

Aine left and Elspeth appreciated a moment to herself. She uttered a quick prayer for strength. With one final glance from her window as sunlight faded away, she realized tomorrow would be the last time she'd enjoy the morning mist on the bay. So sad.

She stepped from her chamber to find Alexander waiting outside her door beside a stranger dressed in the robes of a priest. Apprehension swelled within her chest. Her gaze locked with Alexander's for a moment then he fixed his eyes on her bosom. Unfortunately, the low cut gown pushed her breasts up and made them most obvious. Her cheeks heated and she lowered her gaze to the floor.

"Dearling, you are comely in that gown." Alexander's voice was all sweetness. "May I present my father's cousin, Father Edward.

The priest stepped closer. "I am pleased to perform the wedding ceremony this eve."

Elspeth's gaze jerked to Alexander. "Nae. We are to wed on the morrow."

"We were. That is true. But since Father Edward traveled with my father's entourage, there is no need to wait for your priest to arrive in the morning." He gave her a superior smile. "I have just come from Archibald and he agreed. Besides, the king wishes to ride north at first light."

This wasn't fair. She was to have one more night of solitude.

Alexander's smile took on a lustful gleam. "I ken how eager you are to consummate our vows, dearling."

A sinking feeling came over Elspeth, as if her stomach had dropped to the floor. She swayed and the priest took hold of her arm. "My child, I have come to hear your confession. I understand you tried to lure Alexander to your bed and have been consorting with one of your brother's warriors. There is evil in you that must be forced out." His grip tightened. "You must be purified."

Elspeth tried to pull away, but the priest held her tight and backed her through the open door of her bedchamber. "Sit," he said, pointing to one of the chairs near the hearth.

Alexander entered the chamber and closed the door as she sat. He leaned against the door with his arms crossed, pinning her with his stare. She shifted uneasily in her seat. "Father, I dinnae believe 'tis customary to have a witness to a confession."

The priest rubbed his chin several times, frowning. "That is usually true. However, your betrothed accuses you of coupling with another."

Elspeth's jaw fell. "What?"

"Have you fornicated with a warrior named Finn MacIntyre?" the priest demanded, his lips twisted in disapproval.

"How dare you?" Elspeth started to rise.

The priest placed his hand on her shoulder, gently pushing her back into the chair. "Answer me, before God."

"Nae. I have not."

"We shall see." He stroked his chin again. "Now, you will tell me all you ken about the claymore this warrior brought with him. We believe the man to be a heretic."

Elspeth couldn't fathom the accusation. "How could you think such a thing?"

"That is not for your small female mind to understand. Tell us what you ken and I will grant you absolution."

"I ken nothing more than what I have already told Alexander." She raised her gaze to glare at her betrothed.

"Then we will need to prove your innocence."

"What are you talking about?" Panic nearly choked Elspeth.

Alexander opened the door and a gnarled old woman Elspeth had never seen before entered.

"Who is this?" she asked.

Alexander stepped forward. "She is the Campbell healer. She will prove whether you are chaste or not. I refuse to raise another man's bastard."

"Nae. You cannae do this. I have done nothing wrong." Elspeth's heart tapped a staccato beat within her chest.

"You will submit to the examination, my child. However, I understand your concern. Alexander will leave."

Alexander looked as if he'd object, but after hesitating only a moment, he left the chamber.

"Father, I dinnae wish to wed Alexander."

"Because you have sinned against him?"

"I have not."

"Unless your brother dissolves the contract, you must wed Alexander."

"In the Highlands a maiden cannae be forced." Elspeth held her head high, her stare daring the priest to disagree.

"That is true." The priest's eyes narrowed. "Do you wish

for your brother and your clan to be dishonored before the king?"

"Nae. Of course not."

"Then you must wed Alexander." He waved the old woman forward.

Elspeth succumbed. What else was she to do?

The woman stripped her of her gown and chemise in front of the priest, who watched every movement. Elspeth used her hands and arms to cover her breasts and private patch. Edward Campbell might be a priest, but he was also a man and though he seemed indifferent, he watched with a man's eyes. The old woman examined Elspeth, touching her intimately. Elspeth wanted to scream at the injustice. She'd done nothing wrong.

"Virgin," the woman declared.

"Kneel, child," the priest instructed.

When Elspeth did as ordered, Father Edward approached with a vial. "Uncover yourself. I am the instrument of God."

She dropped her hands to her sides, fighting tears burning her eyes.

He poured the holy water between her breasts and used his thumb to draw the sign of the cross at the base of her neck, mumbling something in Latin. Then he turned his back to her. "You may dress."

Vile man. Elspeth had never been so horrified in her life.

This was no way for a priest to act. He should offer protection, not follow the dictates of a man like Alexander.

Elspeth wished she had laid with Finn, maybe then Alexander wouldn't want her.

With gentle hands the old woman helped Elspeth don her chemise and gown once more. Then the priest ushered Alexander back into the chamber and placed her left hand on her betrothed's right sleeve

"I hate you." She put as much venom in her voice as she could muster.

"At least I now ken only my seed will bring fruit." His smile broadened. "Remember what I told you about our wedding night. I would not anger me if I were you."

Elspeth gasped. "How *dare* you? After what you just put me through."

"Now that you will be mine, I can do with you as I please. Shall we join the others for the celebration, dearling?"

Munn appeared in the almost empty council chamber without making a sound. The same size as the great hall below, but more ornate, the significant room displayed the evidence of the MacLachlan clan's wealth and standing. He puffed out his chest, proud of his clan. Only important councils and festive gatherings occurred in this chamber. Elspeth's wedding banquet was to take place there this very eve.

Not if Munn could stop it.

Peeking from behind his favorite tapestry, depicting scenes of unicorns and faeries, Munn eyed the serving lass who worked to set the tables for the banquet, willing her to leave.

In the ensuing silence, he waited until her steps faded and she descended the wheel stair. He liked this space better than any in the castle. Unlike the great hall below, the council chamber's flooring was laid with sturdy oak, not the cold gray stone found in the rest of the castle. A magnificent hooded fireplace with a pair of columns to either side warmed the room. The jeweled goblets and other fine dinner pieces set out on the tables normally filled the aumbry, the elaborately carved cupboard tucked into one of the walls.

He walked to the center of the chamber and spun. The first breeze he created blew out the candles in the tall metal stands. As he whirled, the swirling air strengthened, knocking the candleholders over and tossing goblets around on tables. The whirlwind grew larger and larger, blowing items off surfaces and toppling benches. Fine pottery and serving platters crashed to the floor, breaking into pieces. Wine flagons spilled, staining the oak flooring blood red.

When the wind settled, nothing remained standing. Overturned tables, benches and chairs littered the room along with all the trappings for the wedding banquet. Even the skillfully crafted tapestries had ripped from the walls.

Munn stood amidst the clutter, rubbing his hands together in glee, pleased with the results of his rage.

"What goes on here?" Archibald bellowed when he and his guests entered the chaos.

CHAPTER SEVENTEEN

Without ambient light from modern urban areas, there were more stars in the night sky than Finn ever remembered seeing. He shifted slightly on the fallen log where he sat. Donald and his men set camp in a clearing within the forest through which they traveled most of the afternoon. Unaccustomed to so much time in the saddle, Finn's butt hurt like hell. He rubbed his chest. He ached there as well since he'd ridden away from Castle Lachlan. He never should have agreed to leave.

Sitting around the fire with Donald and his lads, Finn truly felt the outsider. At the castle, he'd practically forgotten he was from another time and place. Duncan and Jamie, and especially Elspeth made him feel welcome. Even Archibald accepted him into the fold.

Tonight, Donald's gaze was speculative. His lads seemed wary of Finn. The lads were much younger. Finn was closer to Donald's age. Probably due to modern nutrition, Finn was as fit and healthy as the young warriors were, though their muscles were more defined. They'd probably wielded swords since childhood.

Donald scratched his chin then sauntered across the clearing and sat next to Finn on the log. "Well, lad." He placed his hands on his knees, his eyebrows raised. "Are you letting Campbell have the lass, then? I thought you cared for my niece."

Finn didn't know what to say, at a loss as to what to do. He possessed nothing here in this time. Nothing to offer her. The thought occurred to him to take her forward to her parents. But he wasn't even one hundred percent sure he'd be successful with the time gate himself. According to Laurie, the gate was fickle, and when it did work, it was only on a full moon and after you met your destiny.

He stared directly at Donald; sure the man could see the pain in his heart reflected in his eyes.

"Lad, you would be a better husband to Elspeth." Donald stood, brushed pieces of chipped bark from his backside and glanced away, hesitating. He turned back and remorse marked his gaze. "I wish you to ken I never meant any harm to befall Lady Laurie when I sent her away from Castle Lachlan. I merely wanted the feud with the Lamonts to end. The only way I thought for that to happen was for Patrick to wed Isobell Lamont. Now I ken fate made other plans. Archibald will marry Isobell and all will be well. When you next see Lady Laurie, tell her I am verra sorry."

Finn gave a stiff nod, and Donald strode off into the trees.

Staring into the flames of the campfire, Finn struggled with his feelings for what seemed like hours. In reality, no more than a half hour passed. He couldn't let Elspeth marry Alexander. It was wrong. If Finn left soon, he would make it back to Castle Lachlan by morning and stop the wedding. Decision made, he went in search of Donald.

Elspeth followed the priest down the steps of the narrow wheel stair, cautious of her gown. Alexander's presence at her back made her stomach clench. Her legs wobbled as though she were meeting her executioner. Before they made the landing, the chaotic sound of raised voices reached them.

In the hall, they found Archibald waving a parchment

amidst the shocking destruction of the chamber, arguing with Alexander's red-faced father. The king stood a short distance away, watching with a stoic expression.

Alexander pushed Elspeth aside and strode toward the men.

"Cursed hell! What transpires here?" His angry voice joined the cacophony.

She wanted to move closer to hear what they said, but Hector had joined Father Edward and the two men blocked her way. From the stream of shouts, she could make out only the loudest words.

Terminate. Land. Default. Grant. Insult. Contract. Penalty.

The Campbell men in the room gathered behind their chief, stepping over broken pieces of crockery, and the MacLachlan men stood behind Archibald. The king's guards surrounded James.

Shouting escalated.

Elspeth feared a fight would soon break out. She stood on tiptoe, weaving from side to side, trying to see past her watchdogs. More harsh words exchanged. Then the group broke apart, making way for Alexander, his father, King James and Archibald, who left the chamber together. Some pushing and shoving ensued between the remaining clansmen, but the king's guards managed to settle the men down.

"Let me through." Elspeth shoved at the priest's back.

"Nae, lass." He grasped her arm and sat her in a chair Hector righted. "We will remain here until summoned."

Elspeth ground her teeth, annoyed she didn't possess the strength to knock him aside so she could follow the men and learn what caused such an uproar.

Worrying her bottom lip, she waited.

The sound of the heavy oak door slamming shut grated along Archibald's already-coiled muscles. He'd need to be careful not to make a disaster of this out of control affair.

"I dinnae want this discussion to come to blows." King James locked gazes with each man in turn. "Archibald, I will have wine." The king sat in one of the two chairs near the hearth as if there were naught wrong.

Archibald poured the ruby-red claret into a goblet from the flagon he kept on the side table. He wasn't fooled by the king's ease. No matter the evidence, James would manipulate the outcome to serve his desires.

The skin on the back of Archibald's neck prickled. Alexander leaned against the mantle, a smug expression on his face. Archibald could hardly believe the man sneering at him was his long-time friend. His excesses over the last couple of years had carved a change in the man.

Archibald knew now to watch his back.

The Campbell, Alexander's father, stood across the chamber, eyeing the door as if an attacker would soon burst through. An insult to his host.

Before presenting the wine to James, Archibald inhaled several calming breaths.

The king accepted the offered goblet, but took his time tasting the claret. The palpable tension in the chamber escalated with each sip.

Standing with his hands grasped tightly behind his back, Archibald waited.

"State your case," James finally demanded.

Archibald bowed his head with due respect before raising his eyes to meet James's gaze.

"I, Archibald MacLachlan of Strathlachlan, request the crown's permission to terminate the betrothal agreement granted in the Year of Our Lord 1490 between the late Chief Iain MacLachlan of Strathlachlan and the late Chief Colin Campbell, second Earl of Argyll, stipulating the terms of marriage between Elspeth MacLachlan and Alexander Campbell, and do hereby agree to any and all penalties brought forth by the crown. I claim—"

"You cannae break the contract signed by my grandfather." Alexander's interruption was expected, but

Archibald stiffened his already tight muscles just the same. "'Tis my right to—"

James shot Alexander a pointed look, stopping further comment. "The crown wishes to understand why you petition to end said contract, MacLachlan."

Archibald forced down his growing anger. "My sister, Lady Elspeth, nae longer desires to wed Alexander Campbell."

The king chuckled. "What reasons have you, other than the fickle mind of the lass in question? Men are much more capable of making such decisions. He glanced at the other two men for agreement. Both nodded. James continued, "You wish me to grant permission for you to wed the Lamont lass, correct?"

Wary of the king's meaning Archibald swallowed hard before answering. "Aye."

"Then allow the betrothal agreement between your sweet sister and our gallant Alexander to stand."

"In all good conscience, I cannae." Archibald braced himself for James's explosion.

Instead, the king looked to Alexander. "What do you have to say on this matter?"

"The contract was written more than two score years ago. My grandfather bargained for the match in good faith. The agreement should hold."

The king's intense gaze returned to Archibald. "Unless you have another argument—"

"I do. It has come to my attention Alexander offended my sister and my clan by treating Elspeth despicably. He struck her, forced his way into her bedchamber, and attempted rapine upon her person."

"For all the saints. She is to be my wife," Alexander burst out, his voice rising with each word.

Archibald stepped forward. "There is also the land grant to consider. I dispute—"

The king raised his hand for silence. "Enough. Summon Lady Elspeth."

An hour had passed and Elspeth twirled her fingers in her lap, her jaw clenched. She sat before the hearth with Father Edward while Hector stood guard behind them, keeping everyone away from her.

The other Campbells had left the council chamber and several MacLachlan men worked to clear the mess.

The men must have brawled before she and Alexander and the priest arrived in the hall, though none wore bruises to indicate an altercation.

Elspeth glared at Father Edward, motioning to the workers. "Why cannae I help?"

He patted her arm as if she were an ignorant *bairn*. "My dear, we wouldn't want you to dirty your gown before the wedding ceremony."

She glanced across the chamber. There certainly wouldn't be a feast. At least not this eve.

A lump moved beneath one of the fallen tapestries and Elspeth followed the movement with her gaze. Munn's glamour slipped enough for her to see him crawl from under the heavy cloth and scoot through the open doorway. No one else seemed to notice the wee man's escape.

Now she understood why the men wore no bruises. Munn caused the destruction.

At least she had one friend. Aine winked from across the chamber. Two friends. The tight muscles in Elspeth's shoulders eased for the first time since she watched Finn ride away.

She refused to think about his abandonment. She couldn't force him to return her love.

Finally, one of the king's guards arrived with word King James summoned her to Archibald's private chamber. Brushing past the priest and Hector, Elspeth made haste to attend the king. The royal guard followed.

At her soft knock on the study's oak door, James bid her enter. The king sat in one of the chairs before the hearth facing into the room. The other men stood in various places, separated by as much distance as possible in the small chamber. The men's aggression buzzed in the air.

James motioned to the seat beside him.

Elspeth glanced at her brother, who gave her a slight reassuring nod. Her stomach knotted again, and she slipped into the offered chair.

"Lady Elspeth, this was to be a special eve for you. Howbeit, there seems to be a serious misunderstanding between these men." The king waved his arm as if to dismiss their concerns. "Do you wish to marry Alexander?"

Elspeth flicked another glance at her brother. His lips curved slightly and his eyes encouraged her. Much relieved, she gave her attention to the king. "Nae, Sire. I dinnae."

"You men cannae force her. Archibald will pay the penalty for breaking the contract." James stood. "Now, I want to eat."

Elspeth swallowed. Feeling dizzy, she clamped down on the giggle bubbling in her throat. She didn't have to marry the *jerk*.

She liked the word Finn taught her. Before she could think more about the man she loved, Alexander stepped forward, his face a mask of rage. "But the lands I was promised. You told me if I agreed to that ancient contract, married Elspeth and gained her lands, you would—"

James cut him a sharp look. Crimson flushed Alexander's neck and face.

"The contract is terminated." The king's gaze slid to Archibald. "Did you say the banquet victuals will be served in the great hall?"

Archibald smiled. "Aye, Sire."

"May I escort you to the evening meal, Lady Elspeth?" James assisted her from her seat and placed her hand on his arm. "My Janet is likely clamoring to hear our tale."

Elspeth graced the king with her best smile. 'Twas difficult not to grab hold of his arms and spin around the chamber. She was free!

"This is not over, Archibald. We were friends once. Nae longer. I will have my revenge." Alexander stormed from the chamber.

The Campbell gave Archibald a thoughtful look. "The MacLachlans and Campbells have been allies for centuries. You have damaged that alliance this day. Alexander will seek vengeance."

"So be it." Archibald stood tall.

"Foolish lads," Alexander's father admonished before departing the chamber.

"Such unsavory business. Feuds so easily begun." The king shrugged as he guided Elspeth through the threshold.

Caitrina appeared in the largest of the caverns in the maze of caves and tunnels northwest of Castle Carrick. Her nose twitched. The stench of sulfur lingered in the air, though Seumus wasn't present. The wizard had deserted his lair.

She'd missed the opportunity to battle with the squirrelly old man.

Scanning the chamber, she found the table in the center contained the remnants of his attempts to unlock the power of Finn's claymore. *Her claymore.*

Drip. Drip. Drip. The echo from the constant drip of water scraped over Caitrina's nerves. She picked up the jar closest to her and hurled it. Glass shattered against rough stone, splintering, flying in every direction. Thick orange goo oozed along the walls.

That felt good. She stretched her back and picked up a small crock, and threw it across the chamber. Every container on the table met the same fate. When she finished, Caitrina glared at the debris, causing sparks to erupt. As she dissolved into a fine mist, consuming flames spread across the chamber, devouring everything in their path.

Traveling through the void of space, Caitrina sent out her senses to probe for the whereabouts of the wizard and the claymore.

CHAPTER EIGHTEEN

*H*ooves scuffed the ground while Finn and Donald observed Castle Lachlan from a point atop the ridge. Early morning sun endeavored to burn off the mist, casting the stone structure in a white-gold haze. Finn leaned forward in the saddle and shielded his eyes with a cupped hand.

Donald pointed to the cloud of dust and riders heading northeast along the edge of Loch Fyne. At the head of the party, a gold flag emblazoned with the king's red lion rampant flapped in the breeze.

"Lad, appears you are too late. That is the king's entourage leaving."

Finn's lungs froze and a hollow sensation replaced the organ previously beating in his chest. God, he really was a fool.

An hour later, he entered the council chamber, pleased to find Elspeth alone, without Alexander or his irksome men present. She glanced up from her task at his approach.

"So you have returned, have you?"

"I came to stop the wedding."

She continued arranging a collection of crockery on one of the largest tables, some of which lay broken in pieces.

"Guess I'm too late." Finn ran a hand through his

disheveled hair. "I'm sorry."

He couldn't believe he'd waffled on this. The most important decision of his life and he'd blown it. Totally screwed up. Finn rubbed a palm over his aching heart. He'd lost the chance for a life with Elspeth.

She continued sorting through the piles on the table.

Why did she perform chores so soon after her wedding? Where was the groom? Finn scanned the hall before stepping closer to her.

"What are you doing?"

She shrugged. "You really thought to stop the ceremony?"

"I did."

"Why?"

How was he to answer the question? He glanced at his feet, shifted his weight from one leg to the other and raised his gaze to the woman who would always hold his heart.

"I love you." There, he'd said it. Too late, perhaps. He should have told her sooner.

Hands on hips, Elspeth spun around and glared at him. "'Tis easy to say now. Now that 'tis over."

"I know. I know I should've told you before. Told Archibald. Maybe I could have convinced him to allow you to marry me instead of Alexander." Finn shook his head and frowned. "But I had nothing to offer for you."

Elspeth tightened her jaw. A flare of anger flashed in her eyes.

Finn scanned the hall again, hoping no one would find them together. The last thing he wanted was to cause her more trouble.

"Where is your husband? The Campbell galleys are gone. I would've thought you and Alexander would have sailed to Skipness with them."

She didn't answer. Didn't look at him. She just continued rummaging through the plates on the table.

"What are you doing?" He couldn't stop himself from asking again. The party must have been wild for there to be so many broken dishes. And the room reeked of ale.

Several minutes passed. Finally, she turned to him and grinned. Her silver eyes sparkled. "I dinnae have a husband." She picked up an ornate platter and walked to the far end of the table, placing it with others still intact.

Reeling from the gut-punch, he followed. "How? What do you mean?"

Elspeth chuckled. "There was a wee bit of mischief this past night. Alexander had it in his mind to force me to the altar after the pre-wedding banquet."

Finn fisted his hands then relaxed them when he realized he'd clenched them. She moved several more plates into a pile, aggravating the shit out of him.

"Munn had other ideas," she continued. "The wee imp enjoyed a fine time disrupting the feast before it began. The broken crockery is what remains." She waved her arm over the table. "Afterward, an argument broke out between my brother and the Campbell."

"Then what happened?"

"Alexander joined the fray and they retired to Archie's study with the king. They argued for a while behind the closed door of his private chamber. Then James summoned me and asked if I wanted to wed Alexander. I said nae, and James charged Archie a hefty sum for the penalty of breaking the contract." Elspeth faced Finn. "So, as I said, I dinnae have a husband."

"Just like that? Just because you said no?"

With her nod, unprecedented relief washed over Finn, and he reached for her hand. She stepped away.

"Dinnae think I am not angry with you, Finn MacIntyre. For I am." She returned to sorting the dishes, ignoring him.

"I never should have left. I should've at least told you how I felt. Please, forgive me."

She twisted around fast and nailed him in place. He didn't like the expression she wore.

"Are you thinking to ask Archie to allow us to wed? If you are, you can take that thought right out of your head. I will not wed with you."

"I understand you're upset, but I know you feel the same as I." He touched her arm, hoping to convince her to relent. "I love you."

At the sound of boots pounding against oak flooring, Finn shot his gaze across the chamber. Archibald hurried toward them. *Damn. The man had the worst timing.*

Elspeth whirled away from Finn and smiled at her brother. Archibald wore a somewhat sheepish expression.

"I thought to find you alone." He glared at Finn. "I see you did not stay away verra long."

"I came back to stop the wedding and request you allow me the honor of marrying Elspeth."

She tensed, but stayed silent.

Archibald didn't seem surprised by the declaration. The man's eyes narrowed, his gaze speculative as it slid from Elspeth to Finn and back to Elspeth. "Do you wish to wed this worthless man?"

"Nae." Her chin jutted out. "I dinnae wish to marry *any* man."

"MacIntyre, will you leave us so I may speak privately with my sister?"

"There's nae need for him to leave, Archie. I will not change my mind."

"But, Beth—"

She held out her arm to stop her brother. "I plan to enter a convent rather than be forced to wed."

"You cannae," Archibald exclaimed.

"You can't," Finn said at almost the same moment, horrified by the thought of Elspeth as a nun. His earlier sense of relief morphed into annoyance at her blunt refusal of his marriage proposal. He blamed Alexander and the events of the last few days. With time, he was certain he could persuade her to change her mind and agree to marry him. Though not if she hid in a nunnery.

Archibald gently touched Elspeth's arm. She inhaled sharply, but didn't pull away.

"There is nae need for you to enter a convent. I will not

force you to wed. It was a mistake for me to have tried with Alexander. You must understand. 'Twas difficult for me to break the contract father negotiated. My need to honor the old agreement and my believed friendship made me blind to Alexander's treatment of you." He bowed his head then returned his gaze to his sister. "I am sorry. As your guardian, I should have protected you. Can you forgive me?"

Elspeth stared at her brother for a long moment.

"Dinnae look to me to lessen your guilt. You should have believed me. However, you are my brother and I love you. Therefore I will endeavor to forgive you." Tears welled in her eyes, and she presented him with a small smile. "I ken you believed you were performing your duty to both Da and me. I am sure you thought you were doing what was best."

"Aye, I did."

"What made you think again?"

"Munn found a missive from Alexander. Stole it, actually, from the man's bedchamber. It seems Alexander conducted private dealings behind my back. The king agreed to grant the debated lands between MacLachlan country and that of the Campbells to Alexander once he married you. Land our father strongly believed belongs to our clan." Archibald rubbed his brow, hurt evident in the depth of his eyes. "I find it hard to believe Alexander betrayed me. I trusted him."

Archibald hesitated, apparently taking a moment to gain composure.

"When it occurred to me everything you warned me of was true, that Alexander treated you deplorably, I had to petition the king to dissolve father's contract." His eyes pleaded. "Beth, I am verra sorry."

"'Tis fine, now 'tis over. Why did King James give in so easily?"

"I am not sure." Archibald's brow wrinkled. "He threatened to forbid my marriage to Isobell if I chose to cancel your wedding."

"Oh, Archie, nae."

"Nae worry. When I charged that Alexander assaulted

you, James refused to hear any more. That is when he summoned you. I can only guess the king believes a rift between the two clans will benefit him in some way."

"Another feud?" Elspeth sadly shook her head.

"Aye."

"What of Isobell?"

Archibald squared his shoulders and grinned. "James has given his blessing."

The smile Elspeth gave her brother earlier was nothing compared to the brilliant smile she graced him with now. He hugged her in return.

Jealousy gripped Finn. He wished it were he wrapping his arms around Elspeth. If only she'd bestow the warmth of her smile upon him, forgive him, he'd feel encouraged.

Her brother released her and clapped Finn on the shoulder. "Since you have returned and Hector is gone, you can take on the responsibility of Elspeth's safety."

Excellent. He'd have the opportunity to wear Elspeth down, allowing him to convince her they belonged together. Either here or in the future, it didn't matter to him anymore, provided Elspeth was his.

"Why cannae Jamie be my guard? He has been with me for years." Elspeth pursed her lips. Finn raised his gaze heavenward, aware he had his work cut out for him in persuading her to forgive him.

"Jamie has other duties. MacIntyre will be your guard." Archibald didn't stay to hear an argument. He turned on his heel and strode from the chamber.

Finn smiled to himself. Let the seduction begin.

A fortnight later, Elspeth stomped through the passageway. Finn strode a few steps behind, contributing to her confusion.

His heat penetrated her garments as if he pressed against her. She wanted him in a way she never wanted Alexander. Her nipples beaded and the fabric of her gown rubbed against them as she walked, making her moist in the private place between her legs.

She wanted to growl!

Her legs weakened.

Oh, bother. This wouldn't do. These new feelings left her vulnerable. Made her want to forgive Finn. And why did she remain angry with him?

She couldn't trust him with her heart.

If he'd declared his love for her before the wedding debacle, she'd have believed him and confessed her love in return. But for him to show up after the contract was broken and ask Archibald for her hand left her doubting his motives. Was it possible he learned about the land, which made up a large portion of her dowry? After all, he'd spent time with her uncle. The desire for more land was what caused Alexander to act such a scoundrel. Maybe her wealth would tempt Finn just the same.

Elspeth reached deep into herself for strength.

She sensed Finn's every movement. For the past fortnight, the only time he allowed her out of his sight was when she went to the garderobe to use the privy or when she was in her bedchamber.

Hiding in her chamber to avoid the unrelenting man was becoming tiresome.

A smile wanted to burst onto her lips, but she fought it. He certainly tried his best to persuade her to his cause. Persistence seemed to be one of his many traits.

"Lady Elspeth, may I assist you with those?"

She handed two empty leather panniers she intended to use to collect herbs, to Finn. If he wanted to hover, he might as well be useful.

Duncan met them at the beach with another full pannier.

"Victuals," he declared when she raised a brow.

They rowed across to the mainland, where they acquired mounts from the stable for the search of the forest to replenish Aine's store of wild herbs. The cerulean sky cheered Elspeth. Ignoring her male companions, she attempted to enjoy the unusually gentle weather.

The friction of the saddle between her legs bothered her as it never had before, exaggerating the unseemly sensations she experienced around Finn. She shifted her weight, determined to ignore the edgy ache coiling low and tight.

Deer darted from their path as they rode along a meandering trail through the trees. Birds flew from thicket to thicket in advance of their approach. Duncan led, with Finn taking up the rear. She concentrated on her upcoming task, certain she'd locate the plants she sought near her brother's hunting cottage.

They'd ridden quite a distance when Duncan surprised Elspeth by stopping unexpectedly. He reined his horse around to face her. "I dinnae ken what I was thinking to join you. I must return to the castle in all haste. I am to escort Archibald to a meeting with the Lamont. You can continue on without me."

"What about Maclay?" Elspeth asked.

"'Tis good for you to be concerned, lass, but we found nary a trace of the cur since we last battled with his men. You will be perfectly safe with MacIntyre guarding you."

Duncan and Finn shared glances in the annoying way men often did. As if they knew a secret, she didn't.

"Fine." She glared at Finn. "We must hurry. Clouds are moving in and a hint of moisture thickens the air."

Duncan handed the pannier containing the food to Finn and rode in the direction of Castle Lachlan. Elspeth hesitantly continued, unnerved by the thought of being alone with Finn and her desire for him.

They traveled in silence for what seemed an eternity to Finn. He moved uneasily in his saddle. By morning Elspeth would be his or her animosity toward him would deepen.

"Why do you fight against me when you didn't fight against marrying Alexander?"

Elspeth's loud sigh made Finn even more unsure of what he planned. "Wedding Alexander was my duty to my brother, my father, and my clan. I have nae such responsibility where you are concerned." She flicked a glance over her shoulder. "Besides, truth be told, I tried to convince Archie to break the contract before the wedding debacle."

Finn would let it go for now, but he was determined to persuade her to his cause.

He allowed Elspeth to take the lead. They rode deeper into the woods where the trees grew closer together and only a narrow trail existed. The overhanging foliage blocked what little sun escaped the thickening clouds. A chill slid across Finn's skin. Or was it nerves affecting him?

They entered a small clearing and Elspeth waited for him to ride up beside her. She stared at the darkened sky.

"We need to hurry or we will be caught in a storm."

As if on command, the clouds opened, drenching them.

"Too late. Is there some place we can shelter? It is too far to return to the castle."

Finn scanned the edge of the woods. Several paths led into the forest. He wondered which one led to the hunting lodge Duncan described as part of their conspired plan.

"Follow me," Elspeth called to him over the cadence of heavy raindrops striking the leafy canopy.

They rode farther into the forest to where the trail widened and opened into a small glen. A faerie-tale cottage with thatched roof and shuttered windows welcomed, inviting them to enter. Finn couldn't have asked for a more perfect setting to proceed with his seduction.

He hid his smile. Duncan assured him a storm would force them to spend a night alone in a cottage in the woods. Amazing man, that Duncan.

After securing the horses in a byre near the cottage, Finn and Elspeth ran through the pelting rain to the door. He followed her into the single room. The open door didn't provide enough light to discern the features of the interior. Elspeth retrieved a flint and stone from a small wooden box hanging on the wall next to the door along with some candles, which she lit and placed into metal holders on the table.

Although the lighting remained dim, the details of the room came into focus: rough-hewn wood furniture, table and bench, and a reed mat covering an earthen floor.

Finn's pulse jumped at the sight of the cozy bed.

Next to a fire pit in the center of the floor sat a small pile of straw for tinder, twigs and such for kindling, and chopped logs for fuel. Duncan had seen the cottage well provisioned. Elspeth handed Finn the flint and stone, and he started a small fire to handle the chill. Although he hoped later, shared body heat would be enough to keep them warm.

With an over-the-shoulder glance at the woman he loved, his body temperature rose to a point where air conditioning would be preferable to a fire.

Elspeth eyed Finn's broad back suspiciously. How convenient for him that they would be stuck together in the small cottage until the tempest passed. This all seemed a bit contrived. Aine insisting she couldn't wait another day for fresh herbs. Duncan insisting only he could escort them. Then Duncan claiming he needed to return to the castle so he could travel with Archie to meet with the Lamont.

And the storm?

Obviously, no one could contrive a storm, but the bad weather certainly forced her and Finn together. Alone. Something she was positive he wanted.

If she were honest, so did she.

Elspeth had to admit, she wasn't angry with Finn, but with herself for allowing the events with Alexander to worsen as they had. Shivering at the memory of Alexander's brutality, and with the cold, she wished Finn would hurry with the fire.

He stepped back. A tiny yellow flame licked the kindling and smoke filled the room. They both coughed and he glanced around as if searching for something. When he opened the door a crack, the smoke drafted out the small hole in the roof.

Grabbing one of the *plaides* from the bed, he handed it to

her. "We need to get out of our wet clothes. We can wrap ourselves in these dry *plaides* and wait out the storm."

Hmmm. Very convenient. Someone left dry plaids. She hid a smile.

Finn removed the pouch tied at his waist and tossed off his *plaide*. The wet linen of his *leine* stuck to his skin, emphasizing his solid thighs and every other wonderful morsel of his manly assets exposed to her appreciative gaze. Disappointment plagued her when he turned around to remove his *leine*. Then again, as he stripped, the moisture gradually revealed on his bronzed skin glistened in the light of the growing fire.

Elspeth knew she shouldn't watch, but curiosity and lust won out.

Her eyes roamed the length of him. She stole a good long look at his wet shoulders and ran her tongue over her lips. His long hair clung to firm muscles. She wanted to reach out and push aside the tangled strands.

The sight of his tight behind stole her breath. Red-hot desire throbbed within her breast and between her legs. Praise the Saints. She wanted Finn.

Unfortunately, the glorious sight ended too soon. With the dry, wool *plaide* covering all that wonderful skin, he whirled around to face her.

Her heart nearly stopped.

Goodness gracious. The same desire that throbbed within her chest burned in his eyes. She swallowed hard, wanting to reach out and touch him.

He licked his lips. Watching his tongue slide across his mouth did strange things to her. Made her tingle from head to toe.

"Lass, you best get out of that clothing," he said, his tone husky. "I'll turn my back. Wrap yourself in the other dry *plaide*."

She slowly nodded, but couldn't move.

Finally, she dropped her gown and chemise and wrapped the *plaide* around her, pinning it at the shoulder with her brooch. The wool chafed the already sensitive tips of her breasts, and she moaned.

Finn coughed.

"You can turn around. I am covered," her voice sounded as thick as his.

When he faced her, his eyes flared.

"Um, yeah." Finn picked up the full pannier. "We can share the food while we wait."

He emptied the contents onto the table: a hunk of cheese, bread, and a skin of wine. Outside, the storm worsened. Torrents of rain pelted the roof. Wind rattled the shutters. Inside, the thick stone walls and thatched roof ensured security, and the fire provided warmth. Not that she needed extra heat. She all of a sudden felt incredibly hot.

Elspeth sat on the bench and patted the seat next to her. He joined her, and she handed over the wine skin. There gazes held well he took several sips.

She slid a tad closer to Finn on the bench. Tingles danced across her skin where they touched. His audible intake of breath when their hips bumped made her want to giggle. She held in her delight. She wasn't yet ready to let him know she was no longer angry with him, or let him know how much she wanted to be with him.

Before the evening ended, she would take him as her lover.

As his lover, she wouldn't need to worry about his motivation for wanting to marry her. As his lover, she might discover the truth. As his lover, she would learn why the other women wore smiles after being with their men.

Her stomach did a little flip.

As his lover, she would leave this cottage without her maidenhead.

She loved Finn, true. But also, without her virginity she would no longer be a prize on the marriage market.

Finn almost choked on the sweet drink when Elspeth bumped against him. She seemed willing to make the best of their situation. The sight of the scrumptious woman before him left him struggling for breath. She'd draped the tartan fabric toga-style, her brooch pinned at one shoulder, revealing the silky flesh of the other. Several strands of strawberry-blond hair had come loose from her braid to curl around her heart-shaped face, framing her expressive silver eyes. He stared like a lovesick teenager. Would be best to turn away before he made a fool of himself.

Extracting a knife from his boot, he cut a chunk of cheese. After spearing the bite-size piece, he held the point to her. Their gazes met for a sizzling moment before she accepted the proffered portion.

"Cookie provided us with more than enough food for days. What was she thinking?" Elspeth's delicate eyebrows rose in question.

"She expected Duncan to be with us. He can eat as much as three men."

"True." She didn't look convinced, though.

Finn felt a moment of guilt. Somewhere, out in the woods, Duncan—co-conspirer extraordinaire—was getting soaked while keeping guard, making sure Finn's seduction of Elspeth went undisturbed. He owed a great debt to the oversized *teddy bear*.

Elspeth broke off a piece of bread at the same time Finn reached for a piece and their arms brushed. He fought to keep his cool. Each time she reached for something on the table, she rubbed against him. When her breast brushed his arm, her plaid dipped in front, giving him a peek at what awaited him if he were successful with his quest. He stifled a groan. She was killing him without trying.

Within him, an internal battle raged.

He couldn't breathe. Couldn't move. Each time Elspeth brushed against him, razor sharp excitement ripped through him. He began to think her actions intentional. Who was seducing whom?

When their gazes met again, he was positive her actions were deliberate.

He grasped her hand and pressed a kiss on the palm, ending the contact with a swish of his tongue. The hiss of her intake of breath along with her sweet taste teased his senses.

"Elspeth." He waited until she gazed at him. "I love you." He couldn't decipher the emotion within her eyes so he forged on. "Please forgive me for not telling you sooner. For not taking you away from Alexander before he harmed you."

She turned her face away. "I dinnae wish to speak of him."

Finn cringed at the hurt in her voice. "Okay, but I must know. Have you forgiven me?"

When Elspeth glanced at him, her sultry gaze burned him to the core. Maybe he misinterpreted her tone. He shifted slightly on the bench.

"Aye, I have forgiven you and have decided to take you as my lover." Her voice deepened to a husky timbre.

"What?" Her declaration cut deep. Annoyance bubbled in his chest. He wanted so much more from his angel.

"Is not that why we are here? Is not that what you have planned? I am sure you can teach me what I need to ken to please you."

She actually had the gall to flutter her eyelashes. If he weren't so appalled by her announcement, he'd chuckle. He slid slightly away from her on the bench.

"No, that's not what I want. I mean, yes."

Elspeth stared at him as if he didn't make sense. Which he didn't.

"I want you to agree to be my wife. Then we'll be best friends. Life partners. Lovers too." He ran a hand through his hair. "I want your love, Elspeth. Forever. Not a fleeting tumble in the sheets. I don't want to just hook up. I want us to be together forever."

Elspeth scrunched her nose. "Your speech is verra strange."

"Yes, it is." Finn could almost see gears turning in Elspeth's mind.

"Much like Lady Laurie's."

"She is my cousin."

Elspeth bit her lower lip. The sight sent flames rushing through Finn's veins anew. He scooted closer to her and wrapped his arm around her shoulder.

"If I agree, you mustn't beat me," Elspeth declared.

He hated that her experience with Alexander put such a horrible thought in her mind. Finn would never touch her in anger. "I couldn't hurt you like that." He slid his arm down to her waist and gave her a gentle squeeze.

She nodded. "Is it my land that draws you?"

"What land?"

"'Tis of no consequence." She waved her arm to dismiss the subject. He would for now. They could discuss it later. For now, he best act the gentleman.

He rose from the bench and knelt on one knee before Elspeth. "Will you marry me?"

"If I agree, will you teach me to be a good lover?"

"I will. But why do you ask such a thing?"

She hesitated. Color blushed her cheeks. Finn didn't push. He waited, hoping she would confide what troubled her.

"Alexander preferred Jonet rather than me," Elspeth blurted out.

Ahh. That was where her fear lay.

"Angel, never compare me to Alexander. I will only ever want *you*. Never anyone else. Alexander was a blind idiot who didn't know what he had. You are too good for him." *You're probably too good for me too, but I will have you just the same.*

Elspeth's head fell against his chest, and Finn wrapped his arms around her. Over her shoulder, he looked longingly at the bed in the corner.

CHAPTER NINETEEN

*E*lspeth wanted to believe Finn. Could he truly love her?

She rubbed her nose against the *plaide* covering his chest and inhaled his scent—a mixture of wet wool, the pine soap he used, and the storm clung to him. She snuggled close. The beat of his heart against her ear thrilled her. Faerie wings tickled her insides.

Finn eased his embrace and set her back from him. His scorching gaze lingered for a long moment. His hazel eyes mesmerized. Seconds passed and her heart thumped at a rapid pace, matching the tempo of Finn's. A rush of heat curled her toes, rising to envelop her completely.

She struggled to breathe.

Finn grasped her hand and slid his thumb in lazy circles on her palm.

"So what do you say? Will you marry me?"

"I cannae think when you look at me that way."

"Maybe this will help you decide." Finn lowered his head and kissed her.

The feel of his mouth against hers enthralled. She no longer cared if she ever took another breath. Had another thought. The silky friction of his satiny lips gliding over hers was all she needed. Wanted. His tongue skimmed across her lips, and excitement bubbled within her bosom. His kisses traveled to her throat, tiny pecks that slipped lower to her bare shoulder. She hardly noticed when he unclasped the brooch she wore. The *plaide* pooled at her waist.

Cool air hit her breast and her nipples pebbled. Finn smiled wickedly just before his tongue skittered over a puckered tip. She jerked in surprise. "Oh, Finn."

"Shhh, my angel," he murmured.

He rose and once again sat on the bench beside her. His large calloused hands spanned her hips and he pulled her sideways onto his lap.

"Let me love you."

His lips swept across sensitive skin. He suckled one bud and something deep within her core clenched. She thought she would die from pleasure.

She cradled his head, holding him to her bosom. Sensation never imagined before stole over her. She ached with a need she didn't understand. She wanted. Wanted something primal. As his tongue teased, she burrowed tense fingers into silky strands of honey-colored hair and tugged. Hard.

The soft mewing sounds escaping Elspeth's lips drove Finn insane. His pulse throbbed in frantic rhythm. He was close to losing control.

He needed to slow down.

Nuzzling her neck, he inhaled her unique fragrance. Sweet heather invaded his nostrils, driving him mad with desire. He longed to take her to bed, but he feared it might be too soon. He wanted her first time to be a special memory blocking out the rough treatment she endured at the hands of Alexander.

"Finn?"

"Yes?"

He kissed the ivory skin at her throat, and she purred.

"I will agree to wed you if you will take me now, like a real lover."

The passion laced within Elspeth's husky voice sent shock waves of need spiraling through Finn. Blood sizzled in his veins, hardening his body. He moaned and pulled her tighter against him. Her chest pressed into his, the fit perfect. Heartbeats in sync. She wanted him as much as he wanted her.

Finn lifted her into his arms. Stepping over the bench, he almost tripped in his haste to reach the bed. Elspeth giggled and draped her arms around his neck.

He sat her atop the fur covers and crouched on the floor in front of her. "You will marry me." The words meant as a gentle command.

"Aye," Elspeth responded on a breathless whisper.

Grasping both her tiny hands in his much larger ones, he gave her a solemn smile. "Elspeth MacLachlan, with God as my witness, I take thee as my handfasted wife. And to you I promise my love for eternity."

She tilted her head and stared at him quizzically.

"Now you say the same to me." He nodded encouragement.

Comprehension flashed in her eyes, and she smirked. "With God as my witness, I take thee, Finn MacIntyre, as my handfasted husband. To you I vow my love for a year and a day."

"What? Not for eternity?"

She chuckled. "I will let you ken after I see how great a lover you are."

"Sassy wench." Finn dropped her hands and in one quick motion removed the plaid he wore.

Elspeth's wide-eyed stare was almost comical. Even though she tended him when he was ill and seen everything God gave him, she appeared shocked. He glanced down. His erect cock jutted out, reaching for what only she could give him.

What a fool he was. He'd never made love to a virgin. In the past, his lovers were jaded society gals with as much, if not more, sexual experience than he. Elspeth deserved more care. He needed to proceed gently.

Desire brightened her cheeks. Her perky breasts

demanded attention. Need coiled Finn's muscles. His self-imposed celibacy took its toll. A long time had passed since he'd been with a woman. He needed to get his body and mind under control. If he couldn't master his lust, he'd be spent too soon, like an inexperienced teenager.

Thinking of something he didn't like should do the trick. *Cricket.*

Boring game. Really.

He inhaled a deep breath. Getting a needle at the doctor's office.

Now that could deflate any guy.

Sucking more air into his lungs, he sat on the bed next to Elspeth. Her stunned eyes still watched him. She seemed wary, but didn't flinch at his touch.

He took that as a good sign. "We'll take it slow, angel. Turn your back to me and I'll massage your muscles."

Her mouth and throat parched, Elspeth attempted to swallow. The sight of Finn's unbridled lust shocked her at first, but she refused to allow the sudden rush of humiliation and fear from Alexander's assault to spoil her joy with Finn.

With a smile, she twisted her back to him, proof of her trust. She hoped he understood how much she wanted to be with him. Together, they would clear the memories of Alexander and his betrayal.

Finn hesitated. She listened to the rhythm of his ragged breathing, feeling excitement with the realization she affected him as much as he did her.

Still, uncertainty plagued her. What if she couldn't please him?

He tossed her long braid over her shoulder to the front, and she gripped the tail, running it through unsteady fingers. The familiar texture against her palm soothed some of the nervousness.

His hands brushed over her skin, spreading chills that made her shiver. In a good way. She relaxed, allowing his strong fingers to roam over her shoulders.

The throaty sound of his chuckle warmed her heart.

Finn slid his hands across her flesh. His tender ministrations calmed the remaining fears. Each stroke soothed. Craving more of his gentle touch, she leaned into each caress, taking what he offered with pleasure.

His breath tickled her shoulder. Made her nipples harden to tight buds. Made her want more. Everything she'd heard the castle's maids whisper about in hidden corners.

Elspeth tensed in surprise when he leaned forward and licked the sensitive skin along the side of her neck, fire trailing the path of his tongue. Chilling flames shot through her as moist heat circled the recesses of an ear.

Moist heat flared within her womanly core, and she moaned her approval.

With Finn's warmth penetrating her senses, she craved his arms around her, as they'd been that day on the beach. She wanted him to kiss her with the same intensity.

Torn between the tantalizing sensations stirred by his magic touch and her hunger for his kiss, she groaned.

"What do you desire, angel?" Finn murmured.

Deciding she wanted his kiss, she twisted to face him, and froze.

Hungry eyes devoured her. Thrilled her.

She moistened her lips, and his jaw tightened.

"Kiss me."

He dragged her against him and into a not so tender embrace. His lips and tongue demanded, and she became more than willing to succumb. He kissed her with a determination that left them both breathless.

He brushed kisses across her cheeks and forehead and eyelids.

Slow to open her eyes, the sight before her stole her remaining ability to breath. Finn stared with an openness she'd never seen. His soul exposed.

He needed her.

"I want you more than you can imagine. But we must go slow. When we make love this first time, it will hurt you." He gently tapped a finger against her chin. "Only this first time. Never again. I'll try to go slow, to lessen the pain."

"Do you mean, when we mate?"

Finn cringed at her blunt words. "Yes."

He had no cause for concern.

"I ken it will hurt. My mother once explained to me what happens between a husband and wife. Aine reminded me the other night before I was to wed Alexander."

"Let's not talk about that reprobate."

"As you wish." A dark shadow slipped across her heart and she glanced away. The passion she'd felt faded.

"Look at me, angel."

She raised her gaze to Finn. He frowned. "If you'd rather wait…"

She forced her concerns aside. She wanted Finn.

Elspeth tugged the *plaide* from her waist and dropped it to the floor where the wool fabric landed in a wrinkled mess on the reed mat. She didn't care. The man before her was all that mattered. She tentatively touched his arm. "I dinnae want to wait."

Finn hugged her tight against him. Kissed her passionately. He would be the only one of whom she thought.

He broke the kiss and laid beside her. Skin against skin. He peppered kisses over her face before inching his way down her body to lave first one and then the other nipple.

Pure bliss invaded Elspeth's senses when his tongue circled her belly button. She hadn't known how wonderful it would be, to be loved by a warrior like Finn. Running her fingers through his hair, his masculine scent teased her senses again—rain and pine and wool. She silently thanked the fae for gifting him to her.

His kisses singed a path across her body. He knelt afore her on the bed, his head bowed, his tongue tickling the inside of her thigh. The fingers of one of his hands twirled her maiden hairs. So many marvelous sensations raced through Elspeth, she gasped in surprise when his long fingers moved lower to toy within the folds of her womanhood.

He slipped a finger into her and she tensed. He used his other hand to caress her hip. "Easy, angel."

Finn's finger moved gently, repetitively rubbing an unusually sensitive spot. New sensations besieged Elspeth. Slowly, ever-so-slowly, his finger glided in and out. She pressed against his hand, wanting more, though not knowing more of what.

Faster would be good.

When he pulled his hand away, he left her feeling hollow.

Not for long. With two skillful fingers, he teased her responsive flesh. The motion tantalized, and she rocked against his hand. Pressure coiled within her, tighter and tighter. She clutched the bed covering. "Please. Please." She pushed against Finn's hand with everything she had. "Please."

Elspeth begged, her mouth making incoherent sounds, unable to form words. She panted as if she climbed a steep hill, needing desperately to reach the top. In a breath, her world exploded. Blue lights flashed and a harsh guttural sound ripped from her throat.

Moisture slicked Finn's fingers. He licked them one by one and released a manly moan. His eyes rolled before closing, his facial features softened as if in bliss.

Like a blade of tall grass in the sea breeze, Elspeth trembled. She needed…

"Finn, please."

Finn had enjoyed Elspeth's warm silky skin beneath his fingers. But the taste of her in his mouth nearly sent him into orgasm. What would it feel like to fill her to the hilt?

He slowly slid his finger from his mouth. Eyes closed in ecstasy he savored her unique flavor. His desire spiraled upward, growing into ferocious need.

It was time to pleasure his angel and himself fully. The honest passion he found with her delighted him, a sweet innocence entwined with unconscious sensuality. Their union would be hot and playful. Never boring. Life with Elspeth would be fantastic.

Elspeth stared at him with passion-filled eyes. She reached for him. "I need to feel your lips on mine."

Oh, Yeah. He didn't want to miss even a tiny speck of Elspeth's rich bounty.

He rose over her, leaning on his elbows, trying to keep his weight from overwhelming her.

"I'm here, angel. I'll always take care of you." He claimed her mouth. On her soft gasp, he slipped his tongue between her lips to tangle and dance with hers.

He rubbed his erection against her softness and slowly inched into her carnal embrace. She was slick from his fingers, and he easily slid in, until he hit the fiber of her virginity. Struggling to keep control, he rose on quivering-tense forearms and leaned his forehead against hers. "Are you all right?"

"Um hum." Elspeth raised her hips against him.

The action sent sparks from his cock to his heart.

He pulled back then surged forward. Her cry he captured with his mouth, thrusting his tongue in rhythm to their mating.

To his amazement, she moved with him, her pace equal to his. When she shuddered beneath him with a scream, he allowed his own release. Shock waves vibrated through his entire system. He roared his jubilance.

He'd found a home in Elspeth.

Elspeth woke to find Finn crouched, facing the fire. The flickering light bathed the skin across his shoulders in a golden glow. She snuggled deeper into the bedding and enjoyed the view.

The smile he gave her when he turned around was hot enough to melt her. Her cheeks flamed. She could hardly believe what they'd done together during the night. Several times.

He called it making love.

She believed it must be. She'd never imagined feeling anything so glorious.

Elspeth ached a wee between her legs when she moved, but a little discomfort was nothing compared to the wonderful things Finn had done to her and she to him. Her skin warmed when she thought of the several times during the night they'd mated.

Made love.

"Lass, you'd better get up and dress." Finn handed her the slightly damp gown she'd worn the day before. "It's stopped raining. The castle folk will worry about us. We must hurry to return and explain to Archibald we've handfasted."

Elspeth fluttered her lashes at Finn. "We would not want Archie to cut off something important when he tries to kill you for deflowering me."

"You are my wife." He shook his head, a cocky male smile playing on his lips before he looked away. She doubted he was concerned.

They dressed and broke their fast with what remained from the night before. They let the fire burn out, and Finn removed the ashes to a pit in the yard.

When he came back inside, he paced while she collected the few items they used, returning them to the panniers.

"Elspeth." Finn lowered his gaze as if uneasy.

"Aye."

When he glanced at her again, his brow furrowed. "Before we leave, there is something I must tell you."

"What is it?" She stepped toward him, concerned by his tone.

A loud knock startled her, and Finn opened the door to a grinning Duncan.

CHAPTER TWENTY

*O*onagh lounged at the edge of the azure pool. Behind her, diaphanous silk fabric draped the entrance to her antechamber. The luxury within didn't entice.

She glared at the pool. Its usually placid water rippled with each rise of her royal fae temper. A titanic burst of anger spouted a large wave, which rolled across the expanse, spraying spume in all directions. Handmaidens scurried for cover.

Fierce shuddering shook Oonagh. How dare the pesky MacLachlan brownie assist Caitrina with the challenge? That handsome Finn MacIntyre and the MacLachlan lass shared the most ancient of carnal dances—the first phase of the intimate bonding was now complete.

She threw a fire bolt at a weeping cherry tree. Blackened blossoms fell to the ground. Smoke wafted in the air. Her nose pinched from the acrid smell.

Violence did little to quell her escalating rage.

Caitrina may have won the first part of the challenge. Oonagh would not allow the halfling princess to win the second. She'd make sure the couple never conceived.

She curled her lip in distaste with the thought of journeying to the earth realm. But she would do what she must. She'd enhance the evil enchantment enthralling Alexander Campbell.

Though, she'd be careful to evade her consort.

If fortune smiled upon her, he wandered the Emerald Isle far away from Scotland.

For Finvarra, high king of the fae, was surely on earth feeding on the emotions of some beautiful human woman. He would not be pleased to learn of her machinations in the mortal realm. She preferred not to ponder what form his wrath would take if he learned she cheated in the challenge with Caitrina.

Oonagh held little regard for human free will. She'd stolen it from Campbell with barely a thought, using him as a puppet to ensure her victory.

Too bad—he failed.

No matter. Now that he possessed MacIntyre's claymore her pawn would be unstoppable.

She cloaked herself with her favored glamour and withdrew from *Tir-nan-Óg*.

"There is something I must tell you. Things we need decide."

Elspeth glanced up from her needlework. Finn paced the confines of her solar like a trapped animal. *Why so restless?*

He stopped in front of her and crouched, his face level with hers. "I've wanted to discuss something with you since we handfasted."

"What must we decide?" She wished he'd get to the point. "Is this what you wanted to tell me at the cottage when Duncan interrupted us?"

"Yes, I've been trying to talk to you since. The time never seemed right. I thought it best to give us time to settle into our marriage before—"

"We are hardly settled." Heat flushed her cheeks. "It has been less than a sennight since we pledged our hearts."

"I know." Finn ran a hand through his hair.

The morning sun from the window made the honey strands glisten. He was her husband now. For the hundredth time since Duncan came to fetch them and they returned to the castle, she thanked the fae for sending Finn to her.

"Listen. I'm not from here," he said in a rush.

"Is that all?" *No reason for concern.* Elspeth placed the cloth she'd been stitching on the table at her side. She smiled and gave her husband her full attention.

He rose and dropped into the chair next to hers. "Do you know where my cousin Laurie came from before she arrived at Castle Lachlan?"

"I do." Elspeth glanced toward the open doorway fearful someone might walk by and overhear their conversation. "Please, close the door."

Finn nodded, his lips pressed in a tight line. He crossed the chamber, shut the oak door, returned to her side and sat.

"Take your ease. I ken Lady Laurie came from the future to live in France. Are you trying, in your own discomfited way, to tell me that you are also from the future? You need not worry. I guessed such ages ago."

Finn leaned back in his chair, appearing only a trifle relieved. Elspeth's stomach tightened. What else could he possibly want to tell her that had him so troubled?

"Yeah, well, I'm also from the future."

"But after you journeyed from the future, you arrived here from France, as did Lady Laurie."

"Not exactly. We traveled directly here from our time. We never lived in France."

Elspeth shifted her weight atop the cushion she perched upon. "Husband, you are beginning to frighten me. What is it you are trying to tell me?"

"When Patrick and Laurie left Castle Lachlan, Malcolm Maclay and his men separated them from their escort and chased them into the Fir-wood."

"I ken that. When their escort returned without them and we did not find them, we assumed they went to France on their own."

"Not quite." Finn shook his head. "They went to the faerie knoll in Fir-wood and traveled forward to my time."

"Not France?" Elspeth swallowed uneasily. "The twenty-first century?"

"Yes. They've been living there for the last several years along with your parents."

Her parents? A buzzing noise hummed in her ears. She clutched the fabric of her gown over her heart.

"Time passage isn't the same here as in the future—one year here, a couple of months there. It's complicated," Finn said.

"'Tis imposs—" She shut her mouth with a snap. *Not any more impossible than Laurie and Finn traveling through time.* The fae controlled much magic. If she could believe in fae magic, why not believe her parents, and also Patrick, traveled through time?

Finn jumped from his seat and hovered over her. He grasped her trembling hand and squeezed her fingers.

"I attended a celebration in Laurie's garden, and as Patrick made a toast, we saw Malcolm Maclay on the faerie knoll in my time. Your father stopped your brother from running through the time gate after the lunatic. So I ran through instead."

Elspeth pulled her hand away. "Why?"

"I came here to kill Maclay, to avenge what he did to Laurie."

Wild desperation forced Elspeth up, and she paced to the window. She felt Finn's gaze on her, but she couldn't look at him yet.

In the courtyard, her kinsmen moved about, performing chores as if 'twas a normal day. She inhaled several deep breaths. Finally, she calmed enough to turn and face her husband. "If Laurie kenned my parents were alive and living in the future, why did she not tell me? Why would she keep such a secret? She must have kenned I would want her to tell me. How could she have kept the truth from me?"

Finn's intense stare unnerved Elspeth.

"She didn't know then. Not while she was with you. It wasn't until later. After she and Patrick traveled to my time she learned her landlords, Iain and Mairi, were your parents."

"I dinnae understand. If my parents sent for Patrick, why did they not send for the rest of us? How could they have deserted us and allowed us to mourn them?" She crossed her arms over her chest in a self-hug, trying to overcome the terrible sense of betrayal. "Why do they stay there? Why dinnae they come home?"

"I'm not sure how it all works. The faerie knoll, on a full moon, is the time gate. For some reason, your father believes once someone travels forward, they can't return here."

Finn strode to Elspeth and gently dragged her into his arms. She didn't fight him. She leaned against his broad chest.

"Angel, after I kill Maclay, I want you to come with me to the future."

Elspeth pulled away. "How do I ken any of this to be true? You told Archie you came from France. Patrick told me Lady Laurie came from France and was where they were going to live. With her family, he said. Mayhap you lost your senses when you burned with the fever."

"I had to lie to Archibald. I needed to protect my cover. I would never lie to you. Please, I need you to believe me."

"You admit lying to Archie. Why should I believe anything you say, Finn MacIntyre?"

Finn grimaced. "It was wrong to have lied to your brother, but I feared he'd have me condemned to death for what he might mistake as witchcraft."

Elspeth froze. "He would not."

"Are you sure of that?"

"Aye." Moisture pooled in her eyes as the possibility of seeing her parents dawned on her. "I must tell Archie what you have told me. I must tell him our parents live."

Finn reached out his arm, but before he stopped her, she ran from the chamber.

The sound of his fist punching the doorframe didn't slow her down, she hurried along the passageway.

She must tell Archibald. *Her parents are alive!*

❀ ❀ ❀

At Elspeth's exuberant knock on her brother's bedchamber door, he beckoned her enter. Archibald rushed about the large suite, stuffing garments and other travel items into a leather satchel.

"Et-hmm," she loudly cleared her throat to gain his attention.

He stopped and shot her a perturbed look. "What's wrong, Beth?"

"I need to speak with you."

"Tears?" He stepped toward her. "Dinnae tell me you had a fight with Finn. You agreed to the handfast."

"It is not that. I have great news. Finn kens where Ma and Da are."

Archibald's body shuddered once before he stiffened. "Where did he get such information?"

"He says they are with Patrick and Lady Laurie."

"In France? And he is only telling us now?"

"He thought we would not believe him."

Archibald's brow furrowed. "Why not?"

"Because they have traveled through time to the future."

Her brother scowled. "You are not starting that again. I told you before. Lady Laurie was not from the future. 'Tis impossible." He turned away and continued stuffing a pair of *trews* into his travel bag. "I begin to think you have gone addled."

"Please, listen to me. Finn wants me to go to the future with him—to be with Ma and Da."

"I dinnae have time for this, Beth. I plan to sail on the noon tide. I have decided to travel to Arran to fetch Isobell. Uncle Donald is in charge of the castle until I return."

"Uncle Donald?" *No one trusts Uncle Donald.*

The sound of footsteps in the passageway caused them both to look to the doorway.

Finn stood in the threshold with Duncan and Jamie.

"Is it true?" Archibald demanded. "You believe my parents traveled though time and live in some future place?"

Finn glanced uneasily at Duncan and Jamie before nodding. "Aye. Let me explain."

The flush coloring Archibald's neck and face indicated how close he was to losing his temper. Waiting for Finn to speak, Elspeth chewed on her lip. She hoped he could reason with her brother.

"Lady Laurie and I were born in another time. There is a time gate in the woods near where Elspeth found me. My cousin and your brother, Patrick, traveled forward through the gate to where your parents are living. I came back through the gate to seek revenge against Maclay.

The twin's mouths fell open and they stepped away from him. Their eyes clouded with fear.

"You expect me to believe this mad tale," Archibald blustered, his voice rising. "'Tis heresy. I thought better of you."

"Not heresy. Science."

"Sounds like witchery to me." Archibald grabbed his satchel and headed for the door.

"Perhaps magic, but not witchcraft," Finn said, his tone even. "Do not fear what you don't understand."

Her brother stared at Finn for a tense moment, his face reddening more.

"Duncan, throw him in the pit. Then meet me at the boat."

Elspeth grabbed Archibald's sleeve. "Nae, Archie, I did not mean for you to throw him in the pit. I only wanted you to talk to him. To find out about Ma and Da."

Finn didn't even try to fight Duncan's hold. With a look of resignation on his beloved face, he allowed the warrior to take him away by the arm.

"Please! Dinnae throw him in the pit. Listen to what he has to say." The shock of learning the whereabouts of her parents had befuddled her thinking. She hadn't anticipated her brother's angry reaction to the news. Finn had known better. She tugged on her brother's arm.

"I have nae patience for this. Jamie, lock her in her chamber and dinnae let either of them out until I return. I will deal with them then. See to it my uncle understands my orders. The tide will not be in my favor for long. I must leave. Now." Archibald pulled away from Elspeth, and strode from the chamber.

Jamie grasped her elbow. "Come, lass."

"Nae. This is wrong. You must not allow them to keep Finn in that horrible place."

Jamie's features hardened. The pressure on her arm increased.

She pleaded, using her eyes, a glance through her lashes, which usually worked on him when she wanted her own way.

"Dinnae ask me to go against a direct order." His features softened slightly. "I will speak with your uncle but cannae promise he will rule in your favor."

She sighed. "After you do, send him to me."

Elspeth paced the confines of her bedchamber. Three days had passed since Jamie locked her away and set a guard outside her door. The foolish mistake she'd made still haunted her. She never should have blurted what Finn told her to Archibald. She should have stayed with Finn and listened to all he had to say.

They should have discussed the best way to approach Archibald—as husband and wife. She shook her head regretfully. The shock over learning her parents were alive caused her to act without thought.

Since Patrick and Lady Laurie left Castle Lachlan, Archibald was a different man, no longer as understanding as he'd once been. He'd become stiff and unyielding. How he could believe in Munn, but no other magic, truly amazed her.

She picked up a pillow from the window seat and hugged it to her chest. Finn's fresh pine scent lingered on the dark blue velvet. They'd spent the time since they handfasted together in this chamber. Her cheeks heated at the vivid memory of Finn *making love* to her, right here, on this window seat. The ache in her chest made her squeeze the pillow tighter.

The thought of Finn in that dreadful hole broke her heart. She fought tears. She wouldn't cry.

Her uncle had visited shortly after Archibald departed. He patiently listened to her pleas, but in the end, he left Finn in the pit and kept her confined in her velvet prison.

Outside the window, the crescent moon glowed, its silvery reflection glistening on the bay. The day of her twenty-first birth celebration would arrive in a fortnight. With all that happened, there would be no festivities to mark its passing.

The grating slide of the lock and a sharp knock signaled the maid with her evening meal. Elspeth crossed the chamber on slippered feet and flung the door open. Eyes wide with shock, she realized her mistake.

On the threshold stood her worst nightmare.

Alexander grabbed her, silencing her with a hand over her mouth, and dragged her back into the chamber. A horribly scarred man followed, quietly closing the door behind him.

Fear choked Elspeth. Grasping for courage, she dug the sharp point of her elbow into Alexander's ribs. He only grunted. She thrashed within the blackguard's grasp—she had to break free.

CHAPTER TWENTY-ONE

*F*inn scratched a raw patch on his wrist where *something* bit him. His eyes had adjusted to the dimness and he could now decipher forms within his surroundings.

The MacLachlan pit wasn't as bad as he expected. He'd gotten used to the dank stench.

The stone walls oozed moisture and the earthen floor crawled with vermin, but Duncan had given him a cot of sorts to lie on and blankets to keep warm. They lowered food to him in a wooden bucket twice a day and Jamie smuggled him a skin filled with whisky.

The whisky hadn't lasted long. Three days was an eternity in hell.

Finn was smart enough to know there was no way out unless they saw fit to release him. So why had he allowed them to put him in the pit without a fuss?

He trusted them.

Even if he didn't, trying to stop them had made no sense. They'd been determined and he'd been outnumbered. He would have been hurt, and probably would have harmed a number of MacLachlans before they restrained him had he put up a fight.

Yeah, he trusted them to do the right thing.

In the meantime, he was going stir crazy with only rats as companions.

"Lad, are you there?" Donald's voice ricocheted off the walls.

"Of course, I'm here. Where else would I be?" he hollered, his rough voice doing the same bouncy thingy.

"We are dropping a knotted rope for you to climb." Jamie's words circled in his mind before Finn realized what the man said.

Holy halleluiah. They were letting him out.

The end of a heavy rope hit Finn's head. He rubbed his noggin then grabbed hold. Hand over hand, and with his knees, he shimmied up the makeshift ladder. His arms and legs burned from exertion. Having spent several days in the deep, tight hellhole, without the ability to exercise, the climb zapped his strength.

After dragging himself over the edge, he crawled across the stone floor, where Donald helped him sit against the wall while he caught his breath. The shockingly bright light from torches stung his eyes, making them water.

"They have taken her," Jamie said, anguish twisting around his words.

Cobwebs clogged Finn's brain. "Who has taken whom?"

"Are you dimwitted? Alexander and Maclay have stolen our Elspeth," Donald thundered.

"What the hell?" Finn jumped to his feet, an adrenaline kick giving him strength. "Alexander has joined with Maclay?"

"More likely Maclay joined Campbell." Jamie added fuel to the fire burning in Finn's gut.

"Let's go!"

"Ease up, lad." Elspeth's uncle grabbed his arm before he could race off. "We need to devise a plan first and raise a fighting force."

"And you need to bathe," Jamie added with a grimace. "You stink."

"Right." Finn would find Elspeth and, God forgive him, if

Alexander hurt her…Finn wouldn't feel guilty killing the man. And as for Maclay—the man needed to die.

Archibald leaned on the gunwale and scanned the horizon, well aware of the tension emanating from the man who stood beside him. For three days, Duncan remained silent, only speaking when spoken to. The other lads quietly went about the business of rowing the galley away from the isle, ignoring as best they could the two cross men, thusly avoiding the simmering argument.

Not only had Archibald to deal with Duncan's scowls upon their arrival on the Isle of Arran, his furious frustration escalated when he learned Isobell no longer visited her kinswoman. The entire journey had been for naught. Now he must track his betrothed to Lamont country. Something he didn't relish doing.

A curious glance at Duncan caused Archibald to tighten his grip on the rail. His henchman's anger over the way Archibald had treated Elspeth and her new husband added to his remorse. Although Duncan hadn't said anything, the man's disapproval remained palpable.

He didn't require the man's scorn to make him feel guilty. He'd acted harshly. Caught up in his need to fetch Isobell, he'd lashed out at both Finn and Elspeth with severe punishments.

Though, Finn *must* be mad to think people traveled back and forth through time. It wasn't possible. Aye, it would be best to keep the couple apart until they learned if Elspeth carried. Any child begot of their union might inherit Finn's madness.

As soon as Archibald knew for certain there was no bairn, he'd have the handfasted marriage dissolved and send Finn back to France, far away from his sister. Let Patrick deal with the man's brain fever.

Unable to stomach the intense stare of his companion any longer, Archibald sighed heavily. "Speak your mind,

Duncan."

"'Tis nae my place to advise, yet I feel the need to state what troubles me. What you did to Finn was wrong."

"My friend, I appreciate your counsel. I do regret my rash decision to throw Finn into the pit. However, the man is mad and must be kept away from my sister. Such insanity can fester and become dangerous."

"I dinnae think he is a madman."

Archibald gaped at Duncan. "You heard him. He is a lunatic, believing he, Lady Laurie, Patrick and my parents all traveled through time. 'Tis fantasy."

"Aye, I heard what he believes to be true. 'Tis a strange belief. Yet again, I am not so sure what he proposes is impossible. I have seen some strange things in my time. Before Lady Laurie and I were captured by Maclay and taken prisoner, something odd happened that made me think she was one of the fae."

Archibald raised an eyebrow. "One of the fae?"

Duncan's cheeks reddened. "Aye. I thought I saw wings attached to her back. Faerie wings, you ken? She let me believe such foolishness in order to convince me to take her to that cursed faerie knoll."

"She is not a faerie."

"I ken. Yet if you believe in Munn and the goings and comings of the lost *bairns* of the wood…" He shrugged. "I be thinking if the knoll is powerful enough to allow faeries and brownies to travel between the misty land of the fae and our homeland, is it not possible the magic is so strong it could take hold of unsuspecting Highlanders and toss them into another time or place?"

Archibald grunted. He'd need to think on that.

They sailed in silence for a couple of hours until Archibald came to a decision. "We return to Castle Lachlan."

Fetching Isobell would have to wait.

Caitrina slipped past the guard and into the network of

tunnels threading through the bowels of Skipness Castle. She'd used her fae powers to seek out Seumas and failed. Somehow, the wizard managed to block her every intrusion. She doubted his power, of itself, held enough energy to thwart her. Someone of fae blood must be combining forces with him.

Oonagh? The damn queen was cheating again.

An uncontrollable fury raced through Caitrina's veins. She needed to find the sword and end this game. *Now*. Drawing from an inner reserve of resilience, she altered her state of being.

She'd already searched in all the unusual hidey-holes for Seumas, having expected him to conceal the claymore in a sordid hovel of such. So now, she would search the most predictable location.

As mere particles, she glided along the contours of stone, feeling with her fae senses for an anomaly in the pattern of life. A miniscule quiver of power would be enough to alert her to Seumas's lair. And where she found the wizard, she was sure to find the sword she'd enchanted with a kiss.

A shaggy gray rat scurried across the dirt floor. Stopping near the rock wall, the rodent twitched its nose several times before bolting for a fissure within the mortar. Caitrina felt the nearly indiscernible whisper of magic skirr across her mind. Enough to send her molecules chasing after the wizard.

Finn stood in the tub, clenching his fists as Aine's husband, Angus, poured a bucket of warm water over his head, rinsing away the filth of the pit along with the strong soap. He'd wanted to rush headlong after Elspeth. But he conceded the others were right. He needed to cleanse himself of the vermin of the pit.

He took succor from the fact that, while he bathed, Jamie and Donald prepared for a band of men to go after Elspeth.

The fear of Maclay, or possibly even Alexander, hurting her made Finn's gut churn. He grabbed the towel from

Angus and stepped out of the tub, drying his torso as he moved to the bed where a clean *leine* and plaid lay.

Fifteen minutes later, he strode into the noisy council chamber where a force of MacLachlan warriors prepared to go to battle.

Jamie punched his arm. "We will find Herself and bring her home."

"We will." Determination rode Finn's words.

The other emotions, held in check, wound into a tight coil. He braced himself for war as he had in the desert. Tactics might be different, but once trained as a warrior, the discipline never left a man. The skill served him well in the boardroom over the years since. It would serve him again in this battle.

A wisp of uncertainty slipped into his mind. He'd received a serious wound the last time he went after Maclay. Finn brutally pushed the potentially debilitating thought away. He'd trained hard since and his skill with the sword was much improved.

Failure was unacceptable.

Elspeth meant more to him than anything ever had. She filled the dark emptiness within him with light and goodness. He would rescue his angel and make Maclay and Alexander Campbell pay for daring to take her away from him.

Donald joined Finn. "I have sent a fast running gillie to Glasrie, to my cousin Allaine, requesting a fighting force rendezvous with us."

"More men?" Finn glanced around the hall. At least fifty men prepared to join him in his fight. More men would be better.

"Men and horses. We will sail the galleys along the loch, landing near Tarbert. My cousin's lads will meet us there with horses. Then we ride to Skipness and free our Elspeth." Donald slapped Finn on the back and strode away, barking orders as he crossed the room.

Finn slung the same borrowed sword he used before onto his back, missing the familiar weight of his claymore.

Elspeth stared out the glazed tower window of Skipness Castle. The golden brilliance of the setting sun stung her moist eyes and she spun away. The well-appointed chamber was to have been hers after she wed Alexander. Instead, the bedchamber held her prisoner. She had traded one velvet cell for another.

Her stomach roiled from nausea, which still plagued her after all these days. The bang to her head and the stormy crossing of the loch had weakened her. She could still taste the foul rag used to silence her pleas. She lightly touched the tender marks on her wrists where the bindings her captors used had chafed her skin, making it raw.

She hadn't seen Alexander since he carried her gagged and bound and dumped her on the bed. He'd taunted her with the promise of retribution for spurning him, the threat of rape. Each time someone neared the chamber door she froze with dread.

Elspeth started at the sound of heavy footfalls—not the light step of the serving woman. Muffled voices rose in volume. Her heart raced, nearly paralyzing her with fear.

The door opened slowly. Her breath caught and she feared she would faint.

Alexander stepped into the chamber, closed the door, and leaned against the oak panel. His cold gaze slid down her body and back up, lingering on her breasts.

She inhaled a panicked gasp.

His eyes flared and the blackguard smiled. He enjoyed her discomfort.

"Return me to my family." Elspeth pushed aside the terror crippling her and stepped forward, her chin held high.

"You are in nae position to make demands." He cleared the distance between them before she had another thought.

He wrapped his hands around her throat, gently, as if her lover. His thumb massaged the large vein she knew ran to her heart. What did he plan to do to her? Her heart near burst from suspense.

"You were to be mine. Unsoiled by the seed of another man." His fingers tightened a fraction. "I could kill you with my bare hands."

Shock froze her in place.

He increased pressure slowly. She couldn't breath. She clutched at his hands when she realized he wouldn't release her.

"You will do what I ask of you, and with a smile, or I will kill you. Then I will go after your lover. I promise his death will be slow and verra painful."

His grip tightened. Her vision blurred and everything spun. With a growl, he released her and threw her against the bed. Elspeth stumbled and caught hold of the bedpost, gulping air. When the room stopped spinning, she glared at Alexander. He shook his head and waved a finger.

She used every ounce of energy remaining to force her lips into a smile.

"That's better." He strode to the hearth and spun to face her. "Please, have a seat, my lady." He swept a bow and pointed to a chair, his gallantry in contrast to his cold stare.

She staggered to the chair and fell into it, edging back as far away as she could from his threatening presence. "What do you want?" Her voice trembled, as did her hands.

"I want you to use your gift of the sight to find out what King James plans."

"You're mad. 'Tis treason."

"I am sure nary a person will miss your Finn when he disappears from your brother's pit. I will start by tearing out his fingernails, one by one, then—"

"The visions dinnae come by my demand. They are sent."

"You have a sennight to learn how to draw the visions to you." Alexander crossed the chamber and left without a backward glance, the door slamming overloud.

What was she to do?

Five days had passed and no one from Castle Lachlan had come after her. She'd foolishly hoped Finn would rescue her.

How could he? He rotted in her brother's pit.

How could the prophecy given at her birth been so wrong?

She clutched her brooch, seeking her gift. Naught. No visions came upon her. She thought of Finn. His kindness. The way he made her feel when they made love—powerful.

Come to me, my warrior. Save me. Come to me.

A scream pierced his consciousness. Finn woke and realized he'd screamed. Shaking the remnants of the nightmare from his fogged mind, he gazed at several concerned faces. In the light from the fire, two guards plus Jamie and Donald stared at him.

"What ails you, lad? Night terror?" Donald asked.

Finn took a moment to remember where he slept. In the woods, a few miles from Tarbert Castle. He nodded at the men. "Bad dream. Sorry I disturbed you."

"Nae worries. 'Tis your turn to stand guard with Jamie," Donald said. "You probably cannae go back to sleep anyway."

True. Finn rose, but couldn't shake the terror gnawing at his gut.

In his dream, Elspeth called to him as she had in the dreams he'd had in the twenty-first century. On this night, the nightmare grew deadly. He found her crumpled body, tossed from the castle like unwanted rubbish, strangulation marks wringing her lovely neck.

He prayed the nightmare meant nothing.

CHAPTER TWENTY-TWO

*A*fter sailing northwest around the top of the Isle of Arran and crossing the sound, intending to follow the coast of Kintyre north to Loch Fyne, Archibald spied several vessels anchored in a cove to the north of Skipness Castle, well hidden from its three watchtowers.

"Your eyes are keener than mine. What do you make of the activity on yonder shore?"

Duncan cupped a hand over his eyes and muttered a foul curse. "MacLachlan galleys. What are they doing there?"

As their boat glided closer, Archibald recognized the red and gold pennants still attached to masts, billowing in the breeze. Aye, his galleys. His uncle better have a good reason for disobeying him and taking the boats abroad.

"Saint Columba spare me, can I not travel and expect my orders followed?"

Archibald ignored the what-did-you-expect-from-Uncle-Donald look in Duncan's eyes as the man looked down his nose and pursed his lips.

"What else do you see?"

"'Tis a fighting force of kinsman. Donald and Jamie are with them, as is Finn." Duncan leaned farther over the gunwale intent on the men milling about. "And, my God, 'tis cousin Allaine from Glasrie along with his lads and Stephen."

"Lower the sails. Man the oars. Row us into the beach." Anger constricted Archibald's chest as he shouted the orders, making his head throb. He'd given his uncle a direct order to stay at Castle Lachlan and watch over his sister and the castle. So much for believing the man had changed. Could be trusted.

"Must be five score men," Duncan reported.

Archibald rubbed his throbbing temples while his oarsmen hustled to follow his demands. His life had become insanely complicated with too much intrigue. He eyed the chaotic activity on the beach, cursed, and then cursed some more.

"Damn my uncle, what treachery is the man instigating?"

The chief's galley hit the shallows and six men jumped out to secure the boat alongside the others. Allaine and Donald strode toward them, Jamie and Stephen following. Finn held back as if uncertain.

Archibald hoped Elspeth's handfasted husband didn't bolt before they shared words. He hurdled over the side of the galley into the shallow water, making haste to reach the approaching men on shore. Noting the abundance of visible weapons, he hesitated. *Damn.* He'd sailed into a hornet's nest.

"What in blazes goes on here?" he snapped and glared at his uncle.

"Hail cousin, we bear dire tidings." Allaine, always the peacemaker, split from the others and hurried to his side. "Lady Elspeth has been kidnapped by Alexander Campbell and Maclay."

"How?" Archibald closed his eyes, concern and guilt pooling in his gut. "I ordered her kept under guard in her chamber."

At the low growl, he flipped his gaze to Finn's angry stare. The man strode forward, hands fisted and radiating aggression. Donald gripped the man's arm and stopped his advance, murmuring something to him Archibald couldn't hear. Finn held in place though his hostility remained evident.

"You are a young fool, Archie. Your Campbell friend," Donald spit on the ground, "kens the castle same as every MacLachlan. He snuck in with Maclay, incapacitated Jamie and stole our Elspeth. We endeavor to get her back."

Archibald lowered his head, the enormity of his mistakes heavy on his shoulders. This had the potential to end badly and risk war. He refused to think of the potential for Elspeth to be hurt or worse.

"Are you going to stop us?" Finn lunged.

Before Archibald moved into a defensive stance, Duncan tackled Finn. With the smack of fists, grunts and curses, two more guards joined the fray. Once subdued, the guards held Finn and dragged him before Archibald while the lad thrashed between them.

Duncan stepped aside and spat blood. "What in hell is the matter with you? You dinnae go after the chief. 'Twill ring your death knell."

Archibald raised a hand, silencing Duncan. He stared at Finn.

"I made a pledge the day I rescued Lady Laurie from the clutches of Maclay. I vowed to protect her with my life. I would not wish to upset her by killing her kin. 'Twas an error imprisoning you." He offered his arm in apology. "Release him."

The guards stepped away, leaving Finn standing before Archibald. The lad's head hung forward. His breath heaved, in and out, his chest puffing like an overexerted warhorse. Archibald dropped his arm to his side and waited.

Finally, the lad seemed to gain control. He raised his head, his eyes clouded with anguish.

"My only desire is to save Elspeth."

"We are in accord. Will you accept my apology?"

Finn gave an abrupt nod. Both men reached out at the same time, grasping forearms in a warrior's embrace. Stepping back, Archibald glanced at the castle. Betrayal tightened his jaw. He'd believed Alexander a friend before the debacle over Elspeth's betrothal. How could he have been so wrong?

"I may have been wrong about Campbell stealing your sword," he grudgingly admitted.

Finn raised a brow. "You think?"

The sarcasm wasn't lost on Archibald. "Aye. We may find your sword before this is done."

"I certainly hope so."

"Then let us go rescue my sister."

Finn accepted the apology and the extra twenty men Archibald brought to the fight, though he couldn't forget if it hadn't been for Elspeth's kidnapping, he'd still be wasting away in the MacLachlan pit. He needed to take Elspeth away from the ignorance and violence of this time to the future where she'd be safe.

First things, first. They must free her from Alexander's clutches.

Finn stared at the royal fortification known as Skipness Castle and tripped over his modern mind. Doubt plagued him. What was he doing here? Did he really think they could lay siege to a stronghold of the Scottish king without major consequences?

What happened to his resolve not to alter history?

He sighed hard and dragged a hand through his hair. How did he know what was meant to be? What fate decreed?

He shook his head. He could only hope things worked out for the best.

Finn said a silent prayer then turned his attention to matters of the moment.

The main entrance to Skipness was reached by a sea approach, defended by a gate tower with a portcullis, and with machiolation used to drop stones or fire heated sand on attackers. Archibald and Duncan, and five MacLachlan galleys rowed into position to ensure no one approached or escaped the castle by water.

The front gate wouldn't be their means of access. Having fostered under a Campbell master at Skipness, Allaine assured

Finn a weak spot existed at the rear of the castle.

Finn watched the remaining men spread out and disappear into shadows to encircle the rest of the castle. After dark, they would take advantage of the castle's weak point.

"Come, lad." Allaine grasped his shoulder. "We will get your lady back."

Finn followed the older man into the woods. They used available cover, stalking from tree to tree, making their way to the rear of the castle where two additional towers stood guard over a land assault.

From their vantage point in the trees, Finn and his companions could see across the massive field surrounding the rear and sides of the castle and observe if anyone arrived or departed the castle via land.

"There is a bolthole hidden beyond that mound." Allaine leaned close and pointed.

A large raindrop hit Finn's forehead, and he glared at the darkening sky.

Great. Just great.

Patrick MacLachlan's words replayed in his mind. *"You must learn to fight under every circumstance. That includes rain. Could save your miserable life someday."*

Finn's stomach lurched, and nerves made him doubt his ability. His sword skills were impressive when he trained with his claymore. He'd fought like the amateur he was when he used a borrowed sword and ended up injured.

Did his claymore have special powers? Was it the sword in Rory MacNaughton's stories? Could his claymore be enchanted? The lure of such magic would explain why Alexander stole it.

Finn sucked in a breath and let it out slowly, hefting the weight of the borrowed claymore he would use for battle. He'd trained since his recovery like a demon. Would his newfound skills be enough?

They would have to be. He straightened his shoulders.

Horns sounded an alarm from within the castle walls. They no longer had surprise on their side. Finn shot his gaze to the battlements. Through the teeming rain and developing mist, heads and shoulders of guards hovered above the parapet as the Campbell men scrambled to take defensive positions.

Holy shit! Finn gulped.

This was for real. They were laying siege to a castle. He raised his chin, stiffened his resolve.

Finn was prepared to die to gain Elspeth's freedom.

Elspeth pressed a hand against her racing heart, startled by three horn blasts sounding an alarm. She flew to the window and flung open the shutters. Rain sprayed the front of her favorite silver gown. She didn't care if the dress was ruined. Through the mist, her brother's galleys approached. She wanted to rejoice.

He'd come to her rescue.

Holy Mother Mary, she needed to get out of this chamber before Alexander came for her and used her against her brother. If Archibald successfully freed her from Alexander's control, she'd convince her brother to release Finn from the MacLachlan pit and she'd agree to travel with her husband to the future.

Desperation along with hope spurred her on. She must escape.

Elspeth crept to the chamber door. She leaned with her ear pressed to a crack in the heavy oak, the only sound the now familiar creak of floorboards as her guard shifted position. On silent feet, she scurried across the chamber to the desk. With stealth, she searched the drawers for something she could use to break free.

Alexander had been thorough in preparing her chamber. She found nothing of use. Plopping onto the mattress, she released a frustrated breath and ran a determined gaze over the walls of her velvet prison. There must be a way out other than through the bolted door.

She leapt from the bed and starting in one corner of the

chamber, slid her hand over every stone, one by one, hoping to trigger a mechanism to open a hidden doorway into a secret passage. All castles had them within family quarters for urgent escapes. The trick was to find the latch that would set her free.

Screeree.

Elspeth stiffened. Had she heard something?

She held still, straining to hear. *Screeree.* Ah, scratching within the wall. She pulled back a colorful tapestry depicting a bloody battle scene and listened again. *Screeree.* Gooseflesh bubbled on her arms and a chill crawled along her spine.

Lunging forward, she worked the stones, jumping back when a door slid open, exposing a dank passageway. She swallowed hard, searching for courage. Elspeth stiffened her spine, raised her leg to step forward, but before she could enter the passageway, a small pudgy hand reached out, grabbed her by the wrist and yanked her into the dark recess.

Another hand clamped over her mouth, muffling her instinctive scream. "'Tis me. Your loyal Munn."

Elspeth relaxed her body and accepted the brownie's assistance to stand on her own.

"How did you find me?" she whispered, hoping the guard outside the chamber door hadn't heard the commotion.

"Magic." He grasped her hand and tugged her along the dark passageway. He must be able to see better than she. It took all her concentration to follow him without tripping. "Where are you taking me?"

"To Caitrina."

"The faerie?"

"Aye, the *sìthiche* will help you."

Elspeth prayed Caitrina was capable of conjuring miracles.

Alexander stood back from the wall, out of reach of an archer's arrow, and glared at the galleys blockading the entrance to his new home. Anger and fear twisted in his gut. King James would fly into a rage if he learned he kidnapped

Lady Elspeth. He didn't want to think what the king would do to him if the royal resistance received damage in the process of Alexander proving his superiority over the MacLachlans.

How could one woman cause such problems?

He never should have kidnapped Elspeth. Although the broken betrothal angered him, he didn't really want her. Jonet filled his needs.

There were other ways to get even with Archibald. Alexander should have gone for the jugular instead. Brokered a betrothal with Lamont for Isobell to wed a Campbell chieftain.

Isobell wed to another would ruin the high and mighty Archibald MacLachlan. Instead, Alexander stole Elspeth from her home without thinking it through.

The dream made him do it. At least he thought it was a dream.

At the time, it seemed real.

In the dream, the most beautiful woman he'd ever seen seduced him. Her image was blurry now, though he remembered feeling lust and giving her a vow. He promised to keep the MacIntyre warrior and Lady Elspeth apart.

Pledging his troth made sense at the time. Now—not so much.

The sound of approaching boots snapped his gaze to the grimacing Maclay striding toward him from the wheel stair. Just what he needed—more bad news. "What is it, man?"

"Lady Elspeth is gone from her chamber."

Alexander cursed, fisted his hands and gnashed his teeth. "Have you searched?"

"Aye. Do you want to send out guards with dogs?"

"Nae, we need our manpower concentrated on the walls."

"I have other disturbing news." Maclay shifted position and avoided looking him in the eye. "Warriors hide within the trees surrounding the castle."

"Damn MacLachlan. Damn MacIntyre." They had to be who orchestrated this assault. He should have expected as much. Alexander barely resisted kicking the stone wall. "We have so recently arrived. The castle is not yet provisioned to withstand a siege and we lack enough men to counter a heavy attack."

"Perhaps there is another way." Maclay's scarred lip curled into a crooked grin.

"Speak, man."

"Challenge MacIntyre to one-on-one combat. Winner gets the wench."

Alexander digested the suggestion. Maybe he could use Lady Elspeth after all and go through with his original plan of using her gift and the enchanted sword to topple the king, but…

"Lady Elspeth is gone." How had he forgotten? She always foiled his plans.

"The wench cannae get past the guards. She cannae get out of the castle. Besides, her kin dinnae need ken she has gone missing."

"What if I lose? The MacIntyre warrior could demand further retribution."

"How can you lose armed with the enchanted sword?"

"See to it my message is received," Alexander bellowed. "For the right to wed Elspeth MacLachlan, I challenge Finn MacIntyre to single combat to the death."

CHAPTER TWENTY-THREE

Alexander descended dank stairwell after stairwell, deep into the bowels of Skipness Castle. He lengthened his stride when he neared the wizard's new lair. His fingers itched with anticipation. He couldn't wait to wrap his hands around the hilt of the faerie-kissed sword.

He would possess unfathomable power.

With a quick nod to the guard, he set the torch in a holder on the wall and pushed open the oak boards haphazardly lashed together to form a door. "Seumas?"

Dim yellow light from burning candles in niches and hanging overhead proved the chamber empty of its inhabitant. Where in Satan's hell was the wizard? Where in Satan's hell was the sword? "Seumas?" Alexander shouted.

Receiving no response, he stuck his head around the door into the passageway and glowered at the guard, who jumped to attention. "Did you see the wizard?"

"Not since I came on duty, my lord. No one has come or gone."

"Must everyone set out to annoy me?" Alexander snarled. Idiots. He was surrounded by idiots. "Search the castle for the old man. You are of nae use here."

Keeping his rising displeasure in check with much effort,

Alexander watched the man leave then ducked into the wizard's chamber. Herbs hung from rafters, their earthy scent mingling with a flowery fragrance, which seemed somehow familiar. The image of a beautiful emerald-eyed, flame-haired woman teased his thoughts. His blood ran heavy. The fae woman teased him. His annoyance escalated, and he pushed away the ethereal image. He didn't have time for such unattainable foolishness.

Gritting his teeth, he directed his attention to the wizard's work area. Pots and magic apparatus cluttered worktables and shelves. Alexander tossed aside a pile of rags, hoping to uncover the claymore, finding naught.

He searched in barrels and hampers. In cupboards and under tables.

Alexander pushed into the attached sleeping quarters. The wizard's possessions were scattered about in an untidy mess. Piles of leather-bound books lay on the stone floor and shared cluttered tables with rolls of yellowed parchment. Discarded garments draped the lot. In a fit of frustration, Alexander tossed the bedclothes from the narrow mattress to the floor. The claymore had to be there somewhere.

By the time he finished searching both chambers, his jaw hurt from the tight grip he held on his anger. He must find the sword before he met the MacIntyre warrior in personal combat.

The sound of scratching against wood in the passageway drew his attention. Alexander shot his gaze to the door as a rat wearing a wee soiled *leine* scurried through a crack and stopped short. Its beady eyes popped and it hopped into the air when it saw his glare. Then the wee beastie rushed to retreat.

"Whoa, old man." Alexander strode forward.

The rat's whiskers twitched then its garment-covered body stretched and bloated, transforming into the wily wizard.

Alexander clutched the front of Seumus's *leine*, holding the coarse fabric in a tight fist as he leaned his face close to the other man's. "Where. Is. My. Sword?"

The wizard's eyes rounded with fear and a lump at his throat bobbed. He swallowed hard. "Gone."

"Gone where?" Alexander gritted through clenched teeth.

"I napped. When I woke, the sword was gone. Vanished."

"Why should I believe such?"

"'Tis true, I swear." The man trembled in his grasp.

Alexander tossed the old man aside. Seumus hit the wall and slid to sit on the floor.

"If you were not a favorite of my father's I would clamp you in chains."

"Not my fault." Seumus held his hands up in front of him. "Someone stole your sword."

"Who?"

The wizard's lips curled downward and he darted his gaze about the chamber as if he feared others more than he feared Alexander's wrath. "I smelled the cloying scent of *Sithichean* magic when I awoke," Seumus whispered in a quivering voice.

Alexander clenched his fists and uttered foul curses. "Is your magic not stronger?"

The old man's face reddened and he shrank in size, replaced by the sniveling rat. The rat dashed across the floor, slipping through broken mortar to disappear into the stone wall.

"Blasted hell." Alexander stomped from the chamber, up the many stone steps, to the great hall where he found Maclay lounging as if he hadn't a care in the world. "The sword is gone." Alexander glared at the man. "Get off your arse and find it."

With a shrug of one shoulder, the man stood. "Time is running out. You need to devise another plan."

"Are you mad? I am out of options."

"Post an archer in a tree within range of the MacIntyre warrior. If it appears the fight is going his way…" Maclay mimicked shooting an arrow.

"How will we do that? The MacLachlan men will watch everyone who leaves the castle before and during the fight.

They will be on guard against foul play."

"Then invite them in."

"Into the castle? With Elspeth missing? Are you crazy?"

"Finding her is of no import until you win. MacIntyre and MacLachlan have already agreed to your terms. And if the wench escapes, her brother will turn her over to you in order to meet the terms of the agreement or lose his precious honor."

Alexander scratched his chin. Maclay's plan had merit. "See to it then. We will battle at dawn in the courtyard in range of the large oak tree."

Finn spent the night awake, lying on the hard ground, worrying about Elspeth. He refused to fail her. Anxiety hummed in his veins. He took a deep breath in an attempt to center himself. On the third inhale, determination swelled within his chest.

"Ready, lad?" Donald held out a hand and pulled him to his feet.

With a wary eye to the battlements, the MacLachlan warriors crossed the field and entered the castle proper. A crowd milled about, anxious for the fighting to begin. MacLachlans clustered to one side, Campbells on the other. Alexander stood on the bottom step of the keep, his claymore resting at his side. Maclay was nowhere to be seen. Nor was Elspeth.

Finn scanned the warrior-filled courtyard, unhappy with his visiting team status. He'd much prefer a home advantage or the next best tactic of meeting on neutral ground.

As CEO, he preferred meeting on his turf when the outcome of deals was uncertain. If impossible, he pushed for a hotel conference.

He couldn't wait to return to his own world, where he was master of his destiny. Finn sighed heavily. It would be a while before he could go home. Even if he survived this confrontation with Campbell, Maclay still needed to die.

Otherwise, Laurie would never be safe. There would always be the risk Maclay would learn the secret of the time portal. They had spied the man near the enchanted garden gate just prior to Finn's time traveling adventure.

He swallowed to moisten his dry throat. He straightened his shoulders, held his head high, and strode across the stone courtyard, stopping in front of Alexander.

"Where is Elspeth?" He held his borrowed claymore with two hands, point down, in front of him. "I want to see her before we begin."

"She is indisposed at the moment."

"How do I know she is unharmed?" Finn reflexively tightened his hold on the sword.

"She remains unscathed, for now. You will have to trust my word."

"Like I believe assurances from an abuser of women," Finn scoffed.

Alexander's nostrils flared and his face reddened but then he got himself under control. He flicked his gaze to the castle tower. Finn followed the line of the man's gaze to a high window, where he caught a glimpse of blond hair, perhaps lightened by the morning sun. Finn gnashed his molars in frustration. He couldn't be sure it was Elspeth, but had to believe she was okay. He wouldn't be able to breathe if she were hurt or worse.

"Fine. Let's get on with it."

Alexander leapt from the stoop and swirled around into a fighting stance, his claymore extended, pointing toward Finn's eyes. Their gazes locked. Held. Tension escalated.

Finn ran through his mind the hand and foot positions he'd practiced. Mastered. Move by move.

His right hand under the cross guard, his left just above the pommel, he stepped forward with his lead foot into the on-guard position, holding the cross guard at head level and the blade pointing diagonally upward. As they circled, he dropped the blade to a forward position to ward Alexander's first cut with the flat of his blade. The impacting vibration sizzled over Finn's bulging arm muscles, and he twisted his wrists to counterstrike.

The crowd surged as Finn and Alexander fought around small obstacles and avoided a loaded cart.

The dance flowed. Finn's feet slid over the stone paving in patterned moves. He leapt, swinging his hips, giving power to each strike. The cling and clang of steel against steel reverberated in the small courtyard with chops and cuts and wards. Rolling from one blow to another, the zone possessed Finn, thrilled him, until his arms and legs grew weak.

Too late, he realized Alexander's tactic. The man held back, pretending ineptitude, allowing Finn to tire, and then swooped in on the offensive. An excessively aggressive cut whistled along the edge of Finn's sword. He lost his balance and stumbled.

The next cut came from the side. Finn rolled his hips back to avoid getting sliced across the belly. A near miss. He barely warded the next blow.

The crowd roared.

Finn would die. *Damn*. He hadn't meant for things to end this way.

Alexander's next chop arced from above. Finn bounded out of the way, laboring to breathe. The force of the downward momentum imbedded the blade into the wooden frame of a water trough. Alexander struggled to free the sword, his chest heaving, giving Finn time to gulp air, catch his breath.

A flash of light on metal distracted him and he reluctantly flicked his gaze away from his opponent, fearing someone else joined the fray. What the hell? Caitrina stood to the side, at the front of gaping warriors, holding Finn's claymore, its embedded moonstone glowing. She grinned and tossed the sword.

The blade spiraled in slow motion, end over end, through the air.

He jerked his gaze back to Alexander. The man stared at the whirling sword with lust.

Finn read the man's intent, dropped the borrowed sword he held and lunged for his claymore. Before either he or Alexander grabbed hold, a most beautiful woman appeared out of thin air and snatched the spinning sword out of their reach.

She glared at Caitrina.

"The mortals must finish without magic." Then the exquisite blond flashed Finn an enchanting smile.

He inclined his head, accepting what he hoped was encouragement. While Alexander regained his balance, Finn swooped down, retrieved the discarded sword from the ground and spun in time to dodge his opponent's next thrust. The fighting ground on.

Finn's strength ebbed. He needed to make every move count. Sucking as much air into his lungs as he could, he concentrated on his feelings for Elspeth. The way he felt when they were together. He imagined strawberry-blond hair brushing across his bare chest when they made love. He pictured her in his mind. The tilt of her stubborn chin. The curl of her lips when she smiled. The molten fire in her silver eyes.

Her compassion drew him like a moth to flame.

She'd called to him through time and space. She made him whole. He loved her with all his heart.

He caught sight of Elspeth in the crowd. Unsure whether she was real or a figment of his imagination, he pivoted toward Alexander and blocked the man's assault. Finn would finish this for her. He drew willpower from deep within. His blood hummed. Strength returned to his muscles.

The fight raged on. Cuts following chops, he deflected each opposing blow. Gathering his newfound strength, he went on the offensive, counterattacking faster than his opponent. Something whizzed past his head and red-hot pain seared his ear. He disregarded the sting and kept fighting. Sweat ran over his face, dripped into his eyes. He ignored the distraction.

Finn wore Alexander down. The man faltered and

stumbled. His blade slid from his slippery hands. With a diagonal cut, Finn threatened the man's jugular.

The crowd erupted with jeers and cheers.

He froze, breathing hard. Could he kill the man?

Through the roar of raging blood, Finn heard the voice of an angel.

Elspeth stood behind Alexander, her eyes pleading. "Please. Spare his life."

Elspeth couldn't swallow past the lump in her throat. As much as she despised Alexander, she didn't want the man's blood on her husband's hands.

Finn's hate-filled stare burned into the man pinned by his sword.

"You must not take his life." She hoped her plea broke through Finn's battle lust.

A whole-body shudder claimed him. Then without sparing her a glance, he leaned into his sword only hard enough to draw a bead of blood.

"I *should* kill you."

Alexander worked his mouth, but no words passed his lips.

"Don't ever forget, Elspeth is *my* wife." Finn withdrew his blade, spun on his heel, and walked away, leaving Elspeth staring after him. Had she angered him? In time, would he understand?

The boisterous crowd quieted, parted for Finn. The MacLachlan men swarmed her husband, congratulating him, pounding him on his back and shoulders.

She glanced at the man at her feet. Alexander clutched his throat, as if seriously wounded. Tears filled his red-rimmed eyes. She stepped around the whimpering fool and ran after her husband.

Her uncle stopped her before she reached the crowd surrounding Finn. "Leave the lad alone for a wee. Give him time to come back to himself."

"But he is bleeding."

"He will hardly notice until the rage leaves him."

"Do you think I was wrong to ask him to spare Alexander's life?"

"My opinion is of nae matter. You should pose your question to your husband."

"Aye."

Her plea to Finn was the right thing to do. She felt positive he'd regret his action later had he killed Alexander. Once he thought clearly, Finn would see the wisdom in her request.

Another imposing figure muscled his way through the crowd, strode across the courtyard, shoving Campbells and Maclays out of his way, stopping in front of her.

"Are you all right?" Archibald slid his concerned gaze over her. "I owe you an apology. I never should have ordered you and Finn locked up."

She stared long and hard at her brother. He'd changed much since becoming clan chief. He had believed he meant well and done the right thing. Could she forgive his domineering ways?

"Will you imprison us again?" Elspeth lifted her chin to level her eyes on her brother.

"Nae, 'twas a mistake. I hope you can find it in your heart to forgive me once again."

Elspeth leapt into his embrace. "I love you, brother mine."

Archibald cleared his throat, patted her back and gave her a squeeze before releasing her.

Seeing Finn standing behind her brother, his expression guarded, made her stomach tighten. Archibald stepped out of the way, and she gently touched the side of Finn's face where blood from the grazing arrow welled. "You are bleeding."

"Ouch!" His eyes widened when she withdrew bloody fingers. "How?"

Elspeth pointed to the dead archer beneath the oak tree.

Uncle Donald stepped forward. "Someone shot him as he pulled back on his bow, aiming for your heart. The arrow

231

missed its mark and grazed near your ear instead."

Finn brushed his fingers over the shallow wound. "I didn't feel it before, but I do now."

"You are lucky to be alive, lad." Donald glanced from Finn to Elspeth and back. "I think you two need a few private minutes. I will keep the others away."

"Does it hurt much?" Elspeth asked after her uncle strode off, stalling, trying to think of what to say to explain why she begged he spare Alexander's life.

"Nah, I'm okay." Finn leaned in close and opened his arms.

She stepped into his sweaty embrace. "Are you angry with me?"

"Whatever for? Wasn't your fault you were kidnapped."

"Nae, for requesting you spare Alexander's life."

Finn held her at arms length. Warmth shone in his beloved hazel eyes. "You were right to stop me. I would regret killing the man later had I acted in the heat of the fight." His grip tightened on her arms. "You won't be safe unless I take you to my time. Will you travel with me to the future?"

Elspeth didn't hesitate. "Aye, I will happily accompany you to your home."

Finn's lips, soft and sweet, slid across hers in a tender mating. She moaned and leaned in, pouring her relief and love for him into the kiss. He took them deeper, delving into the recesses of her mouth. Her head buzzed with pleasure, and she matched his urgency, twirling her tongue with his as heat raced to her toes. She melted, wanting more.

"Stop him!"

The bellow shocked them apart, and they spun in unison toward the sharp voice. A MacLachlan warrior waved his claymore in the air, his angry stare directed at the horse and rider galloping away as if chased by a *banshee*, a faerie harbinger of death keening at his heels.

Maclay was escaping.

CHAPTER TWENTY-FOUR

*M*acLachlan warriors bolted for their horses. Finn was torn. Elspeth clung to his arm.

"Come now, lad," Donald bellowed before dashing across the field to where the horses remained tethered.

"I must go." Finn hated to leave her, but Maclay wouldn't wait.

Elspeth raised her chin, her jaw tight. "I am coming with you."

"No, you aren't." He removed her hand from his arm, adamant she remain behind. He couldn't take her where he was going. Who knew how long it would take to catch up with Maclay? Who knew what dangers awaited?

Archibald stepped forward and gently grasped her arm. "Beth, stay with me. I sail for home."

"Finn…" Elspeth held out her arm in entreaty. "Please."

"I need to do this, and need to know you're safe."

Allaine MacLachlan dashed by with several men, Stephen MacEwen on their heels. Stephen slowed. "The bastard is getting away. Hurry!" Then he, too, ran toward the horses.

Campbell's men grumbled amongst themselves. None moved to follow, leaving Maclay to the MacLachlans and fate.

"I can't take you with me. I'll be back soon." Finn sidestepped away, talking to Elspeth as he moved.

"What are you waiting for? We need to leave!" Jamie hurried past.

Archibald caught Finn's gaze. "Go. I will take care of Beth and see to it Alexander is punished."

Finn stared at Elspeth for a moment then sprinted across the field, chasing Jamie. He mounted the horse held out to him by one of the lads and jerked a glance over his shoulder. Elspeth strained against her brother's grip, trying to break free. Though they didn't always agree, he needed to trust Archibald to keep her safe.

With a kick to his flank, Finn encouraged the horse into action, and they shot after the MacLachlan men. He hoped his wife wasn't foolish enough to try to escape and follow them.

Tears swam in Elspeth's eyes as the men rode away. She blinked several times, refusing to shed them. Finn looked back once then kept going. *Infuriating man.* Anger roiled to the surface, and she kicked her brother in the shins.

"Ouch." He pursed his lips, but didn't lesson the hold on her arm. "You cannot go where he is going."

"Why not?" she demanded.

"Because…" Archibald's face reddened, and he sputtered, "It is too dangerous."

Elspeth let her shoulders slump. It wasn't fair men were so much stronger. "What if Finn gets hurt? What if he needs my healing skills?"

Her brother's scowl softened. "Our lads will stand with him. He will fight better if he kens you are safe at home."

"I will take you to him." Caitrina joined them, leading two beautiful horses.

"Oh, please, do." Hope leapt within Elspeth's chest.

Archibald jerked his gaze to the faerie and shook his head. "Revenge is not pretty. What will happen between Finn and Maclay is not meant for the tender sensibilities of well-bred ladies."

"After what I have been through with Alexander, you dare to speak such?"

Caitrina grasped the golden bridle of a handsome white steed. The bridle shimmered in the light and golden bells plaited in the stallion's mane tinkled when he shook his head. From a jewel-encrusted sheath attached to the horse's saddle, Caitrina withdrew Finn's moonstone-adorned sword. She held the claymore in the air with two hands, the gem glowing bright.

"I take Finn the sword of the fae and his wife. 'Twill be best for you to say your goodbyes. Elspeth will not return to Castle Lachlan. Fate has other plans for her and Finn and their future son."

Moisture filled Elspeth's eyes once again. This time with wonder and happiness. She would have a son. Finn would survive.

Archibald sighed heavily once he realized he wouldn't win the argument. He stared at Caitrina. She nodded as if she read his thoughts.

"Elspeth is going to that future place." Not a question from her brother—a statement. Aye, Archibald had changed much.

Tiny faerie wings tickled the inside of Elspeth's belly as anticipation grew. "I love you, brother mine." She wrapped her arms around his waist, stood on the tips of her toes and kissed his cheek.

"And I, you." He wrapped his arms around her and hugged her close.

Do you really believe our parents live in the future?" he asked after he released her.

"I will tell them you miss them."

Archibald gave an abrupt nod, cupped his hands and helped Elspeth mount the gray horse Caitrina provided. Though not as grandly adorned as his companion, the stallion stood tall and proud.

Elspeth patted his neck and murmured nonsensical words

to calm him, or was it she who needed calming?

Caitrina gracefully leapt into the saddle, spoke to the animal in a strange language, and horse and rider surged forward, flying across the open field at a gallop. Caitrina's long red hair billowed behind her with the wind.

"Go." Archibald smacked the gray's rump, sending Elspeth's horse into motion. "God be with you."

Finn glanced behind them for the umpteenth time.

"What's wrong?" Stephen asked from his position riding beside him.

"I fear we're being followed." The back of Finn's neck had felt like ants marched across it since they rode away from Skipness Castle.

Stephen twisted around in his saddle. "I see naught but the dust kicked up by our horses."

"Must be my imagination."

"I am not one to dismiss the warnings of my gut, nor will I disregard what you suspect. We should send a scout to confirm none of Campbell's men are in pursuit." Stephen kicked his horse and galloped ahead to talk to Donald and Allaine, and set a man to the task.

The scout found no sign men followed.

One day led into the next, and next, and next.

Finn scratched the back of his neck unable to shake the sense someone tracked them. Setting aside his suspicion, he leaned forward in the saddle and stared at the endless grass. The trail they followed weaved, circled, disappeared and reappeared.

Then disappeared again.

Ten days passed before the MacLachlan men found fresh tracks leading into the forest east of the Fir-wood. At some point during the pursuit, Maclay rendezvoused with men loyal to him and they now camped near steep cliffs overlooking a ravine and the river.

Finn crept on his belly, hidden within underbrush at the

edge of Maclay's camp. Moving silently over the layer of dead leaves, he eased next to Stephen. "How many?"

"We are evenly matched. Our twelve against his twenty."

Finn's gut clenched, not quite even, but he respected the abilities of his Highlander friends. He felt proud to fight beside them again. He had faith they would prevail.

His muscles tensed and he bared his teeth when Maclay walked into his line of vision. He had to force himself not to lunge for the man. Stephen placed a reassuring hand on his upper arm, and Finn released the breath jammed in his lungs.

Stephen squeezed his arm in signal, and they crabbed backward out of the thicket and ghosted through the trees for the quarter mile to where the rest of the MacLachlan men waited.

"What did you learn?" Allaine asked when they joined the others.

"Twenty men. Heavily armed," Stephen reported.

"Maclay is with them," Finn said through gritted teeth.

"Good." Donald swept his gaze over the early evening sky. Shades of vermilion colored the western horizon.

"Gloaming will fall within a few hours. We should attack after dark. After they have filled their bellies with meat and whisky and they snore in their plaids, we can ambush them." He rubbed his chin. "The moon is waxing, will be full tomorrow, and since nae clouds clutter the sky, we should have enough light to fight. What do you think, lad?"

Finn started and eyed the man, surprised Donald asked his opinion.

"Although we all despise Maclay, the right to take him down is yours as Lady Laurie's kin."

"Then we attack after nightfall, after the moon brightens the sky." Finn nodded, determined to finish this tonight. He wanted to collect Elspeth and move on with their life together. Take her home to the future, away from the brutality of the past.

An hour slipped by. Two. Finn paced, restless, edgy with anticipation. Dusk approached with chilled air and lengthening shadows. Still they waited.

When the other men hunkered down, huddled within their wool plaids, Finn developed a sweat. Downwind from the enemy camp, he inhaled wood smoke and the scent of roasting meat. He tried to ignore his growling stomach. Oatcakes didn't do much to curb one's appetite.

The lads assigned to watch the comings and goings at Maclay's camp were relieved. Still they waited.

Another couple of hours passed. Finn was ready to climb out of his skin.

"Easy, lad," Donald warned. "Will not be long now, we only wait for the rabble to sleep."

"Aye." Finn should be used to waiting. In the corporate world, he was known for his tenacity, waiting out his opponents during negotiations to make the best deal.

The need for revenge didn't seem to work the same way. At least not for him. He was twitchy with impatience.

A twig snapped, shooting Finn's gaze to the darkening woods. Allaine strode from the trees, returning from scouting the enemy's camp. "'Tis time."

Finally. Finn inhaled several deep breaths, leaning on his military training, summoning his confidence, allowing it to emerge and harden.

He wished they had night goggles, instead of relying on moonlight. Thinking fast, he retrieved a white *leine* from his bedroll and shredded the fabric into several strips. Handing a couple to Allaine, he said, "Each man is to tie a strip around their left arm. That way, we'll know friend from foe."

The MacLachlan men guided their horse into the trees, scattering the animals so the enemy couldn't capture the horses as a group. Stomach tight, Finn looped his reins over a low-hanging branch. He removed the sheath containing the borrowed claymore from his horse, and strapped it to his back. His mouth and throat suddenly dry, he swallowed hard.

He would end this now—for Patrick, for Laurie.

Dressed in cattle-hide breeches and leather shirt instead of *leine* and plaid, Finn joined Stephen deeper in the trees.

"Are you ready?" Stephen asked.

"Aye." Restless anticipation hummed along Finn's nerves. "Let's get this done."

Stephen nodded and they padded through the woods in silence. Smoldering campfires fouled the air near the enemy's camp. Stephen kept close to Finn. His birdcall signaled the others to encircle the clearing. Maclay had stationed two guards on the peripheral of the camp, easily taken down with a clout to the head. Finn had insisted no one be killed unnecessarily.

Only Maclay needed to meet his maker.

Hidden in the shadow of a large tree, Finn studied the lay of the campsite lit by the nearly-full moon. Embers burned in the pit-fires. He counted eight wool-wrapped men lying close to the sparse heat of one pit and ten near another, uttering loud snores. With the two guards taken out, two men were left unaccounted for. Maybe they both slept in the makeshift tent off to the side.

A cough came from the far side of the clearing. Finn jerked his gaze to the sound. A tipsy man staggered into the bushes and pissed. In a flash, a MacLachlan warrior clocked him over the head with the pommel of his sword. The man's body hit the ground hard.

Finn held his breath. If anyone remained awake, they certainly heard the thump.

The flap of the tent opened, and Maclay stuck out his head. Wasting no time, Finn whistled, and the MacLachlan warriors burst from hiding.

The men near the fire-pit woke, drawing weapons from within the folds of their plaids.

War cries rent the air. Battle erupted.

One goal consumed Finn. Take down Maclay.

Finn darted across the clearing, drawing his sword from the sheath strapped to his back as he ran. Maclay growled and met the aggressive first cut with the flat of his sword. The reverberation vibrated up Finn's arm, causing him to grit his teeth. The clang of steel rang in his ears, deafening him to the chaos surrounding him.

Both men circled. Taunted. "I want naught less than absolute vengeance against the MacLachlans," Maclay raged.

"And I want revenge for what you did to my cousin, Lady Laurie MacLachlan."

"Naught but a whore." Maclay spat on the ground.

"Go to hell." Finn charged, warded Maclay's blow and body-slammed the man. Maclay staggered back. Planting his feet, Finn sliced the sword down and took a chunk out of the bastard's thigh.

Blood spewed, spattering his face and arms. Curses polluted the air. Finn leapt back, dodging the sloppy counterstrike. Maclay raised his weapon, presenting Finn an opportunity.

Sweat burned his eyes, but he controlled the fight. Taking a gamble, Finn raised his claymore and thrust to the throat, a move only used by the most experienced fighters.

Caught unprepared, Maclay swiveled his hips and leaned his upper body back out of harm's way, swung his sword in an arc to counter, lost his balance and his torso heaved unwieldy to the side. He tried to throw his weight in the other direction, but the momentum caused him to slip and slide backwards. Unable to recover, his injured leg weak, he went over the side, arms flailing.

Finn ran to the edge of the cliff and looked over. Dislodged stones rolled and bounced off boulders to land far below. Broken branches and debris declared the path of the bastard's descent. Leaning farther over, Finn glimpsed the prone body lying in a pile of rubble, a leg twisted in an unnatural position.

"No one could survive a fall like that," Stephen said.

Finn flinched at the sound of the man's voice, unaware the blond warrior joined him.

When he shook his head to shed his battle rage, he realized the clearing was quiet. The fighting had ended. Maclay's men were dead except for the two guards and the man who'd taken a piss in the bushes. The MacLachlan's lost one of their own.

The loss of life would haunt Finn for the rest of his days.

Elspeth stomped through the moonlit forest, leading her horse, glaring at the back of Caitrina's head. "I thought you were taking me to Finn. We have traveled in their dust for ten days, and still we have not met up with him and the other MacLachlan warriors."

Maybe her husband had been right. Maybe she should have stayed with her brother.

"Shh!" Caitrina snapped and halted.

What now?

Then she heard it. Steel clanging against steel. The sound of many swords.

Elspeth froze. Her heart raced. An intense sounding battle ensued not far from where she and Caitrina stood. Elspeth's mouth went dry. Was Finn fighting? "What do we do?"

"We wait until they finish."

How could she wait, believing Finn was involved? His life at risk? Elspeth dropped the reins and reached for the hilt of the sword attached to Caitrina's horse. "He needs his sword."

Caitrina wrapped her hand around Elspeth's wrist, stopping her. "He proved during his fight with Alexander, he doesn't require my magic."

"Then why bring him the claymore?"

"The sword is for your son's destiny. Trust in your husband."

Elspeth overlooked the comment about her unborn son's future, instead envisioning Finn's sandy hair falling into his hazel eyes and his smile. His gentle touch. His determination to do what he believed right. She loved him. How could she not trust in him?

The clang of swords stilled. Elspeth couldn't wait another moment. She dashed through the wood toward the shouts of men, undergrowth tugging at her skirt, praying she heard MacLachlan voices.

She burst from the trees into a bloody field filled with dead bodies. Men from her clan ambled around, bruised, but not beaten.

Then she saw *him* standing with Stephen and Jamie.

The love of her life—uninjured.

A shiver skittered across Finn's shoulders, and he spun into a crouch, his sword raised forward in front of him, ready to face another foe.

His angel flew at him. He tossed the claymore aside, and Elspeth leapt into his arms, her unexpected weight sending him back a step, almost knocking him to the ground. He planted his feet firm. Found his balance and grasped her taut butt with his palms, drawing her tight against his sweat-covered body.

God, he loved this woman.

"You live." She grazed his cheek with her delicate touch, getting blood on her fingers, then slammed her lips against his. Finn inhaled her taste, and she slid her tongue into the moist recesses of his mouth.

Holy shit. A sizzle shot to his cock. He lost himself in his woman's kiss.

One of the other warriors cleared his throat. A male chuckle followed. He didn't care. Elspeth was safe in his arms, kissing him. Maclay was dead. They could go home.

When the kiss ended and they finally opened their eyes and pulled apart, they faced twelve grins. Caitrina had joined the others.

"I thought you would both fall dead from lack of breath," Allaine said good-naturedly.

Elspeth blushed, and Finn lowered his head so she didn't see his proud smile.

"You didn't stay with your brother." Though he didn't like that she disobeyed him, he was damn glad to see her.

She lowered her eyes, but he caught her happy smile.

Donald slapped his back. "Where to now, lad?"

Finn raised a brow to Elspeth. "We leave for France," she

said.

"I will see you on your journey," Stephen offered.

Caitrina stepped forward with Finn's sheathed sword, the moonstone in its cross-section winking at him. The weapon had caused so much trouble. Alexander's greed—the desire to possess the claymore—caused the man to hurt Elspeth. Finn almost didn't want the damn thing anymore.

"This belongs to you," she said. "It holds your son's destiny."

Finn tensed. His eyes nearly popped. His son? He flicked his gaze to Elspeth. She inclined her head and he accepted the claymore without reservation.

Satisfaction marked Caitrina's smile. "I will travel with you on your journey home."

Their escort decided upon, they said their goodbyes to the rest of the MacLachlan warriors.

Jamie hugged Elspeth in burly arms. She kissed both his cheeks. "I will miss you."

"And I you, sweet lass."

Finn accepted Jamie's arm grasp. "Give our regards to Duncan."

"Aye, please," Elspeth said from where she stood at his side.

Donald and Allain, one at a time, clasped Finn's arm in a warrior's embrace. Finn's throat closed, he hated that he and Elspeth would never see these men again.

"What will happen with Alexander?" he asked. "Although I couldn't take his life, he needs punishing."

"Nae worries. Although Alexander is the king's man, so is Archie. He will see the king exacts a heavy toll against Campbell for his crimes," Donald said. "The man will be less likely in the future to steal another's wife."

Caitrina had disappeared during the good byes. She returned with two beautiful horses. One white and one gray. Elspeth stroked the gray's face, taken with the animal.

"A belated wedding gift." Caitrina handed the reins of the gray over to Finn.

Elspeth's eyes widened. "Thank you." Caitrina lowered her gaze, seeming embarrassed by the gratitude.

Finn lifted Elspeth and she swung a leg over the horse's back and settled into the saddle.

Stephen led his and Finn's horses into the clearing. Finn removed the bloodied leather top he wore, wiped the blood from his face and chest with a cloth and pulled his spare *leine* from the saddlebags, tugging it on over his head before mounting.

As they rode away, he twisted in the saddle and raised his arm in farewell. He turned to Stephen. "Do you know where we are going?"

"Aye, the *Sithichean Sluaigh*, the cursed faerie knoll where Iain and Lady Mairi and Patrick and Lady Laurie vanished. I expect you and Elspeth will disappear too."

Obviously well familiar with the terrain, Caitrina led them through the night forest with ease. They huddled in their wools, chilled by the fog. As dawn broke, they came upon the familiar grassy mound.

Finn hoped the magic worked. Laurie claimed it could be unpredictable. He slid from his horse then assisted Elspeth and Caitrina to the ground. Stephen remained in the saddle.

"Tell Patrick, my cousin…I wish him well." His voice cracked. "*Slàinte mhòr!*"

"Good health!" Finn returned.

Stephen reined his horse around, spurred the beast and rode away into the morning mist.

"Shall we go, angel? I'll take you to your parents." Finn placed his hand on Elspeth's waist.

"I will always follow you." She blessed him with a heart-stopping smile, though her eyes remained round and anxious.

Caitrina strode onto the mound, leading her mount. "Wait," Finn said. "It won't be a full moon until tonight."

"You travel with me. I can bend the magic to my will," Caitrina assured them.

Elspeth moistened her lips and hesitantly gazed at Finn through her lashes. "Then it is time?"

His heart went out to her. He'd make her a good life in the future.

"Are you ready?"

"Aye." She straightened her back and held her head high.

"Hold tight, lass." Finn released her waist, grasped her hand, and together they led their horses onto the faerie knoll.

CHAPTER TWENTY-FIVE

Present day, Anderson Creek, North Carolina

Foxgloves closed for the evening over an hour ago. Jillian O'Donnell extended her arm and reached with the long wand to water a hanging fuchsia planter. She savored the quiet of the greenhouse and the playful red, white, and blue dangling flowers. With a sigh, she moved to the next basket, dripping water along the way, and caught the scent of petunias.

Left to her own devices, too much alone time forced her to think. She'd made an absolute ass of herself at her business partner's garden party on Thursday night, trying to attract Finn's attention. Thankfully, Laurie wasn't mad about the expensive Talavera urn Jillian broke in her haste to reach Finn before he took off. The next morning, she'd told her partner to dock her pay for the busted ceramic planter, but Laurie waved her off, preoccupied by more important matters.

The weirdest thing—Finn *had* taken off.

That night, Jillian had finished cleaning up the damaged plant, dirt, and pottery shards with the help of a few friendly guests and joined other guests for toasts when Patrick stopped mid-sentence. Laurie had gone pale, and Patrick got into what looked like a heated argument with his father. Jillian had tried to get closer to find out what was going on, but Finn's friend, Douglas, blocked her. She only heard a few nonsensical words in the Gaelic language they often spoke.

Then Finn rushed by, ran through the garden gate and disappeared into the mountain fog.

He hadn't shown up for the rest of the festival, which ended today. *Very odd.*

The other strange thing was Caitrina was also gone, though Jillian doubted Finn and Caitrina were together; she'd only ever seen animosity between the two. Maybe they'd both been avoiding her, and Laurie, and the rest of their friends.

The cell phone in her pocket vibrated. Jillian flicked off the water flow and gripped the water wand under one arm while retrieving the phone with the other hand. *Drats.* Kyle. She was tempted to let the call drop into voice mail, but her tenacious younger brother would just call back. "Yeah."

He wanted her to take a vacation and go camping and bicycling on a rail-trail along a river somewhere in West Virginia. She didn't want to go. She hated to leave Anderson Creek. It was as if she was glued in place, unable to leave, always hoping Finn would visit and finally notice her and ask her out.

Pathetic.

"I really can't get away from work right now. You know this is our busiest season. Yeah. Well, I'm scheduled to teach some workshops in August. Yeah. Maybe in the fall."

Ugh. She hated when he slipped into persuasive mode. No wonder he was a good salesman.

"Whatever. I have to get back to work."

No way was she going on vacation with her brother in September. Finn would probably be visiting. Jillian shoved the phone into her back pocket, moved on to the next hanging basket and flipped on the water.

God, when would she get it into her thick head Finn would never ask her out?

❀ ❀ ❀

Finn landed knees first then palms-down in soft dirt. He raised his head, his heart pounding uncomfortably as he glanced around the familiar garden. He'd made it back. But where was Elspeth? Caitrina? Their horses?

Just then, Elspeth plopped next to him, landing on her butt in the freshly turned soil of his cousin's garden with a grunt. *Thank God, they'd made it. Together.* He'd thought he lost her when his grip on her hand failed during the crazy spinning that was time travel.

"Are you okay?" He grasped her upper arm. Elspeth nodded, her eyes dazed.

He released his hold and jumped to his feet, a bit wobbly until he gained his balance. He reached for her hand and pulled her up. She took a step and stumbled into him.

Finn held his wife in a shaky embrace. *Thank you, God.*

"Are we in the twenty-first century?" Elspeth murmured against his chest.

He leaned back and held her at arm's length to look at her. "Yeah, we are."

She trembled for a moment then took hold of herself and gave him a tentative smile. "Where are Caitrina and the horses?"

"I don't know."

He glanced around the garden. The profusion of bright-colored flowers indicated he'd returned to summer. The sun sat low in the western sky. Must be late afternoon, soon to be early evening. *Okay, now what?* He released Elspeth, and she brushed the dirt from her backside.

Through one of the frosted windows, he noticed movement within the greenhouse. "Wait here," he said to Elspeth as he guided her to a cement bench. "I won't be gone long."

"Where are you going?" She dropped to the seat and stared at him through eyes a bit wild.

"Don't worry, you're safe." He leaned down and pressed

his lips to hers in a reassuring kiss. "I won't be long." He traversed the path to the greenhouse and flung the door open.

Damn. Jillian busily watered plants.

"Hey, where is everyone?" he asked.

She gasped, dropped the water wand and spun to face him, her palm pressed against her heart over her white cotton tank top.

"Sorry. Didn't mean to scare you."

Her eyes narrowed. "Nice disappearing act. I saw you take off through the gate and run into the woods. After Iain and Douglas performed their mock fight, I went looking for you, but couldn't find you. Where did you go?" She shoved her hands into the front pockets of her khaki-colored short shorts and stared at him.

Finn sighed. The guys must have covered up his leaving by performing. But that didn't explain where everyone was or why it didn't seem as if he'd been gone that long. "I was around," he hedged.

She pouted. "Well, I didn't see you all weekend." Her gaze flew to the door. Elspeth had followed him. Jillian looked her up and down and curled her lip. "Nice getup. Too bad you're too late."

Elspeth gaped at the five-foot tall woman.

"What do you mean?" Finn asked, drawing Jillian's attention back to him.

"Don't mess with me. You know the games ended today."

"So, today's Sunday?"

"Of course. Where have you been, in a time warp or something?"

He shifted uneasily, glad she didn't know how close to the mark she'd hit with her question. "So, Jillian, where are Laurie and Patrick?"

"The family went to the festival grounds to wait for the piper like they always do."

Finn relaxed. "Do you think Mairi and Iain went too?"

"I'd imagine. You know it's a family tradition to go hear

the ghost play."

Finn smiled at Elspeth and reached for her hand. "Come. We'll find your parents."

"Hey. Don't you plan to introduce me to your *friend?*"

"Oh. Sorry. This is Elspeth, Mairi and Iain's daughter. She's just arrived from…Scotland." Finn smiled at his bemused wife. "This is Jillian. She helps Laurie in the garden."

"Ex-cuse me. I'm her *business partner.*" Jillian glared at him. It seemed the little mouse had found her roar.

"Yeah, of course. If you'll excuse us, we'll be on our way." He hurried Elspeth to the exit.

Elspeth didn't care for the way the other woman stared at Finn, but she allowed him to drag her from the strange many-windowed building into the garden where the shock of blooms in every imaginable color startled the eye. The heady fragrance stole her breath. The garden must be the most beautiful place in the world.

But that woman was…

"Stop for a moment." She dug her heels in and held in place. "Who was that woman?"

Finn stiffened and spun to face her. "I told you, she's a friend of Laurie's."

That might be true, but the woman was interested in him in a way Elspeth didn't like, of that she was certain. The thought of Alexander with Jonet made her stomach queasy.

Finn was nothing like Alexander. Elspeth had nothing to worry about with her husband. He was a good man. He would remain faithful.

"Where are we going?" she asked.

"To find your parents." Finn tugged gently on her hand. "Come on. I think they are at the field, waiting for the ghost piper to make his annual appearance."

"Ghost?" She shivered.

Finn grinned. "Not really a ghost. Someone pretending to be. It's fun for the kids. And I guess for the adults too."

"Kids?" *Goats?*

"*Bairns.*"

Elspeth swallowed uneasily and swept her clammy hand over her gown. She'd need to learn much to live in this place. "I'm frightened," she admitted.

Finn stepped in close and wrapped his arms around her. "Don't worry. I'll help you make the transition. Patrick is here. Laurie. Your mother and father. You'll do fine."

She wasn't convinced. He kissed her forehead then pulled away.

"Let's go find your parents." Finn guided her across a gravel expanse to a strange device. "Thank God, my pickup is still parked where I left it."

"Is that a war machine?" she stepped back, uneasy.

"Nah. A truck. Think of it as an enclosed cart without a horse. It will take us to your parents." Finn opened the side of the contrivance as if it were a door. She only hesitated for a minute before sliding into the interior. Everything seemed so foreign. Excitement chased away her fear. Eager to see her parents, she jounced on the springy seat. Finn dashed around to the other side, opened another door, and slid onto the seat next to her. He reached across and snapped a cloth belt over her chest. "You ready?"

She nodded, enjoying the newness of everything.

Finn squeezed her hand then flipped open a small compartment in front of her and extracted a folded piece of heavy leather. "Thank God. My wallet is where I left it."

"Wallet?"

He chuckled. "Don't worry. You'll quickly learn our strange terms. Think of a wallet as a small sporran. A place for keeping money and important papers."

"Oh."

He secured a matching cloth belt over his chest, inserted a strange-looking key into a column attached to a wheel and twisted. The metal beast roared to life.

"You'd think I never left."

Elspeth startled and jerked her eyes to him. "'Tis loud."

"It'll quiet some once it warms up." He patted her thigh. "Think of it as a great adventure."

She smiled at the man who held her heart. The beast lunged forward and she held her breath for a moment.

"And we're off," Finn said.

Amazing. The gravel trail they followed meandered around a large wildflower meadow. After maneuvering a sharp curve, a large wooden castle came into view.

"That's the Whispering Pines Inn. The B&B your parents own." Finn glanced sideways at her.

She wrinkled her brow. Her parents would never be proprietors of an inn. Her father was a clan chief.

"They provide rooms with beds and breakfast for vacationers...travelers."

"My parents? You jest."

"They'll tell you about it, I'm sure."

Life must be much different in this time.

They continued past the wooden inn painted multiple colors—she liked the lavender very much—along the gravel path until they turned onto a hard black surface and their speed increased.

Oh. My. Goodness. Elspeth pressed her hands against the front of the...truck he called it. "Can we go faster?"

"You bet." Finn grinned and they flew like the wind.

Elspeth clapped her hands, giddy, enjoying watching the landscape whiz by.

Such marvels exist in this time and place.

Anticipation swelled within her chest. She could hardly sit still. She would soon see her parents again. She'd missed them terribly after they'd gone missing. Would they be the same? She'd changed much since last they'd seen her. Would they be happy she wed with Finn?

"You're pensive all of a sudden. What are you thinking about, angel?" Concern edged Finn's voice.

His hands wrapped the large wheel, which he used to make the horseless cart go in one direction or another. "Dinnae worry. I am fine. I was thinking about seeing my mother and father."

He twisted the wheel hard and the truck left the firm black trail for one of packed dirt bordered by large trees. The many hollows in the ground made the truck jump and made her bounce in her seat.

"Almost there. You'll see them soon," Finn said as they entered a clearing.

Strangely dressed people milled around campfires in front of tents. A few trucks sat nearby, each different in shape and color. Unease replaced the excitement she'd felt earlier. What would these people think of her? She didn't know anything about their ways. She didn't even dress like them.

Neither did Finn.

Finn parked the truck in the camping area not far from where he'd pitched his tent what seemed like forever ago. He hastened around the front, opened the passenger door and helped Elspeth to her feet.

"Let's go." He clasped her tiny hand within his. "We'll walk to the field from here."

As they passed one of the few remaining campsites—most attendees departed early on the last day of the festival—Amy Ferguson untangled herself from the group she talked with and ran over to them.

She did a shimmy and tugged on her tight, short skirt. The strappy t-shirt she wore had a Celtic knot printed across her breasts. Finn refrained from rolling his eyes.

"I can't believe this." Overly excited, she could hardly stand still. "I found out who you are."

Finn cringed.

"I Googled you."

"You can't believe everything you read on the internet," he said.

Amy ignored the comment and continued speaking. "You're *the* Finn MacIntyre. The one who is CEO and President of *MacIntyre Consulting*."

The words were on the tip of Finn's tongue to disavow

her assertion.

"I saw your picture and read how you were voted the most eligible bachelor in Manhattan by some glitzy magazine." She exhaled a puff of air that blew her hair out of her eyes and fluttered her eyelashes at him.

So much for denying the truth.

"Wow. I can hardly believe I know you. You're famous," she gushed. "Who's that? A new girlfriend?" Her frown curled her lips in the most unbecoming way when she noticed Elspeth standing behind him.

"Sorry, Amy, I should have introduced you. This is Elspeth, Mairi and Iain's daughter.

Elspeth dropped into a quick curtsy. "A pleasure to meet you."

Amy looked her up and down. "Nice costume. Too bad the games are over."

Elspeth glanced at Finn with uncertainty then smiled sweetly at the annoying woman. He'd have a lot of explaining to do once they were alone. He couldn't tell Amy they were husband and wife. At least, not until he spoke with Iain and attained permission to make their marriage public. They would have to come up with a plan to explain Elspeth's sudden appearance and the fact they were married.

Geez. He hoped Iain would be okay with him as a son-in-law. Iain might not approve of the handfasting, but because of the circumstances, he'd have to understand.

Finn hadn't thought about his father-in-law's possible reaction until now. They'd work it out and he'd take care of Elspeth.

When Patrick unexpectedly showed up with Laurie from the past, Finn used the firm's connections to get all the papers Patrick needed to blend into this time. He could do the same for his wife. Her father also had connections, though he kept them quiet and Finn didn't know the source. He didn't want to know the source.

Finn wrapped his arm around his wife's waist to show Amy that Elspeth belonged to him. He felt a perverted pleasure when the woman's eyes narrowed. He didn't care what she thought. "Excuse us. We're in a hurry to find Elspeth's parents."

"You'll come back later for the farewell bonfire?"

"Maybe. Gotta go." Finn ushered Elspeth past Amy and quickly whisked her away. Once they were out of earshot, she halted.

Finn sighed heavily and stopped walking, but didn't say anything. He couldn't blame Elspeth if she felt put out. The women of this time were much more aggressive than those of her time. Amy was a bitch.

"I dinnae understand." Elspeth twisted her hand in the fabric of her gown. "The women here are beautiful and they dress...scantily. They look at you with open lust."

"Ignore them. You are the only one I care about."

She lowered her gaze to the skirt of her gown. "My garments are..."

"Don't worry about it. We'll buy you some modern clothes." Though they wouldn't be as revealing as Amy's. The ways of the past held certain merit.

"But..."

"Later. Let's find your parents."

CHAPTER TWENTY-SIX

Strathlachlan, Late Summer, 1511

Stephen burst from the trees to face a cusp in his life. He slowed to a stop at the crossroad. Morning sun warmed his back, but didn't ease the tension in his shoulders. Did he turn left to Castle Lachlan and his childhood haunts or right to Allaine's keep?

With Patrick and Elspeth gone, he had little desire to return home. His parent's were dead. He had no siblings. He and Archibald had never been close. The man might be his chief, but out of respect, he'd given Stephen the consideration to choose his next duty.

From his vantage point atop the ridge, Castle Lachlan's shadow shimmied in the glistening waters of Loch Fyne. Shaggy black cattle grazed in nearby fields. He rubbed the ache in his chest. He missed Patrick. The horse fussed, tugging at the bit, sensing his rider's discontent.

Stephen was tempted to return to the *Sithichean Sluaigh* and force the damn fae magic to work for him too. *Foolish thought.* He tried to follow Patrick and Lady Laurie years ago with no success. The same would likely be true if he attempted to follow Finn and Elspeth.

He couldn't remain here all day. He needed to make a decision. His homeland meant everything to him. At least it had before Patrick left. Now Stephen felt lost. Making matters worse, royal rumors spread fear throughout the countryside. Scotland and England were headed for a confrontation.

Stephen sighed heavily, made a clicking sound with his tongue and reined the stallion to the right, away from bittersweet memories and toward an unclear future.

MacRae's Field, North Carolina

The sun slipped behind the mountain and the air chilled.

Finn took Elspeth's hand and hurried her the remaining distance. As they crossed the running track, she tugged on his arm. "Wait. I am out of breath."

They stopped, allowing her a moment to regain her composure. He scanned the grounds.

The festive trappings from the games were gone. In the middle of the field, seated in an array of bright-colored folding chairs—the kind that came in bags—were about seventy people scattered in family groups.

Only took Finn a second to spot the MacLachlan clan. The twins ran around the four adults, wooden swords swinging.

Doubt crept into his mind. Would Elspeth's family be happy to see her, or angry he'd uprooted her from the past? They'd find out soon. "Come on. There they are." He pointed toward her parents.

Elspeth's joyous grin when she located them eased Finn's concern. If need be, they would convince her family this was the right time for her to live in. He wanted her to be happy.

She hiked up the skirt of her gown and dashed across the field, he following behind.

"Ma! Da!" she screamed.

Seventy heads turned to stare.

Iain, Mairi, Patrick and Laurie jumped from their seats, eyes wide and mouths dropped open. Iain knocked a couple of chairs out of the way, and Mairi stepped forward.

"Beth?" She wobbled, and Iain supported her with an arm around her shoulder.

Tears fell over both their faces, and they opened their arms as Elspeth hurled against them. The twin lads yelled a war cry, shocking Patrick and Laurie out of their gape. Patrick grabbed one son as he ran toward the weeping huddle.

"My God, Finn, what have you done?" Laurie held his gaze while capturing the other lad by his nape.

"Long story." He ran a hand over his face.

"Who's the lady making Grandpa and Grandma cry?" Iain, the grandson, asked, glaring in Elspeth's direction.

"Your Auntie Elspeth." Laurie turned Young Iain to face her and squatted so she could gaze into his eyes. "They're crying happy tears. Do you understand?"

"Oh." He twisted his upper body to look at his grandparents and Elspeth with bewilderment. Then he grimaced in the way little boys did when they thought grownups were acting stupid.

Finn laughed. Iain pulled away from his mother and lunged for Finn. He wrapped the boy in his arms. Laurie stood and rolled her neck. "You okay?" he asked.

"Yeah. Just tired. The boys are a handful." She rubbed her lower back.

"Where is your daughter?"

"With Emily at the inn."

Young Iain tugged on the sleeve of Finn's leine, and Finn stared into inquisitive blue eyes the same color as Patrick's. "Where ya been, Uncle Finn? You promised to play warrior with me and Scott."

"I will. Tomorrow." He'd keep the date as long as Iain didn't chew him up and spit him out. Finn eyed his new father-in-law. The man exuded strength, a force to be reckoned with.

The daughter of one of the other reenactors, sat nearby with some friends, listening. She jumped up and joined them. "Hey, Finn." She gave him a finger wave then hunched down to Young Iain's level and gently touched his arm. "Would you and your brother like to come over by us and wait for the piper? My friend is telling ghost stories."

The little boy nodded and pulled out of Finn's embrace. He took her hand, then she collected his twin from Patrick and led the lads away. Patrick joined his parents and sister in the hug-a-thon.

"Spill it," Laurie demanded.

"Maclay is dead."

She clutched her hand to her heart. "You killed him?"

"Yeah."

Her relief was palpable. "There's more."

"How do you know?"

"The trepidation in your eyes."

"Yeah, okay, but I'd rather wait to tell everyone at the same time."

She nodded. "All right."

Finn turned toward Elspeth and her family and received a speculative glance from her father. Tonight would be interesting. Finn slid his gaze to his wife and let it linger.

Elspeth could barely see her mother and father and brother through the tears swimming in her eyes. She swiped her sleeve across her face, uncaring the fabric might get damaged. Finn planned to buy her new garments. The thought of dressing like the other women she'd seen made her cheeks hot.

"Let me look at you." Her mother held her at arm's length.

Her mother wasn't dressed as the others, but Elspeth liked her lavender gown. Although seeing her ankles and calves was a wee shocking.

"Glad I am to see you, daughter." Her father awkwardly patted her on the shoulder.

He didn't look much different in his *leine* and *plaide*. But Patrick wore blue *trews* made from a type of fabric she'd never seen before. And Lady Laurie dressed the same, like a lad.

Elspeth did her best to appear serene and hide her bewilderment.

Patrick grinned like a fool. "Get lost at the *Sithichean Sluaigh* did you, wee sister? Will Archibald be following?"

She snorted. She couldn't help it. The thought of Archibald doing something so outlandish made her laugh.

Her mother released her. "Is Archibald well?"

"Aye, but he has become a *mùigean*, a surly old goat."

"That is an understatement," Finn said as he joined them.

Laurie's brow wrinkled. She glanced at the others sitting nearby. "Is something wrong at Castle Lachlan?"

"It's a long story," Finn said.

"You said that before." Laurie pursed her lips.

"So I did."

"Perhaps we should save the tales for home," Patrick suggested, indicating with a tilt of his head the strangers staring at them and listening.

From a chair nearby, a tiny head swung around. "Shh!" The wee lass held a finger to her lips. "He won't come if you keep talking."

Gloaming with its dimness made it difficult to discern the *bairn's* other features.

"Who?" Elspeth asked.

"The ghost piper, silly. Why do you think we're waiting here? My mother said he'll only come if we're quiet."

"I see," Elspeth bit back a laugh.

"We should head for home." Patrick folded one of the strange chairs they'd been sitting on and shoved it into a sheath.

"I'll bring the twins home after the piper plays," the young woman who had corralled the lads earlier offered. Elspeth wanted to meet them. Hug them. Though acquainting herself with her nephews could come later.

"Thank you. That's sweet of you, Krystle." Laurie picked up a basket from the ground and slipped it over her arm. "We'll be at the inn."

Elspeth glanced around. "Is there something I can do to help?"

"We've got it covered," Laurie said.

Finn reached out, and Elspeth clasped his hand. He drew her close and draped his arm around her shoulders.

Her father's stare slid from her to her husband.

"So that is how it is." He studied Finn, his gaze intense. "I believe we have much to discuss, lad."

Her stomach tightened. Was her father angry?

Iain's tone made Finn tense. He glanced at his wife, tucked in the crook of his arm. She worried her lip nervously.

"I'll explain everything when we get to the inn," he assured her.

Before her father stopped them, Finn escorted Elspeth across the field, rehearsing in his mind what he'd say to Iain when they reached the inn.

Darkness fell quick in the mountains. They couldn't see very well so they had to wait by the running track for the others who carried flashlights.

Elspeth gasped when her family joined them. "What is that?"

"A magic torch." Though they couldn't see Patrick's grin, it was evident in his voice.

"You are laughing at me," Elspeth complained.

"Hardly, I am just so happy to see you."

"You have changed much."

Finn gave Elspeth's hand a gentle squeeze, hoping to stop her from saying too much before they got to the inn.

"He has changed," she said. "He is not as stern as I remember."

"Aye, I am different." Patrick agreed. "Life here is unlike what you are used to."

"This isn't the time or place to discuss this." Finn looked

over Patrick's shoulder, wondering what was keeping Iain and Mairi."

"Nae worries. My father parked elsewhere. You are safe for the moment." Patrick slapped Finn's back hard. "Glad to see you, lad."

"I wish you would stop calling me lad. I'm older than you."

"So you say."

"Can we borrow a flashlight?"

"Are you never prepared, lad?"

Finn cringed, but let the comment slide when Patrick handed over the Maglite.

Iain appeared behind Patrick. "I think Elspeth should ride with us."

"I don't think—"

An eerie skirl of pipes came from the distance, getting louder, stopping Finn mid-sentence. "Look!" Elspeth's voice rose with excitement. "In the trees."

They looked across the field. A bright, glowing-figure bobbed through the woods.

Laurie laughed. "The ghost piper has arrived."

"His music is hauntingly beautiful," Elspeth noted, a hitch in her voice.

The whine of bagpipes always gave Finn the chills. Tonight was no different. When the music stopped, the glowing presence disappeared. Finn squinted when the overhead lights kicked on with an electrical sizzle, flooding the field with illumination. Elspeth gasped and wrapped her hands around his waist, holding tight.

Iain growled, low and deep. Mairi, who'd appeared while the piper played, gently touched his arm and he quieted.

Patrick had the nerve to hoot. Finn wanted to strangle his friend.

Great. Just great. Iain was going to kill him when he heard their story.

"My truck is in the camping area. I'll bring Elspeth by the inn." Finn stared at Iain, daring the man to disagree.

Mairi grasped Iain's arm before he responded to the unspoken challenge and guided him away.

"See you at the inn," Laurie said. "Should be great theater."

"Come on, angel." Finn guided Elspeth toward the camping area.

They walked to his campsite in silence. If things went well, they'd spend the night at the inn, but he needed a few things from his tent. A change of clothes and his ditty bag for starters.

If things went south, they'd go to one of those chain hotels. He wasn't making Elspeth sleep in a tent on her first night in the twenty-first century.

He ducked into the vestibule and snatched his gear while Elspeth waited outside.

"My father would never hurt you," she said when he returned to her side.

Finn wasn't so sure.

CHAPTER TWENTY-SEVEN

*F*inn preceded his father-in-law—the man might not know it yet, but he would soon—into the inn's study. The lemony scent of furniture polish tweaked Finn's nostrils, and he fought a sneeze. Iain slid the pocket door shut. The cherry-wood panel squealed, hitting the jamb with a thud, smashing the silence and setting Finn's strung-out nerves on edge.

"Sit." Iain waved his arm to one of the wing chairs in front of the huge mahogany desk. The man hadn't cracked a smile since Finn and Elspeth arrived at the inn. Though polite, his brusque manner did little to encourage.

Finn dropped onto the wine leather. The fight with Alexander, the long days searching for Maclay and the resulting battle, along with traveling through time, were taking their toll. He stayed alert through force of will alone, stalked by weariness.

He needed to sleep, and soon, but Finn didn't want to go to bed alone.

Would Iain uphold the handfasting? The fear he might not had Finn's stomach acid spiking.

Iain rounded the immense spread of polished wood and eased into the large chair on the other side, seizing the position of power. "Well, lad, what have you to say for yourself?"

Finn swallowed past the lump in his throat. Where to begin? *Oh, what the heck.* "Maclay is dead," he blurted, blunt as when he told Laurie.

Iain's eyes widened and he leaned back in his chair, but recovered quickly, his features blanking. "That is good." He steepled his hands in front of him on the desk. "Patrick and Laurie will be much relieved."

"I couldn't let the lowlife get away with what he did to my cousin. Had Maclay learned the secret of the faerie knoll...well, it no longer matters."

"True enough." Iain held Finn with his gaze. "Now, explain why you believe 'tis your right to roam your hands over my daughter."

"We're married. We handfasted. I'd like your permission to make it official in this time. That is, once we get the legal papers Elspeth needs to live here."

Finn shrank back from Iain's roar. The furious man sprang from his chair. He bent forward, hands flat on the surface of the desk, white knuckles contrasting with dark wood. "She was to wed Alexander Campbell."

Finn rose to his feet, maintaining eye contact with his father-in-law. "Sit and calm yourself. Mairi will kill me if you have a coronary. I'll try to explain."

They sank to their chairs, though Iain begrudgingly. "Did Archibald give his permission?"

Finn glanced at the corner of the room where the decorative crown molding met the ceiling then flicked his gaze back to Iain. "After the fact."

"At least you are honest." Iain swirled his gaze around the room as if searching for something. "Perhaps we should discuss this with swords."

"Hear me out."

Iain waved his hand in a rolling manner, motioning Finn to get on with it.

"Marrying Elspeth wasn't what I intended when I ran

through the gate." Finn dragged fingers through his dirty hair. God, he needed a shower. "I'd planned to take revenge against Maclay and hurry back through the gate, but things happened."

Iain gave him a good once over with a critical eye. "Not sure why I did not notice before, but you appear to have been fighting."

"More than you can imagine."

"Explain."

"I'm not sure where to start." Finn shook his head.

"The beginning would be best."

"Then I guess the tale starts when Elspeth called to me from her time."

"What are you talking about?" Iain demanded, eyes narrowed.

Finn flinched. "I didn't know it was your daughter calling to me in my dreams until I traveled through the gate and woke at Castle Lachlan with Elspeth sitting nearby, waiting for me to rouse. I tried to keep my distance. I did. Alexander treated her poorly. And then when I was injured during a battle with Maclay's men, she nursed me back to health and…well, we discovered an affinity."

"So you liked each other. Not enough reason to break the contract I put into effect to secure her future."

"There's more. She planned to go through with the wedding to Alexander up to the last minute even though he shamed her. For Christ sake, Iain, she caught him in *the act* with another woman."

"That is unfortunate."

"He tried to force her to marry him. He attempted to rape Elspeth."

Iain's neck and face flushed red and he tightened his fists. "Did you kill the bastard?"

"No. Archibald was guilting her into going through with the wedding, and she told me to stay out of it."

"What?" Iain leapt from his chair again. "What was my son thinking?"

266

"He said he couldn't break the contract. Alexander can be persuasive. He convinced Archibald that Elspeth exaggerated."

"Scoundrel!"

"That is an understatement. Anyhow, Archibald ordered me to leave when he learned Elspeth and me...well, I left, but I couldn't stay away. I love her, Iain. I couldn't let her wed Alexander. Not with the way he treated her." Finn scraped a hand over his face, remembering the pain of standing by and watching Alexander mistreat Elspeth. "When I returned I learned the wedding had already been stopped. Munn had disrupted the pre-wedding feast by knocking over tables and tossing everything—food, wine, serving platters—on the floor. Somehow, the little man found proof Alexander plotted against Archibald. The king allowed the bridal contract to be broken for a penalty payment from Archibald."

"So you handfasted with her then?"

"Not right away. She was angry with me for leaving and not fighting for her." Finn looked at the floor then back at Iain. "I had a lot of convincing to do."

"She gave you a tough time? Aye?"

"She did."

Iain grinned.

"The story doesn't end there," Finn said.

"Nae?"

"When I told Elspeth you and Mairi were living in my time, she told Archibald. He had Elspeth locked in her room and threw me in the pit, believing me mad. While Archibald was gone, Alexander kidnapped Elspeth."

"And you didn't kill him then?"

"I fought with him and won, but I couldn't kill the man."

"Ach, you and your modern sensibilities." Iain's brow furrowed. "Yet you killed Maclay."

"Yeah. Maclay needed killing. Alexander?" Finn made an iffy motion with his hand. "Not so much. Besides, Elspeth begged me not to kill the man. And I didn't want Archibald to have to answer to the king for my actions."

Iain shook his head. "What was Archibald thinking to have tried to force Elspeth?"

"He has other things on his mind."

"What say you?"

"Isobell."

"She is being difficult?"

"You could say that. We can discuss his tribulations tomorrow." Finn shifted his weight in the chair, extending his cramped legs. "So will you give us your blessing?"

"Aye. You will make her a better husband. I never cared much for Alexander after he grew into a man."

"I vow to you, I'll make her happy."

Iain locked gazes with Finn. "You had better, lad. You had better, or I will come after you with my sword."

Finn rose and extended his hand. Iain came around the desk and shook it, slipping from a modern handshake into a warriors embrace.

"Where will you live? I dinnae like the thought of her in New York City."

"It's where my company is. We'll need to live there at least part of the year."

"Leave her here then for a while with me and her mother until she adjusts. Give her time to learn modern ways. She'll be safer here with people who understand what she is going through."

"She belongs with me."

"Dinnae be stubborn, lad. She kens naught of this time."

"Look whose talking about being obstinate."

"Give her time. 'Tis all I ask. Let her decide when she is ready to face the outside world."

Although Iain had a valid point, Finn didn't want to go to New York without Elspeth. They had handfasted. They should be together. In his mind they were married, dammit.

"I'll compromise. We'll stay here for three months then move to New York. We'll return at the end of the handfast period and officially wed here at the inn."

"We'll discuss this again in three months time. If she still wants you, I will consider agreeing to a marriage. We will negotiate terms after that." Iain always had to get in the last word. For now, Finn allowed it. But when three months passed, he and Elspeth were moving to New York.

Elspeth sat on a plump floral—sofa, her mother called it—worrying her lower lip, her mother's arm reassuringly draped around her shoulders. Finn and her father had been behind the closed door for a long time.

"I dinnae understand Father's anger."

"Ah, well, he did not like the way Finn touched you. You are betrothed to Alexander Campbell and are to wed after your twenty-first birth celebration."

"Nae longer."

"What do you mean, dear heart?"

"My birth celebration has already passed."

"And you are not wed to Alexander?" Her mother asked, tone sharp.

Elspeth closed her eyes and shook her head.

"Tell me what happened," her mother urged in a calmer voice.

"It was horrible. He changed so much. He tried to force…" Elspeth covered her face with her hands. She hated the memory of his hands touching her. Shoving her against the bed, his fingers seeking between her legs. His mouth wet against hers, his tongue…

She inwardly shuddered yet refused to linger on the past. Finn was gentle. She'd only think about the way they were together. "I dinnae want to talk about it."

"Are you sure?"

"Aye."

The arm around her squeezed comfortingly then relaxed. Her mother seeming relieved not to learn more. Elspeth raised her gaze to her mother's serene face, remembering how she felt when she learned her parents went missing. How her heart ached for years after they didn't come back.

"Why did you not send for me when Laurie came for Patrick?"

Remorse strained her mother's expression. "Dinnae think we did not want you here with us. We did. Patrick though…well, we learned through some books he was never listed as clan chief. Caitrina confirmed he was meant to live his life here. But we thought your future was with Alexander in the past."

Tears welled, and Elspeth swallowed through a throat gone tight.

"Had I known Mairi and Iain were your parents, I would have told you," Laurie said from across the room where she sat with Patrick and their wee baby daughter.

"I did not learn the truth until we were already here," her brother said.

"What do you think is happening in there?" Elspeth asked.

Patrick chuckled awkwardly. "Dinnae worry. They went into the study without their swords."

"I am tired of men deciding my future." Elspeth leapt from the sofa and strode across the chamber, skirting the fine furniture. She stared at the closed wooden panel, hesitated, lost her nerve.

Neither her father nor Finn would appreciate her interrupting. She was in a new time and place; she wasn't going to be submissive like before. She stiffened her resolve and knocked—not softly but with vigor.

Annoyance rode the voice bidding her enter. She found her father and Finn embracing when she slid the door open, as she had seen him do earlier, and peered inside.

Finn smiled warmly. "Hi, angel."

His tired greeting stole her ire and replaced it with concern. He looked like he was about to collapse.

"Are you well?"

"Just tired."

"What have you been discussing?" She eyed her father, trying to determine his temper.

Finn slid an arm around her waist. "Our future."

Her father ambled from the study, a smug expression on his face, and nodded to her mother. Elspeth glanced from one to the other. Then she pulled away from Finn and swung around to face him. "Dinnae be making choices for me." She fisted her hands at her waist. "I want to contribute to the decision making."

"See what happens when one allows one's children to mingle with moderns," her father complained to her mother.

She turned her glare on him. She didn't understand his wording, but she knew he made fun of her because Patrick laughed.

Finn cleared his throat. "Can we discuss this in private, angel."

"Fine." She crossed her arms.

"Mairi, where do you want us?" Finn clasped Elspeth's elbow and guided her toward the magnificent wooden stairs.

"Where are we going?" She stopped moving and stared at Finn.

"To bed." Finn whispered near her ear, taking the first step, hoping he wouldn't fall over before he made it up the stairs and hit the mattress.

"Most of our guests checked out this morning. Your usual room is made up." Mairi twittered nervously. "I will send up some food. You are probably starving from all the excitement."

"Thanks," Finn said to his mother-in-law before turning to his annoyed wife. "You must be as tired as I am. Let's sleep on things and we'll discuss our plans in the morning after we've both had a good night's sleep."

Elspeth gave a quick nod and allowed him to escort her up the stairs. He wanted to sweep her into his arms and carry her to bed, but didn't have the strength. When they reached the room he usually stayed in while visiting, he slipped the card key into the slot and let Elspeth precede him into the room. Her gasp of surprise sent warm shivers over his spine.

"Lovely," she said.

"You like? It's a bit on the masculine side compared to the rest of the inn."

Mairi decorated the room he'd chosen for himself in shades of deep green and wine with beige. A jolt of rich gold here and there added power to the mix. Elspeth glided across the room to the bed and swept the tips of her fingers over the plaid duvet. The warmth he felt before turned hot, heating his blood when she twisted around and jounced her bum on the mattress. Her suggestive smile sent molten fire to his groin and he growled.

"Oh, man. You're killing me, angel."

She flashed her lashes at him, not the least penitent. In three strides, he stood before her, and dropped into a crouch. Her eyes darkened, and she grabbed the hem of his shirt, pulling the fabric over his head. Before his next breath, her fingers splayed his bare chest, soothing him, setting him on fire.

He leaned forward and met her lips in an open-mouthed kiss. The rasp of her tongue against his sent tingling sensation to the soles of his feet. Maybe he wasn't so tired.

"Want to take a shower with me?"

"Shower?"

"A modern way of bathing."

Her wicked grin curled his toes. "We can bathe together?"

"Oh, yeah." He took her hand, rose and tugged her toward the bathroom.

The reason he'd selected this suite over the others with their claw foot tubs that women found romantic was its mega-large tile shower with six heads. He was more than ready to introduce Elspeth to the pleasures of the contemporary world.

CHAPTER TWENTY-EIGHT

*E*lspeth glanced across the chamber she would share with her husband. Her gaze lingered on the bed. A thrill tingled at the back of her neck, teasing fine hairs on her nape, making the tips of her breasts harden and ache. Ache for Finn's touch.

He tugged on her hand. Anticipation welled in her chest, catching her breath. She followed him through a doorway, curious what they'd find inside, what they'd *do* inside. Finn snapped a wee lever on the inside wall and the room came to life. Light gleamed from the ceiling, from torches on the walls, illuminating a wall-sized mirror reflecting their bedraggled images. Across from the looking glass, a wall made of glass blocks sparkled.

Her gasp of surprise loudened, sounding deeper in the strange chamber. "Magic?" She lifted her gaze to Finn.

"No." A smile creased his eyes. "Electricity. Come in. Nothing in the room will harm you. I'll explain what everything is."

Elspeth stepped up to the low wooden cupboard spanning the width of the huge mirror. She slid a hand over her rumpled and dirty gown. What must people have thought when they'd seen them earlier? Their disreputable reflections explained the strange looks they'd received.

"Don't worry." Finn joined her before the mirror. "We'll borrow an outfit from Laurie until we go shopping and buy you new clothes."

Outfit? Would she ever learn all the strange words they use in this time? Refusing to become overwhelmed, she took a deep breath and exhaled her worries.

Finn pointed to two shiny basins imbedded in the gray, heavily veined, stone top of the wooden cupboard. "Sinks." He reached forward and twisted a metal knob. "Right for cold."

Water flowed from a spigot mounted on one of the... *sinks.*

He flicked his wrist and turned another knob. "Left for hot. Hot is what I am for you."

His gaze burned her, and heat suffused her neck and face. "I know that was lame, but, Elspeth, I'm...so glad you came home with me."

"Me, also," she managed through a mouth gone dry.

"Right." Finn cleared his throat and his gaze swept the chamber, landing on an odd-looking seat. Was he as nervous as she?

He lifted its lid. "Toilet instead of bedpan."

He pressed a lever and the seat roared. She jumped back, but curiosity made her step forward and peer into the oval opening. Water spiraled through the apparatus.

"Oh my!" She jerked her gaze to Finn's face, her fears nearly forgotten with the excitement of discovering new wonders.

He smiled faintly. "You sit on it and...you know...when you're done, you flush. Press the lever and everything washes away."

"May I use it now?"

"Of course, I'll just...yeah...give you a moment." He backed out of the doorway, leaving her alone in the unusual chamber.

She stepped out of her filthy, torn gown, dropped it onto the unusual stone floor, and kicked it into a corner. The damaged fabric wasn't fit for rags, besides the gown would be of no use to her in this time and place. She wanted to don garments like Laurie and the other young women she'd seen at the festival grounds.

Elspeth used the odd seat Finn named a toilet and giggled with glee when she pushed down on the lever and the water roared and washed the bowl clean.

Astonishing. A marvel indeed.

Wearing only her ragged chemise, she poked her head around the doorstop and spied Finn pacing the bedchamber, his rear to her. After taking a moment to admire and confirm, once again, he possessed a firm backside she wanted to grab and hold onto, she slid her gaze upward. Light and shadow played across the muscles on his broad back.

Her stomach fluttered. He was her man. The man who fought against unfathomable odds and won.

"I am done. Can we wash now?" She couldn't wait to run a wet cloth over his smooth flesh. The thought brought heat to her cheeks.

Finn swung around and stared. She glanced down. The rosy tips of her breasts were visible through the sheer cotton she wore. He uttered a noise deep in his throat and stood before her. She hadn't had the time to blink. He sought her gaze.

"Yeah, we'll shower. But first..." He lowered his head and brushed her lips with his. Strength left her and she leaned into him, wanting the reassurance of his touch. He pulled her tight against his body. The warmth of his love enveloped her, easing her apprehension.

Their kiss deepened. An intoxicating play of tongues and lips and teeth. When they broke apart, they both breathed hard.

"Shower now, loving after." Finn gently backed her into the bathing chamber.

He unlaced the *trews* he wore and his thick arousal burst from the leather. Elspeth swallowed as the garment revealed his muscular thighs, calves, then fell to the floor. Her sigh was that of a young maiden.

She moistened her puffy lips. Anticipation escalated. He reached for the hem of her chemise and pulled the soft fabric over her head, tossing it atop her discarded gown. Taking her gently by the hand, he led her across the chamber to where the glass blocks reflected the light. Her gaze dropped to his firm backside and she reached out to touch him, but stopped, suddenly awkward in the strange chamber.

Finn extended his arm behind the glass blocks, twisted a knob and water sprayed from the sides of an area enclosed by the glass. "'Tis like a spring rain."

He grasped her upper arms, stepped backward and walked her into the waterfall, his gaze intent on hers.

Warm water sprinkled over their bodies. "I like this way of bathing," she said, unable to express the extent of wonderment within her.

"Thought you might." He released her arms and slid a finger along her cheek, spreading tingles in its wake, along the length of her neck to brush the top of her breasts with reverent tenderness. His low hiss set her heart to racing. "God, you're beautiful."

Heat flamed over the flesh where his touch lingered, having nothing to do with the warmth of the water sluicing over her sensitized skin.

Her legs wobbled and Finn wrapped an arm around her waist. "Stay with me."

"Oh, aye," she murmured.

Finn's wicked grin sent a shiver up her spine even though the water felt hotter.

"Are you warm?" he asked.

"Aye."

"Good."

He nudged her backward until she leaned against one of the walls. Then he moved in tight, pinning her arms to her side, hip to hip, skin to skin. His arousal poked against her belly, full and thick.

Desire raced through her like a raging bonfire. He rested

his forehead against hers. "I want you so bad it hurts."

"Then have me."

His hands gripped her hips. Then he slowly lowered himself, kissing a trail of fire over her belly, along the inside of a thigh.

Moisture pooled, low and sweet, making her want—

He swept his tongue over her private place, sending tantalizing desire to her core. She bucked against his mouth, gripped his hair, begged for more.

He gave her everything. He lapped and licked and flicked his tongue against her most sensitive spot. She flattened her hands against the wet wall and shouted his name. "Finn, please!"

He sucked her hard. When she thought she'd had all she could endure, something broke loose within her. Shooting stars burst behind her eyelids.

Her cry of release echoed off the strange stone walls.

Finn leaned back on his haunches. Elspeth's womanly scent filled his nostrils. Her taste coated his throat. He wanted to go down on her again.

He stared at the ecstasy glowing on her face. She was the most beautiful woman in the world in his eyes. More than that—he loved her sweetness. Her strength. The way she was learning to stand up for herself.

It might be primitive of him, but he couldn't wait for their child to grow healthy within her womb.

Maybe they could start working at creating a baby tonight. He stood, and she stepped into his embrace. "You okay?" he asked.

Oh, aye." She bobbed her head.

He snuggled her close. Felt the rapid beat of her heart. Then it slowed to an even thump…thump…thump.

He held her at arm's length. "Wash now."

Although he was hard and needy, he'd wait until they made it to the bed where he could love his wife through the night. And perhaps together create a new life.

He released his hold and collected the soap from the tray in the tile wall. He lathered his hands and handed her the bar.

She lifted it to her nose and sniffed. "Cinnamon and...something I cannot define."

"Our manufacturers create many different scents."

"Lovely." She smiled. "'Twas what you smelled like when first I found you."

He raised his brow skeptically. "I doubt that."

"Well, 'twas the scent beneath the odor of masculine sweat."

"I'd been fighting...and spent time unconscious in the shallows of the stream where you found me."

"I did not mean to—"

He didn't wait for her to finish, instead swept his soapy hands over her shoulders, down her arms, moved closer and massaged her breasts.

He savored her hiss of pleasure. The feel of her curves combined with her sensual purr jerked his cock to full attention. He ached to press her against the wall and drive into her until they were both spent.

Not to be outdone, she slipped a soapy hand around his cock, slid its length, teased the weeping tip.

His knees buckled. He shot his arm out and pressed his palm against the wall to support his weight.

The shower washed away the suds, and she lowered herself, sucked him into her mouth and worked him with her lips and tongue. Holy shit. Lightning streaked through his veins, blasted into his cock, blew a hole in his control.

Agony. Blessed agony.

Pleasure-pain pushed him to the edge. He couldn't breathe. Couldn't think. He was losing his mind.

Now! He had to get inside her now.

He gripped her hips. Their gazes locked in communion. Her sexy chuckle urged him on as he slid her up his body. She wrapped her legs around his waist. Held tight.

He thrust deep, using the wall to hold her in place.

His rhythm became violent. She stayed with him,

encouraging him to give more. Everything.

She came, screaming his name. His orgasm rolled through his cock like a rocket blasting off. Lights burst behind his eyelids, and he roared her name as his sperm shot deep into her womb.

When his heart slowed enough for him to think again, he eased Elspeth down his length. Her feet touched the tile and she wobbled, went limp against his chest, her breath whispering over his wet skin. Goose flesh covered his body.

"Wow. That was great."

"Aye."

He raised her chin. Kissed her hard on the mouth. "You all right?"

"Oh, aye." Her breathy response and glazed eyes spoke volumes.

"Come on. Let's dry off and go to bed." He shut off the water, and they left the shower enclosure. On the way through the bathroom, he snatched two towels from the warming rack and wrapped Elspeth in the thick, forest-green cotton.

She squeezed the bath sheet with her fingers. "Verra luxurious. You and my family live like royalty."

"Yeah. I'm afraid I took it for granted before I came to your time. I took a lot for granted." Her gaze held his. "You must be tired. It's been a long day and we've had much excitement these past few days." He held out his hand. "Let's retire."

Hours later, after making love with his wife multiple times, he held her within the crook of his arm, fast asleep. He brushed a stray hair from her soft cheek. A twinge of guilt pinched near his heart. She'd said she wanted a *bairn*. As much as he wanted a child with Elspeth, and soon, that wasn't the only reason he planted his sperm deep within her womb.

Iain would be less likely to forbid their formal marriage at the end of the handfast period if there was a small lad or lass involved.

With the full moon high in the sky, Caitrina appeared on the faerie knoll just beyond Foxgloves's garden gate, leading three prime specimens of Scottish Highland breeding. Her own beast had made the trip on many occasions, but the other two stallions were skittish after traveling through time. She walked them around the enclosed garden and into the fenced meadow, allowing them space to run.

She leaned on the fence and watched the animals work off their anxious energy, allowing her thoughts to wander.

A chill slid over her shoulders when she realized she wasn't alone. A quick sniff of the air and she recognized the cologne. She stiffened, but didn't turn to him.

"Douglas, I ken you are there."

Heat seeped into her skin as he leaned next to her, brushing arm against arm. She didn't move away, refusing to give him any indication he got to her.

"What do you want?" She asked, keeping her voice steady, though desire kindled in her blood.

"I've been looking for you."

"Have you?"

"Aye. Where have you been? You missed the festival."

"How do you know that?"

He raised a sardonic brow. Even if not for the full moon, her faerie sight would allow her to see his mocking expression.

"I had other things to attend to," she said, though she didn't owe him an explanation.

"Acquiring pricey horseflesh no longer bred, except by a very few? Sold to even fewer." His tone sounded accusative.

"You have seen my stallion before."

What was he getting at? What did he think he knew?

"That I have. It's the other two horses causing me to wonder where you've been. I saw Finn disappear through the gate and he's returned with a lass resembling our Mairi. Know anything about where he's been and why he returned with a MacLachlan woman?"

"Just what are you implying?"

"Oh, I dinnae ken. Seems odd to see two ancient horses in Iain's meadow."

"Dinnae be ridiculous. There is naught unusual about these horses being here. And you can't count. All three horses are the same breed."

"You and I both ken there is something very different about your steed."

"Ridiculous. I've just returned from purchasing the horses in Kentucky." She lowered her gaze so he wouldn't see the lie in her eyes.

He gripped her arm, his fingers bruising skin. "Beware, lass. You're playing with a power stronger than your own."

Caitrina shrugged out of his grasp. He couldn't possibly know who she was.

Could he?

Finn liked seeing Elspeth in his robe. The oxblood silk grazed her ankles. When she sat on the mattress and reached to the nightstand for the comb he gave her, the front slid open to display a delicious length of ivory skin. His gaze swept ankle to calf to thigh. Although he was fully sated from their night of lovemaking, blood rushed to his cock and his erection kicked.

"What will I do for garments?" she asked.

It took a moment to get with the program and understand her question. He'd prefer to keep her out of clothes for a while longer.

"Dinnae look at me that way. My ma and da will never forgive us if we dinnae break our fast with them."

"We will, but..." He held out his arms. "Let me hold you for a minute."

She rose from the bed and walked into his embrace. God had seen fit to bless him. He slid his palms over the curve of her hips, loving the feel of her in his arms.

The ringing of the phone on the dresser jolted them apart. "What is that?"

Finn held up a finger, picked up the receiver, expecting Iain or Mairi to be on the other end, reminding him and Elspeth to come down for breakfast. "Yeah?"

When he heard the voice on the other end, he kept his curse to himself. Unfortunately, the caller wasn't one of his in-laws.

CHAPTER TWENTY-NINE

Two Weeks Later, Manhattan...

I still can't believe you convinced Iain to let you take Elspeth to New York without giving her time to adjust."

Finn leaned back in the leather desk chair, phone receiver clenched between his shoulder and ear, staring out the window. He couldn't believe he sat in the corner office of *MacIntyre Consulting*, looking at the dark streets and buildings of Manhattan either. It was as if he were living in someone else's skin.

Only a couple of weeks ago he'd been in sixteenth century Scotland, wielding a sword.

"Finn, are you there?" Laurie asked.

"Yeah." He swiveled the chair to face his desk, shifted the phone to his other ear and doodled on a pad of lined paper. "It wasn't as if Iain had a choice. Elspeth refused to stay behind."

Thank God. He couldn't imagine living away from her, especially with the stress his business partners added to his burdens.

"Well, I hope she is okay. How is she adapting?"

"Just fine."

Not exactly the truth. In reality, she was a tad glum all the time. And angry with him most of the time. He figured there was no reason to upset the rest of the clan. She'd get used to her new life soon.

Finn heard the gift shop's door chime through the phone line.

"Better go," Laurie said. "A customer walked in and we're closing in a half-hour."

"Yeah, sure. I'll talk to you later."

Finn hung up the phone relieved he got off before Laurie started in on him for the umpteenth time about him and Elspeth returning to North Carolina for a visit.

He couldn't take her back until things got better between them. If he did, Iain would pick up on the friction and forbid a formal marriage at the end of the handfast period. If only Finn could get her pregnant.

His sigh sounded hollow in the quiet office. It wasn't through lack of trying. Seemed the only good thing they had going for them was sex. His cock stirred at the notion. He checked the time on the computer. Nearly eight-thirty.

Shit. He was late again. He really sucked at being a husband.

An hour later, Finn dropped his briefcase onto a chair near the door and loosened his silk tie. Elspeth stood in the foyer, staring at him. Barefoot, dressed in dark leggings and an oversized lavender t-shirt, her hair in a long braid, she looked darned cute.

Only problem, his precious angel wore a cross-frown. He obviously upset her again.

Not that he blamed her for being angry. He stayed at the office longer than he intended, but he didn't trust the financial report his two partners pulled together. Something wasn't right. He couldn't put his finger on exactly what bothered him. Though he was certain something about the numbers was wrong.

They swore to its accuracy.

Adding to his worries, his lawyer was missing. Jim Devlin had been a good buddy since college. Joined the firm when Finn took over as president. He'd called Finn in North Carolina the morning after Finn and Elspeth returned from the past with a cryptic warning that Finn needed to get back to the office ASAP.

By the time Finn returned to Manhattan, Jim had gone missing and Finn's two business partners feigned ignorance as to where the firm's lawyer went and why.

It wasn't like Jim to go out of town without telling someone at the office and checking in on a regular basis. His administrative assistant had no clue where the man had gone. Worried there might have been foul play, Finn intended to dig deeper.

"You are late again." Elspeth's accusation brought his thoughts home.

"I know. I'm sorry." He crossed the distance to where she stood.

He knew he expected a lot from her. But the other members of her family who had come forward in time and adapted to the twenty-first century were proof she could too.

Finn reached out and touched her cheek. "Have you eaten, angel?"

She lowered her gaze to the wood floor, but he caught the sheen of tears in her silver eyes.

"What happened?"

She sniffled and raised her head, tilting her chin defiantly. "I placed the frozen brick into the magic oven like you told me, but nothing happened. It is a dripping mess."

"No worries, sweetheart. I'll make something for both of us."

"You should not need too."

"It's not a problem."

"Yes it is. I am worthless in this time," she screeched and broke away from him. Before he could stop her, she darted down the hall. A few seconds later, the bedroom door slammed.

He balled his hands on his waist. There wasn't time to deal with her hysterics. He needed Elspeth to adjust so he could concentrate on all the shit at the office.

Finn sighed and headed for the kitchen. He'd give her a little while to get a grip on herself then he'd go talk to her. What could he do to make things easier on her? He didn't have a single idea.

The door to the microwave hung open. Inside sat the thawed frozen dinner still within its cardboard container with liquid oozing from the corners. Elspeth had forgotten to open the container before putting the meal in the oven. It didn't look like she'd turned the oven on. She must have forgotten the instructions he gave her.

Maybe it was time to hire a cook. That was what his wife was used to in Scotland.

For now, he had a dinner to prepare. Finn opened the cabinet, took out a box of rigatoni and a jar of roasted garlic flavored pasta sauce, and placed them on the counter. He retrieved a stockpot with a lid from under the counter, filled it with water and set it to boil.

In the fridge, he found a salad and some left over veggies from the weekend.

Using the heavy maple cutting board, he made short work of processing the vegetables.

He grabbed a deep-sided frying pan from the rack over the six-burner stove and added about a tablespoon of virgin olive oil to it. With a flick of the wrist, he turned on the gas and heated the oil. The onion went in first. When limp, he added the diced zucchini and chopped mushrooms. Took a few minutes for the fungi to cook down. Then he added the pasta sauce, placed a glass cover on the pan and let the contents simmer.

When he twisted to the side to toss the pasta into the boiling water, he spotted Elspeth out of the corner of his eye, leaning on the doorjamb, watching him, a sorrowful expression on her face.

"I am sorry for my terse words," she said. "I want to learn how to cook."

He dropped the pasta in the pot, set the timer and faced her. "Okay. On the weekends, I'll teach you what little I know about cooking." Though he'd already tried and the outcome had been burned food and hurt feelings.

"I saw on the talking picture box that a person can go to a school to learn how to cook."

"That's what you want to do?"

"Aye." Elspeth's jaw clenched tight.

"All right. I'll look into it tomorrow." He handed her the salad bowl. "Would you take this into the dining room and set the table? I'll be finished here in a few minutes."

He hoped a cooking instructor had better luck than he, teaching Elspeth to cook.

Elspeth hated *the city*.

Two sennight had passed since she came to Finn's time. On the occasions he'd taken her out—without a guard, she couldn't venture forth alone—she'd been overcome by the heat and stench. He said it was because of a garbage strike. Even with the rubbish gone, she didn't think she'd like the place.

There was no garden. Naught for her to do but stay inside and ply her skill at needlework.

That's why she wanted to learn how to cook. For the past sennight, Chef Jacque had come everyday to teach her.

She stared at the ingredients sitting on the kitchen counter and sighed. She'd told Finn to be home for dinner at seven. She might be having trouble learning how to cook, but she had mastered reading time on the clock. At least she had something of which to be proud.

Now, if only she could become skilled in the kitchen.

She had three hours to prepare the meal she'd planned with her instructor. Chef Jacque promised it wouldn't take that long, but she didn't want to risk Finn getting home before she was finished. If he watched her, she'd ruin their meal.

She intended to cook lamb stew. How difficult could that be? She'd seen Cookie and Aine make venison stew on many occasions at Castle Lachlan. Chef Jacque said it was peasant food, but they often ate similar fare at the castle and she'd seen Finn devour everything placed before him. She was determined to master the recipe.

Elspeth placed a large onion on the cutting board, took hold of the sharp knife and started slicing. Tears burned her eyes, but she kept chopping.

"Ouch!" Blood oozed from a cut on her left thumb. She dropped the knife and headed to the bathing chamber for her healing basket so she could wrap a rag around the wound.

By the time Finn got home from work, Elspeth had three fingers wrapped with rags, burn ointment smeared on her inner arm, but stew simmered on the stove.

"Hey, angel, smells great in here," he said as he entered the kitchen.

The loss of blood was worth hearing him say those words.

"I hope you like dinner." She hid her hands behind her back.

He lifted the lid and inhaled a deep whiff of the savory-smelling stew. "I'm sure it will be great."

"Wash up and sit at the table and I will serve."

"How about kissing your husband first." He pulled her into his arms, kissed her hard on the mouth, and managed to sit her on the counter top while standing between her legs.

She twirled her arms around his neck, her legs around his waist and melted into the kiss. Finn's warm lips were at her throat, grazing the edge of her blouse. Her breasts ached, wanting attention. She slanted her mouth, opened her lips, teased him with her tongue.

His manly groan was satisfying indeed.

"Maybe dinner can wait," he murmured into her ear before biting the lobe.

A whimper was all she could manage in response. He

ended the kiss, grabbed her wrists and unwrapped her arms from his neck.

She stiffened, waiting.

"What the hell did you do?" His accusing tone was like a splash of cold water from an icy loch.

She shrank back from him. She tried to tug her arms out of his grip, but he wouldn't let go. He carefully unwrapped each of the rags and studied her injuries. "That's it. We're hiring a cook."

"Nae! I can manage."

"Obviously not."

Frustrated tears sprang to her eyes. She couldn't help it. She'd tried so hard to make them a nice dinner. And now, he was angry.

"Please," she implored, using her eyes to sway him. "Go sit in the dining room and let me serve dinner."

"After I tend to your hands."

He was gentle. He used some magic strips to protect the cuts, but left the burn alone. At least he trusted her healing skills.

They both remained quiet while they ate the salad and stew she prepared.

"The stew is great, Elspeth," Finn broke the silence. He used a piece of crusty bread to clean the gravy from his bowl.

"So we dinnae need to hire a cook?"

"We'll see. Come on, I'll help you clean up." He pulled her from the chair and together they gathered the dishes.

At least he liked the stew. Maybe after she cooked a few more good meals, he'd give up wanting to hire a cook.

"Hey, I forgot to mention I have a surprise for you," Finn said as he loaded the dish washing machine. She hadn't mastered that apparatus yet.

Feeling buoyed by the success of dinner, she smiled. "What?"

"If I tell you, it won't be a surprise."

CHAPTER THIRTY

*T*hree days later, Finn paced his office like a caged lion. He glanced at the packages on the credenza and rubbed his chest where a twinge of guilt pinched. Not because he'd purchased the presents but that he planned time away from the office with Jim still missing.

Torn between the needs of his wife and that of his friend and business, he brooded, plagued by the press of his responsibilities. In frustration, he plunged into the leather desk chair and leaned on the intercom button to his admin. "Any word on Mr. Devlin?"

"No. His assistant hasn't heard anything."

"Okay. Thanks."

If he didn't learn Jim's whereabouts by tomorrow, he'd hire a private investigator. Wouldn't be the first time the firm used one. Finn procured one himself when he searched for his cousin, Laurie, a couple years ago.

Not that it had done any good in Laurie's case. Hard for a PI to find an individual traveling through time.

That thought birthed another. *What if?*

Nah. He shook his head. *Unlikely.*

He walked out of his office shortly past noon, planning to be gone for the rest of the day. An event totally out of character, especially under the circumstances. Still, he had to smile. Tonight would be special.

Briefcase in hand, he passed the desk of his admin on the way to the elevator.

"Hey. Are you leaving for the day?" She stared, bug-eyed.

"Yup. I'll be unreachable until tomorrow morning."

Her shock tickled his need for freedom and he quickened his pace. He carried a box under his left arm containing the silver sequined gown he bought the day before. The magnificent moonstone necklace and earrings he purchased to complement the dress were tucked in a velvet case within the briefcase he held on his right. There was no point in being wealthy if you didn't spend extravagantly on your wife.

Not that she would expect him to lavish her with gifts. She wasn't like the grasping women he'd known. His mind conjured the image of Amy Ferguson. He shook off the shudder skittering across his shoulder blades and entered the elevator.

Elspeth deserved the surprise he had in store for her.

As a sustaining patron of the New York Philharmonic, he garnered a special invitation to an exclusive champagne gala and private chamber music performance in the Kaplan Penthouse. Being CEO of a highly successful New York consulting firm had its benefits.

Tonight would be his first *date* with Elspeth in the twenty-first century and he planned to wine and dine her and introduce her to his world.

He figured he owed her a special night out for putting up with his long hours at the office and for her being alone so much. Never mind the debacle over her cooking skills.

She'd been working with Chef Jacque and was making simple meals each night. Finn still thought they should hire a cook for the bulk of their needs, but he was humoring her for now. Luck was with him. He caught a taxi when he hit the street.

A half hour later, Finn stepped off the elevator in their building and strode along the hall to their apartment. Before he reached their door, fire alarms blared.

Shit. What had she done this time?

He darted down the remainder of the hall and nearly broke in the apartment door, trying to gain access. He tossed aside the package and briefcase and dashed across the foyer then skidded around the corner into the dining room, coming to a dead stop.

Smoke wafted from the kitchen. "Elspeth!" he yelled, heart in throat.

She burst through the swinging door, clutching a fire extinguisher in her hands, her eyes wide and scared. Flour coated her hair and dark smudges marred the beauty of her face.

"I put the fire out." She coughed.

Great. Just great.

He picked up the ringing phone. "Yeah."

The voice on the other end of the line sounded panicked.

"We have everything under control. No, you don't need to come up. I've got it handled." Finn slammed down the receiver and counted to ten before looking at Elspeth.

"I burned the bread I was baking," she said in a quiet voice.

"Are you all right?"

"Aye, but the kitchen is a wee mess."

"We'll deal with it. What matters is you didn't get hurt."

"Nae. Only my pride is injured. Who was on the phone?"

"Building security. Our smoke detector triggered their alarm panel."

"I am sorry."

"Well, let's see what needs to be done." Finn followed Elspeth into the kitchen. After assessing the minor damage, he pulled out his cell phone and called the cleaning agency he used. "This is Finn MacIntyre. We had a small oven fire. Can you send someone over to clean the mess? Great. Thanks."

Elspeth stared at the oven, her expression forlorn.

"How did you know how to use that?" Finn pointed to the extinguisher she still clutched in her hands.

She carefully laid it on the granite counter. "'Twas the first thing Chef Jacque taught me."

"Smart man." Finn attempted a smile though his heart still raced from the fear rushing through his veins. He didn't want to imagine what could have happened to Elspeth if the fire had grown out of control.

She picked up a dishrag. He removed it from her hands. "Don't bother. The cleaning company will take care of the mess. We're going out tonight and you need to bathe and," he tugged on her braid, "wash your hair."

Her silver eyes brightened. "We are going out?"

"Yeah. We'll go to Central Park for a carriage ride, then dinner at the Park Grille, and afterward a champagne gala at the Philharmonic."

She smiled. "I have never done any of those things."

"You'll enjoy the night." He planned for the evening to be romantic. Every woman's dream.

"What shall I wear?" she asked, looking worried.

"That is part of the surprise." Finn squeezed Elspeth's hand.

A while later, Elspeth stepped from the bathing chamber wearing Finn's robe, her wet hair wrapped in a thick drying cloth. She couldn't believe he behaved so reasonably about her blunder in the kitchen. The image of the flaming bread pan remained imbedded in her mind. The thought of what could have happened made her shudder.

Living in his time sometimes seemed beyond her ability.

"Sit over here. I'll comb out your hair. I'd like you to wear it unbound."

Elspeth gasped, her gaze shooting to Finn, unaware he'd returned to their chamber from the guest chamber where he'd bathed. He wore snug—pants he'd called them—and a white shirt with tucks down the front exposing his throat. Desire sparked, and she wanted to kiss the exposed skin. She refrained from getting too close, knowing where her passion would lead.

They would never go to dinner. And she wanted to get out of the stifling apartment. Away from the cloying odor of her latest failure.

"Come on. Sit." He patted the padded bench he'd pulled in front of a mirror.

"As you wish." She sat and unwrapped the toweling from her hair. The damp strawberry-blond strands fell around her shoulders in disarray.

She met Finn's gaze in the mirror. He winked then ran the comb through her hair, careful of the knots.

Tension eased with his gentle ministrations. Her mind wandered, here and there and back again, refusing to linger on her inadequacies.

What had he purchased for her to wear? She couldn't imagine.

What did a person wear for a carriage ride, dinner, and philymonic? She wasn't sure what a philymonic was, but she'd enjoy a carriage ride and dinner.

"Finished." Finn put down the comb.

"Thank you."

"You are very welcome, angel." He kneaded her shoulders.

She liked the feel of his big hands. The thought made her breasts tingle.

"Don't look like that or we'll never leave the apartment tonight."

She lowered her lashes and hid a smile. She could wait. Later, after they returned from their evening out, she'd unleash her passion on her husband. That would be her surprise for him.

He bent his head and kissed her cheek. "Time for your gift."

Finn presented her with a large white box tied with a blue velvet ribbon. In her time, they would have had to travel to the Glasgow fair to find something so fine. She untied the bow and ran the ribbon through her fingers. "Shall I wear this weaved through my hair?"

"Not today."

She set the ribbon aside, saving it for another day, and stared at the box.

"Aren't you going to open it?"

She lifted the lid and pushed away the paper wrapping. "Oh, my!" Tears swam in her eyes.

She lifted the sparkling fabric from the box and held it up. Her heart fluttered in her chest as the gown flowed to the floor. "Beautiful. I have never owned anything so lovely."

Finn helped her don the dress. The silk lining teased her skin as he slipped it over her head and secured the magic fastener in back. Something he called a zipper.

The gown fit like a second skin, making her imagine she was beautiful. She gasped when she glanced in the looking glass. She looked beautiful.

Finn stepped up behind her and she caught his admiring gaze in the mirror. He reached around her neck and clasped a string of moonstones at her throat. She reached up and grasped one of the cool stones. "For me?"

"There is no one else in the room."

"True," she said, awed by his generosity. Then he clipped a couple more stones to each of her earlobes, and she cried in earnest.

"Have I welcomed you properly to the twenty-first century with my gifts?"

"Oh, aye. They are splendid."

Finn handed her a tissue, and she wiped below her eyes.

"I'm having a matching ring made to present as a betrothal ring for our formal marriage."

"You are verra considerate, husband."

"How do you plan to thank me?"

She twisted around, twirled her arms about his neck, and found his lips with her kiss.

He held her at arm's length. "Hold that thought for later."

A shimmy of anticipation flowed through her. *Aye, later.*

After Finn finished dressing, buttoning his shirt so she could no longer glimpse his throat, adding a wide black ribbon under his collar tied in an elaborate bow, and donning a black jacket, they were off.

The yellow conveyance—a taxi—whisked them across town to a place Finn named Central Park.

Finn held out a hand. The soles of Elspeth's silver silk pumps touched the sidewalk, and he assisted her from the taxi. She'd gushed over the shoes when he presented them to her. She made life fun. She marveled over things that he took for granted. He couldn't imagine living without her.

Iain had better agree to their formal marriage when the time came. Though only God knew how Finn would wait until then to officially claim her as his bride. Living together just wasn't the same. Sure, they were handfasted, but that meant nothing in the twenty-first century.

When they returned home tonight, they'd work at making a child. Slipping a hand within his jacket, he discreetly adjusted the family jewels.

The sparkle in Elspeth's eyes as she took in the sight of Central Park matched the dazzle of her silver gown. She gasped when they approached the horse drawn carriage and the driver with his black top hat and contagious smile. "How marvelous."

He grasped her elbow and guided her to the carriage. She brushed her hand along the horse's flank. The old mare twisted her head then returned to chomping at the feedbag set before her, unconcerned by the attention.

Finn handed the driver his business card, having previously arranged the ride, and assisted Elspeth onto the worn leather seat. As he set his foot on the step to join her, the hairs at his nape stood on end. He whipped his head around and froze.

Couldn't be. A man who looked remarkably like Douglas returned his stare then vanished into the milling crowd.

"Is something wrong?" Elspeth asked, her brow wrinkled with concern.

"I thought…thought I saw a friend. One of the reenactors

from Anderson Creek. The one who sold me the magic sword."

"Why would he be here?"

"I don't know. Probably wasn't him." Finn shook his head. "I must be mistaken. More than likely was someone else."

With a strong resemblance to Douglas?

What would he be doing in New York? If he were in town on a buying trip for the *Celtic Image* shop, he would have called to let Finn know he was in town. He wouldn't be stalking Finn and Elspeth.

Finn swung up into the carriage and sat next to his wife. "Are you cold? I didn't think to get a shawl to match your gown."

"Nae, the late afternoon air is pleasant."

"Good." He slipped an arm around her shoulders. "Besides, I can keep you warm." Her purr heated his blood as she cuddled against his side.

The driver leapt onto his seat and clicked his tongue for the horse to proceed. They made a circuit through the park, returning to where they began an hour later.

Finn scanned the crowd. No sign of the man he thought he saw.

At the Park Grille, Elspeth took Finn's arm, and they followed a gentleman into a dining chamber where well-dressed patrons sat at linen draped tables. Dark wood paneled the walls. Magnificent torches hung from the ceiling, providing a warmly-lit atmosphere.

She did her best not to gawk at the lavish surroundings. She'd seen pictures of similar dining chambers in a picture book Finn had at home. *Architectural Interiors*, she thought it was titled. She squeezed the wool fabric wrapping her shoulders, the soft blue shawl Finn purchased for her after leaving the park, hoping to stifle the jittery sensation in her belly.

Women stared as she and Finn walked through the

dinning chamber, their gazes eating him alive then settling on her in envy. Let them ogle. He belonged to her. Their escort reached for her shawl, but she held tight to the fabric, afraid she'd feel exposed without the covering.

"The lady will keep her wrap. Feels a bit chilly in here, doesn't it, my dear?"

Elspeth nodded, glad Finn was aware of her unease.

They were seated at a fine table, aglow with crystal glassware reflecting the amber light, and bedecked with silver fit for the king.

Another man approached the table. "My name is Edmund. I'll be your server for the evening. May I bring cocktails…or perhaps a bottle of fine wine?"

Finn reviewed a book listing the many different wines offered. He selected a bottle of brut champagne. The bottle arrived in a silver bucket filled with ice.

Bubbles teased her nose when she took her first sip, forcing her to stifle a sneeze.

The server returned a short while later. "Are you ready to order?"

"Would you like me to order for you, my dear?" Finn leaned close and murmured.

"Oh, aye."

Elspeth had learned much about present day cuisine and serving from Chef Jacque, but lacked confidence to order for herself. Her skin heated with embarrassment. She dreaded admitting to her mentor the failure with the fresh baked bread. Cookie made loaves for the entire clan at Castle Lachlan. Elspeth should be able to master the making of one loaf for her and Finn to share every couple of days.

Finn's gaze lingered on her, making her skin heat in a different way. He seemed to have other things on his mind. She moistened her suddenly dry lips. Finn's eyes flared.

The waiter cleared his throat.

"Ah, yes," Finn said, his sinful gaze dropping to the menu book. "We shall start with spinach salad. Please serve the warm bacon dressing on the side."

"Yes, sir. And for the main course?"

"The lady will have the salmon with tomato relish. I, the porcini-rubbed Delmonico. And serve us both French green beans with shallots as a side."

"Shall be my pleasure." The waiter nodded and backed away.

Elspeth exhaled a frustrated breath, feeling needy between her legs, wishing they were home alone.

"Is anything wrong?" Finn asked, touching her arm.

"Nae. Everything is lovely."

"I'm glad." He gave her a tender pat as the waiter returned with their salads.

They ate in silence for a few minutes then Finn lowered his fork to the plate. "I've invited a few people over for a party next Friday night. Please don't take offense, but I think I'll need to hire a chef or a caterer to prepare the food."

It galled Elspeth to agree. "Perhaps Chef Jacque."

"Sure. If he's available."

After they finished the main course, the waiter came by with the dessert tray—everything looked scrumptious—Elspeth settled on fresh berries served with cream.

"I'll have black coffee and Nocello," Finn said.

The berry dessert tasted like a bit of heaven.

"What is that you are drinking?" she asked.

"Walnut flavored liqueur. Would you care for a taste? It's sweet."

The liquid slid over her tongue, tasting better than honey.

"I've so enjoyed dinner," Elspeth gushed.

Finn squeezed her fingers. "I'm glad, but the best of the evening is yet to come."

Finn escorted Elspeth through the mingling crowd and into the music room. About fifty chairs were arranged in a semi-circle around the front of a small grouping of music stands. Their seats were third row center.

He seated Elspeth. "I'll go get us a glass of champagne.

Will you be all right here alone?"

"Of course."

"Be right back."

"Dinnae worry. I will be fine."

Finn headed for the bar set up in the reception area then glanced back to Elspeth, making sure she was okay. When he turned around to proceed, he stumbled into a soft body.

"Wow. Amy. What a surprise. What are you doing in New York?" He glanced past the woman, trying to figure out which poor guy was her escort.

She gazed at him through mascara-caked lashes and batted her eyelids. "Aren't you glad to see me?" She pursed her lips into what she probably thought a sexy pout.

Heat raced through Finn, and he tugged at the collar of his tuxedo shirt. "Wh-why, sure. What are you doing here?"

"Seeing a concert, silly."

"Of course you are."

Finn continued to scan the room, trying to figure out with whom Amy came. Who he could unload her on.

"I hear congratulations are in order," she said rather cattily.

"For what?"

"Your engagement."

"Thank you." He shuffled his feet. "Well, the concert will start soon so I better get back to my seat." He stepped away toward the music room door.

"I'll see you at home then."

Finn stopped and turned to face her. "Home? What are you talking about?"

"I moved to New York and leased the apartment next to yours." Having released that volley with a smug smile, she stepped past him and walked into the music room.

He stared after her for several minutes his mouth agape.

He gathered himself, collected two glasses of champagne and returned to his and Elspeth's seats where he found his wife speaking to an elderly couple seated next to her.

Finn scanned the room. Amy was nowhere in sight. The

crowd wasn't large enough for her to hide within it. Where was she? A shiver snaked down his spine.

Was he being stalked?

Seemed an odd coincidence the woman would be living in the next apartment over from him and Elspeth. Amy had better not intend to cause them grief.

CHAPTER THIRTY-ONE

*L*oud tapping on the apartment door caused Finn to raise his gaze from the Sunday morning news blog he read on his tablet device. Elspeth wore a puzzled expression, her brow creased. She looked cute in black silk pajama pants and an oversized white hoodie, her long braid hanging to one side.

"Who do you think it is?" she asked.

He shrugged, somewhat annoyed. He'd no idea who knocked. No one had called from the concierge desk to announce a visitor. Still dressed in his favorite green and blue MacIntyre plaid PJ bottoms, though well past noon, he padded barefoot across the polished wood floor to check the security monitor.

Shit. Amy.

What was she doing at the door? The answer wasn't a stretch. *Stalker.*

He'd hoped after he returned with Elspeth from the past, women would stop pursuing him. He needed to make it known he was unavailable.

The other evening at the Philharmonic, Amy mentioned hearing he was engaged. Where had she gotten her information? His in-laws wouldn't spread rumors. No one else knew the situation between him and Elspeth. He hadn't even notified his father since David MacIntyre was out on an African dig and unreachable.

Maybe Finn should ask Iain's permission to officially announce an engagement to society. Put it in the papers and all the other places such things were announced. Surely, Laurie could help with the particulars. She was once a debutante.

Though believing he had a romantic partner didn't seem to stop Amy from bothering them. More knocking made him grind his molars. Drawing in a long breath, he cracked the door.

"Hi! Thought I'd drop by to meet your fiancée." Amy attempted to lean around Finn and see into the apartment. He dodged her efforts.

"As you can see," he swept his hand the length of his body, "we're still in our pajamas."

"Doesn't matter to me." Amy smiled brightly, ogling his bare chest.

Of course, it didn't. *Dammit to hell.*

"Finn, who's at the door?" Elspeth called as she approached.

When he turned around to address her, Amy slid past into the front hall.

"Hi, I'm Amy. A good friend of Finn's from way back." Her tone implied more than friends.

"Only since last summer." He gritted his teeth, barely managing a polite smile.

He strode past the women into the living room and grabbed a wrinkled oxford shirt from the back of the leather sofa, shrugged into it, and secured most of the buttons to cover his chest. The two women followed him into the room.

"Would you care for a cup of tea—coffee?" Elspeth hesitantly asked Amy.

"Sure. Java would be great. I brought homemade cranberry-orange scones to share." She held out a covered plate he hadn't noticed before. "Thought you might like them. I'm dying to get to know you."

Amy's fake grin would annoy a heavenly angel. His angel moistened her lips nervously, desperate to please. *Damn Amy!*

"Set them on the dining room table. I will get the coffee." Elspeth headed toward the kitchen. "Finn just made a fresh pot," she said, over her shoulder, and slipped through the swinging door.

Amy raised her brows. "You have hidden talents."

He tightened his jaw. The woman would drive anyone mad. She brushed past him and strutted into the next room. He followed to the doorway.

She set the plate on the dining table and swung around to face him. "Nice digs. I love the antique cherry furniture." He bet she did. *Gold-digger.*

Finn glanced back at the kitchen door. Good. Elspeth was out of ear range. She didn't need to hear what he had to say. He flipped his gaze back to Amy and lowered his voice. "What are you doing here?"

"Being neighborly." She lowered her lashes, feigning innocence.

"Are you sure you haven't an ulterior motive?"

"Now why would you suspect me of duplicity?"

"You have a reputation." He strode to within a foot of her, crowding her, hoping to make her uncomfortable. Maybe she would leave.

"Lies." She tossed her hair and struck a pose, hip stuck out, hand at waist. "You can't believe everything you hear."

"I'm warning you." His temper simmered just below the surface. So what if it exploded? He gripped her wrist, rougher than intended.

"About what?" She tugged her arm, attempting to break his hold. When she couldn't, she jutted her chin forward and scowled.

He shook the arm he held. "Don't play dumb. You know what I mean."

"I don't."

"Come now, Amy, you can't expect me to believe your appearance here is a coincidence."

"Let go of my arm, Finn, or I'll scream."

They glared into each other's eyes, playing chicken.

Finally, he released her with a flick of his wrist, gently casting her off. Just in time. Elspeth returned with a serving tray containing the coffee pot and three mugs, which she set on the dining room table next to Amy's scones. Highland hospitality unwarranted for their unwanted guest.

Amy wore a smug smile as if she won round one.

Finn wasn't sure what game they played, but he'd be damned before he let her win. He'd need to keep an eye on his new neighbor. Make sure she wasn't out to cause trouble.

He cracked his neck, hoping to let off steam. Maybe he read too much into her actions.

"Please, sit, Amy." Elspeth pointed to a chair at the side of the table. "I will pour. Do you take cream—sugar?"

"Black is fine. I need to watch my figure." Amy perched on the offered chair, and Elspeth placed a cup of hot brew in front of her. Chef Jacque made progress with Elspeth. She'd be quite the social hostess in time. An asset for his business.

Not that it mattered. He loved her as she was.

She placed a mug at his usual place, rolled her eyes at him and prepared tea for herself. She was no fool.

He sat and poured himself coffee.

"I love your long hair. I've never seen hair so long." Amy squeezed Elspeth's braid then picked up her mug and sipped. Finn wished Amy would keep her hands to herself. He didn't like her touching Elspeth.

"Thank you." Elspeth blushed.

"I'd grow mine long, but long, straight hair is so out of style," Amy added maliciously. "Yours is longer than any I've seen."

Finn noted the sheen in Elspeth's eyes. He wanted to strangle the bitch for upsetting her.

He saw red as the two women continued chatting. How could he get rid of the woman?

❀ ❀ ❀

A couple of days later, Elspeth pursed her lips and stared into the looking glass, feeling lonely and miserable. Finn was late again. Cold and impersonal, this future didn't meet with her expectations. As much as she loved her husband, and had been glad to see her parents, and Patrick and Laurie again, she missed Scotland, Castle Lachlan, and most of all, her garden. New York City was bleak and unfriendly.

And she wanted to tear her hair out.

She removed the tie from the end of the offending braid, ran her fingers through the weave and let the strands fall about her shoulders. Scissors held in a tight grip, she was tempted to sheer the unruly locks, but hesitated, refusing to shed the tears burning her eyes.

She wanted one of those cute hairstyles like the ones on the pages of a fashion magazine. Amy recommended Elspeth visit a beauty salon. Maybe her new friend was right.

Elspeth glared at her image in the mirror. Maybe Finn would like her better if she looked more like modern women. Maybe he wouldn't stay at work so late if he found her more attractive. Maybe he would come home from work early for a change so he wasn't too tired to make love.

Decision made, she returned the scissor to the drawer in the dressing table. Back stiff, head held high, she marched out of the apartment, strode down the hall and knocked on Amy's door.

Jim Devlin remained missing.

Finn leaned back in the taxi seat, loosened his tie and undid the top button of his shirt. The private investigator he hired promised results, but warned the search might take time.

Time might be a luxury they could ill afford. Finn had a bad feeling about Jim's disappearance.

The cab pulled up to the curb in front of his apartment building and Finn hopped out. He glanced up at the stars. Oh heck, how had he lost track of the time. Elspeth was certain to be disappointed he was late for dinner. Really late. Again. *Hope she ate without me.* When he entered the apartment, he stilled, frozen in place, certain something was wrong.

Sobbing sounds came from the bedroom. What calamity had Elspeth gotten into this time? At least smoke didn't foul the air. Thank God for small favors.

A few long strides had him at the doorway to their room. Shit!

His wife sat on the floor in a yoga position, the hood of her sweatshirt covering her lowered head, her shoulders hunched and shuddering with the force of her mournful sobs.

Finn went to her, crouched in front of her, reached out a hand, hesitant, as if approaching a wounded animal. He gently touched her denim-covered knee. "What's wrong, angel?"

She raised her gaze, her eyes dark and haunted.

Fear knotted in his gut. "What happened?"

In slow motion, she raised her hands and pushed back the hood.

"Ah, shit. What have you done?" That was a stupid question. She'd cut her hair.

"You dinnae like it." The crying started again in earnest.

He sat, wrapped his arms around her and pulled her onto his lap.

"Shush. Don't cry. I didn't say I didn't like it." He rocked her. "Was a shock is all."

Elspeth burrowed her head into his shoulder, still weeping.

"Why did you cut you hair?" he asked gently, stroking her blunt-cut hair.

She sniffled. "Long hair is out of style."

Amy. Finn kept his growl to himself. The woman meant trouble.

"I like your new haircut," he murmured near his wife's ear, hoping to make her feel better. "It's sexy."

She leaned back to look into his eyes. "Really?"

"Sure." He kissed the tip of her nose. "Now, let's go dry your tears and have dinner."

"I donated my hair to charity." She pulled a receipt from her pocket as they rose, and handed it to him.

She was such a generous soul. He hated the idea of Amy making her feel bad about herself. He tugged on a lock. "I really do like it."

"Thank you." She wiped the moisture from her eyes with the handkerchief he provided. "I spoke to Chef Jacque, he'll help me prepare for the party on Friday."

"Sounds good." He followed Elspeth into the kitchen relieved she'd changed the subject.

He grabbed a bowl from under the counter then opened the refrigerator and collected salad fixings.

After some serious cutting and chopping, Finn glanced up from tossing the salad. Elspeth scooted around the kitchen, preparing dinner. She seemed recovered from her crying jag. The new haircut looked great on her, but he wanted Amy to stay away from his wife.

"Maybe you shouldn't spend time with Amy."

"Why not?"

"I don't trust her."

"Why? She seems nice. And I have nae friends here."

"It's just that, well, she reminds me of Alexander's friend Jonet."

Elspeth's brow furrowed. "Dinnae be silly, they are naught alike."

Early Friday morning, Elspeth wandered along a path in Central Park, trying to figure out what to do about her dilemma. Shortly after Finn left for work, Chef Jacque called and cancelled. A family matter had arisen and the chef would be unable to help prepare the food for Finn's party tonight.

She worried her bottom lip. What was she to do? If she handled the food preparation alone and something went wrong, she'd make a fool of herself and embarrass Finn in front of his guests. Trying to calm down, she inhaled a deep breath of air laced with the woodsy scents of autumn. Even with the potential for disaster tonight, she was happy to be free of the apartment's confines and the smelly streets of their neighborhood for a short time.

Central Park was the only place in New York that felt at all like home. Well, not truly like home. At least, she was outdoors. She sighed. Soon she'd need to return to the apartment and begin cooking.

The morning sun warmed her face and she managed a small smile.

Nannies walked past with baby carriages. A couple of joggers ran by. When Elspeth rounded a bend, she found her and Finn's new neighbor sitting on a bench weeping. She rushed over to console Amy. "What is the matter?" She joined the woman on the bench.

"I moved here to work in *Le Grand Café*, that posh restaurant over on Fifth Ave., but the board of health closed the place down so I'm out a job. My parents paid for my apartment for six months. I have to stay in New York, but I don't have any money to live on."

"Finn's been considering hiring a cook. Maybe you could work for us until you find another restaurant in need of an apprentice chef," Elspeth said.

"Really?" Amy's eyes brightened. "Do you think I could work for you and Finn?"

"Aye," Elspeth said, though her insides squirmed. Maybe she shouldn't commit to such an arrangement without first discussing the matter with Finn. Would he be angry?

"You're a lifesaver." Amy beamed.

Too late to back out now.

"Are you available today? Finn is having a party tonight and Chef Jacque, my cooking instructor, needed to cancel. I am afraid I will be unable to handle the food preparation for the party by myself."

"Sure. I'll help." Amy's expression reminded Elspeth of a child who'd gotten away with stealing something.

Worried she'd made a mistake hiring Amy, she glanced away, only to notice a large man wearing a red and green kilt, watching them. When he saw her looking at him, he slipped into the trees, out of sight.

Odd. Men didn't wear kilts in New York.

She couldn't get a sense as to whether he meant them harm or nae. Her gift had completely deserted her since she handfasted with Finn.

"Do you have the party menu planned? Have you done the grocery shopping?" Amy's questions startled Elspeth and she faced the woman.

"We only need prepare the food."

"Great. Let's go." Amy leapt from the bench.

Elspeth swept her gaze to the spot where the man had stood. "Did you see the man who was standing in the shadows watching us?"

"I didn't see any guy. You're probably paranoid 'cause you're not used to living in the city. The town your parents live in is rather rural."

"Perhaps." A man had been watching. Elspeth was positive. Who was he? Why was he interested in them?

"We better hurry if you want everything ready for when the guests arrive."

"Of course." Elspeth shook off her unease and walked with Amy toward the cabstand.

Finn hung up the phone and clenched his fists.

What was Amy up to? What was Caitrina up to?

He received two irritating phone calls during the day. The first, this morning, from his wife, announcing she hired Amy as their cook. Although he was annoyed with Elspeth and needed to figure out how to get rid of Amy, the second call from Douglas proved more disturbing.

Finn's friend had found torn fabric near Laurie's garden gate. A ragged piece of gray wool gabardine, like from a man's suit. Douglas worried someone might have wandered through the time gate. Of course, nothing would happen unless the person walked through on a full moon.

And only if Caitrina cast her darned faerie magic.

The annoying faerie was missing. Douglas believed she was in New York, trying to keep Amy away from Finn and Elspeth.

Too late for that. Amy was in their apartment, helping his wife prepare for the party tonight. Why Caitrina felt the need to get involved was an unknown. He ran a hand over his face, regretting scheduling the party. The last thing he needed was for his unusual life to blow up in front of his New York friends and business associates.

Releasing a deep sigh, he shoved some unread papers into his briefcase. At least he hadn't completely lost his mind. He'd been right when he thought he saw Douglas in Central Park the afternoon they'd gone for the carriage ride. The man was searching for Caitrina. God help her when he found her. Douglas was livid.

Not Finn's problem at the moment. He had enough to worry about with Amy in his home with Elspeth.

Finn checked his watch. Nearly six. Guests would start arriving at seven. He shrugged into his suit jacket, grabbed his briefcase and headed for the door.

When he arrived home, he found Elspeth standing outside the kitchen door, an unhappy expression on her pretty face.

"What's the matter, angel?"

"Amy refuses to allow me to help. She claims I get in the way."

"It's your kitchen. You hired her."

"I ken that." Elspeth's lip quivered. "I feel so useless."

Placing his arms around her, he pulled her close and hugged her tight. She gave him a squeeze back then tilted her head to look at him.

"I am worthless in your time."

"Not to me." He kissed the tip of her nose. "The adjustment is difficult, I know. But you'll find your niche just like your parents and Patrick did."

"I hope you are right." She pulled away, and her chin lifted. "We are expecting guests and I need to dress."

"That's my girl." He tweaked her nose.

She smiled, and melted his heart.

Her hips swayed as she sashayed away. Damn, she looked great in tight jeans. His body tightened. He wanted to get inside those jeans.

More than ready to follow her, the ringing of the phone stopped him mid-step. Damn. The party. The first of the guests had arrived.

Elspeth returned to the living room, wearing the little black dress she'd begged Finn to purchase for her. She tugged on the hem, wishing to make it longer. When she let go, it clung to her legs, several inches above the knee. The dress had looked great on the salesperson. Now, Elspeth wasn't so sure she liked exposing so much of her skin.

Finn whistled as she approached, his smile wide.

Then again, he seemed to like the way she looked. She twirled her short hair for affect.

"You look terrific."

"Thank you." She reached up on tiptoes and brushed his lips with hers.

He leaned into her and took the kiss deeper. She pressed into him, absorbing his strength. She would need it for the evening ahead.

The sound of a clearing throat broke them apart. An extremely tall, broad man, dressed in a modern kilt and heavy knit sweater, grinned.

Finn chuckled. "Elspeth, this is my very good friend. Douglas McKinnon."

She smiled and was surprised when he bowed over her hand as the Highlanders of her time did.

The man in the park.

"I saw you this morning, in the park, in the shadows near the trees. You were watching me."

"Guilty as accused."

"Why? Why were you watching me?"

Finn's eyes narrowed. "Yeah, Douglas. Why were you in the park, stalking my wife? How'd you know it was her? That she was there?"

Douglas chuckled. "Don't get your panties in a bind, big guy. Iain showed me a picture he took before you left North Carolina. Asked me to look in on Elspeth. When I saw her leave the apartment, I followed. I thought I was discreet. Guess not."

Finn's phone rang. "If you'll excuse me, there are probably more guests on their way up."

Turning his head slightly toward Elspeth so his friend couldn't see, he mouthed, "Will you be all right with Douglas?"

Elspeth nodded. Douglas reminded her of the men of her clan. She glanced at him from under her lashes.

"Would you care to sit with me, lass? I bring greetings from your parents."

"News?"

"Greetings and gossip. Shall we find a quiet place to sit?" Douglas waved his arm and she led him into Finn's study where the closed door dulled the noise from the other guests.

Several hours later, Elspeth hesitated in the front hall, not wanting to rejoin the party. The only person she'd felt comfortable with was Finn's friend, Douglas, and he'd already left for the night. How long would the remaining guests stay?

She felt so out-of-place, like…the penguins at the Central Park Zoo. She hoped the party ended soon.

A loud knocking on the apartment door made her jump. She jerked her head to the door then swept it to the doorway of the living room. Finn's friends conversed in small groups. No one paid her any mind, or acknowledged the persistent rapping.

Seeing no other option, she opened the door.

"Well, well, well. What have we here? Had I known Finn

invited such lovely dessert, I would have arrived sooner."

The leering man leaned against the doorframe, grinning like a fool.

"Tim, I didn't think you were coming." Finn strode into the hall.

The man swayed, as sloppy as a drunken warrior. Elspeth wondered who he was.

Finn lunged to the man's side and used his body to prop the man up. "Come on, I think we need to get some coffee in you."

The two men staggered into the kitchen, Finn taking most of the man's weight.

Elspeth made small talk with an older man who attended the party with a much younger woman. He was pleasant and attentive, but Elspeth's gaze kept slipping to the swinging door and the kitchen.

When Amy strutted out, she made her excuses and headed for the kitchen. She cracked the door, ready to enter, hesitating when she overhead Finn and his guest talking.

"Finn, you're a lucky guy. You've a beautiful young fiancée for your arm."

Her husband's eyes narrowed to slits, his jaw tightened, hands fisted at his sides. Why did the comment make him angry? Didn't he think her beautiful? Elspeth bit her lip, desperate to hear what else they would say.

The daggers Finn shot from his eyes didn't stop the other man. He kept speaking as if what he had to say was vitally important. "Every successful executive should have a beautiful wife, of course. And a sexy cook to bed. You've the best of both worlds, I think."

Elspeth froze, unable to breath, her heart shattering into a million pieces. Finn was bedding Amy. No wonder he claimed to work late most nights. She quietly slipped away, desperate to flee. Amy was like Jonet, and Finn no better than Alexander.

CHAPTER THIRTY-TWO

*E*lspeth feigned sleep when Finn came to their bedchamber. He padded past the bed and into the bath chamber. At the spatter of running water, she rolled to face the wall away from his side of the bed and the open door. The last thing she wanted to see was his perfect body—golden skin—as he undressed. She muffled sobs into the pillow, hoping the shower would also hide the sound of her pitiful tears.

After a short time, he climbed into bed beside her. She held perfectly still, going limp when he pulled her back against his chest and nuzzled her neck. She hated the needy desire that pulsed through her at his touch. Finn's betrayal was so much worse than what Alexander perpetrated against her. She loved Finn. The thought of him with Amy made Elspeth's stomach knot and her throat clog. The modern world closed in on her. She needed to get away. Return to her time where life made sense.

How would she make it through the night? His body pressed against hers. How would she survive the rest of her life without him? When his breathing evened and she knew he slept, she sniffled and slipped from his embrace. Through the night, she held her tears deep within her heart.

Early in the morning, he slid from the bed in silence, believing she slept.

She sighed with a painful kind of relief when the apartment door shut and he was on his way. Thank the saints. He had an early Saturday morning meeting at the office about his missing lawyer. She waited until the lock clicked, waited a few minutes more, then leapt from the bed. She needed to get out of the apartment, away from her life with Finn.

She moved as if in a fog while she dressed in a pair of jeans, a white v-neck sweater, and the navy wool blazer Finn bought for her. She sat on the bed and tugged on a pair of boots of the finest leather. Her gaze swept the chamber they shared. Nothing belonged to her. Finn purchased everything.

In her time, she would have brought land to the marriage. Here she had naught.

The wee carved chest on the dressing table caught her gaze. Well, not everything had been given to her by Finn. She still had the moonstone brooch her mother had given her when she'd become a woman. Too bad Elspeth had lost her visions.

Maybe she would have foreseen Finn's betrayal.

She removed the brooch from the box and fastened it to the lapel of her blazer. She didn't bother to take the other moonstone jewelry Finn had given her. The only things she'd take were the garments on her back and the credit card he'd taught her to use.

She'd convince her da to pay Finn back after she walked though the time gate.

A final perusal of the apartment tore at her heart. She would never return. Elspeth raised her chin and stepped through the doorway into the hall and her uncertain future. Her hands fisted as she passed Amy's apartment door. Damn the witch!

Elspeth marched past and pushed the button for the moving box, swallowing uneasily. She hated riding the thing, but there were too many stairs down to street level. She hesitated for a moment in the building foyer, letting her stomach settle.

Once on the street, she stopped cold. Where could she go? How would she get to North Carolina and the time gate? If she called her parents for help, they would phone Finn and inform him of her plans. She couldn't bear to face him.

She glanced up and down the avenue. There must be a place she could go and think.

People strolled by without a care in the world, unaware of her turmoil. Elspeth wandered along Second Avenue then turned the corner onto East Sixty-Second Street walking in the direction of Central Park. Always nervous in the city's crowds, she kept an eye on the paned glass windows she passed, watching for anyone who might get too close and wish her harm. Where was a guardsman when you needed one? Jamie? How thoughtlessly she walked away from her old life.

Who was she fooling? Certainly not herself. She'd wanted to see her parents, Patrick and Laurie, and her niece and nephews. And she'd wanted to spend the rest of her life with Finn.

She'd better not dwell on what should have been or she'd lose her nerve.

Elspeth headed for the coffee shop Finn had taken her to on the previous Sunday. She didn't know where else to go. The only thing she really liked about New York were the coffee establishments. The tantalizing aroma of roasted beans filled her senses as she entered the bustling shop.

Glancing around, she stumbled over her feet. The sight of the man sitting at one of the far tables almost had her running back out the door. Too late. He waved her over.

What was Douglas MacKinnon doing here?

Oh bother, she'd need to say hello so he wouldn't think anything wrong.

"Mornin'. How are you this fine day?" He stood as she approached.

Elspeth inhaled deep through her nose, trying not to burst into tears.

"What ever is the matter, lass?"

He pulled out a chair for her, and she sat. He returned to his seat and stared at her, making her squirm at the intensity in his gaze. His eyes darkened and a frown curved his lips downward.

"Something terrible must have happened to put such sadness in your eyes." Not only did he see the shame in her eyes. She felt as if Douglas saw right into her soul. "Perhaps I can help."

"I dinnae—"

He clasped her hand on the table and some of the tightness in her chest eased.

"I'm a good listener and I wouldn't share anything you confide in me."

"But my problem is with Finn and he is your friend."

"I wish to be your friend too. Tell me your sorrows and I will help if I can."

"I need to go to my parents."

"Ah, I see." His mouth thinned. "Does Finn know you intend to return to Andersen Creek?"

She lowered her gaze and shook her head.

"What has the knucklehead done?"

"Finn is not the man I thought he was. Here, in Manhattan, he is cold and unfeeling."

"He's under a lot of pressure with the business and—"

"I ken that. That is no excuse to take a mistress."

"What?" Douglas made a growling sound deep in his throat. "Who?"

"Our neighbor. Amy."

"The lad *is* a fool." He lunged to his feet and reached out his hand. "Come. I have a friend with a plane. We'll be in Anderson Creek well before dinner time."

"Mr. MacIntyre?"

Finn glanced up from the disturbing papers on his desk. His administrative assistant stood in the threshold of his office suite, smiling.

"Yes?" He'd need to remember to give her a bonus for all the nights and weekends she worked.

"There's a call on line one from your cousin, Laurie. She says it's important."

Finn glanced at his watch. He had five minutes before he was due in the boardroom. "I'll take the call, but don't put anymore through."

"Yes, sir." His assistant left.

Finn pressed the line button and picked up the receiver. "Hey, Laurie. What's so important you're calling me at the office on a Saturday afternoon?"

"I should ask you what you're doing in the office on a Saturday afternoon. But I'm sure it's something important. It always is."

"Long story. I'll tell you next time we talk." He cracked his neck, hoping to release some of the pressure building from the bad feeling he had about the unexpected emergency board meeting. "Listen, I'm really in a hurry. What's up?"

"Brigit at *Le Petite Café* is giving cooking classes."

"You called to tell me that?"

"Elspeth has signed up for a month-long session."

"So she plans to travel south and visit with her parents and take some cooking lessons while she's there. Sounds good to me. Although a month is a bit long. I'll certainly miss her." Using his shoulder to hold the phone receiver, he shoved several reports into his valise.

"Finn, you don't understand. She's already here."

"What!" His gut clenched.

"I thought you might be ignorant of the fact. She showed up at the inn late this afternoon, her eyes red and puffy from crying. She was behind closed doors with Iain and Mairi then went to the village with her mother and signed up for the classes." Laurie's tone of voice made her words resemble an accusation, making him flinch. "What happened?"

"She didn't tell me she was leaving." He sighed, rubbing the ache at the back of his neck. How could she have, he hadn't really talked to her in days. Except about the fiasco with her hair and the damned party that had turned out to be a major mistake.

"Don't worry. She told me you were busy with work and she just needed to get away from the big bad city for a while." Laurie chuckled softly. "I think she must be having a tough time adapting. Patrick did too. I'm sure it's nothing more than that. We'll keep an eye on her."

Finn sighed. His assistant was back at the door, signaling for him to get a move on. "Okay, then. I need to run. Tell her I'll call later and I'll come down Thursday night and we'll spend a long weekend together, relaxing."

Laurie snorted. "Yeah, right. See you then. Bye." At the sound of his cousin's hang-up, he placed the receiver in the cradle, grabbed his valise, and hurried toward the boardroom.

He could only imagine why the board called this meeting. Didn't matter. The fact his wife traveled alone to her parent's home made his blood boil.

Alone. What had she been thinking? Why hadn't she told him of her plans?

This didn't bode well for the success of their marriage. He shook his head, needing to get his head back in the game.

Finn stepped through the conference room doorway and scanned those already gathered. The fine hairs on the back of his neck stood at attention and his nerves coiled tighter. The men and women in the room seemed wary to look him in the eye.

As he approached the large oval table, Tim jumped from Finn's usual seat. "Sorry. I thought you might not show."

Finn frowned. "Why would you think that?"

The jerk shrugged, ambled to the far end of the table and sat to the right of the chairman. Tim's smirk set Finn's teeth on edge. *Just great!* Finn braced for a power play.

CHAPTER THIRTY-THREE

*F*inn's shoulders sagged, the weight of his problems heavy, as if they had physical substance. He still couldn't believe Elspeth left without telling him. Traveled alone. He'd called her parent's inn several times after the disturbing board meeting, but she refused to speak to him.

What had set her off?

Iain and Mairi were mute on the subject. They said to give her time. Time for what? Finn wanted her back where she belonged, with him.

Christ. What a hellacious day. He sighed, totally at a loss. How much worse could things get?

He slid his key into the lock of the apartment door and entered to lonely silence. God, he missed her. He tossed his briefcase on the nearest chair. The ringing of the house phone jarred his senses, and he scrambled to answer the damned thing. Maybe Elspeth changed her mind and wanted to speak to him.

He darted into the living room and grabbed the phone. "Hello." He didn't care how eager he sounded.

"Glad to hear from me, are you? Heard you made a mess of my company."

Finn fell back into the sofa. The sound of his father's

gravelly voice a shock. "Dad, where are you?"

"London. Your partners' lawyer called, claiming they're proceeding with a buyout offer. Are they muscling you out?"

"Guess you could say that."

"What do you plan to do about it?"

He dragged a hand over his face. "I don't know. I have other more pressing problems. Personal ones."

His father chuckled. "One of those socialites finally snare you?"

"No. It's a long story. I have a wife. Sort of. She's left me. I want her back."

"Good God, Finn. My flight leaves on the half hour. Hold on until I get there."

The phone went dead. Finn didn't know whether to laugh or scream or stamp his feet.

Roll out the red carpet. *David MacIntyre is returning to Manhattan.* Dad to the rescue.

Finn made tight fists. If it weren't for the fact the company had been in the family for umpteen years, he wouldn't care about losing control of the firm. But disappointing his father made him feel like a wayward child who'd failed a term at school. Maybe two terms.

Finn strode to the bar and poured a whisky, tossing the shot back. The liquid provided a slow burn as it slid down his throat. The second, he drank more slowly. After a third, he was ready for the forgetfulness only sleep would provide.

Slow even steps took him to the bedroom. He dreaded sleeping alone. Why had Elspeth left him?

As he stepped into their dark bedroom, his internal alarm system went on full alert. He wasn't alone. He slowly bent to retrieve the knife secured at his calf. He hadn't been without a weapon since returning from the sixteenth century. He'd feel vulnerable without the touch of cold steel against his skin. Gripping the blade, he switched on the light.

Shit! His stomach slid south.

Stretched out on his and Elspeth's bed like an artist's nude, Amy smiled, her eyes alight and mischievous. "Hey, sexy." Her voice was a seductive purr. The sound made him feel cold. Hollow.

"What the hell are you doing here? Put your clothes back on." Anger edged his tone. Amy would be wise to take heed.

Finn tucked the blade back in place and marched to the bedside chair where she had laid out her clothing and held them out to her, refusing to give her the modesty of looking away.

"Why?" She moistened her lips, making them shine. "You know I can make you feel *real* good."

"I don't want to be with you."

"Really? I thought you would like company since your so-called fiancée left with that handsome friend of yours from North Carolina."

"Douglas?" *No way*. Finn shoved the clothing at her and stepped out of reach.

"Yeah. That's his name."

The betrayal struck him in the chest, shredding his heart. Thankfully, Amy dressed quickly.

When she was fully dressed, he breathed easier. Yet a pain in his chest remained. Had Amy something to do with Elspeth's leaving?

"How do you know she left with Douglas?"

"I was in *International Java* and overheard them making plans to leave together. They didn't see me."

That bit of news went down his gullet like liquid filled with shattered glass. He wished he'd stayed in the living room, drank the bottle of whisky, and passed out. He glared at Amy. "How did you get in here, anyway?"

"Elspeth gave me a key."

"Give it to me." He held out his hand.

Amy threw the apartment key at his feet. "Fine. Just let me gather my things from the kitchen and I'll get out of your life. You'll regret snubbing me though."

"Don't threaten me."

"It's a promise—not a threat." She brushed passed him and marched into the kitchen.

He met her in the front hall a few minutes later, and she left the apartment in a huff.

With the door locked behind her, he leaned back against it. How had his life become so complicated? He didn't believe there was anything romantic between Douglas and Elspeth. Certainly not. Douglas was in love with Caitrina. And Elspeth...

Finn hoped she was still in love with him.

She must have asked Douglas to take her to her parents. But why?

Early in the morning, Amy watched Finn jump into a cab at the curb on the street below. Fury stiffened her stance when she thought of his rejection. How could he prefer that simpering Scottish woman?

He'd regret spurning her.

She muscled open the window. The drop to the street was considerable. One false move, one mistake, and she might kill herself. No. She knew what she was doing.

With a bracing breath, she shimmied her butt out onto the ledge. Finding handholds, she rose to her feet, facing the building. Light breeze tickled her exposed skin, but she didn't dare shiver and lose her balance. Clutching the decorative trim above her head and flexing the toes of her climbing shoes, she felt for the edge of the ledge with her heels.

Plenty of room. How much more difficult could this be than a climbing wall?

Piece of cake. She could do this.

Amy slowly shuffled her feet, reaching from handhold to handhold as she spidered across the face of the building. *Please. No one look up and see me.*

Relief eased the tension in her muscles when she reached the window to Finn's kitchen. The window she'd left open the night before when she went to collect her cook kit. There had been a fifty percent chance Finn would discover it left open and shut the damn thing.

Luck was on her side. She smiled.

Holding onto window trim, she eased herself down and through the window. The apartment was quiet. She'd need to be quick and return the way she came. She didn't want to risk setting off the door alarm.

It was the work of a moment to reprogram the house phone, forwarding all incoming calls on Finn and Elspeth's— she wrinkled her nose—private line to her cell. When finished, she wiped the phone with a handkerchief. Did the same to the inside of the window frame and climbed through. It was tougher to wipe the outside of the frame.

Shit! She dropped her handkerchief. She held stone-still while it fluttered to the sidewalk below. Thank God, passersby ignored the cloth.

Amy released her held breath and worked her way toward her apartment window.

She glanced to the side. Two feet remained until she reached the safety of her apartment. She slid her left foot along the ledge, reached for the next handhold and—

Slipped.

God, no!

Thrown off balance and dangling precariously, she scrambled to catch herself with one arm while the fingers of her other hand scraped across rough stone, searching for purchase. Heart beating in overdrive, she grabbed for a protruding piece of trim and leaned hard against the building, holding on with straining muscles.

Shaking with effort, she pulled her dangling leg back up onto the ledge. Amy glanced at the street below through wet eyes and almost lost it. It took several deep breaths before she calmed enough to move again.

When she reached the open window to her apartment, she hurried through and fell to the floor in a trembling heap. She lay there, taking deep breaths and feeling the secure hard floor beneath her.

A long time passed before her ringing cell phone jolted her into action. She grabbed it from the counter, swallowed hard to level her voice, and answered, "Hello."

Elspeth's hesitant, "Who is this?" from the other end made the dangerous trip across the ledge well worth the risk.

"Amy. Amy Ferguson. Who's this?"

Yes! Success. The hang up click made Amy grin with satisfaction.

Elspeth dropped onto the garden bench at the sound of Amy's voice on the other end of the line. Devastated, her chest ached. How could Finn be so unfeeling as to keep that woman in their home?

Tears slid along her cheeks as the portable phone dropped from her hand to the ground. She'd tried to stick to her resolution not to speak to Finn. But she missed him desperately. Faerie wings of anticipation fluttered in her belly when she called him. She'd hoped she'd misconstrued what she'd overheard at the party.

She'd been a fool to place so much trust in Finn. Was he in love with Amy?

The thought of the two of them together made the breakfast in Elspeth's stomach curdle.

"What's happened?"

She raised tear-filled eyes. Laurie hurried toward her along the garden path, concern etched in her features.

"I dialed Finn's number the way my mother taught me." Elspeth's voice hitched.

Laurie glanced at the phone on the ground. "Did you get a wrong number?"

"Not exactly."

"What do you mean?"

"Amy Ferguson answered the phone at our apartment."

"Why would she be there?" Laurie's brow furrowed and she tilted her head in question.

"She and Finn are having an affair. He is no different than Alexander."

"I'm shocked. This is so unlike him." Laurie frowned,

shaking her head. "I'm truly sorry."

"Aye, me also." Elspeth moved uneasily on the bench, picked up the discarded phone and held on tight.

"What will you do now?"

"I'll return to my own time."

"You could stay here. It would make your parents happy. And you've signed up for cooking classes. Why not make the best of what this time has to offer?"

"I have no place in this time."

"Let me talk to Finn."

"Nae!"

"Why not?"

"'Tis too humiliating."

"Okay, but I don't think you should go back in time. Perhaps you could work in my garden center. After all, your garden at Castle Lachlan was exquisite."

Elspeth loosened her grip on the phone. Perhaps she could stay at the inn with her parents. She wouldn't have to leave them and miss them for the rest of her life. She could work with plants once again. The thought of supporting herself with a job was daunting, yet exciting.

"Honest? I could work for you and Patrick?"

"Sure."

For the first time in days, Elspeth wanted to stay in the twenty-first century. She didn't need Finn. After all, they weren't truly wed. Her father could declare the handfast null and void.

Finn smoothed his features and opened the door. David MacIntyre hadn't aged a day since the last time he saw him. How long ago was that? Had to be at least three years since he saw his father in person. His dad had a few more lines around his hazel eyes and a few gray hairs. True.

For the most part his father was a mirror image of himself, though older with a dark tan from spending so much time outdoors in the hot sun.

Had the fear of losing control of the family firm finally dragged the man away from Africa and the digs he'd made famous in archeology circles?

"Good to see you, son."

"You, too, Dad. Come in."

His father crossed the threshold and swept his gaze around the apartment. "Looks the same."

"Where are your bags?"

"I stopped by the office."

"Yeah?" Finn braced for a lecture.

"Your admin asked me to tell you they've had news about Jim."

"Jim? Have they found him?"

"Someone claims to have seen him in Scotland near Castle Lachlan."

"Why the hell would he go there without telling anyone? And for what purpose?"

"No one seems to know."

"Strange." Finn rubbed the ache in the back of his neck. "So where are your bags?"

"I checked into a hotel on the way here. I didn't want to interrupt your love nest."

"What do you mean?"

"When I called from the airport a woman answered your phone. She said her name was Amy Ferguson. Claimed to be your fiancée. I assume she is the woman you referred to on the phone and you've repaired your differences."

No wonder Elspeth refused to speak to him. Finn glared at the house phone in his apartment. "My handfasted wife's name is Elspeth. Elspeth MacIntyre, previously of Clan MacLachlan. She's left me and returned to her parents in North Carolina."

"Well, they're both of Scottish descent, at least." His father chuckled and strode to the wet bar and poured two whiskies then handed one to Finn.

"Are you sure a woman answered my phone?"

"Yes."

Finn pulled out his cell and dialed the house phone. After two rings, Amy answered the phone. "How the hell are you answering my phone?"

Damn it to hell. She hung up on him.

"I can't believe it. Somehow Amy managed to get my phone diverted to her cell."

"I would have thought with all that has happened since you became so sought after by women you would have learned how desperate they can become when wealth is involved." His father shook his head.

"I feel like everyone is out to scam me."

"It comes with the territory."

"How did you stand it?"

"Was easier when your mother was alive. Later, I left a lot. And that I am sorry for, son."

"I admit I used to resent your trips abroad. Now I understand."

"I'm glad." His father took a sip from his drink. "So what about the company?"

"I told you, they're trying to force me out."

"Tim has always coveted your position in the firm, and if he has the board supporting him, we're in for one heck of a fight. Is your heart in it, son?"

Finn hesitated for longer than appropriate. He loved his father and didn't want to disappoint him, but he didn't want to fight to keep possession of the firm and continue leading it. He wanted a quieter life with his wife in the country. Now, if only he could figure out how to get his father to take over the company and figure out how to reconcile with Elspeth.

CHAPTER THIRTY-FOUR

The Village of Anderson Creek, North Carolina

*C*aitrina watched Douglas flip the sign hanging on the inside of the door of the *Celtic Image* shop from open to closed. She swallowed uneasily, considering the risks of vanishing in front of him. The last thing she wanted was for him to learn her secret.

Douglas slowly turned and leaned back against the locked door. Her pulse quickened, making her lightheaded. Or was it all in her mind? He made her crazy.

"Have you nothing to say for yourself, lass?" His irate gaze bored into her.

"About what?" She moistened parched lips, not liking the sensation of feeling like a rabbit caught in a snare.

"About where you have been and what you have been doing. Why did you go to New York City?"

"I have no idea what you're talking about." She attempted to smooth her features.

"I believe you know exactly to what I refer. I followed you to New York, but you managed to stay several steps ahead of me. What mischief were you conjuring?" He advanced toward her as he spoke.

She took a step backward and bumped into a glass display

case containing fine crafted Celtic jewelry. He moved in tight. She could hardly breathe.

Conjuring? What a strange word choice. He couldn't possibly know of her origins.

The rapping on the door startled them both. Finn stood on the other side of the glass.

"Saved by the knock." She laughed lightly, relieved. She hadn't needed to *conjure* magic to create an interruption. "Aren't you going to let him in? He looks miffed."

"I'm sure he is." Douglas strode to the door. Before he opened it, he threw a warning look over his shoulder, pinning her with his stare. "We're not finished, princess. I want answers."

Princess? Her breath froze in her lungs. Just what did Douglas know about her?

He opened the door and Finn rushed in. "Caitrina." Finn inclined his head to her, and then he glared at Douglas. "We need to have words."

Douglas shut the door, leaving the closed sign in place. "What's on your mind?" He crossed his arms over his thick chest.

"Why did you escort Elspeth to Anderson Creek without my knowledge? Why didn't you tell me? I thought we were friends." Finn's fists clenched.

"Take it easy. We are friends."

Caitrina edged closer to the door, hoping the men wouldn't notice her escape.

Douglas shot a look in her direction, stopping her just short of freedom. "Don't go anywhere. I think you are involved in this."

Finn jerked his gaze to her. "What did you do, Caitrina?"

"Nothing. I tried to get rid of Amy, but she's persistent. And poor Elspeth was feeling insecure."

"Why would she feel that way?" Finn demanded.

"Because you're having an affair with Amy Ferguson," Douglas accused.

Finn's mouth fell open. Then he shut it with a snap. "I'm

not. How could you think such a horrific thing?"

Caitrina exchanged glances with Douglas. He shook his head, so she remained silent, allowing him to take the lead. Maybe he could clear up this mess. Help her get Finn and Elspeth back together, enabling her to win the queen's challenge.

"Amy's been spending a lot of time at your apartment."

"Only to help Elspeth with the party."

"During the party, Elspeth overheard you and your business partner talking about you bedding Amy."

"You've got to be kidding me." Finn threw an arm in the air in annoyance. "Tim made an incorrect assumption. I've only gone out with Amy once. Last summer. We never slept together. That fool was needling me at the party about having two women for sex."

"Elspeth believes it true."

"Great. Just great." Finn paced a few steps away, his head down, and then returned.

"Maybe I can help." Caitrina glanced at Douglas for agreement. "Today's cooking class at *Le Petite Café* should be about finished. Why don't I go get Elspeth and bring her here? Then she and Finn can talk." *And I can ensure they get back together.*

Douglas gave her a barely perceptible nod, and she let herself out the door. Now, all she needed do was convince Elspeth to return with her. Why were mortals allowed free will?

Finn paced the confines of the shop. Maybe it was providence, his being there. What goes round certainly comes round. He glanced at the empty wall over the checkout counter where his claymore hung the first time he entered the store. This was the place where it all started. *Magic.* Maybe he could use the magic to win Elspeth back.

Or maybe he just needed to convince her of his love. He spun around when the door opened. She stepped through, looking like an angel, even with the frown on her lips and the annoyed furrow puckering her brow. Caitrina followed her in then locked the door.

"Come on, Douglas. I think they need some alone time." Douglas and Caitrina disappeared into the back room.

"Bet they listen to every word," Finn said. Elspeth just stared at him, her eyes glistening.

"Hi." He started again. Maybe a lame beginning, but he didn't know how else to start the conversation they needed to have. "We need to talk."

Elspeth looked away and ran her fingers over the wool of some tartan scarves on a nearby table. A sure sign she was nervous.

He took a deep breath. "I'm sorry you overheard the false claim made by Tim. I'm not sleeping with Amy. You're the only one for me."

Elspeth raised her gaze to him, glared at him through moist lashes. "But she answered the phone in our apartment when I called you."

"Yeah. Shit!" He ran a hand through his hair. "Listen, somehow she got into the apartment and programmed the phone to send the calls to her cell."

"Really? Why would she do that?"

"She wanted to get you angry so you would leave." He stepped in close, placed his hands on her shoulders, looked her in the eyes. "I love you. I'd never cheat on you."

She stared at him for a long moment then her features softened. "I love you too, but…"

"I don't like the sound of that *but*." Elspeth opened her mouth to speak, but he raised a hand to stop her. "Before you explain, let me tell you a wee tale."

"If you feel you must."

"I must." He cleared his throat. "The faeries of the ancient Highlands had an affinity for moonstones. Enamored by the pale color resembling moonlight, they found the best of these stones on the shores of their faerie paradise, *Tir-nan-Óg*."

Elspeth raised a brow. Her lips trembled as if she fought a

smile.

"A faerie princess spelled some of the moonstones with magical powers. To some, she gave the ability to reunite lost lovers." He reached into his pocket and pulled out the box containing the wedding ring he'd bought for her in Manhattan, opened it, and placed it on the display table next to them. Her eyes went wide. He grasped her right hand and placed it over his heart. "This ring will be the symbol of my love for you, if you will marry me for real, in front of God and your family."

"You ken I want to."

"But…"

"Aye."

"Okay, so what is your *but?*"

"Being away from New York City has been wonderful. I hate the city."

"I know. I've decided we'll live here."

"What about your business?"

"I've spoken with my father and Laurie. We've decided to sell the firm."

"Really?"

"Yeah. Both my father and Laurie bolted out on the business and made new lives and my heart isn't in it. It would be best for all concerned if we let it go."

"What will you do instead?"

"I'm not sure—"

"You can become my partner." Douglas ambled out of the backroom, Caitrina following, a grin on her face. "I've been looking for someone to handle business in the US while I spend time in Scotland, searching for antique merchandise."

"You did listen to everything we said."

Neither of them looked repentant.

"We're just glad everything is good with the two of you." Douglas smiled.

"So when is the real wedding?" Caitrina asked.

"She hasn't said yes yet." Finn placed his hands on Elspeth's shoulder. "Well, what do you say? Will you marry me?"

"Oh, aye, I will marry you."

He pulled her into his arms and kissed her thoroughly before placing her back on her feet. "Shall we go speak to your father and convince him to let us wed before the end of the handfast period?"

"Aye." Elspeth leaned into him for another breath-stealing kiss.

Whispering Pines Inn, two months later...

Even though he was a twenty-first century man, Finn liked the fact Elspeth had only belonged to him. He was the only man who had kissed and caressed her most private places.

The feeling was primitive. He was an arrogant hypocrite, but he was glad of his possession. She belonged to him, and there was no way he would ever let her go. Tears of joy moistened his eyes as he watched his angel enter the parlor on the arm of her father, her silver wedding gown shimmering in the artificial light. Her eyes glistened as their gazes met.

Iain leaned in close to Finn's ear as he placed her hand in Finn's. "You better take good care of my wee lass. I would not wish to bring my claymore down upon your head."

Finn gave the man an abrupt nod and grasped Elspeth's hand. Her joyous smile made his heart swell. Blinded by her essence, he barely heard the words of the priest, though he recited his vows with feeling.

"With this ring, I thee wed." He slid the moonstone ring on her finger.

The love in her gaze humbled him.

She was his destiny. He would love her forever.

CHAPTER THIRTY-FIVE

Grandfather Mountain

Where is he? Caitrina crossed the high meadow, searching for Tristan.

Instead of finding her beloved falcon, the queen appeared before her, resplendent in her silvery glamour. Oonagh raised a delicate brow.

Caitrina hated the queen's expression. She hated the queen.

"Tell me who you've decided will be the toughest challenge, the couple hardest to match, the match that will end my banishment."

Caitrina suppressed an urge to glare at the uncooperative queen, knowing the final match would be the most difficult of the three.

She needed to learn what unlikely couple the queen had chosen so she could start making plans. The final match would certainly be fraught with complexity.

Oonagh smiled. "You are very sure of yourself, princess, believing you will successfully complete the next match also."

"Final match," Caitrina asserted.

"Of course, we did agree on three." Anger flashed in the

queen's sapphire eyes for the briefest moment, quickly replaced by indifference.

"Several men come to mind. And the women who defy them. They would make for stimulating play." The queen tapped silver-painted fingernails against the side of her jaw. "Yes. Interesting."

"Who?"

"For me to know and for you to discover. On your own." The queen's image flickered, faded, vanished.

"Urgh." Caitrina spun away. Her heart jumped in surprise, a scream caught in her throat.

"Easy, lass." Douglas grabbed her by the upper arms. "I wouldn't want you to fall off this ridge."

"Take your hands off of me, you Neanderthal."

He pulled her against his thick chest. Fates, he felt good. "What were you doing with the queen?" he demanded.

She gasped. How could he possibly know of Oonagh?

Caitrina leaned her head back and stared into his amber eyes, searching for truth. "Who are you?"

"Someone to watch over you."

He lowered his head and kissed her hard on the lips, curling her toes.

Fir-wood, Strathlachlan, August 1513

Munn stood at the center of the *Sithichean Sluaigh* and concentrated. He needed to discover the secret of the faerie knoll.

Damn the fae and their travel spells.

How did Caitrina pass through time and space between realms? Did she recite a spell or use some other more archaic form of magic?

He'd felt the magic vibrate over his skin once, when Caitrina banished him to the Sands of Time. If only he could remember the chant that teased his mind while he hurled through space to the in-between realm filled with sand.

He needed to journey to Caitrina or bring her to him and inform her that he learned the queen's choices for the next match. It wouldn't be easy. Caitrina needed to prepare.

Munn couldn't allow the queen to win the last match, not with his fate entwined with that of the faerie princess.

EPILOGUE

The village of Andersen Creek, North Carolina

*F*inn leaned against the nursery doorframe, a comfortable smile tugging at his lips, the worry and the waiting ended. Elspeth cradled their child, Colin, within her arms, rocking him gently to keep the young lad asleep.

All of a sudden, an unexpected fragrance infused the room, though the windows remained closed tight to keep out an autumn morning chill. Honeysuckle? Not quite, but similar. Finn straightened, sniffing the air, glancing from side to side, tension escalating.

Tendrils of mist appeared, deepening to a fog in the center, and within the swirling mass a human shape formed. His mouth went dry, his pulse rate climbed. He pushed away from the doorway and without conscious thought, pulled a dirk from his boot, ready, and strode into the room determined to protect his wife and son from all potential threats.

Elspeth raised a hand, warning him back. Her serene smile remained in place as she shook her head, unconcerned.

When the haze cleared, a white-haired woman wearing a gray silk gown was revealed.

One of the fae, most certainly.

"Welcome to our home, ancient one," Elspeth said.

The old woman glided across the room to mother and child and tugged the receiving blanket away from the boy's face. "He will grow brawn like his father, I dare say." Her ageless green gaze flicked to Finn. "See he learns the way of a warrior."

Finn nodded, unsure what he promised.

The elder faerie brushed her fingers along Elspeth's cheek. "When you were a wee *bairn*, I came to your mother and foretold the prophecy that has come to fruition."

Finn swallowed hard, worry returning in a rush.

The woman directed her attention to Colin, drawing a symbol on the boy's forehead with her finger. "On the day of your twenty-first birth celebration, you will take up the faerie-kissed sword and bring end to the violence."

With that said, the faerie dissolved into nothingness.

Finn wanted to believe the elder faerie had never been there, but her cloying fragrance lingered in the air. *Great. Just great.*

"What do you make of that?" he paced to Elspeth's side and glanced at his son.

"Our son is destined for greatness."

Several hours later, Elspeth inhaled the floral scent playing on the breeze and noted Caitrina standing with Douglas. Apparently, they were on speaking terms again.

She waved to the couple then joined the others gathered. Happiness made her gay. Her son's christening was complete and the party just begun. Laurie's garden was ablaze with autumn color, the perfect setting for the celebration.

Elspeth worried for the future of her son as any mother would, but MacIntyre and MacLachlan blood ran heavy in his veins. He would grow and prove the strength of his Highland ancestors.

At peace with the future, she nodded to her husband to

begin. Their gazes locked for a sexually charged moment, a commitment made for later.

Finn turned to the crowd and raised his glass in toast. Hesitated. His brow furrowed and his lips turned down in a confused frown. He leaned his head to the side as if listening and shot his gaze to the back of the garden.

His face blanched.

"What's wrong?" She stepped into him, hoping the guests hadn't realized something was amiss.

Someone coughed. Another cleared their throat.

Finn blinked.

"I thought I saw Maclay on the mound just beyond the garden gate." His voice quivered, a hoarse whisper.

She swallowed uneasily and followed his gaze to the faerie knoll, to the wood beyond. No one lingered there, only wispy tendrils of mist, the beginnings of an early evening fog.

"I dinnae see anyone." She kept her voice low, hoping no one overheard the conversation.

"I must have imagined it." He squinted at the gate.

"Aye." She grasped his wrist, drawing his attention to her. "The ancient one's prophesy has given you the willies."

"Probably," he agreed with a grimace.

Her father raised his glass, taking control of the awkward moment. "To our wee Colin, may his future shine bright, beyond all expectation."

Glasses clinked.

Finn's color returned and a wry smile of acceptance curved his lips. "A toast to my angel for gifting me a son." He held forward his champagne glass.

More clinking in the background. Elspeth couldn't look away from the man who made her heart sing. She was where she belonged with the man she loved.

With a promising smile, her husband grasped her empty hand, and together they gazed into the frilly blue basinet at their precious wee lad, peacefully sleeping, unaware of his destiny.

Just Wait for Me

A Highland Gardens Novel
Book 3

Coming Soon
from
Dawn Marie Hamilton

www.dawnmariehamilton.com

Turn the page for a sneak peek…

PROLOGUE

9 September 1513 near the village of Branxton

The king is dead.

Anguish tore from her halfling soul with a fae scream that reverberated over the field of devastation like rolling thunder.

Silence ensued. Men frozen in fear.

Caitrina dropped to her knees beside the redheaded warrior. She ran gentle fingers along the bloodied curve of his handsome face. Damn Oonagh! Damn the fae queen! She'd refused to allow Caitrina to intervene in the politics of the mortals and prevent this tragedy.

Now, the king lay dead, fatally wounded by an arrow and a bill.

Be damned the English and their nasty weapon—the bill, a staff mounted with hooked chopping blade and pointed projections. The Scots hadn't stood a chance against the onslaught in this slippery, hilly terrain with their cumbersome pikes.

Heart broken, she cradled the man to her breast. Such greatness lost. Tears spilled unchecked onto his precious face. Too late. Even the magic tears of a *Sithichean* princess couldn't revive the king.

"Caitrina! Let us be away from here." The *brùnaidh*, the Maclachlan Clan brownie, fussed at her back. "We must remove Stephen from the field before the English learn he lives and plunge a bill into his chest."

She ignored the wee man. How would the Scots forge forward without their beloved king—with only a *bairn* and the sister of the despised English monarch to guide them?

"If we lose Stephen you will never regain your rightful place."

Ah, yes. Oonagh and her stupid matchmaking challenge must be dealt with. Caitrina released James from her embrace and eased him back to the ground. "Sleep in peace, oh greatest king."

The metallic tang of blood fouled the air. She rose and moved through the death and destruction. Oonagh had tricked her. Led her to believe after three matches she'd be free to return and live in *Tir-nan-óg*, the beloved faerie paradise, land o' heart's desire. But Oonagh refused to reveal which match was the third and final. The one that would free Caitrina from servitude to the queen.

"Needs be we hurry!" Munn side-stepped one of the petrified English knights.

They found Stephen's prone form not far from that of his king. Caitrina rolled him over and took stock of his injuries. Thanks be to Danu, the blond warrior would live. She cloaked the three of them in fae mist and whisked them away on the fetid breeze to the healing caves of the Gray Women.

The battle field returned to morbid activity—an agony of pain.

CHAPTER ONE

Present Day, Greenbriar River Trail, West Virginia

"Rattlesnake!"

Jillian pedaled as fast as she could, past the autumn-tinted trees, to catch up to her brother, the rat. Why must he always speed ahead, leaving her in the dust?

"Kyle O'Donnell, did you hear me? I said...no, I screamed...rattlesnake."

As she rode the dusty mountain bike alongside, he slowed. "You overreact."

"Do not. There was a rattlesnake on the trail. What if the nasty snake bit me, and you were so far ahead you didn't know? The poison would be all through my system before help arrived."

Kyle chuckled. "That snake was more afraid of you than you of it. Relax."

She knew that, but wanted to make a point. "Why do you always dart ahead?"

"Because you're a slowpoke." He gave her a toothy grin. "I always wait for you to catch up. Don't I?"

Jillian gnashed her teeth. Why must he be so difficult? After all, Kyle was the one who had begged her to come on this stupid cycling trip. The least he could do was ride at her pace.

Who would have thought that at twenty-eight, and as a co-owner of a successful garden business, she still chased after her thirty-year-old sibling? She'd only agreed to join Kyle because she'd needed to get away. Away from all the happy-happy between Finn and Elspeth.

"Come on, the tunnel isn't far. Let's race." Her brother sped ahead again.

Jillian sighed and took her sweet time to catch up. Fifteen minutes later, she crossed the weathered old train trestle and arrived at the spot where Kyle waited, sporting an exasperated expression.

"Took you long enough."

Oh, how she wanted to kick him. Instead, she blew a kiss.

He brushed strands of annoyingly perfect sun-bleached, blond hair out of disgustingly gorgeous chocolate eyes and laughed. "Let's take a break before we ride through the tunnel."

So not fair. He got all the good looks and all their parent's attention. Geez. She was pathetic. Really. She needed to get over the past.

While they munched trail mix, Jillian covertly glanced into the rocky opening. The mouth of the abandoned train tunnel was dim and ominous. Water trickled from fissures in the stone walls and ceiling. A damp breeze wafting from the entrance brought with it a musty odor that drilled into her nostrils and sent a chill over her spine.

Did she want to ride through that murky place?

"Must we go through there? Couldn't we go back now and return to the last campsite? Enjoy the afternoon in the sun?"

"Don't you want to see what's on the other side?"

She stared into the dank tunnel. "Not really."

"Don't be a spoil sport. We haven't ridden enough miles today. I promise, after we go through the tunnel, we'll only ride another five. I heard there is a nice campground near a quaint town. Can you say restaurant?"

Jillian didn't want to go any farther, but knew there was

no use arguing. She'd never get Kyle to turn back. They would ride all the way to the southern end of the trail as planned.

She righted her bike and started walking toward the gloomy entrance. Clouds stole over the sun, making it difficult to see anything within. Jillian shivered. The hairs on her arms stood on end. Something didn't feel right about this place.

"Ready?" Kyle asked.

"No."

"Come on, Jilly. It'll be fun."

A couple on a silver tandem bicycle rode from the tunnel, waving as they passed. Sunshine reappeared from the clouds.

"See? It's safe," Kyle said.

"All right. But I'm going to walk my bike through. Just wait for me on the other side."

Kyle pedaled off, popped a wheelie, and entered the odious opening.

Jillian pulled a headlamp out of her pack, secured it over her baseball cap, and flicked it on. Inhaling deeply, she slowly walked her bike into the dark.

The beam of light bounced off brick walls and earthen floor. In the far distance, hazy sunlight indicated the other end of the tunnel. Okay, she could do this. There was nothing here to fear. She proceeded carefully, taking shallow breaths. About a quarter of the way through, rough rock replaced brick on the walls. A blast of super-cold air hit her side.

She shined the light into what appeared to be a passageway. Narrow and foreboding. Suddenly, something pressed against her back. A hand? Her pulse quickened. Whoa! A dizzy sensation swamped her senses. She stumbled. Lost hold of the bike. Fell—or was she being pulled?

She tumbled into the mysterious opening. Falling downward, her body became weightless as she plummeted down…down…down…into a black void. Colorful lights erupted in her mind. A horrible buzzing assaulted her ears.

She screamed, but no sound passed her parched lips.

A piercing white light appeared, drawing her to it. She closed her eyes, but felt no relief. Pain burst behind heavy lids, making her head throb relentlessly. Bile burned her throat. Just when the agony became too much to endure, the cruel light exploded into a zillion pieces.

Blue stars twinkled in a peaceful midnight sky. Her mind blanked.

Panting, Jillian crouched, tips of fingers pressed against the earth for balance. The nauseous sensation gradually subsided and she attempted to stand. Vertigo forced her to her knees, and her stomach lurched again.

Breathe, Jillian. Breathe.

She inhaled deep breaths, trying to calm down. The nausea finally passed and she sat against the rough trunk of a tree. Exhaustion tempted her to curl up and sleep. But she needed to hurry and catch up with…Kyle.

Where was he? Where was she?

Jillian didn't recognize the surroundings. The towering evergreens were larger than any she'd ever seen before, heavy needles blocking a majority of the late afternoon light. The dense forest wasn't like any they'd cycled through on this trip.

She started to shake. This was no time to come unglued. She inhaled a deep, calming breath. Think, Jillian, analyze the situation. *How did you get here?* Her last memory was entering the train tunnel and falling. Had someone shoved her? She'd thought she felt the pressure of a hand on her back as she'd fallen forward.

Strange. Who would have pushed her? No one came to mind. They'd only seen the couple on the tandem, riding the other way. No other cyclists or hikers.

Frowning, she removed one of the water bottles attached to her pack, took a long swig, and accessed the height of the sun. There wasn't much time before it would get dark. She scanned the area. Great. Her bike was missing and there was no sign of a trail.

Nerves taut, she swallowed hard. She would not submit to

fear. If she started walking, surely she'd come across a road or some such thing. *Right?*

Jillian walked until she couldn't take another step. Her feet hurt. Sneakers were little protection against the rough, rocky terrain. The sun was setting, and she was lost. Completely and utterly lost, but she refused to panic. She would find a safe place to settle in for the night. Tomorrow she was sure to find some sign of civilization.

On a scree covered slope, she spotted a protected area under an overhanging ledge. She scrambled up the incline, slipping and sliding, scraping knees and hands. She had fleece cover-ups, a wind jacket, and a space blanket in her pack. Pulling out the silver cloth, she laid it on the ground. She slipped into the fleece and zipped the jacket snug as the sun disappeared over the horizon.

Wanting to save the batteries in the headlamp, she ate a power bar in the dark. She wrapped the blanket around her, and used the pack as a pillow. She hummed. When that didn't ease the jitters, she made up silly stories as a distraction. Small stones dug into her side, but finally, exhaustion took hold and she slept.

Thunder from a passing storm woke her at some point. The feeling someone watched skittered over her nerves. She blinked, trying to adjust her vision to the dark. Nighttime forest sounds heightened her anxiety. She expected to see glowing animal eyes. But no, as far as she could tell, she was alone.

Nervous and stiff, it took a while to fall asleep again only to startle awake before dawn. The storm had passed and a bright silver moon slid in and out of clouds, creating shifting shadows. An odd disfiguration of bark at the bottom of a nearby tree caught Jillian's attention. The scarred wood appeared as a young boy's face.

Staring hard at the tree, she smiled as the face changed in the moon's unpredictable light. Two distinctly different faces appeared imbedded in the rough bark. The first, a boy with a pudgy nose and big sad eyes, and the second—

She must be dehydrated. Delusional. Imagining faces imbedded in a perfectly normal tree. Jillian huddled deeper into the cocoon the space blanket provided and tried to fall back to sleep.

Sleep wouldn't come so she glanced at the tree again. A third face appeared in the texture of the old oak. This one had a scarred forehead and a crooked mouth.

Such fanciful thoughts. She snorted. Here she was lost and alone in the woods and she was killing time imagining faces in a tree trunk. Sleep was what she needed. In her mind, she counted plants on a potting bench in the greenhouse at *Foxgloves*—one hundred thirty two, thirty three, thirty four.

Finally, Jillian dozed off again.

When she woke a third time, a chill had seeped into her bones. She sat up and pulled the space blanket more snuggly around her. The tree looked different in the white light of morning and another image appeared. This tiny face had an elongated nose and wisps of blond hair dangled across its brow. Jillian covered her mouth to stifle a giggle. She'd recently read a book about faeries and changelings and stolen children. She imagined that the hobgoblins lived in this tree. That stolen boys—

The snap of a branch made her jump. Her stomach knotted.

Standing before her was a gnarled little man. No more than four feet tall, he nearly blended into the surrounding woods. The peculiar clothes he wore matched the colors of the forest. And his dusty brown skin had wrinkles upon wrinkles. Elf-like ears stuck out from beneath a pointed cap. But what startled her most, were the unusual blue-green eyes that bore into her.

The man reminded her of a sketch she'd seen while babysitting. Little Allison MacLachlan loved the story of *Rumpelstiltskin*.

Jillian clutched the space blanket in fists and gawked at the man. He stared back. Unnerving seconds passed in silence. Abruptly, the strange fellow lunged forward and yanked on the blanket, almost snatching it away.

"What do you think you're doing? Leave my blanket alone." She rose into a crouch, holding tight to the silver cloth while he continued to tug. When the man let go, Jillian fell backward unto her rump. "Dammit."

His eyes narrowed. "Be you a witch?"

"What?" She shook her head. "Of course not."

He circled around. "Then who are you to have spun such a plaid. You are nae one of the *Sithichean*. Are you?"

Her thoughts whirled. "A what?"

"A *Sithichean*, one of the faeries of these hills." A wave of an arm encompassed the surrounding terrain.

Jillian ran fingers along the edge of the space blanket. "This isn't a plaid."

The man glowered.

Ridiculous. "Who are you?"

"That is none of your mind. My lad be needing that plaid." He grabbed for the blanket again.

She drew it close to her chest, refusing to let go. Jillian wasn't about to let the crazy little man steal it. "I asked who you are."

He raised his chin defiantly. "You tell me first."

"Oh, all right. I'm tired of this game." Jillian threw up her arms in exasperation. "I'm Jillian O'Donnell. I'm lost. Perhaps you can direct me to the nearest road?"

A mischievous glint flashed in the man's eyes. "There are none, but if you give me that plaid, I'll tell you where to find a game trail."

"Will that take me into town?"

"None here or about. Nearest village is three days walk over yonder ridge." He pointed off to the left.

While she glanced that way, the man snatched the blanket and disappeared into the wood.

Hands fisted on hips Jillian glared at the trees. "Damned little man."

❀ ❀ ❀

There wasn't a spot on Stephen's black and blue body that didn't hurt. The battle had been a bloodbath. Although his wounds weren't too serious, he ached everywhere.

And his leg—would be awhile before it healed.

His memory burned with the haunting sight of his dead monarch. Stephen had never expected events to unfold as they had. King James the IV of Scotland, dead on the battlefield beside so many of the kingdom's finest warriors.

After lying unconscious among the dead, Stephen had managed to escape the chaos of the field with the help of Munn, the MacLachlan Clan brounie, and found shelter in the caves of the Gray Women. Stephen didn't remember how they'd managed the feat, but here he was, hidden away from those who'd wish him ill.

Stifling a groan, he shifted the bum leg and reached for what Munn procured. His fingers slid over an unusual, shiny fabric. "What the devil? Where did you get this bewitched cloth?"

Munn looked away, and an uncomfortable dread ran through Stephen. The brownie scraped a foot in the dirt. Stephen's teeth chattered so he wrapped the strange cloth around his upper body. Whether from witch or fae, he was cold and needed any warmth the strange fabric could provide.

"Munn? Where did you get it?"

"Forest."

"Who did you steal it from?"

"Borrowed." Blue-green eyes flashed. "There be a lass in the wood. Dressed as a lad."

"What were you thinking, wee man? We don't want to be discovered." Stephen swallowed uneasily. "Is the wench English?"

Munn curled his body away and looked over his shoulder at Stephen as if bracing for a blow. "Foreign. Like Lady Laurie."

Stephen inhaled sharply. *Like Lady Laurie?* Was it possible? "Fetch her here."

"'Twould be a mistake."

"Do as I say. But be careful. We dinnae want the English to find us."

With a deep grumble, Munn scurried out of the cave.

Stephen scrubbed the stubble on his chin. Could another time traveler have appeared at the *Sithichean Sluaigh*, the faerie mound near Castle Lachlan? If so, how would she have gotten here? 'Twas quite a distance from Strathlachlan.

Hmmm. Would the lass be as intriguing as Lady Laurie?

Just Beyond the Garden Gate
Book One, Highland Gardens Series

by Dawn Marie Hamilton

Time Travel Fantasy Romance

Determined to regain her royal status, a banished faerie princess accepts a challenge from the High-Queen of the Fae to unite an unlikely couple while the clan brownie attempts to thwart her.

Passion ignites when a faerie-shove propels burned-out business consultant Laurie Bernard through the garden gate, back through time, and into the embrace of Patrick MacLachlan. The arrogant clan chief doesn't know what to make of the lass in his arms, especially when he recognizes the brooch she wears as the one his stepmother wore when she and his father disappeared.

With the fae interfering at every opportunity, the couple must learn to trust one another while they battle an enemy clan, expose a traitor within their midst and discover the true fate of the missing parents. Can they learn the most important truth—love transcends time?

Journey from the lush gardens of the Blue Ridge Mountains of North Carolina to the Scottish Highlands of 1509 with *Just Beyond the Garden Gate*.

Sea Panther

Book One, Crimson Storm Series

by Dawn Marie Hamilton

Paranormal Romance

2013 Golden Heart® finalist for Best Paranormal Romance

Can love mend a fractured soul?

After evading arrest for Jacobite activities, Scottish nobleman Robert MacLachlan turns privateer. A Caribbean Voodoo priestess curses him to an eternal existence as a vampire shifter torn between the dual natures of a Florida panther and an immortal blood-thirsting man. For centuries, he seeks to reverse the black magic whilst maintaining his honor. Cruising the twenty-first century Atlantic, he becomes shorthanded to sail his 90-foot yacht, *Sea Panther*. The last thing he wants is a female crewmember and the call of her blood.

Although she swore never to sail again after her father died in a sailing accident, Kimberly Scot answers the captain's crew wanted ad to escape a hit man. She's lost everything, her fiancé, her job, and most of her money, along with money belonging to her ex-clients. A taste of Kimberly's blood convinces Robert she is the one woman who can claim the panther's heart. To break the curse, they travel back in time to where it all began—Jamaica 1715.

Future Works:

Time Travel Fantasy Romance

Just Wait for Me
Book Three, Highland Gardens Series

Just in Time for a Highland Christmas
A Highland Gardens Novella

Paranormal Romance

Raven's Revenge
Book Two, Crimson Storm Series

ABOUT THE AUTHOR

Dawn Marie Hamilton dares you to dream. She is a 2013 RWA® Golden Heart® Finalist who pens Scottish-inspired fantasy and paranormal romance. Some of her tales are rife with mischief-making faeries, brownies, and other fae creatures. More tormented souls—shape shifters, vampires, and maybe a zombie or two—stalk across the pages of other stories. She is a member of The Golden Network, Fantasy, Futuristic & Paranormal, Celtic Hearts, and From the Heart chapters of RWA. When not writing, she's cooking, gardening, or paddling the local creeks of Southern Maryland with her husband.

Visit Dawn Marie on the web at dawnmariehamilton.com.